ELIZABETH NOYES

Imperfect Trust

Imperfect Trust

© 2015 Elizabeth Noyes

ISBN-13: 978-1-938092-87-9

ISBN-10: 1938092872

All rights reserved. No part of this publication may be reproduced or transmitted in any form or by any means without written permission from the publisher.

Scripture verses are taken from Holman Christian Standard Bible (HCSB) Copyright © 1999, 2000, 2002, 2003, 2009 by Holman Bible Publishers, Nashville Tennessee. All rights reserved.

This book is a work of fiction. Names, characters, places, and incidents are either products of the author's imagination or used fictitiously. Any similarity to actual people and/or events is purely coincidental.

Published by Write Integrity Press, 2631 Holly Springs Parkway, Box 35, Holly Springs, GA 30142.

www.WriteIntegrity.com

Printed in the United States of America.

Acknowledgements

It is impossible to adequately convey the depth of my appreciation for the incredible group of people I call my Sounding Board, but I'm going to try. First though, let me give you the definition of a sounding board: 1) a thin, resonant plate of wood forming part of a musical instrument, and so placed as **to enhance the power and quality of the tone**; 2) a person or persons whose reactions serve as a **measure of the effectiveness of the methods, ideas**, etc., put forth; and 3) a person or group that **propagates ideas, opinions, solutions, suggestions**, etc.

My heartfelt thanks go out to:

Gene Valaquin – Gene's technical savvy and suggestions were invaluable in getting this story off the ground. Thanks for the great ideas!

Emily Grey – *"Do you need that?"* A critique partner who makes me cry, makes me think, makes me question, makes me go deeper, makes me revise and revise again—and always with a kindness that won't allow me to pout. How can I not love her?

My many **Critique Partners** – I am always mystified how six different people can offer six different perspectives, focus on six different areas, and offer so much value. Do I use all their suggestions? No. Do I use most of them? At least ninety percent.

Barry Thomason – Beta Reader extraordinaire and someone I've come to depend on to catch all those pesky little boo-boos every writer seems to skim right over.

Brenda Curtis – Always willing to jump in when needed, to give support even without knowing it's needed, and to offer up the best eye.

Shari Nardello – Superb beta reader, constant supporter, and amazing daughter who's not afraid to tell you like it is.

Paul Noyes – My super hero and go-to techie guy. He always reads my first draft, second draft, third draft, tenth draft … and always with eagerness. A balm to a needy ego. And never a complaint.

And to the many others too numerous to name who supported, encouraged, and helped me through this excruciating process we call writing. I love you all.

Chapter One

Raindrops shimmered in the van's headlights, hanging like glittery diamonds suspended in time. A child's delight.

Lucy blinked and broke the unwelcome connection with the past. She hadn't thought of *that* night in years. Outside, the iridescent raindrops splattered against the windshield, coalesced into rivulets, and slid down the glass. The unwanted memories went with them.

A quick glance in the rearview mirror showed absolute blackness. She'd seen no other traffic for a long while. Not surprising. Intel reported the area abandoned by the county during a downturn in the economy a few years back. Only warehouses remained in this forsaken part of Atlanta now, derelict and far gone in Mother Nature's reclamation project.

The rain fell in a fine mist now, enough to keep the wipers on intermittent as she strained to see the almost invisible center strip. She rubbed her left shoulder, aware of the dull ache there. Wet weather seemed to exacerbate the old injury. Cold, too. The white-knuckled grip she'd had on the steering wheel for the past hour probably didn't help either. There'd be no more martial arts competitions for her. And no more boss after tomorrow, either.

A tiny, self-satisfied smile formed. The video game world offered more than anything the government would pay. They had their chance.

Despite having aced all the physical requirements for rookie agents, despite her marksmanship records, and martial

Imperfect Trust

arts successes, the Bureau of International Intelligence had stuck her in a windowless computer lab to analyze and exploit network weaknesses all over the globe. A gerbil wheel for the technology rat. They'd denied her requests to move into the field again and again, and instead turned her into the very thing she'd run from. A hacker.

Too bad she got her one and only field assignment now. At the end. Thanks to Ed.

Strains of *Bad Boy, Bad Boy* filled the vehicle. Ed had scowled something fierce when he learned she'd assigned the theme song from *Cops* for his ringtone.

She grabbed the cell phone from the cup holder. "Hi, Ed."

"You're late."

Ed Whitaker, thirty-year veteran of the Bureau of International Intelligence, North American Corridor, and the special agent in charge assigned to the Cypher case. Ed would never be accused of making polite conversation. Just the facts, ma'am.

"Visibility's bad. Wait. I see the abandoned gas station. Less than a half mile now."

"About time."

She rolled her eyes at the authoritative tone.

"Delacroix will meet you at the surveillance point to help hook up the cables before he takes up over-watch position. Get the files, give the signal, and get out. Nothing more. Del will tail you back to headquarters. Got it?"

Of course she got it. He knew about her near-perfect recall, not to mention he'd harped on the same thing during the last dozen briefings for tonight's mission.

A nervous flutter in her belly had her taking a deep breath. The only difference with this assignment was she'd traded her lab in the Bureau's Atlanta office for one inside the armored van. And they'd issued her a gun. Not that she'd have a chance to use it.

"Lucy. You copy?" By the numbers, that was Ed.

"Yeah, I copy."

"Good. We go silent now. Shoulder mic for emergency only."

A dial-tone hummed in her ear.

"Bye to you, too," she grumbled and powered down the phone. Right on time, the rain stopped. For once, the weather cooperated with Ed's meticulous planning.

Outside, night relinquished its hold on the world. Monday dawned gray and dreary. She turned the big van dubbed Bubba into the abandoned warehouse complex. Could the setup be more perfect? The absence of civilians translated to no collateral damage. Down and dirty. Take 'em in or take 'em out.

After three long years of chasing the wily Cypher and always coming up a little too late and a whole lot short, Ed finally got smart. He'd brought Lucy in but kept her involvement quiet. Only he knew the details of what she would attempt on this sting. Ed wanted to nab Cypher, but he wanted the drug dealer's files more.

Goose bumps pebbled Lucy's skin. Cypher conducted million-dollar deals through cyberspace. If Ed was right, the clever drug dealer used a program long considered a pipedream. He could track computer signals to their precise geographic coordinates, which would explain how he always stayed one step ahead of the authorities.

Quicksilver employed the same premise, but with a twist. There'd been no time to run more than a few laboratory simulations, though. Would her program work the way it was supposed to in a live environment?

The van's heater blasted the spring chill from the air but did nada to dispel her nerves. Quicksilver had to work. Ed needed closure on this case. And she wanted to leave the Bureau with a bang.

Imperfect Trust

Lucy drove through the industrial complex, following the route scouted earlier by the recon team. She found the designated dead-end street positioned well away from the area of action, and backed the customized van along the road until the pavement ended. Bubba might not look like much on the outside with the missing hubcaps and assorted dents, scrapes, and rust spots, but he had moxie where it counted.

The battered white Econoline E-350 stood seventy-inches high and one hundred inches long, and boasted a 6.8-liter V10 engine with 305 horsepower and a body lined with lightweight ballistic material that could deter armor-piercing slugs. Only a rocket launcher at point-blank range could penetrate Bubba's hide or the polycarbonate armored windows.

Cypher's arrival was pinpointed for eleven thirty that morning. If they didn't get him this time, they'd burned a reliable informant for nothing.

In Ed's typical over-prep fashion, he'd sent in Todd Delacroix the night before, the team's communications tech. Del, as the other members of the team called him, planted cameras and laid landlines that would connect with Bubba's generator-powered control center. The rest of the team had arrived onsite earlier, around 4:00 a.m. Ed wanted everyone in place, even if it meant a long wait. He didn't take chances.

As the creaks and pings of Bubba's cooling engine faded, Lucy reached for the hundredth time to the small holster under her arm. With practiced hands, she lifted the gun free, pulled the slide back, and checked the ammo load.

The shoulder mic crackled. "Lucy?"

Ed's whispered growl made every one of her muscles tense. Breaking radio silence meant bad things. She tapped the speaker button to un-mute and answered. "Yeah?"

"You in position?"

"Just cut the engine."

"Change of plans. Target is imminent. Six minutes out.

Del is on his way to you. He'll need your help." Ed disconnected.

Her heart went into overdrive. Cypher was *hours* too early. She yanked the keys from the ignition, opened the driver's door, and dropped to the ground. The automatic lock engaged behind her.

Off to the right, a flashlight beam bobbed through the woods. Del, fresh from the training academy in Alexandria, Virginia, was a technology rat like her, but with outside privileges. Discrimination? Oh, yeah, but a battle she hadn't won. Besides, she couldn't do half the stuff he did.

If Cypher could drill down to the exact coordinates of an active IP address as Ed suspected, then Del's handiwork would provide eyes for the team without a traceable computer signal to give them away. A few more days and she might have perfected a mask for electronic camera feeds. Instead, they used the hardwired method. It was messy and archaic, but effective, given Cypher's focus on technology.

Lucy met Del at the rear of the van.

"Connect the lines while I cover them." He handed off a handful of quarter-inch cables. "The wire colors match the connectors, red to red, blue to blue."

He didn't wait for her answer. This might be Del's first field op, but he performed like a veteran. But did he understand that bad guys don't play by the rules?

Lucy clenched a small flashlight between her teeth and set to work, pairing the color-coded wires and twisting them around their contact points.

Back inside the van, she opened the panel to the cargo area and stepped through to the technical surveillance observation post—TSOP, Ed called it. After the panel swooshed closed, low-wattage lights flickered on.

A one-way glass window ran along one side of the cargo area. A desk-high counter filled the length on the other side.

Imperfect Trust

Two thirty-two-inch LED monitors were mounted there, each with a laptop docked in front.

Lucy powered up both computers. When the cursor appeared in the middle of the left screen, she spoke. "Watch Dog, sync to camera connections. Display feeds one through six."

The screen on the left filled with a series of picture-in-picture video streams showing views of the tree-lined approach from the main road, the front entrance to the warehouse, a rear entry view, two perspectives of the rear loading docks, and one of the empty truck lots. *Thank you, Del.*

On the second monitor, the crux of the operation, two words blinked in the middle of the screen.

Authorization required.

"Quicksilver JG6725."

A new word popped up, keyed to her specific voice patterns.

Authenticated.

"Quicksilver, open command sequence."

Today's deal could send millions of dollars to an untraceable bank account on Grand Cayman. Worse, the transaction could flood the eastern seaboard with a supply of illicit drugs.

A question appeared on the screen. *Activate?*

On her directive, Quicksilver would latch onto Cypher's computer signal without being detected. Then, camouflaged by the source computer's own attributes, her Trojan program would slide down the captured signal right into the heart of Cypher's operating system. From there, she could copy all readable and executable files, download them to a cache on her computer, and transmit them to the Bureau's field office in Atlanta.

The cursor blinked in a steady rhythm.

Movement on the multi-picture surveillance monitor drew

her attention. Four cars rolled from one screen to another until they stopped at the loading dock. Two men per car. Eight total. Six of them brandished what looked like assault weapons. The seventh man, the driver, held a handgun while the last man carried a briefcase.

"Watch Dog, zoom in twenty-five percent on feed five. Zoom in forty percent."

The man with the briefcase wore a baseball cap that obscured his features but increased magnification blurred the pixilation too much. "Watch Dog, camera feed five zoom out to normal."

The man opened the briefcase, removed a laptop, and set it on the hood of the SUV. He connected a small tripod with an umbrella-like attachment, and then his fingers began moving over the keyboard.

Oh, yeah, this had to be their target. "Quicksilver, identify computer signals within five-hundred yard radius."

Five seconds passed before three IP addresses appeared on the right monitor. Two belonged to her computers, plus one unknown.

191.156.1.12.

"Quicksilver, acquire signal for one-nine-one point one-five-six point one point one-two."

A circular arrow began spinning on the screen. The moment of truth had arrived. If Cypher discovered the tampering, the op would turn ugly fast. Lucy held her breath and watched the men on the screen. They appeared alert and cautious, constantly scanning the area, but nothing more.

Fifteen seconds passed.

"C'mon, c'mon."

At thirty seconds, words replaced the circle. *Signal acquired.*

She let out an audible breath when there was no reaction from Cypher or his men. "Quicksilver, launch Hermes."

Hopefully, the Greek patron god of thieves would favor them today.

A full minute passed. A bead of sweat trickled down her temple. Lucy wiped it away with her shirtsleeve. Back in the lab, the connection had been instantaneous.

Another thirty seconds went by before a series of file names and paths spilled onto the screen, rolling up and off the page too fast to follow.

"Quicksilver, open BII portal. Transfer cached files."

A pop-up appeared, showing the transfer connection between the two machines. Relief flooded through her.

She looked at the surveillance screen again and choked off the short-lived relief. Cypher's men swarmed around like someone had kicked their hornets' nest. What happened? She'd taken such care to mask Quicksilver's signal.

Realization came with a groan. She'd spent so much time masking Quicksilver's entry, she hadn't thought once about the return transmission *from* Cypher's computer. *Stupid. A novice's mistake.* Of course, he would know if his own machine communicated out.

A bar at the bottom of the screen slowly filled with green. Four percent. Not nearly enough.

On the surveillance monitor, laptop guy pointed toward the woods, right at her. He said something to his men and six of them took off at a dead run.

Lucy thumbed her mic. "Uh, Ed?"

"You got the files already?"

"Transfer is in process, but I think Cypher's men are on to us. Six of them are heading my way."

On the monitor, Cypher's frenzied fingers stabbed at the keyboard. He stepped back, hands gripping his head. And then he grabbed the laptop and hurled it to the ground. One doozy of a control-alt-delete.

On Lucy's screen, the files continued to scroll. Amazing.

He'd trashed his laptop, but the impact didn't break the connection.

"Stay put, Lucy. We're moving in."

Cypher gathered the broken laptop pieces, stuffed them back in the briefcase, snatched up the rest of the equipment, and climbed inside the SUV. The driver sped off, spewing gravel in their wake.

"Cypher is on the move. He and the driver took off in a dark blue Escalade. If they go too far, I'll lose the signal."

"Roger. Alpha Team move to intercept. Bravo and Charlie stay with the plan. Lucy, it's time for you to go."

"The upload isn't complete." The bar had climbed to twenty-three percent. Still not enough. "I need more time."

One of the surveillance pictures showed Cypher's car stopped in front of the warehouse. Instead of turning right toward the exit, the driver went left. Toward her.

"Ed, he's coming this way." She wasn't supposed to be involved in the action.

The SUV disappeared off the monitor. Less than a minute passed before a vehicle screeched to a halt and blocked Bubba's exit. The driver leapt out, a lethal-looking machine pistol in hand, and sprinted out of sight. Laptop guy—he had to be Cypher—got out also, using his door as a shield, holding a handgun.

A moment later a hail of bullets struck Bubba's passenger door.

Lucy screamed. Her heart pounded. "Ed, they're shooting."

"Easy, Lucy. You're safe in the van. Just stay put."

The six thugs who'd run off emerged from the woods. Two of them half-dragged, half-carried a captive between them.

Their prisoner struggled—until a third man clubbed him in the back of his head. He collapsed only to be yanked upright.

Imperfect Trust

"Nooooo." Bile burned her throat. This couldn't be happening.

"What?" Ed demanded.

She could hardly choke the words out. "They've got ... Del."

Another dozen men converged on the scene, some with drawn handguns while others wielded weapons right out of a Tom Clancy movie. Cypher had brought his own SWAT team.

Her mouth dried up.

"Hold it together, Lucy."

"Ed, I count eighteen ... nineteen ... no, make that twenty men. Repeat, two-zero men, all of them heavily armed."

One of Cypher's thugs crept to the van and pounded on the window where she knelt.

She jumped. They couldn't see in, but knew she was there. He motioned for her to come out.

She shook her head. Not happening. "They want me to come out."

"Negative. Do not leave the van. That is an order."

Outside, one of Del's captors stretched his arm out to one side.

Pffft!

A shriek shattered the silence. Del collapsed to the ground, doubled over.

Lucy jerked back from the window, collided with the counter, and fell. On hands and knees, she crawled to the trashcan and retched.

"Talk to me, Lucy," Ed demanded.

She wiped her mouth with a sleeve, praying she wouldn't puke again. Tears streamed down her face. "T-they shot him," she managed to say. "Cypher put a g-gun to Del's hand and p-pulled the trigger." Her stomach lurched.

The same thug banged on the window again.

She crawled to the window and looked out. "Oh, God, please, no." She slapped her hand against the window.

They'd lifted Del to his feet. Cypher stood by his side. The baseball cap still hid most of the drug dealer's features, but she had no difficulty reading his lips. He pressed the gun against Del's thigh and looked at the van. He held up his index finger and mouthed, "One."

A vise had settled around her chest.

He raised a second finger. "Two."

"Nooooo!" Her fists hammered against the glass.

"Three minutes, Lucy. Hold on."

Del didn't have three minutes. He didn't have three seconds. She glanced at the computer. Fifty-two percent.

Outside, Cypher added a third finger and gave her a Boy Scout salute. "Three."

"No." She wept.

Pffft.

Del jerked and screamed again before collapsing on the ground. Anguished cries filled her ears.

Lucy sank to her knees, face buried in her hands, sobbing.

"Lucy," Ed shouted.

"Oh, God, Ed, he shot Del in the leg. He's killing him!"

"Listen to me, girl. You can't help him."

Another slap on the glass.

She couldn't turn away. She owed Del that much.

Del's captors held him upright again, though he slumped in their arms, head hanging limp against his chest. Blood dripped from his mangled hand. More blood soaked his pants. Pooled on the ground.

Cypher jabbed the weapon in Del's belly, under the flak vest.

Checkmate. If she left Bubba they both might die, but if she stayed put—

No. She had to try. A quick glance at the master computer.

Sixty-three percent.

She set her pistol on the counter. The weapon would be useless against so many. Opening the front panel, she screamed, "Wait, I'm coming."

The killers trained their guns on her as she clambered into the front of the van.

"Open the door."

"Lucy, do not leave the van." Ed's ferocity came through the mic loud and clear. "Acknowledge."

Her heart pounded like an insane woodpecker. "He'll kill Del."

"One." Cypher jammed the gun harder into Del's torso, making him groan.

"Lucy, you will stay put. That's an order."

"Two."

"I'll stall them. Please hurry." Fishing the van keys from her pocket, she dropped them on the floor. "Don't shoot. I'm coming."

"Don't do it, Lucy," Ed shouted.

Before she could change her mind, Lucy unlocked and opened the door. Her feet hit the ground, and she slammed the door behind her. The automatic lock clicked.

One man rushed forward, shoved Lucy out of the way, and yanked on the van's door, cursing when it didn't open. He fired his weapon at Bubba, but the bullets ricocheted off the armored skin.

Lucy went down hard. White-hot pain streaked through her shoulder—the all-too-familiar agony of a shoulder separation.

Strong hands grabbed Lucy and flipped her onto her back. Pain became agony and cascaded through her.

"Well, well, who do we have here?"

Cypher. It had to be.

He straddled her stomach and brushed a strand of hair

from her face. "Little Lucy Kiddron, the brat genius."

His voice was familiar, but the agony in her arm demanded all of her attention.

He poked her injured shoulder. "Are you still trying to play with the big boys?"

She couldn't hold back a scream.

Knuckles brushed her cheek then, his touch gentle. "Look at me, Lucy. Open your eyes."

She whimpered, not wanting to put a face to the nightmare.

"Gotta go, Boss," someone shouted. "Now."

The man astride her belly laughed. He jabbed her shoulder again. "Come on, look at me."

"Aaagh!" Somehow she opened her eyes.

"Better."

She looked up into eyes the color of midnight. Beautiful eyes framed by long lashes. Jensen Argault. The college genius from her past. He'd presented his hypothesis for tracking computer signatures. A flawed theory she'd debunked, embarrassing him in the process.

Jensen was Cypher.

"You stole my code, didn't you? I should put a bullet in you for that alone." He smiled. "I'll leave you a little present instead." A wicked-looking knife blade snicked open. "And a promise."

Lucy's heart pummeled against her ribs. She couldn't breathe, couldn't move.

"Run, Lucy." Jensen sliced open the front of her shirt. "Hide." He dragged the flat of the blade across her throat. "I like the hunt. And I'll kill anyone who gets in my way."

"Please. Please don't."

His smile would put angels to shame. "Begging is nice. Remember that when I come for you."

The tip of the blade bit into the soft skin of her chest.

Imperfect Trust

Chapter Two

A mélange of odors assailed her—pine-scented cleanser that didn't quite mask the reek of urine, medicinal smells, flowers, and that indefinable odor of sickness. She hated hospitals.

The orderly pushing Lucy's wheelchair paused at the nurse's station while Officer Gomez, the retired policeman assigned to guard her in the hospital, ducked inside her room. He returned a moment later with an, "All clear, Ms. Kiddron."

Guard or jailer? His presence both comforted and annoyed. Ed's team had captured most of Cypher's thugs, but the drug dealer and a few of his cronies managed to slip away like wraiths. Again.

And Ed put *her* in protective custody. Something was wrong when the victim went to jail while the bad guy roamed free.

Cypher was Jensen Argault. She shook her head, still finding it difficult to wrap her mind around the knowledge. Her fingers hovered near the bandage over her heart.

The stout officer returned to his post outside her door while the orderly pushed the wheelchair into the room and set the handbrake. "Here you go, Miss Lucy."

"Thank you, Antoine."

Lucy stared out the room's lone window at stained rooftops, dirty brick walls, and a somber sky. Grady Hospital had a top-notch reputation as a trauma center, and the staff was great, but the old building was long overdue for a facelift, inside and out. The facility wouldn't score a single star on the hotel rating scale.

Turning to her bed, she settled in for a nap she knew wouldn't come.

Half an hour later, a young woman tapped on the door and entered the room. Trim and athletic, she wore a short white lab jacket over jeans ... and cowboy boots?

"Lucy Kiddron? Hi, my name's Cassie Cameron. I'm a physical therapist with Dr. Beaumont's group. He asked me to work up a post-op rehab plan for you." She waved a clipboard.

Thank goodness. As soon as this last checkbox got ticked off, Lucy could get out of here.

The young woman motioned Lucy to sit in the chair beside the bed.

"What are you going to do?" Lucy swung her legs over the side of the bed.

"Not much." The physical therapist helped Lucy to the chair. "See how far I can twist your arm before you scream."

Lucy took a step back. Her mouth fell open.

"Kidding," Cassie laughed. "Just wanted to see how loopy you are. Some of the stuff they prescribe here could disable an elephant. Not that you're an elephant."

"Thanks. I think." Lucy clutched the open-backed hospital gown in her good hand and sat on the edge of the guest chair. "I can't place your accent. Where are you from?"

The dark-haired girl's laugh lightened Lucy's mood. "*My* accent? You can't be serious." Cassie removed Lucy's sling with firm but gentle hands. "*You're* the one with the drawl. I'm from Idaho. We don't have accents."

"Down here you do. What brought you to Atlanta?" Lucy didn't make friends easily, could number them on one hand. But this girl with her brash attitude reminded Lucy a little of herself. She liked Cassie Cameron. Maybe they could get to know one another during the therapy sessions.

"I'm doing an internship with Dr. B's group. Six more

weeks 'til I head home. Now, keep your elbow bent and lift your arm out to the side, high as you can."

Okay, no long-term friendship here but she still liked the girl. Lucy raised her elbow three inches before she grimaced. "An internship, huh? You're still in school?"

"That's far enough. You can lower your arm." Cassie scribbled something on her clipboard. "I'll finish my doctorate this fall at the University of Idaho. Describe the pain for me."

"A dull ache most of the time. Sharp and burning when I move it." Lucy touched high on the left side of her neck. "It radiates from here all the way down to my wrist at times."

Still making notes, Cassie nodded. "Keep your arm down by your side, but move it backward as far as you can. Don't force it. Stop when it hurts. That's good, now forward. Okay, try to reach across your chest. How'd you injure your shoulder?"

"I've had two other dislocations," Lucy said through clenched teeth. "The first was a car wreck, a long time ago. The second happened six months ago in a Karate competition. This time I ... uh ... fell."

Cassie's fingers probed and drew a wince. "I've never seen a shoulder float this free in the socket. That's not good."

"Yeah, well, it hurts, too. Dr. Beaumont's got me scheduled for surgery next week."

After having her bend, stretch, and contort like a pretzel, Cassie announced, "We're done. Let's get you back in bed."

She helped Lucy into the sling again. "Let me finish my notes, and I'll get out of your hair. Be sure you wear the sling all the time, take the pain medication Dr. B will give you, and I'll see you after your surgery."

Lucy hugged her achy arm to her chest and adjusted the bed's position so she could sit upright.

Cassie used the rolling tray-table to finish her notes.

Imperfect Trust

A thump came from the hall, followed by a muffled gurgle. The door to Lucy's room opened and a man in blue scrubs slipped inside. He wore a surgical mask, a tissue-thin cap over his hair, and held one arm behind his back.

Cassie looked up with a frown. "Can I help you?"

The man ignored her, his stare fixed on Lucy. His eyes blazed with a manic intensity.

Lucy tugged the bed covers higher.

"I told you I would find you." The baritone held dark promise.

Lucy fumbled for the bedside remote. This couldn't be happening.

Jensen Argault lowered the surgical mask and smiled. He brought his hand from behind his back and flourished a bloody knife.

"Hey," Cassie yelled. She'd grabbed the wheeled table and rammed it at the intruder. A vase of flowers crashed to the ground.

Lucy's lungs remembered their primary function. "Nooooo!" She screamed, loud enough to rival a police siren. Where was the guard? The nurses? She jabbed the call button.

Jensen's focus shifted from Lucy to Cassie. He pointed the knife at her. "You are in my way."

Lucy's heart pounded. A roaring sound filled her ears.

The bedside intercom blared. "Nurses' station."

"Help," Lucy shrieked. "Help me."

"Get security," Cassie shouted. "Hurry."

Argault made another move toward the bed, but Cassie jabbed him with the table. He retreated, rubbing his hip. "You'll pay for that."

He turned toward Lucy and gave her that awful three-fingered Boy Scout salute. "Another time, brat."

He slipped out the door.

Long hours later, after the last policeman left her hospital room and a new guard had taken up position outside the door, Ed and Cassie remained.

"I can't believe he killed Officer Gomez. Right outside my room." The horror leached into Lucy's voice. "I don't understand how someone didn't see."

"The scrubs he wore let him hide in plain sight," Ed said from his chair by the bed. "The policeman, the nurses ... no one gave him a second look."

"Cassie did."

"It was the surgical mask." Cassie rose from her chair in the corner where the detectives had subjected her to the same intensive grilling they'd given Lucy. "They're pretty commonplace around the hospital, but you don't wear them outside the OR. Around your neck maybe but not over your face."

"Well, it won't happen again. With his bank accounts cut off, Cypher will soon become desperate. He'll make mistakes," Ed continued. "Don't worry, Lucy. We'll catch him."

Lucy rubbed her temple. How could she *not* worry? "Ed, you still don't get it. It's not about the money. Losing those Cayman accounts won't stop him. I told you, I knew Jensen in college. He's selfish, cruel, cunning, and manipulative. Add in computer genius with an IQ of 175-plus and an advanced degree in psychology, and you have a psychopathic nightmare. He gets off on the power."

Ed frowned. "You think it's all a game for him?"

Lucy nodded. "I know it is." She was weary of talking about Jensen, about Cypher. "Tell me about Todd. Is he here at Grady?"

The lines around Ed's eyes deepened, adding to the overall impression of weariness. "He arrived here minutes ahead of you. The ER docs stabilized him and treated his leg wound. The bullet went straight through. There's a lot of

Imperfect Trust

muscle damage, but it didn't nick bone or blood vessels, which is a miracle. His hand's a mess, though. They shipped him to Emory University Hospital to see a vascular specialist. And yeah, before you ask, I put a guard on him, too."

A weight lifted from Lucy's chest. Del faced a long recovery, but he was alive. She'd made the right decision. "What about my laptop? Is it secure?"

"Locked up in the swat van. I'll put it in my office safe tomorrow. Look Lucy, you'll need help before and after your surgery. Phyllis and I want you to stay with us."

She shook her head. "I'm not putting you or your family at risk, Ed. Did we get the files?"

He released a long, drawn out breath and let his shoulders slump. "Yeah. Your program worked like magic." Ed stood and rolled his neck in circles, making the cervical joints pop. "You took a huge risk today, Lucy. One that could've gotten you killed. If you worked for me, I'd put you on toilet detail for the next twenty-five years."

The twinkle in his eyes belied the gruffness of his tone.

"Cypher might've gotten away again," he went on. "But his drug operation is history for the foreseeable future. Delacroix owes you. I owe you." Ed leaned down. "You turned out okay, Lucy. I always knew you would. I'm proud of you."

After Ed departed, Lucy hobbled from the bed to the small closet to get her backpack and tattered clothing.

"What are you doing?"

Lucy looked up in surprise. Cassie had been so quiet hidden away in the corner that Lucy forgot she was there. "You heard what I said. Jensen will hurt anyone who gets in his way. I have to leave." She tossed the blood-stained shirt on the bed. Her upper lip curled at the thought of wearing it again.

"Um, I don't think running is such a good idea. You're not in the best shape, Lucy. Let the police handle this. Let them do their job."

"You mean like today?"

Cassie pursed her lips. "You have a point, but you can't very well waltz out of here wearing those rags. The new guard will have Ed on the phone before you reach the end of the hall. And what about your shoulder? Where will you go?"

Valid points. With no immediate answer. She met Cassie's stare. "I could use your help."

"Uh-uh, no way. I'm pretty sure there's something in my Code of Ethics that says 'thou shalt not help foolish girls commit suicide.'"

"Listen. By now, Cypher—Jensen—has ferreted out every detail of my life. He'll know where I live, all my contacts, the kind of cereal I eat for breakfast, that I'm allergic to chocolate. I can't go home. Can't call my friends, or even use my cell phone. Heck, he's probably hidden a tracking device on my car. I have to get away. Now. While he thinks I'm an easy target."

Cassie stared at her, one eyebrow raised. "You're allergic to chocolate?" She threw her hands up in the air and shook her head. "Look, I hate to break it to you, but you *are* an easy target. I mean, look at you. You've got a bum shoulder, you're weaker than a virgin daiquiri, and I doubt you have ten bucks in your pocket. I repeat: where will you go?"

"Getting my shoulder fixed won't matter if I'm dead. I just need someplace to hide until I can come up with a plan."

"I get what you're saying, but you haven't thought this through." Cassie's lips thinned.

"I'll think it through later. Right now, I have to slip away while he thinks I'm incapacitated."

It wasn't fair. She'd known Cassie for only a few hours, and yet a bond had formed between them. Now, their fledgling friendship wouldn't have a chance to get off the ground.

"I know somewhere you'd be safe," Cassie said. She looked anything but happy about it.

Lucy looked up with a spark of hope. "Where?"

"Hastings Bluff. My home. I've got an apartment there. You can't drive or use a credit card to book a flight, but you can buy a bus ticket. Cash can't be traced." Cassie pursed her lips and tapped her chin. "The sheriff there is a friend of mine. There's also an army of hardcore cowboys who'd love to correct Mr. Cypher's inadequate upbringing, and that includes my dad and three brothers. You see, Lucy, in Idaho we don't tolerate jerks that like to hurt women or children."

"I don't want to drag your family into my mess."

"Well, whether you want it or not, you need help. Idaho is like two thousand miles away. My hometown is so far off the beaten path you can't find it unless you're looking for it. Even then you might miss it. This Cypher jerk will stick out in Hastings Bluff like a pig in my mother's parlor."

Idaho. Jensen Argault would never think to look for her there.

She fingered the flash drive in the backpack's front zipper pocket. Her most important files were on the tiny device—the framework of her new video game, *LA Kidd,* and the source code for Quicksilver. "Your mother has a parlor?"

Cassie rolled her eyes.

"I need clothes. Could you get me some scrubs?" She dropped her cell phone in the drawer of the bedside table. She couldn't take it with her. "I need money. Is there a Bank of America nearby?" Her mind raced with possibilities.

"Scrubs shirts are all pullover. Too difficult with your shoulder messed up, not to mention how much attention you'd draw wearing them on a long bus trip. I have a change of clothes in my locker. You get cleaned up and pack your stuff while I run next door to the office." She slipped out of the room.

Lucy used the toothbrush, toothpaste, and comb provided by the hospital. Travel would be like this, slow and one-handed, and without pain medication. She rubbed her aching shoulder and had almost talked herself out of the crazy venture when Cassie returned ten minutes later.

"I have jeans, a button-up shirt, and some slip-on Keds that should fit." She laid the clothes out on the bed along with an oversized plaid shirt and a fleece-lined denim jacket before dumping Lucy's rags in the trashcan. "Springtime in Idaho is a lot colder than here. My brother's flannel shirt will be warm enough on the bus, but you'll need the jacket outside the farther north you go."

"Thanks."

With Cassie's help, Lucy changed into the new duds, slipped on her old dirty socks, and donned the heeless sneakers. "I'm beginning to think this might work. So, how do I get past the guard?"

Cassie's sly look would've made a fox proud. "I'll leave first. When you hear a loud racket, wait ten seconds and peek out. If the guard is gone, go left down the hall and out through the double doors. Follow the signs to Radiology. I'll meet you there and take you out the employee entrance. My car's in a parking lot not far away."

"How in the world do I find my way to Idaho?"

"We'll look up the closest bus station on my phone while we search for a bank. First, I need to call someone." She pulled her cell phone from another pocket and dialed.

"Uh ..." Lucy wasn't sure about letting anyone else in on their plans.

"James? Hi, it's Cassie. I need a favor." Silence. "That's not true. I don't only call you when I want something." Another pause. "Well, yeah, I do need something *this* time. I loaned my apartment to a friend. Will you give her my spare key when she arrives? It will take her a few days to get there." Cassie shrugged. "I don't know, as long as she wants." More silence. "Great, her name is Lucy. I'll give her your cell number. Thanks, James."

She ended the call, scribbled a name and number on a piece of paper, and stuffed the note in the pocket of Lucy's jeans. "Don't lose this. Call Sheriff James Evers when you arrive. He's a good man to have on your side, but it's your decision how much you want to tell him. You should change buses a few times." Cassie pulled a folded baseball cap from a hip pocket, tugged it over Lucy's head, and threaded her ponytail through the back opening.

Emotion made Lucy's throat tighten. She caught her new friend's hand and squeezed. "I don't know how to thank you."

Cassie gave her a careful hug. "Stay safe, that's how. Now, let's do this before somebody comes in." She slipped out the door.

Lucy blinked away tears. She hadn't cried in years and couldn't afford such a weakness now. She grabbed the backpack and positioned herself by the door. What kind of commotion did Cassie have in mind?

A crash resounded from down the hall.

Lucy flinched.

Voices shouted.

A peek through the narrow crack of the not-quite-closed door allowed Lucy to see a dark blue uniform dash by. This was it.

After a count of ten, she eased the door open and peeked to the right. Plastic basins, urinals, and bedpans—some still rolling—littered a twenty-foot swath of the hallway. Cassie flailed in the middle of the mess. Two nurses waded through the clutter and went to her aid while the policeman hurried toward them.

Pulse racing, Lucy stepped into the hallway, ducked her head, and walked in the opposite direction. The urge to run almost overpowered the need for nonchalance. She reached the end of the hall and pressed the big, flat button on the wall that opened the automatic doors. A quick look behind brought a sigh of relief.

Cassie was on her knees with the nurses, gathering up the scattered items. The policeman wrestled with the shelving unit. No one saw Lucy dart through the doors.

After one wrong turn, she backtracked, found the Radiology waiting room, took a seat in the far corner, and hid behind a magazine. Her pulse never slowed. Minutes felt like hours.

"There you are. C'mon. Let's go."

Lucy jumped. Never had someone looked more like an answer to a prayer. She followed Cassie through the maze of corridors and out onto the sidewalks of downtown Atlanta.

"Three blocks to the parking lot. Can you make it?" Cassie hooked her arm through Lucy's good one.

"Other than Jell-O legs, a stomach that wants to turn itself inside out, and a demon poking my shoulder with a pitchfork, I'm fine. I can make it." She hoped she could make it.

When they reached the car, Cassie handed Lucy her phone. "Find the closest Greyhound station while I get us out of here. We're going to Buckhead. I know where the Bank of America is there."

Fifteen minutes later, Lucy went inside the bank and withdrew five-thousand dollars in twenties. She stuffed a wad in her jeans, some more in the button pocket of the denim shirt, and the rest she stashed in the bottom of the backpack.

They made another stop at Target where she picked up a cheap phone with prepaid minutes, a change of clothes, a bottle of ibuprofen, snacks, and some bottled water. After that, they headed for the Greyhound station on Forsyth Street.

When Cassie pulled to the curb in front of the bus station, Lucy reached over and squeezed her new friend's hand. "I don't know how to thank you."

Cassie gave her a gentle hug in return. "Promise me you'll be careful."

"Always."

Leaving the safety of the little Civic required every scrap of Lucy's courage. How was she going to make it two thousand miles to Idaho?

Chapter Three

The doorbell chimed, announcing a visitor to Cameron Security Services. Voices murmured from the reception area followed by soft laughter. A few seconds more and footsteps started down the hall.

Wade pushed back from his desk with a groan, his concentration broken. They didn't get many drop-in visitors. Most clients came by referral.

He glanced at the clock on the wall and gave a low whistle. No wonder his spine creaked like the third stair step at home. Sitting hunched over in front of the computer for five hours straight would do that to you. Whoever had come to visit had good timing. It was past time he took a break.

Maybe it was also past time to give up on this snipe hunt. He'd spent the past year searching for whatever it was his ex had inserted into his computer system, and had nada to show for the effort. Sometimes he wondered if it really happened.

"Wade?" Mallory rapped on his open door. "Miz Tillberry stopped by to see you."

He lifted one eyebrow in surprise. Agnes Tillberry was the English teacher when he and his brothers were in school, and later the principal of Hastings Bluff High School when his sisters got there. In her seventies now, she didn't get out much anymore. Whatever brought her here today must be important.

Agnes Tillberry stepped into his office. Whipcord thin and about as substantial as a dandelion puff, she greeted him with a smile. "Hello, Wade. If I'm interrupting I can come anoth—"

He hurried over and took her arm. "Nonsense, Miz Tillberry. Come on in and have a seat."

She patted his hand and followed him to the guest chair. "Thanks, Mal."

His sister and temporary office manager waved and walked away.

Once his visitor was seated, Wade took the chair behind the desk. "How's that new computer working for you?"

He'd given Miz Tillberry a new Dell laptop with the biggest monitor he could find for Valentine's Day. Even so, she still had to crank up the zoom. Hard to believe those piercing hazel eyes were failing.

Her cheeks turned rosy, but delight sparkled in her eyes. "You are such a thoughtful young man. Do you know I can talk with my great-granddaughter on the computer now? And see her? It's like I'm right there in their living room in Seattle with them. I love it."

Wade smiled, warmed by her obvious enjoyment.

"I'm so excited about the wedding," she went on. "TJ is perfect for your brother, Garrett. You know they asked me to sit with your family at the service. So sweet."

Wade settled back in his chair. Miz Tillberry didn't do chatty. Her prattle this morning made him nervous. "Of course you'll sit with us at my brother's wedding," he assured her. "You became part of the family after you kicked my butt and put me on the straight and narrow back in high school. If not for you ... well, let's say Mom and Dad are mighty grateful my name isn't a bunch of numbers, and that I don't have to wear an orange jumpsuit."

"Well, orange isn't your color." Her lips twitched. "You were always smarter than the others in your grade and so bored with the curriculum. A dangerous combination. I still remember all the mischief you masterminded ... and how you snickered when your friends got blamed for it. That is, until you got caught. Remember that night, Wade?"

He shook his head. "I'll never live it down. Peggy Sue Renfroe hates me to this day. She said I ruined her life."

Mrs. Tillberry raised her hands and swayed side-to-side, doing a credible imitation of the oldies tune Wade had sung at halftime during the homecoming football game so long ago.

"I don't know what I was thinking. "He laughed. "Mom still swears they heard me three miles away at the ranch."

Mrs. Tillberry joined in with his laughter. "Cody Cameron didn't know whether to be proud of how his son hijacked the stadium's sound system or angry that you blew it up."

"Peggy Sue wasn't too thrilled either."

"Neither were her parents. Or the booster club, football team, fire department, and Pastor Westmoreland."

"Dad threatened to let them put me in jail. It took me forever to pay off the damages."

"I can't believe so much time has passed. What's it been, fifteen years? And now we have another Wade finishing up his junior year."

Here it comes. He cocked one eyebrow and waited her out.

"Casey Petersen is a lot like you were—skinny, angry, bored, too much time on his hands, and smarter than the rest of the students combined. Rupert Black called me this morning for advice. He's the current principal and remembered when I faced a similar problem with you back when I held his position. He's afraid Casey has done something foolish that could get him hurt."

Ahhh, the boy needed to hear from someone who'd been down that road. Wade could do that. Put a little fear in him. "Got an attitude, huh?" Wade recalled a few of his own misadventures. The only difference was he'd had an older brother who was bigger than everybody else. Sounded like

Mrs. Tillberry's pet might not be as lucky. "You want me to talk some sense into him?"

She nodded. "Yes, but there's more. Casey is very good with computers, but he has a chip on his shoulder."

Miz Tillberry had a way of looking at you as if she could strip your soul naked and make you confess to things you never did. Those gray-green eyes were focused on him now. "I don't know that talk will be enough at this point. You see, three of the football players confronted him last week with an ultimatum—hack into the school network and raise their math grades ... or else. You can imagine his answer."

Wade pursed his lips and nodded, wondering where she was going.

"Casey came to school yesterday with a black eye, a busted lip, and limping like he knew firsthand how bad my arthritis can get."

"He say what happened?"

"Of course not. But a group of students did and reported it. Unfortunately, by the time help arrived, those boys had left Casey on his face in the dirt." A twinkle sparked in her eyes. "He got the last laugh though."

"Okay, I'll bite. What'd he do that's probably gonna earn him another beating?"

She covered her mouth in a useless attempt to hide her delight. "Mind you, we can't prove a thing, but *someone* hacked into the school system last night and changed some of the students' grades. I thought Principal Black's heart would fail when he told me about it this morning."

"Let me guess—the same three who beat the snot out of Casey"

Her long neck dipped in another nod.

"And instead of improved scores, I'll bet they're now *failing* in math."

She tittered like a schoolgirl. "Oh, more than that. It

appears those three have failed every subject, PE included, since the school system put its records online two years ago. Worse, the school board commissioner received an anonymous e-mail last night questioning their graduation qualifications."

Wade's stomach ached from the laughter he held back. He bit his bottom lip. Dadgum, but he liked this kid.

"Unfortunately, the original records don't seem to exist anymore, electronic or paper. The commissioner has no choice but to suspend them pending a special investigation into their academic standing."

He did laugh then. "And that's a problem because ...?"

"All three of those boys have football scholarships."

His laughter came to an abrupt halt. A prank was a prank, but this could affect lives. Casey's included. "You talk to this Casey's parents?"

Mrs. Tillberry sighed. "Parent. Singular. His mother works two jobs. She has no idea how to deal with a son who's smarter than she is."

"What about the father?"

"I don't know that she's ever mentioned his name."

Wade pursed his lips, aware that Miz Tillberry had led him along like a blind mule. Next, she'd be asking him to—

"I thought you might have some work Casey could do around here." She waved one hand in a vague gesture. "He needs a role model, a man who can influence him in a positive way."

It took all Wade's willpower to not groan. Miz Tillberry wanted him to adopt a rebellious, sullen teenager. Become a father figure to a kid who'd gotten too big for his own britches, and yet was too dumb to get out of the way of an enraged bull—or in this case, three bulls.

He'd pay whatever it cost, do any physical job she asked. But this? He was thirty-two dysfunctional years old and could claim one mangled long-term relationship with a woman. What did he know about a snarky teen? Wade needed another emotional involvement like he needed a new pair of pink roller skates. "Look, Miz Tillberry, I'd like ..."

Disappointment radiated from the fragile woman. Her smile dimmed as she fumbled to rise. "It's okay, Wade. I know it's a lot to ask. We'll figure something else out. You've been so kind all these years. I never want to impose on you."

"Hold on, Miz Tillberry." She'd always made him look outside himself. He hated feeling like a jerk. "You didn't let me finish."

She looked at him with a mixture of resignation and hope.

"As I was saying, I'd like to help and ... I'm glad you thought of me." He tugged at his suddenly too-tight shirt collar. "Send Casey over tomorrow after school lets out. If we can come to an agreement and his mama's okay with an afterschool job, I'll put him to work."

Miz Tillberry's lips twitched, deepening the wrinkles around her mouth and eyes.

He might regret his decision later, but right now, right this minute, he'd change his name to Florence if it would keep the smile on her face.

"Supper was a good idea, Mal. It's good to get out."

Wade cut into his T-bone, took a bite, and almost moaned out loud. Beef Barons had the best beefsteak in the county, well worth the eighteen-mile drive to the neighboring town of Challis. Even better, he could actually enjoy the meal without an interruption every five minutes by well-intentioned but nosy friends.

"I'm proud of you, Wade."

He stopped chewing, his mouth full of half-masticated steak. None of his siblings were good at feelings. Wariness filled him as he stared at his sister. Somehow he got the chunk of meat to go down. "Mmm. This is really good."

"Don't choke." Mallory giggled. "You try to come across all gruff and tough, but I'm not a bit surprised you took on Miz Tillberry's juvenile delinquent. I just wanted to say I'm glad you're my brother."

Wade squirmed. Who was this stranger sitting across the table from him? Camerons didn't do the touchy-feely thing. "Kid needs a job, and we can use the help."

She shook her head. "You're a fake, Wade Alexander Cameron, and a bad liar, too. It's way more than that."

He stared, at a loss for words.

"You have a soft spot for people in trouble. I think that's why you took Sarah in after you got out of the Army and she left the CIA. And why you let her go when she tried to hack into your computer. You should have let James arrest her. As sheriff, the decision was his to make. Not yours."

Sweat beaded on his forehead. He needed to put an end to Mallory's misplaced hero worship. If she knew a tenth of what he'd done while in service …

"Not going there."

"She conspired with a known terrorist to steal your programming. You've refused to talk about what happened, but we both know Sarah Porter belongs in jail for what she did. She and Azizi probably wanted it for the Afghani mafia. And let's not mention she cheated on you."

"Afghanistan doesn't have a mafia. What they have is much worse. And I agree, let's not mention the cheating."

Mallory had it right. Sarah should be in jail on federal charges. Not by his hand, though.

"C'mon, Wade. Talk to me." Mallory reached across the table. "Whatever's got you tied in knots, you have to let it go. I want to help."

He patted her hand but then released it and leaned back in his chair. The guilt he carried from that final mission was a scar on his soul. He'd gotten a purple heart and a medical discharge while too many of his men had died that day.

Mallory withdrew her hand, but her sad eyes never left his face.

"She saved my life, Mal. The bullet I took on that last mission should have been the end. Instead of heading for safety like she should have, Sarah took out two shooters and somehow got me on my feet and out of there. Am I supposed to just forget that?"

Their orders were simple—stay low. Keep moving. Avoid contact with the natives at all costs. Simple orders ... until they stumbled on the goat herder hidden in a shallow depression. A boy. Maybe ten years old.

Wade's hand strayed to the puckered scar on his side. The other members of their team had been wiped out. And the Taliban executed the boy anyway.

"You think letting her go evens the score?"

"I don't know." He shrugged. "Maybe."

Something about their escape had always bothered him. It was too easy.

"Well, it was a good thing you upgraded your security before she made her move." Mallory wouldn't back down.

"Yeah. A good thing." Except he didn't upgrade the security system. He'd written a whole new program instead. Because he didn't trust her.

"All right, Mr. Monotone. No more talk about Sarah. For what it's worth, I think you'll make a great mentor."

Wade grinned and tried for a lighter tone. "There's not a soul in the world who can tell Miz Tillberry no when she's set on something."

Mallory laughed. "Remember the botanical gardens she bullied Councilman Vincent into funding? And the bronze sculpture she had the city council commission for the town square? I swear if Miz Tillberry was twenty-five years younger and you were twenty-five years older, we'd have a match made in heaven."

"Hmph." Slicing through the meat on his plate, he leaned in and took another bite.

"So, shouldn't you have found whatever it is Sarah put in your computer by now?"

He chewed and swallowed. "When did you get so smart, little sister?"

She dropped her eyes. "Always been smart," she mumbled. "Can I help it if none of you ever bothered to notice?"

The accusation and hurt in her tone made him uncomfortable. Realizing she was right didn't sit well either. He studied her for several long moments before responding. "Well, to answer your question, I'll keep searching 'til I find whatever *it* is. I have to."

The planted file had to be a backdoor and sooner or later Sarah would find a way in.

But why had she waited six months?

"What about Kevin Fowler? Do you know his plans?" she asked.

Wade shrugged. He'd alerted the former Bureau of International Intelligence agent when the first attack occurred but hadn't heard from him since. "I wish James hadn't called him in."

Wade shook his head. Did Fowler really believe he would sell classified technology to a terrorist like Ullah Ahmad Azizi and endanger U.S. soldiers?

Mallory must have sensed his darkening mood. "Let's change the subject. I have a favor to ask. Will you teach me how to play *LA Kidd*?"

Mal wanted to play a video game? Now, *that* he didn't expect. "Unlike us guys, you hate computer games, Sis." The rosy flush in her cheeks provided a clue. "Ah, I get it. A way to get closer to our esteemed sheriff."

The blush deepened to fiery red. "No. Not at all. I'm just tired of feeling left out."

A laugh bubbled up, but Wade choked it back. Once Sarah was out of the picture, his family had gone on about their business. Not that he blamed them. He hid his feelings well—except Mallory saw through his defensive facade. She'd waltzed in, taken charge of his business, and kept it afloat while he floundered through an emotional quagmire. He owed his sister.

"Okay. I'll help. I have to tell you, though. The blogs claim no one can beat it. I've never gotten past level ninety-nine, so they may be right."

Mallory lifted an eyebrow. "You think it was designed that way? I'll bet the kid Miz Tillberry's sending over can help. Sounds like something right up his alley."

"Let's see if Casey sticks first. So, why didn't you ask James?" He raised his eyebrows, expecting another blush.

She studied her plate again, her posture drooping. "He's still at work. Has to wait for someone coming in on the bus, part of his 'sheriff-ly' duties. I swear the man is married to his job. Besides, I don't want to impose on our friendship "

Friendship. Right. He managed not to snort. His baby sister and the town sheriff were made for each other. He suspected Mallory knew it. James, on the other hand, seemed clueless.

Wade signaled for the check. "Let's go. I need to talk to Jonas. He thinks old man Hughes is ready to close the deal to breed five of his mares with Hercules, but he needs me to hold his hand."

"I thought Garrett handled the contracts now that Dad's retired and you're spending most days at the office." Mallory laid her napkin aside and stood.

"Garrett and his bride-to-be are in Idaho Falls today picking out …" Wade grinned and made air quotes with his fingers. "*Window treatments* for their new home."

Imperfect Trust

Chapter Four

She shouldn't have bought the milk.

Lucy paid the cashier and picked up the plastic bag containing the box of cereal and loaf of bread with her left hand. Even that insignificant weight put a strain on her shoulder. Clenching her teeth, she hefted the second heavier bag with the quart of milk and a jar of peanut butter in her right hand, and headed for the exit.

The automatic door of the IGA Foodliner swished open to bright morning sunshine and clear blue skies. And cold. She shivered despite the flannel shirt one of Cassie's brothers had unknowingly donated. Atlanta seemed almost tropical compared to Idaho. Maybe the cooler temperature would distract her from the ache in her arm. And maybe she should have worn the darn sling after all.

Hastings Bluff, Idaho. Small Town, USA with its two-story pillared courthouse on the square, a Main Street with parking spaces on the slant, and a combined hardware and feed store circa 1940 where old men played checkers on the front porch. They even had an honest-to-goodness Five and Dime Store on the corner. Throw in the few three-story modern office buildings, a McDonald's with an indoor playground, a combination bank and post office, a few boutiques, a library, and the Wal-Mart Supercenter her bus had passed on the way into town, and Hastings Bluff had it all. A confluence of Americana, Old West, and modern-day cowboys.

Lucy stared down the long sidewalk, frowning hard, her thoughts already focused on taking a break. The distance

Imperfect Trust

hadn't seemed so far when she started out, eight city blocks, or so. No more than a mile from Cassie's apartment to the grocery store and another mile back. An easy stroll—with empty arms.

Her shoulder burned now. The fire increased with each stride. A week had passed with no noticeable improvement to the injury. She suspected Dr. Beaumont was right as usual. Surgery couldn't be avoided this time. But risk a hospital stay? Not a chance. Not now. She'd be like a kid behind the drapes who thought she was hidden when her feet were sticking out. Hospital records would be child's play for Jensen Argault.

She looked around again, always aware of her surroundings. Was she safe even now?

Two blocks farther she set the grocery bags on a bench and pressed a palm to her throbbing shoulder. All the previous separations had hurt, but nothing like this. At this rate, she might make it back to the apartment by sunset.

She'd lied to Ed when she called him from Chattanooga, and again from Denver. Told him the pain was nothing. He'd scolded and threatened to put out a nationwide all-points bulletin, but she wouldn't tell him her destination. The fewer people who knew the better.

The disposable phone purchased in Atlanta got tossed in the trash after those two calls. No trails, no phone tracking. She bought a replacement in Salt Lake City, but Ed hadn't asked her whereabouts that time. He knew she wouldn't tell him. Or did he suspect the security of the lines in his office? Or maybe he was relieved to be rid of her.

The Calico Diner beckoned from a short distance ahead. Situated across the street from the sheriff's office, it looked to be about halfway to the apartment. She set shorter goals now, resting her arm between milestones.

Her stomach chose that moment to protest the length of time since the cheese crackers she'd eaten on the bus the night before. Sheriff Evers had bragged about the pie at the diner. A cup of coffee sounded pretty good, too.

The diner appeared busy, though at half past nine in the morning, more patrons poured out than in. Lucy set off again, taking both plastic bags in her right hand this time, her left arm hugged tight to her side.

A shiny black pickup pulled abreast of her. The two men in the truck stared, marking her every step. In front of the diner, the driver maneuvered the vehicle into one of the slanted parking spaces and the men got out … and turned toward her. They stared with way too much interest. Big men. Like professional linebacker big. They wore dark suits. And sunglasses.

Fear, the new resident in her head, seized control.

The sheriff claimed strangers, those from the city in particular, stood out around these parts. Lucy might be an outsider, but even she could tell how out of place they looked.

Her breathing escalated to ragged pants. She'd arrived in town less than twenty-four hours ago. Could he have found her this fast?

She slowed her pace and tried to calm her breathing, all the while glancing around for someone, anyone who might help. The little can of mace in her pocket wouldn't provide much of a defense. Her eyes locked on the sheriff's office across the street.

The men started toward her, blocking the sidewalk. Those blasted shades might hide their eyes but not the determined set of their jaws. One stood taller than the other, and bulkier. Not that the smaller one could be considered small. Both towered over her. They had to be Jensen's men. No one else here had given her a second look.

Inhale. Exhale. Focus. She was a trained BII agent. She could protect herself from muscle-bound cretins. *One-handed?*

Lucy shoved her left hand into her jeans pocket, ignoring

the pain, and pulled out the small canister of pepper spray. If she caught them off guard, sprayed them both, she could dash across the street to the sheriff's office.

The two men slowed. The big guy reached for her. "Hey there, little lady. Let me take those bags for you."

The smaller man, who'd remained a step behind, frowned. "Hold on a minute, Wade. I don't think—"

Gripping the plastic handles of the grocery bags in her right hand, Lucy put everything she had into the swing. The big guy danced back, but the bags smacked him square in the chest. The flimsy plastic tore. The milk carton exploded. White froth spewed everywhere.

"Hey." Big Guy yelled, wiping at his face and clothes. "What'd you do that for?"

The smaller man who'd hesitated to approach removed his glasses and made a grab for her, his arms flung wide. "Hey, hey, easy now."

She couldn't let him get those beefy arms around her.

A quick transfer and she held the little canister in her good hand. A stream of liquid shot out. *Bingo.* Direct hit in both eyes.

Small Guy fell back with a howl, clawing at his face.

She pointed the spray at the milk-spattered man and shot another stream at his face.

Big Guy dodged away. His sunglasses, still in place, shielded his eyes but his feet got tangled up in the scattered groceries. He slipped in the milk puddle and went down hard. He sprang to his feet with a snarl and snatched his glasses off. Fury ignited in deep blue eyes. He lunged for her.

Lucy eluded him, surprised a man his size could move so fast.

A few feet away, his friend howled. "I can't see. She blinded me." Small Guy scrubbed at his eyes with his fist and fell to his knees. His curses sizzled in the air.

Lucy looked from the wailing man to the one who stalked her. *So this was how a rabbit felt.*

Big Guy glanced back at his injured buddy, at her, back to him. Finally, he turned and picked his way through the remains of the groceries to kneel by the injured man's side. "Somebody get me water, quick," he yelled at the gathered crowd.

The paralysis snapped. Lucy sprinted for the sheriff's office—and stepped into the road right in front of a truck.

The driver slammed on his brakes, horn blaring. His front bumper missed her by inches. He leaned out the window, waved a fist, and yelled a few choice words, some she'd never heard before.

Her legs trembled as she started for the sheriff's office again. They wouldn't dare follow her there.

On the far side of the road, she risked a glance over her shoulder. Oh mercy, the big guy was coming.

She tripped and fell.

The sting of skinned knees lasted a split second—until her palms shot out in reflex and hit the sidewalk. Agony stabbed through her shoulder. Tears streamed down her face. She couldn't get her breath for a long moment.

With her lower lip clenched between her teeth, she struggled to her feet with her arm clutched tight to her middle. *Almost there.*

Somehow she made it up the two steps, threw the door open, and burst inside. "Sheriff!"

The office was empty.

CCC

Wade's heart faltered when the crazy woman darted out in front of Fred Robertson's truck. Primal instincts he didn't know he had roared to life. He started forward, intending to haul her to safety and shake some sense into her. What—or who—had her so spooked she lost all common sense?

Jonas grabbed his arm. "Wade?"

Imperfect Trust

Turning away with reluctance, Wade said, "Yeah, Buddy. I'm here." Jo needed him more than he needed to catch that little wildcat. Besides, she wouldn't get far. Not in this town.

DeeDee Guthrie, owner of the diner, hurried over, lugging two water pitchers filled to the brim. Another woman, a real looker with long flaxen hair tied back in a braid, followed on DeeDee's heels. She carried another pitcher of water and an armload of napkins.

"Shea, grab his head," DeeDee instructed the blonde.

The girl wrapped an arm around Jonas's neck and fisted his hair to pull his head back.

He collapsed back against the young woman, arms flailing.

"Jonas, hold still," DeeDee scolded. "We're trying to help you. Keep your eyes open. I'm gonna pour water over them. Wash that stuff out."

"You okay, Jo?" Wade patted his brother's arm and glanced back across the street.

"I got this, sweetie," DeeDee said. "Go find out what put that girl's panties in a twist."

"Yeah." Jonas snarled out through clenched teeth. "And then I want to talk to her."

Wade studied his brother's swollen eyes and red face. "Don't worry. I got this."

He'd taken one step into the street when the girl tripped over the far curb. She didn't get up right away, but then she was scurrying up the steps and into the sheriff's office.

Ha. Like James would protect her after what she did to Jonas. She was a fierce little thing, he'd give her that. But there wasn't a place in town she could hide.

The look on her face when she looked back one more time made him check his stride. He hadn't seen fear like that since Afghanistan.

The door closed behind her.

When he reached the other side of the street, Wade didn't bother with the steps. One stride and he grabbed the door handle and yanked. It didn't budge. She'd locked it. And didn't that add fuel to an already raging fire?

Jiggling the knob didn't work. He pounded on the door with his fist. "Open up," he yelled.

Nothing.

He reared back and rammed one shoulder against the door. The frame rattled. He hit it again and felt it give. "I said, open the door. Now."

Still nothing. Another heave-ho would do it. James would be ticked off and would send him a bill for the damages. Wade didn't care, as long as he caught the girl before she found a way out through the rear.

The wood splintered.

Wade stumbled in through the ruined door and spotted his prey hobbling toward the break room.

She looked back and saw him, her big, beautiful eyes filled with terror.

"Hey, hold on." He lunged forward and caught her arm ... and the world tilted. One moment his hand held her slim bicep, and the next his feet left the ground. He flew through the air. Upside down. And then falling. He hit the floor hard and all the breath in his lungs whooshed out. She'd flipped him. *Him.*

"Stop it. Right now."

James's voice didn't penetrate the red fog of anger and embarrassment that snared Wade. No way he'd let her get away again.

She staggered toward the kitchen, doubled over and making sounds like a wounded animal.

With a roar, he got his feet under him and dove at her.

"No, man. Don't do it. She's hurt."

James's admonition registered. Wade didn't tackle the woman outright. She was just a little thing. Instead, he snagged

Imperfect Trust

her ankle. He wanted to stop her, not hurt her.

She fell and landed hard on her left side. Her shriek cut off in mid-cry—when her head hit the floor.

"You fool. What's gotten into you, Wade? Didn't you hear me yell? Lucy's under my protection. She's hurt and you ... you ..."

Lucy? Wade felt like he'd swallowed a cat that was doing its darndest to claw its way back out.

She lay sprawled on the floor, not moving.

He scurried to the unconscious woman's side, panic expanding in his gut. She was under James's protection. From what?

Jonas barreled through the demolished door, wet shirt and suit jacket molded to his body. Eyes red and swollen, he radiated anger. "Where is she?" he snarled.

Wade knelt beside Lucy, sickened by the unnatural angle of her left arm. Shoulders shouldn't look that way.

His fingers found the pulse in her neck. Fast. Too fast. And uneven. He cupped her cheek. The baby-soft skin was ashen, cool to his touch.

"Wade? She okay?" James crowded in behind him. "Wade?"

"We're gonna need Doc Burdette."

CCC

Wade peeked inside the hospital-style room Doc Burdette had in the back of his office for the rare occasion when a patient needed a bed but not a hospital. The woman—Lucy—looked fragile lying there with her long brown hair spread out around her. Asleep, without the pinched look of terror and pain, she looked sweet. Innocent.

"You sure you didn't give her too much of that stuff, Doc? She's not very big." Wade looked at his watch again and started to pace. Miz Tillberry's teenage computer genius was due at his office soon. He snorted. Not a chance he'd leave here until he knew the girl would be okay.

Behind him in the hallway, Jonas snickered. "Don't know as I would've said that."

The doctor ignored them. He placed a stethoscope on the girl's chest and then took his time jotting notes in the chart before he fixed Wade with a stare that did indeed make him wish he'd kept his mouth shut. "First off, no one is very big compared to you. Second, if you hadn't manhandled her, she wouldn't be here. I've never known you to assault a woman before, Wade Cameron." The doctor turned and pinned Jonas with a stare. "Unlike your brother."

"Hey!" Indignation replaced Jonas's laughter. "Lyddie Thatcher outweighed me by at least fifty pounds, and she started it. Besides, we were kids."

Wade bit the inside of his mouth to stifle a chuckle. Lyddie had beaten the tar out of Jonas several times in second grade. Tired of getting pounded, his little brother had punched her. Once, but hard enough to make her nose bleed and earn him another whupping at home. Their dad raised his sons to respect women, whether they deserved it or not.

He shuddered at the thought of his dad's reaction and shoved his hands in his pockets. "Wasn't assault."

Doc Burdette harrumphed. He might be dwarfed in size by the Cameron men, but the old man left no doubt who was in charge in his office or what he thought of Wade's actions.

"Well, it's apparent her shoulder was injured prior to today's encounter. It's also obvious from the dark circles under her eyes that she's exhausted. We'll let her sleep as long as she needs." He pointed a finger. "And don't question my decisions."

Wade nodded. His eyes flickered toward the girl. What had possessed him to tackle the girl? He couldn't remember the last time he'd lost control like that.

Imperfect Trust

Doc waved his arms and shooed Wade and Jonas away. "What she doesn't need is to wake up with a couple of brutes in her room. Since you two don't have anything better to do than hang around and get in my way, you can fix the broken step out front. Go get your tools, boys. I'll let you know if anything changes here."

Outside, Jonas told Wade, "I'll get the tools."

Wade cocked an eyebrow at him.

"Hey, I'm not messing up my good suit. Yours is already ruined so you can pry up the board and hammer in the replacement."

"It was your idea to dress up for the appointment with Wyman Hughes and his lawyer this morning. Not that it did us any good." Wade looked down at his clothes. A donation for the rag bin. "Let's make it fast. I've got an appointment at the office in an hour."

Jonas set off at a jog to where he'd parked his truck in front of the diner, while Wade shrugged out of the milk-stained and ripped jacket and draped it across the porch rail.

James pulled up in his sheriff's cruiser a few moments later. "She still out?" He opened the door and stepped from the Explorer, took one look at Wade's clothes, and frowned. "You know you got a rip in your suit pants?"

Wade examined the tear over his knee. "Doc says she's exhausted and needs rest." He unbuttoned his cuffs and rolled up his shirtsleeves before kneeling on the ground to pry away the cracked step. Man, he hated carpentry work. "You gonna tell me why she's in Hastings Bluff, how it is you know her, and what you're protecting her from?"

"Cassie called about a week ago. Said a friend needed a place to stay and would I hand over the apartment key." James tipped his hat back. "Lucy showed up last night looking like she'd spent the last five days and nights on a bus."

"That's it?"

James nodded.

"Any idea why she maced Jonas and then skedaddled away like I meant to barbeque her for dinner?" Wade couldn't explain why, but Lucy running from him didn't sit well.

"Sounds like she felt threatened," James said.

"By a complete stranger? C'mon. I see women I don't know every time I visit Idaho Falls or Boise. Never sent one screaming for her life before today."

"My guess is she's running. I tried to call Cass last night after Lucy arrived. Tried again about fifteen minutes ago but your sister's not answering."

Jonas parked his truck behind the police car and got out. "What do you need?" He lifted the lid of the tool box in the bed of the black F-250.

"Give me a claw hammer to pull out the nails. Go ask Doc if he's got any boards in the garage we can use to replace it."

"There's some scrap lumber in the storage shed behind my office," James said. "I'm sure you can scrounge up something there."

Wade took the hammer from his brother. "Jo, you heard from Cassie lately?"

"Uh, no. Why would I?"

"She sent Lucy here," James said.

Easygoing Jonas disappeared. "Is Cassie in trouble?"

A cell phone trilled. Wade reached for his jacket while James and Jonas searched through their pants pockets.

"Mine." James held up his phone. "It's Cassie."

He took the call and put it on speaker. "Hey, little girl, your ears must be burning. Wade, Jonas, and I were just talking about you."

Her groan came loud and clear over the line. "Did you have to drag them into this? You know how they get."

Jonas rolled his eyes, releasing some of his tension.

Imperfect Trust

"Yeah, well, I'm the same way about people I care for," James answered. "Call it a man thing. Now tell me about your little friend."

"Lucy made it?"

"She came in on the eight o'clock bus last night. Now spill."

"What'd she tell you?"

"You already know the answer. I can't help her if I don't know what's going on."

"You were supposed to call me when she arrived," Cassie whined.

"I did call. You didn't answer."

"All right, I'll tell you what I know, just don't go all Rambo on me."

"Cass." James's voice resonated with warning.

"Okay, okay. Lucy was involved in a drug deal that went wrong. Now that crazy psycho, Cypher, is after her."

Chapter Five

Wade grabbed James's wrist and yelled at the cell phone. "You sent someone involved with a drug dealer here? To our home?"

Jerking his arm free, James thumbed up the volume. "Ignore your brothers, Cassie."

"Trouble. I knew it the minute we spotted her," Jonas barked. "Explains why she acted like a frightened rabbit, too. She's on the run."

"Who's after her, Cass?" Wade demanded. "Why is she afraid?" Wade demanded.

"If my two neurotic brothers will shut up for a moment, I'll tell you what I know. And you better not have scared her."

James made a slashing motion across his throat at Wade and his brother. "Go on, sweetheart."

Cassie waited a moment before continuing. "Okay. Lucy was admitted to Grady Hospital with a dislocated shoulder and assorted cuts and bruises. Dr. Beaumont, one of the orthopedists in the group I work for, assigned me to her case and asked me to do a physical assessment. The evaluation helps us establish a patient's pre-op threshold, which in turn tells us how far we can push with a post-op physical therapy plan. Dr. Beaumont treats the whole body, not just the injury. Anyway, I went to her hospital room. That's where I met her."

Jonas rolled his eyes. Smart and hardworking described Cassie perfectly, but the girl sure liked the sound of her own voice.

Imperfect Trust

"Just the facts, Cass," Wade told her. "We don't need a dissertation."

A miffed sound came over the line. "Well, now I understand why you guys can't keep a girlfriend. You need to practice the art of conversation."

Jonas made a rude noise.

Wade closed his eyes, barely managing to stifle a groan.

James frowned. "Cassie ..."

"All right," she huffed. "Some government agency planned a drug bust. It's the dealer that's been on all the news stations for the last week. They call him Cypher because he's some kind of computer genius. Anyway, Lucy was involved somehow and got hurt."

"Why'd you send her here?" James asked.

"As I was saying, Dr. Beaumont assigned me to Lucy's case. When I went to her room, I had to show my ID to the guard. I went in, did the assessment, and then we talked. I really like her, James."

"Wait, what? She had a guard?" Jonas barked.

"Guard? What guard?" Wade's brain lit up like a spotlight. This kept getting better and better.

James pinched the bridge of his nose and shook his head.

"Well, of course, she had a guard," Cassie explained. "Not that it stopped him, that Cypher guy. He put on scrubs and wore a surgical mask. The staff must have th-thought he was one of th-them."

Wade's ears perked up. Was that a tremor in Cassie's voice?

"We found out later he k-k-killed the guard before he came into Lucy's room."

Definitely a stammer. His little sister was upset. After multiple tours to Afghanistan, Wade thought he'd seen and heard it all. But the image his sister's words evoked, the fear in her voice ... His stomach lurched, threatening to reject what might be left of the early morning coffee and donut. From the gut-punch reaction of James and his brother, they might be helping him wash off Doc's sidewalk.

"What happened next?" James growled. His voice had dropped a full octave. Not a good sign. When James went all guttural, blood usually followed.

"He came in and just stood there, staring at Lucy. You remember the summer we crossed paths with that rabid fox?" Cassie asked. "The ropes of slobber hanging from its mouth? Ugh. It walked all funny and stiff, off balance. Worse was the way it stared at Jo like the rest of us didn't exist. That's how this guy acted, fixated on Lucy, with a knife in his hand. He never once looked at me. Until I shoved the tray-table at him."

Wade locked eyes with his brother and saw his own open-mouthed disbelief reflected.

Jonas opened his mouth, closed it, spun in a circle, and then clapped both hands on top of his head.

James made a zip-it gesture. He took a deep breath and, to his credit, sounded almost normal when he spoke.

"Cassie, honey, why did you shove a table at a man with a knife?"

"He'd started toward Lucy. He said awful things."

Jonas flung his arms out and looked to the heavens. A firecracker with its fuse lit. He should explode any minute now.

"I couldn't just stand there and watch him hurt her. I mean, she was trapped in a bed with the rails up. And her arm in a sling." Cassie's voice dropped to a whisper before it rose again. "So I whacked him. With the table. There was a vase of flowers on it, Gerbera daisies, I think. They fell off and shattered on the floor. That's when Lucy screamed and punched the nurse's call button. I might have screamed a little, too."

Wade leaned over, hands braced on his knees. His little sister had been threatened by a madman wielding a blade.

She'd fought him off with a ... table. He shuddered. The visual would haunt him for a long time.

A vein throbbed in James's neck. His voice remained calm, though it dropped again. "What happened next, Cass?"

"He, Cypher, pointed the knife at me. Said I couldn't protect Lucy from him. No one could. I think all the screams frightened him off, though, because he left then. Poof. One second he's there, the next he's gone."

James's grip on the phone turned his knuckles white. "Go on."

"The nurses didn't come in right away. I think they were distracted by the guard's body." Cassie's voice broke on a sob.

Wade took the phone before James crushed it in his fist. "Take a deep breath, Sis. It's okay. You're safe now. Lucy's safe."

"Lucy doesn't have any family, Wade. No close friends. And the police proved they can't protect her. She made up her mind to run with or without my help, so I thought maybe if she went far enough ... I mean, who'd think to look for her in Idaho?"

Wade looked at his brother and then at James.

"She kept saying she had to leave before he killed someone else to get to her," Cassie went on. "But she's hurt and all alone, and scared, too. I told her she'd be safe with you guys." There was an audible sniff this time.

Tough-as-nails Cassie who'd whacked him and Jonas upside the head with a broom when they were kids and her half their size. He'd never known her to back down from anything. Hearing the fear in her voice now—

"Anyway, that's why I sent her to Hastings Bluff. I thought ..." Her voice broke again. "Guess I was wrong."

"You made yourself a target, Cass." Jonas blasted. "Dad's gonna yank your butt home when he hears about this. I don't even want to think about what Derek will do."

"Don't you dare tell Mom and Dad. I worked too hard to land this internship. I will *not* leave with only a few weeks left." Feisty Cassie had returned. "And I don't give a fig what Derek Naughton thinks. Besides, I've got my own assigned bodyguard now."

Wade whispered away from the speaker. "If they couldn't protect Lucy, why would Cass think they can keep her safe?"

"That settles it. She's coming home," Jonas declared.

James pursed his lips and made a rude sound. "You think Cassie would listen to either of you? Derek, on the other hand, won't take any of her guff. He'll make her listen."

Wade closed his eyes and counted to ten. He didn't want to tell their dad, but he sure as heck didn't want to be the one to tell Derek, Cassie's sometime boyfriend. Those two had danced around each other ever since Derek landed in Hastings Bluff a little over a year ago. As James's newest deputy and with Cassie's tendency to ignore the speed limit, they'd knocked heads more than a few times. And his sister had the points on her driver's record to show for it.

Wade looked at his brother, not surprised when Jonas smirked in agreement. "Yeah, let's send Derek."

Uncovering the phone's speaker, Wade said, "All right, little sis. Since you're only there another six weeks and they've given you a bodyguard, we won't tell Mom or Dad ... on two conditions. First, your bodyguard is in charge. You do what he says, when he says, and you go nowhere without him. Got it?"

"Waaade."

He could picture her now—lower lip stuck out, hurt puppy look, long lashes fluttering. She and her twin, Mallory, had owned all three brothers from the time they could toddle about. But not this time.

"And you will call me once a week to check in. I want a phone call every Monday morning, Cass. I won't bend on this.

Imperfect Trust

You miss one time and I tell Dad." Wade didn't dare warn her that Derek would soon be her new bodyguard.

"Will you look after Lucy for me like I promised?"

"Of course," James answered.

"Thank you, James. Wade, I will call you every Monday. I get all tingly knowing you worry about me."

Jonas made a gagging sound.

"Good-bye, brat." Wade disconnected the call and handed the phone back to James.

"It's back to the office for me." James slipped the cell phone in his pocket and opened the cruiser door. "I've got a deputy to brief about a special assignment down south."

"I'll come with you and see if I can find that replacement board for Doc's step." Jonas climbed in the passenger side of James's cruiser.

When Jonas hadn't returned by the time Wade finished ripping away the broken step, he went inside to check on the patient.

"She's been stirring," Doc told him.

"Her shoulder gonna be okay?"

"Don't know. A good cough will pop it out of joint again. She needs surgery, but even then there's a possibility she might already have permanent damage."

"No," a muffled voice said behind them.

The two men turned toward the sound.

"Well, it looks like Sleeping Beauty has awakened." Doc moved to the bedside.

Wade remained at the door and studied the patient. Her hair was a tangled mess, but the lustrous shade reminded him of the way his dun-colored stallion's coat glistened like spun gold in bright sunlight. He suspected her hair would too.

"No surgery," she croaked again. Big brown eyes, heavy with sleep, struggled to hold his gaze.

Whispers lured Lucy from the depths of slumber. Two voices. Masculine. One soft spoken, with a higher pitch. The other one deeper, comforting.

Lucy gave up trying to recapture oblivion. She opened her eyes and blinked. "No. No surgery."

A smallish man wearing a long, white coat patted her hand. "We'll worry about that later, Lucy. Now, how's your shoulder?"

She couldn't move her arm. Maybe a good thing, since the deep-seated ache in her shoulder promised worse pain if she did. "Hurts."

"I strapped your arm down so you can't aggravate it. You need rest. I'm Dr. Wilton Burdette, by the way."

"She's staying in Cassie's apartment," the very large man standing in the doorway said. "I figure she'll need help so I called out to the ranch. Mom's on her way." He took a tentative step into the room.

"You." Lucy hissed. This was one of the men ... Weak and disoriented, her heart racing, she scuttled like a two-legged crab toward the far side of her bed.

He retreated, hands up in the air.

The doctor leaned over her. "Be still before you hurt yourself, Lucy. You're safe."

"Where am I? Where are my clothes?" She tugged the sheet higher over the thin, cotton gown.

"You're in my office." Dr. Burdette jerked a thumb at the door. "Goliath here and his brother brought you in after you fell."

She glared at the man in the doorway. "I didn't fall. He tackled me."

"Yeah, well you hit me with a bag of groceries first, tiger. And then you tried to blind my brother with pepper spray."

"Be quiet, both of you." The doctor's head didn't reach the big guy's shoulder, but he left no doubt who ran this show.

Imperfect Trust

"This is Wade Cameron, a friend of Sheriff Evers, who I believe you've already met. Wade says his sister sent you."

Cameron? "You're Cassie's brother?"

Wade nodded and inched forward again.

Lucy studied his face. He had close-cropped, dark brown hair, not as dark as Cassie's, but the blue eyes matched. Now that she looked at him without suspicion tainting her vision, she saw the resemblance. Her body sagged with relief.

"As I was saying, Wade and his brother, Jonas, brought you to my office. They've been under foot ever since."

"How long is ever since?"

The doctor glanced at his watch. "Going on six hours."

Half the day? Lucy relaxed her death grip on the sheet. Perhaps she'd been a little rash in her assessment of the two men.

Wade Cameron had a strong jaw and square chin that screamed arrogance, and he looked like he wasn't afraid of anything. Or anyone. Goliath seemed an apt description. Better than Big Guy.

"Care to explain why you attacked me and my brother? Without provocation, I might add." His deep voice matched the domineering attitude.

"Is he all right? Your brother?"

"Yeah. Mad, but he'll get over it." Wade edged closer.

Her mouth had the feel of cotton balls. So dry. She started to ask for water when an unpleasant odor made her nose wrinkle. "What's that smell?"

The doctor burst out laughing. "That would be Wade, here."

Wade rolled his eyes, color flushing his cheeks.

Another laugh echoed from the hall. A younger, somewhat smaller version of Goliath stuck his head in. He wore a grin, despite having bloodshot and swollen eyes.

"Don't tell me," Lucy said. "Another Cameron."

Wade chuckled at his brother's offended expression. "I suppose we have to claim him. This is my brother, Jonas."

"Don't get sassy, little lady. I still owe you." Jonas's grin changed to a menacing leer, but somehow, the threat didn't reach his eyes.

"I'm sure it was an unfortunate misunderstanding," Dr. Burdette said.

"Yeah, hers." Jonas shifted his glare to the doctor. "We wanted to help her with her groceries."

"Help?" Lucy's chin lifted. "You drove by so slow a tree could outrun you. The way you stared made my skin crawl, and then you parked that monster truck, jumped out, and cut me off on the sidewalk." She pointed a finger at Goliath—Wade. "That's when *he* tried to grab me."

"You always jump to conclusions?" Jonas asked.

"You both wore suits."

Jonas did a doubletake. "What's that got to do with anything?"

"The sheriff said strangers stood out around here. I haven't seen any men in suits. I thought you were ... thugs." Her chin lifted a little higher.

"Thugs?" Jonas took two aggressive steps forward.

Wade pressed a hand against his brother chest. "Cassie told us how you were involved in a drug bust. Is that why you're running?" His eyes changed to blue ice.

Lucy's mouth fell open. What had Cassie told them to provoke such animosity? "Got it all figured out, huh? Well, since you've made up your minds, there's no need for me to stick around. Go away. I need to get dressed."

Wade muscled the doctor aside and leaned over her bed, coming nose-to-nose with her. "You put my sister in the crosshairs of a murderer. Now my family's in danger. You're not going anywhere until I get answers."

Imperfect Trust

Too close. She couldn't breathe. He sucked all the air from the room. Instinct and years of self-defense classes took over. She reared back and head-butted him. "Get out of my face."

"Ow!" One meaty hand came up to cover his nose, but he took a step back.

Lucy did the scuttling move again to put more distance between them.

"Back off, Wade." Jonas tugged at his brother's arm.

The diminutive doctor stepped aside, eyes wide.

"I *am* leaving," she said with more confidence than she felt. "Tell your sister thanks for nothing." She threw the covers off, swung her legs over the side of the bed, sat up, and forced Wade to retreat another step. The overhead lights spun like a kaleidoscope. Her bare feet touched the icy floor. If she could get her feet under her, get moving, everything would— Sound roared in her ears.

"She's going down," Jonas yelled.

Strong arms caught her when she toppled forward, lifted her with little effort, and settled her back in the softness of the bed. A pungent odor burned her nostrils. She batted the smelling salts away.

"What is all this?" A small tornado of a woman pushed through the men. "Time for you boys to leave. Wait out front because I'm not through with you." Her nose wrinkled. "Wade, Son. You need to wash up."

Wade scowled while Jonas snickered again, but both men hurried from the room muttering, "Yes, ma'am."

When the door closed behind them, the woman turned to Lucy. She had brown hair going silver at the temples, but her deep blue eyes commanded attention. "Wilton, why did you let them bully this poor girl?"

The doctor chuckled. "Lucy, meet Cate Cameron, a force of nature."

"Another Cameron?" She already felt outnumbered. Now the odds leaned more toward overwhelmed. "How many more of you are there?"

Cate's laugh, like Cassie's, was light and airy. "Well, you've met two of my sons, Wade and Jonas. There's also my husband, Cody, our oldest son, Garrett, and his fiancée, TJ, and the twins, Cassidy and Mallory. I understand you met Cassie in Atlanta."

Lucy nodded.

Turning her sights on the doctor, Cate demanded, "Tell me, short and quick, Wilton. What's wrong with Lucy, and what does she need by way of medication and care?"

He didn't hesitate. "Her shoulder's torn up. The ligaments are looser than Polly Prescott's lips. She needs surgery, but Lucy says that's not an option right now."

Lucy stared aghast as the doctor discussed her medical condition with a stranger. Wasn't that against the law?

Cate's eyes flashed with fire when she pointed at Lucy's sling. At least three of her children had inherited that marvelous blue color. "Did my son do this?"

"No, ma'am." Lucy was tired of being talked over. "My shoulder was already injured when he decided to tackle me."

Cate's generous lips flattened out.

"Keep her arm immobile." Doc Burdette didn't miss a beat. "No movement whatsoever, not even to hold a book. I've strapped her down pretty good, but she can remove the sling to shower. Keep it cinched tight otherwise. I want to see her again in a week."

"A week?" Lucy cried.

"Pills?" Cate asked.

The doctor handed Cate a small bottle. "Got these ready for her. She needs one now. It'll make the drive more tolerable. Another tonight before bedtime, and then one every eight hours as needed for pain. Keep her in bed, if you can. She needs the rest."

Had the whole world gone insane? Lucy swung her legs over the side of the bed again, slower this time. "Thank you for taking care of me, Dr. Burdette, but I have a bus to catch."

Cate set a canvas tote bag on Lucy's bed. "That all, Doc?"

"Pretty much. She had some stitches, but I took those out while she slept."

Lucy head jerked around to stare at the doctor. *He knew.* Her hand hovered over the cuts Jensen had inflicted over her heart.

Dr. Burdette leaned down and whispered. "Nothing a little plastic surgery won't take care of. When you're ready, of course."

"I'll take it from here." Cate steered the doctor toward the door. "Tell Wade and Jonas we'll be out in a minute. They can help Lucy to my car and then collect her stuff from the apartment."

"Mrs. Cameron, I appreciate your good intentions," Lucy said. "But I don't need your sons' help."

"Of course you don't. And it's Cate, not Mrs. Cameron. I brought some of Cassie's sweats. The pants will do, but I think we'll keep this fancy hospital gown for now, and wrap a blanket around you. There's a guest suite at the ranch on the first floor. It's all set up for you. We'll have you settled there in no time. Now, let's get you changed before those boys barge in. Patience isn't something the Cameron men know. Tell me, have you ever been around horses?"

Chapter Six

Wade sucked on his finger and trudged toward his office. He knew better than to hurry a construction job. Now, he had the hammer-smashed finger to prove it. Not that a broken porch step could be considered construction work. And rushing hadn't made a whit of difference. He was still late for the appointment with Miz Tillbury's pet student.

Two elderly ladies stood on the sidewalk ahead. They raked him from head to toe. Mavis Dalrymple and Rosa Bea Thompson, both spinsters and the gossip queens of Hastings Bluff. Great. Their salacious accounts of Sarah's betrayal had endured for months. No telling what they'd say about his disreputable appearance today.

He tipped his hat in passing. "Ladies."

Miss Mavis sniffed and stuck her nose so high in the air it was a wonder she didn't wrench her neck. And Miss Rosa Bea ... An involuntary shiver made its way down his spine from the frosty look she cast his way.

Their obvious disapproval made him chuckle. He hated being the focus of the town's rumor mill, but this time he couldn't work himself up enough to care.

Three blocks past the Calico Diner, he crossed the street to his office. No one would dare intrude here, not with his sister on guard at the entrance.

Mallory—quiet, prissy, and the exact opposite of her twin. Education came easy for her. She was elected class president and named valedictorian her senior year. Cassidy had to work for her grades, but she'd been elected prom queen and won

Imperfect Trust

both the barrel racing and calf roping crowns that year. And moved out of the house a week after graduation into that ratty little apartment in town. Like she couldn't wait to get away.

Wade didn't know what happened between his sisters. They used to be inseparable. Now, the family only saw Cass on holidays and an occasional visit.

Thank goodness Mallory came home after college, though. Without her, his business would have folded with the Sarah fiasco. *Had he ever told Mal that?*

She greeted him when he came through the door, and nodded toward the small seating area where a teenager lounged in one of the chairs. "Casey Petersen is here to see you."

Wade studied the lanky frame slumped low in the chair—ragged sneakers propped on the coffee table, threadbare jeans with too many rips to be fashionable, a too-tight tee shirt stretched across a bony chest, and shaggy hair that had to be a year or more overdue on a haircut. "You the kid got his rear end kicked at school?"

Keen brown eyes stared back, doing their own appraisal. "Dude, looks like they got you, too."

Mallory snickered.

Wade gave his sister the stink eye. This smart-aleck didn't need her encouragement. "No, *dude*. I got mine kicked by a girl."

"A girl, huh?" Casey wrinkled his nose. "She make you puke or something? 'Cause man, you don't smell so good."

Wade sucked in an exasperated breath and caught a whiff of the spoiled milk stench. He exhaled with slow deliberation and focused on not shattering his molars. "You." He pointed at Mallory who had a hand cupped over her mouth. "Hold my calls. And you." He pointed at the kid. "Come with me."

Without waiting for either to respond, Wade marched off down the hall.

In his office, he hung the tattered jacket on the back of the door and motioned the boy to sit. When he turned, his mouth dropped.

The boy's spine was curled like a bow, his backside hanging off the seat. Knobby knees splayed wide, gangly arms hung off each side of the chair, and his neck—Wade couldn't help but wince—was bent at a ridiculous angle so his head rested flush against the seat back.

"Straight." Wade growled at the boneless, teenaged mass, irritated by the kid's obvious lack of respect. Or was it envy? Five minutes in that position would render him unable to straighten up for hours, maybe days.

The kid looked up with a bewildered frown. "Huh?"

"In *my* office, you *sit* in a chair. Straight. Now put your butt on the seat." He sucked in another ragged breath and let it out in a ten-second count. Nothing had gone right today—the breeding deal down the toilet, the run-in with Lucy, his good suit ruined, Doc's scathing reprimand, Cassidy's call that freaked him out, the chunk of hide his mother had taken, not to mention the disdain from the old biddies outside the office. Those two would slice, dice, and serve him up tomorrow with a dash of cumin.

None of it the kid's fault.

Wade had been that boy once upon a time. Stupidity was a teenager's rite of passage and impossible to avoid. He swore to keep a civil tone, even if it killed him.

Casey pushed upright, red-faced and rigid. Jaw clenched and eyes hooded, he was as untrusting as one of the wild mustangs and looked about as likely to bolt.

Time for damage control. First, though, to have any chance at a working relationship, the kid needed to understand where he stood in the order of things.

Wade settled into his chair behind the desk.

Imperfect Trust

Casey might be scrawny with arms like toothpicks, but he had a man-sized attitude. A few more birthdays would take care of his physical limitations, but he needed to learn discipline and self-control real soon, before his belligerence got him into serious trouble.

"Casey, right?"

"Yeah."

Dad always said time would take care of the misunderstandings between generations, and right now, Wade believed it. He was becoming his father, and the kid's clipped answers didn't sit well.

Lifting one eyebrow, Wade fixed him with a stare and waited.

A few seconds passed before Casey said, "Uh, yes, sir?"

Good. A quick learner. Wade relaxed the tiniest bit. "Why are you here?"

The boy seemed surprised by the question. "Mrs. Tillberry sent me."

"You always do what you're told?"

His face reddened even more. "She thinks I need a job or something. Said you'd give me one."

"Is that what you want?"

A frown drew Casey's brows together, confusion plain on his face. He was younger than Wade first thought, not in years but in social maturity.

"Let's try again. Why are you here? If a job is all you want, I can get you on at the Triple C Ranch mucking stalls. The work's hard, dirty, and smelly, but it pays more."

The kid's sullen expression turned unsure. "Mrs. Tillberry said you run a security business. With computers. I'm good with computers."

Better, but it still didn't answer the question. "So, you want an easy job where you can sit inside and play computer games all day?" Wade leaned forward, waiting with his arms on the desk, fingers interlaced.

"No. I mean, I like games well enough, but I'm really good with computers. I thought you might need someone like me, someone who could help." Casey threw up his hands in the air. "You know what? Forget it, man. My mistake." He rose to his feet ready to storm out.

"Sit down, Casey."

The kid's response was a sulky glare.

"Please."

The kid took his seat again—and sat straight this time.

Wade let out a silent, relieved sigh. "You got a computer at home?"

"No ... sir. I use the ones at school."

Wade could live with the surly tone. For now. Besides, he hadn't earned the kid's respect yet. And trust was a two-way street. "You involved in any activities outside of school? Baseball? Rodeo?"

Casey's shaggy hair fell in his eyes when he shook his head. "No, sir."

"What kind of grades do you get?"

"Mostly A's, though I got a D in P.E. last semester."

"Why?"

"Skipping. Phys Ed is last period. I don't do the jock thing."

Hmm. Honesty. This could work. "That where you had the run-in?"

"Yes, sir."

"Okay, here's the deal. Cameron Security Services is a small business. Everybody works their tail off here. We tag mostly cows and horses, but we've also done a bison herd. The technology uses signals from the transponder chips inserted under the animals' skin. That lets us keep tabs on their whereabouts and even track a few vital signs. If your mama is

Imperfect Trust

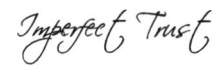

okay with you having an afterschool job, you can work for me in the office."

Casey gave a cautious nod.

"You'll work here from school closing 'til we close at five thirty and answer to Mallory. Homework gets done first. After that, there'll be a list of chores to do around the office."

Casey didn't say anything, but at least he didn't jump up to leave again.

"I won't lie. It's hard work for minimum wage. You'll empty trash, scrub the toilet, sweep the floors, stock supplies, run errands, load inventory, and clean the trucks after a job. In other words, do whatever needs doing. If you prove yourself, I'll add some computer work, teach you about the business, how to run reports and read incoming data. Later on, when you're ready, I might include you in a roundup when we tag the animals."

He had the kid's attention now. "I understand you have an aptitude for computers. What I don't know is if you're mature enough to grasp that what I say goes, whether you can be trusted to not only do the work, but do it well. One mistake can mean a loss of thousands of dollars, or worse, cattle. You live here, so you know the value of each animal."

"Why are you doing this?" Casey turned Wade's own question back on him. "Did you make this job up? Because I don't need charity."

Good. The boy had pride. "No free ride here, Casey. You'll earn every penny. But to answer your question, business is good. I need more help. Miz Tillberry thinks you're worth the bother, and her word is good enough for me, but your success here will depend on how well you respect the rules."

"What rules?"

Of course. Authority put the kibosh on everything a teenage boy wanted to do. Well, he'd have to come to terms with society sooner or later. It would go easier if he learned under a firm but fair hand that had his best interests at heart.

"My rules—no drugs, booze, smoking, sniffing, or dipping. You don't goof off in school or after. No skipping and no fights. You arrive on time, to both school and work, and keep your grades up. Do your work and keep your nose clean. Your loyalty is to your mama first and then to me and Mallory."

"Let me get this straight, you'll pay me squat, and I'm grounded for, like, ever?"

"Hey, I'm the one that's got his neck on the line, not you." Wade fought to keep a straight face. "Look at it this way—you got anything better to do? Earn my trust, do a good job, and you get more responsibility. Maybe a pay raise. In return, you get paid for work you enjoy and finish school without having a football player in your face every day. Might even be a way to get to college."

Casey blinked.

"Go home and talk it over with your mother. You decide to give it a try, be here after school tomorrow. We'll see if Miz Tillberry can work some magic and get you out of last period."

The boy sat for a long moment. He looked unsure and vulnerable. When he finally stood, he said. "Thank you, Mr. Cameron. I'll think about what you said."

Wade stuck his right hand out for a handshake and had to hide a grimace. "Tighten up your grip, Casey."

Casey's grip firmed.

"That's better. Weak handshakes are for boys. I only hire men. And Mr. Cameron is my dad. Call me Wade." He gave two short pumps and let go.

Satisfaction filled Wade when the young man stood a little taller and squared his shoulders. "Oh, and Casey? Put the school records back the way they were. You made your point."

Imperfect Trust

Casey nodded and smiled, a bare twist of the lips and only for a second, but it revealed a newfound confidence.

Mallory came into Wade's office after Casey's departure, her blue eyes twinkling. "Wow, who was that young man? And what did you do with the punk?"

Wade grinned. "Miz Tillberry said it best. It takes one to know one. I've already been down the path he's on, and believe me, he don't want to go that way."

"Here are your phone messages. You need to return the first two as soon as possible. The others can wait until tomorrow. I'll have a stack of checks for you to sign in the morning." Her nose wrinkled. "Wade—"

He held his hand up. "I know. I stink."

"Yeah. Well, what I really want to know is how the meeting with Wyman Hughes went. And why you look like you lost a round with a wildcat."

"Not a wildcat. A tiger." He grinned then, remembering the fierce young woman with the gorgeous eyes who'd turned him upside down—literally. Might as well give Mallory the details. She'd hear twelve different versions by this time tomorrow.

"Tell you what, I rode in with Jo. You let me drive your little truck and I'll give you all the juicy details on the way home."

"Juicy is good."

"You okay?" Wade turned down the long drive that led to the Triple C Ranch. At some point while he recounted his day, Mallory had gone quiet.

"Fine."

Uh-oh. Fine uttered in that tone of voice was female-speak for *I'm ticked off, I won't tell you why, and somebody's gonna pay.*

"So," Wade said as he tiptoed through the unexpected minefield. "We have a houseguest for an indeterminate time. You know how Mom always champions underdogs."

Mallory wasn't ready to let go of her funk. "She's only doing it because Cassidy backed us all into a corner. I mean, what do we know about this Lucy person—other than she's involved with drugs?"

"She's hurt, has a really nasty guy after her, and has no family or anyone else she can turn to. She needs help and knows it, and isn't happy about it."

"Wade, you do realize Cassidy's not the greatest judge of character? We have to think about what's best for the family."

Whoa. Two things jumped out at him. First, Mallory had been bringing strays home since she was a kid. Shoot, they still had Edwina, one of Harry Lassiter's goats she'd rescued from a bog almost ten years ago. Why was she so dead-set against Lucy before she'd even met her? And second, why did he only now realize Mal called her twin, Cassidy? Never Cass or Cassie. Or Sis.

"Think about it," Mallory went on. "She sprayed Jonas with mace and got you mad enough to knock her down. She must be bad news, because you don't do things like that."

His face burned. "I didn't knock her down. Well, I did, but she was already hurt. Wait, that's not what I meant."

With a well-practiced toss of her long hair over one shoulder, Mallory made an unladylike snort. "How long before her druggie friends show up here? Before James and his men have to get involved? Oh, I forgot. James is already involved."

Ahhh, this little snit was about the sheriff. Wade covered his smile by faking a yawn. Any show of humor at this point would set his sister off. "James is coming out to the house tonight. We can ask him about Lucy then."

The look she turned his way made Wade wish he'd kept his mouth shut. If he tried to be conciliatory now she'd draw blood. Best let it go. He owed his little sister too much to upset her anymore.

The Triple C arch appeared ahead. Home sweet home. He and his brothers and sisters were born and raised on the ranch and, except for Cassie, they all still lived there. That would change again when Garrett and TJ got married and moved across the valley into their new home. Still close by. But not the same as being all together under one roof.

Mallory's thundercloud must be contagious. Thinking about Garrett and TJ and their wedding next month sent Wade's thoughts down a dark path. Had things worked out differently, *he*'d be married and in his own home now. *Was he jealous?*

He'd plunged headlong into the relationship with Sarah, despite his family's reservations. Did he still want marriage? And a family of his own? Maybe. A little. But not anytime soon.

He switched off the radio, unable to stomach the words about love gone wrong. What if he hadn't caught Sarah trying to jack his computers? Where would he be today?

Wade shook off the train of thought and concentrated on the road. He'd rolled the dice and danced with the devil more than a few times over the years, but marriage to Sarah ... He shuddered. That was one waltz he was relieved to have missed.

"What?" Mallory snipped.

"Nothing."

They finished the ride in silence until Wade pulled up near the front door. Might be prudent to let the pyrotechnics proceed without him. He climbed out and walked around to open Mallory's door. "Tell Mom I'll be in soon as I put your truck away."

Mallory sniffed and headed for the front door.

He drove Mallory's pickup to the nearby red barn where the family kept their horses and personal vehicles. He'd call

James and warn him off until tomorrow. Lucy might be the excuse for his visit, but Wade would bet money his sassy little sister was the real draw. Sparks had arced between James and Mallory for months. Be a shame to see his buddy crash and burn tonight, although it would serve him right the way he dragged his feet with her.

Sometime later, when he thought enough time had passed, Wade made his way to the rear door of the ranch house. His cell phone rang as he started up the back stairs. "What's up, Jo?"

"You were right about Wyman Hughes. The old bandit called and said he'd be out tonight to sign the papers. At our price."

Wade whistled. "Well now, little brother, that's some very good news for the hind end of a sorry day. Where are you, and when's Wyman getting here?"

"I'm over at the big barn, about to leave. Wyman said to look for him around eight thirty. Need you to print out another contract since the original one got soaked with milk." A snicker followed the request.

"Keep laughing, funny boy. You owe me for this deal with Wyman."

"I do indeed. But you have to admit, the whole Lucy incident is funny. Except for her getting hurt, of course. If she'd had a dagger, I swear that little filly would have gutted you back at Doc's. And now she's bedded down at our ranch." Jonas's snicker became an outright chuckle. "Should be a fun few days while she recovers. Pretty little thing."

"Lucy's not a horse and she's off limits, Romeo."

Jonas laughed again. "That goes for you, too. By the way, Mom wants somebody to watch over Lucy through the night. Doesn't want her to wake up and not know where she is. You drew the nightshift."

Imperfect Trust

Chapter Seven

A fragrance drew Lucy from the depths. Clean sheets and sunshine. She took a deeper breath. And lavender. Mama loved lavender.

Her eyes blinked open and registered the unfamiliar surroundings even as her child's face lifted to a summer sky that wasn't there. Stuck between past and present, with sunshine warming her skin and grass that tickled her bare toes, her younger self danced in circles and handed clothespins to Mama to pin the sheets on the clothesline.

Lucy pushed the bittersweet memories away and snuggled deeper into the bed, but a more urgent need insinuated itself. Accepting the inevitable, she looked around the room only to realize she had no idea where she was. Wary now, she studied the shadowy shapes around her. A bedside table. A lamp. Two windows on the near wall where muted moonlight filtered in through sheer white curtains. Across the room, a door stood ajar. A sliver of light spilled out. Ahhh, a bathroom. Which meant this was a bedroom, but not sterile like a hospital or impersonal like a hotel.

A creak shredded whatever threads of sleep lingered. Lucy jerked around at the sound and winced, a not so subtle reminder of her injured shoulder. She stilled, held her breath, and waited for the noise to repeat.

Small sounds intruded, innocuous enough to blend in unless you listened for them. A wind-up clock on the bedside table ticked the seconds away. A tree limb outside the window rasped against the glass. A sorrowful moan from the wind.

Imperfect Trust

Somewhere in another part of the house, an appliance kicked on with a steady hum. Night sounds. Normal sounds.

Normal for here, maybe. Wherever here was.

Her long exhale sounded loud in the stillness. She lay on her right side with a pillow wedged behind her back for support. Sweet relief flooded her when she realized *here* was someone's home and that same someone had tried to make her comfortable.

Cassie's mom.

The haze in her mind cleared and the previous day's events clicked into place. "Stay with us. Just until you get back on your feet," Mrs. Cameron—Cate—had argued.

At that moment, Lucy would have traded her last granola bar for a hot shower and a night free from worry over Jensen Argault. A day to rest up wouldn't hurt. Maybe two. And Cassie had sworn she'd be safe at her family's ranch. The days of travel and the relentless ache in her shoulder had exacted a toll. Lucy caved.

A picture of Cassie's brother formed in her mind as she lay awake in the darkness. Big Guy. Wade.

Outside, in the distance, an animal bayed, a sad, keening wail like nothing she'd ever heard. A coyote? A wolf? No matter. An army of cowboys surrounded her here. How long had it been since she felt this safe?

A snore ripped apart the quiet.

Lucy's lungs seized, but her heart bolted in a mad sprint. She turned her head toward the dark corner.

Across the room, a shadow stirred ... and snored again. Louder this time.

Coherent thought disintegrated like ice under a spray of hot water. A single imperative took control—flee. Lucy tossed the covers aside and struggled to sit up. The movement sent a spear of pain through her poor, abused shoulder. She choked back a cry and got to her feet. The pain ratcheted higher. Her head spun, legs buckled.

Strong arms, familiar arms caught her, pressed her against a hard chest. "Hey, hey, hey, settle down. It's okay. You're safe," a deep voice soothed. "Shhh, I've got you."

A man. A *big* man. She stopped struggling. There'd be no fighting her way out this time, not as weak as she was. "Who …?"

"Wade Cameron, remember? You ran into me and my brother in town yesterday. My mom brought you home from Doc's office. You're at our ranch. Now, let's sit you down before you keel over. I'll grab your pain pills and some water." He eased her down onto the side of the bed and knelt in front of her. "Better?"

Cassie's brother. Wade was the bigger of the two brothers she'd met and the one who'd tackled her in the sheriff's office. She'd been so sure Jensen had sent them. "Wait. Bathroom."

His lips parted in a grin. "Okay."

Jerk.

When he slid one arm behind her back and tried to put his other arm under her legs, she balked and pushed his hands away. "I can walk."

The smug look faded a little. "All right, but I'm holding on to you. Grab hold. I'll help you up."

Lucy took his hand and let him tug her upright. A cool draft touched her legs. The soft, cotton shirt she wore reached only mid-thigh. "What on earth have I got on?"

"One of my tee shirts."

His shirt? She wanted to crawl back in bed and pull the covers over her head.

"You were wearing my favorite plaid shirt when we met." He laughed outright this time. "Cass was always stealing my clothes. Don't fret. Mom helped you change. She said you needed something big enough to allow easy movement for your arm."

He'd given her his clothes, and she'd slugged him with a bag a groceries in return. Now, she needed his help to get to the bathroom. Hopefully, the dim light hid the burn in her cheeks.

She took a tentative step, grateful when the floor didn't rise up this time, and let him lead her to the open door across the room. When he tried to enter behind her, she slapped a palm against his broad chest. "Ladies room, Big Guy. Not for cowboys."

He didn't budge.

This close to him, she had to look up. Way up. Gads he was tall. And broad. The light confirmed what she remembered. Dark brown hair shorn close. A strong jaw in need of a razor. And blue eyes that burned a hole in her soul.

"Mom will skin me alive if you hurt yourself."

"Then you'll make a nice rug in front of the fireplace." She made another ineffective attempt to shove him.

He hesitated and finally stepped away. "Okay, but don't lock the door."

"Sure thing." She closed the door in his face and turned the latch.

Heavy footsteps made several passes outside the bathroom door. "Lucy?" He tapped on the door.

She ignored him, washed and dried her hands, and cringed at what she saw in the mirror. Her hair was pressed flat on one side, with several strands stuck to her forehead and cheek. On the other ... Ugh. Electroshock didn't look good on her.

He rattled the doorknob. "You okay in there?"

She replaced the hand towel and unlocked the door ... and had to stifle a giggle when he all but fell into the bathroom. The man's glower might make babies cry, but he didn't frighten her anymore. "I'd like one of those pain pills now."

Simple words, but the thunderclouds he wore dispersed in a blink. With his arm snaked around her waist again, he helped her back to bed.

The brief exertion left her exhausted but also grateful for Wade's help. "Would you help me with the pillows, please? I'd like to sit up until the meds kick in."

He adjusted the pillows and smoothed her covers before fetching the pills.

She accepted the medication and the water he offered, all too aware of the warm hand on her back.

"Want to tell me why you thought it a good idea to assault someone twice your size with a quart of milk?" The corner of his mouth twitched.

Any answer she gave would only lead to more questions. The less any of them knew about her, the better chance she had of keeping them off Jensen Argault's radar. "Why are you in my bedroom in the middle of the night? Am I under house arrest or something? And while you're at it, do the men in this town make it a habit to terrorize defenseless women?"

One of his thick eyebrows lifted. "First off, it isn't *your* bedroom. My mother didn't want her *guest* to wake up in a strange place and scream the house down. No, you're not under arrest, though you probably ought to be locked up for your own good. And no, the men of Hastings Bluff do not scare strange women, not even those who claim to be defenseless."

She nodded. Wade had drawn babysitter duty. Probably under duress, though his poker face revealed nothing. Still, his actions confused her. All care and concern one moment and then as suspicious as the father of a teenage girl on her first date the next.

"For the record," he went on, "my brother and I didn't mean to scare you. But it's obvious someone has. Who are you running from, Lucy? And why?" His voice dropped an octave, took on an authoritative tone that made his questions sound more like demands.

"It's complicated." She almost said more but clamped her mouth shut instead. What was she doing? He made her want to tell him everything. The man should have *dangerous* stamped on his forehead.

Lucy returned his stare without blinking. She knew how to play this game. Wade Cameron might be intimidating, but she'd dealt with bullies before. They backed off when you confronted them. "If you didn't mean any harm, why chase me across the street? And let's not forget the body slam."

Wade didn't back off. If anything he loomed larger. "You were struggling with your groceries. We wanted to help. You attacked us and then you ran. And you body slammed me first."

"I get it. Red flag, angry bull. Mighty hunter stalking his prey. The thrill of the chase and all those other manly urges. Couldn't help it, right?" She released a soft chuckle and shook her head. Why did she have this perverse desire to provoke him?

His jaw clenched, and for a moment, she thought he might ruin those perfect teeth. His silent struggle for control made her a tad uneasy, but then he laughed, too. A soft, throaty caress. "You left Atlanta with a backpack. Why didn't you go to your own family for help? Or the police? Why travel thousands of miles to hide among perfect strangers?"

The questions struck like a barrage of bullets. "Not all that perfect," she muttered.

The pulsing vein in his neck gave the only indication that his control wasn't solid. "What trouble are you in, Lucy? Why did Cassie send you to us?"

It was a mistake coming here. She'd known it from the start, but she'd let fear override her good sense. A day, no more, and she'd leave. Find another rock to crawl under. For now, the less he knew the better for him and his family.

She lifted her chin high and snipped, "My business is none of your concern. Why do you even care? And for the record, Cassie didn't send me to you. Maybe the better question is why would she ask the sheriff for help and not her own family?" Lucy regretted the cheap shot as soon as the words left her mouth.

One moment Wade stood at ease near the foot of her bed; the next, he was in her face, so close she could have kissed him. Or bitten his nose. His rocklike countenance was gone. Anger radiated from him like heat shimmers that hid a desert oasis. "I care when danger knocks on my front door and threatens the people I love. Danger you brought here."

She shrank into the pillows, fearful he'd been pushed past his limit. Injured, pinned down, she hated her vulnerability. And he knew it.

"I want answers, Lucy Kiddron," he demanded. "Tell me what I want to know, or I'll get them another way."

She blinked. She hadn't given her last name to anyone, not even to the sheriff. If Wade went snooping, he could land them all in a murderer's crosshairs. Maybe if she gave him a few answers, enough to placate him until she could skip town. "How did you find out my name?"

Wade moved away from the bed and scrubbed a hand through his hair. He hated seeing Lucy cringe from him, but she set off every one of his hot buttons. He wanted to like her, wanted to believe in her innocence, but she was so darned evasive. And prickly. Stubborn, too. How could he help her if he didn't know what frightened her?

To give them both a little space, he retreated to the far corner where he'd spent most of the night. The job his mother assigned him was simple: watch over Lucy and keep her safe. He dragged the chair across the room and positioned it by her bed. Not so close he made her uncomfortable but near enough

Imperfect Trust

he could study her reactions. Did she know her face revealed every thought and emotion? He sat in the chair and let his eyes drift to the soft curve of her cheek, her chin …

"What?" she demanded in a surly tone.

He jerked his wayward thoughts under control and glanced at his watch. Ten minutes, fifteen tops, before the pain meds kicked in. Slouching with his legs stretched out, he crossed one ankle over the other. Yesterday, she'd interpreted his and Jonas's actions as a threat. Her first response was to fight, and then she ran. What would she do if he backed her into a corner?

Something foolish, no doubt. The little flares of panic he'd glimpsed told him he didn't want to find out. Perhaps if he took an indirect approach. Non-threatening.

He folded his arms over his chest, thought how she might interpret his body language, and let his hands drop to his lap instead. "What do you say we start over, tiger? I ask a question; you answer. You ask a question; I answer. No accusations. No opinions. No judgment. Just facts. Truth in its rawest form." "Let's start simple. What do you do for a living?"

Lucy held his stare but didn't answer. The gears grinding inside her head were almost audible.

Wade settled deeper into the chair, antsy for answers, but prepared to wait her out. Despite what his mother thought about him and his brothers, patience was a requirement for any soldier who wanted to survive a warzone.

A full minute passed before she squirmed. Another thirty seconds came and went before she spoke. "I'm kind of a technology consultant. I, uh, work on computer security systems. What do you do besides live on a ranch and molest innocent women?

Satisfaction filled him. Lucy wasn't so tough. He laughed and shook his head, ignoring her jabs. "I run a small security and monitoring business out of an office in town. We provide large livestock operations with inventory management and herd tracking. It's not big enough yet to consume all my time, but I have hopes. Meanwhile, I help out here where I can, but ranching is not my passion. Not like it is for Dad and my brothers."

Her eyebrows lifted, the delicate arches providing a perfect frame for her Bambi eyes.

Wade pushed on. "So, you met my sister in Atlanta. Does that mean you live and work there?"

Her eyes dropped to the sheet clutched in her right hand. "I went to Georgia Tech in Atlanta. Got a job there after graduation. I can work from pretty much anywhere with an Internet connection." She glanced up with, a quizzical expression. "How does your security program work?"

An honest answer, but not the whole truth. Like it was second nature for her to hide. And she didn't trust him. Not that he trusted her either. Trust didn't happen overnight, and he had a niggling suspicion that in Lucy's case time was a luxury they didn't have. Her second question gave him hope they shared some common ground.

He smiled. "We insert a transponder chip under the skin of the animals, mostly horses or cattle, though I recently got a contract for a herd of bison over in Wyoming." He laughed. "The chip allows us to track them by satellite and monitor a few vital signs. The computer sends an alert if the animal leaves a predefined area or if the readings fall out of normal range. It's a new technology, but with a positive impact on our multimillion dollar rustling problem."

"Wow. Rustlers. Like the Old West."

Wade ignored her digs. "Okay, my turn. Are you married, engaged, involved, or otherwise entangled? I can't figure out why someone as pretty as you is out here in the middle of nowhere all alone. This is dangerous territory for anyone not familiar with it."

Imperfect Trust

The night's diminished light reduced the color spectrum to shades of gray, but he had no doubt Lucy's cheeks turned as pink as the tea roses his mother cultivated in her garden. He liked when his compliments flustered a woman. And while this little dab of a woman didn't fit his usual preferences, she had an alluring wholesomeness at odds with the secrets she hid.

"That's not an appropriate question, but no. There's no one. What kind of operating system do you have? Do you use canned programs or write your own? How old is your business? What security applications and devices do you use?"

Well, she sure didn't fit the square hole he'd pegged her for. Most women would go a little flirty after a man expressed interest, ask about his availability in return. Not Lucy. She steered right back to the computer stuff. He didn't know whether to be insulted by her lack of interest in him as a man or flattered because his business piqued her curiosity. "There you go again, not playing by the rules."

Lucy's expression closed up.

"We take turns, remember?" He couldn't let her withdraw. "One question, one answer. You asked four. I'll answer them, but then I get four."

She hesitated but then gave a short, sharp nod.

"Okay, I opened my office doors two years ago. Developed my own programs. Wrote them in C to run on an OpenBSD operating system with fixed length buffers. C is such a rudimentary language, though. Too well known and too easy to compromise, and I wanted something more robust, more defensible. And geared toward satellite technology." He shrugged. "So I created a proprietary program language based on a little-known script called Grail and eventually I rewrote all my programs in the new language."

"You know Grail?" Lucy asked in a breathless whisper. "The one NASA uses to track satellites? I thought it was a myth." She leaned forward, eyes wide.

Wade's jaw dropped. Who was this woman, this complex bundle of contradiction and knowledge? Grail was a classified machine language developed by the government, impervious to cyber-attack and, more importantly, unknown to the civilian sector. Or so he'd thought. He knew of only two satellites equipped with the clandestine hardware. Both had been dedicated to the Afghan theater. They used a top secret radio wave tracking program and stealth motion detection technology that allowed Wade and his team to see real-time enemy movements over a wide region.

How did she know about Grail and its application? Did her presence here, now, have anything to do with his cyber-attacks? "Yeah, well, the government frowns on civilians having knowledge of its secrets. You shouldn't know about it, much less speak of it. My program is much simpler. I call it Switchback."

A puzzled look crossed her pretty face. "Switch … what?"

"Switchback. Like a crooked mountain road." He drew a zigzag line in the air with his finger. "Because the path isn't straightforward."

"Oh," she said with a distracted nod.

"My turn. What do you do security-wise? How long have you been at it? How old are you, and what is it about me that spooks you so bad?"

A fake yawn stretched her mouth wide. "I'm really tired. I'd like to rest now."

He made a tsking sound and wagged his finger. "Play fair, tiger. I answered your questions."

This woman demanded every ounce of his patience, so he waited again while her crazy-smart mind churned. She'd been hurt in a drug deal, frightened enough to leave her life behind and go off-grid on a moment's notice, and refused much needed medical attention. He needed to know what was driving her.

When she spoke again, he had to lean forward to hear her whisper.

"I perform external security tests and probe for weaknesses," she mumbled. "At least I did. I'm not sure what I'm doing now. I turned twenty-four last month, and you don't scare me, Wade Cameron. But large men don't realize how they overwhelm and intimidate."

He did. And he wasn't afraid to use his size advantage. But then her first answer registered. "Wait. You said you test … you probe …" His voice took on a tenor of disbelief. "You break into computers? You're a *hacker*?"

Lucy didn't respond. Neither did she look away, but ferocity flickered in her eyes. Not shame, that was for darn sure.

Deep seated anger surged forth. Of course, she wouldn't be ashamed. Hackers all thought of themselves as white hats. They claimed good guy status to justify when they crossed ethical lines for the good of the industry. He knew better. The lines between white, gray, and black hats were blurry at best, and easily adjusted to suit their desire. Hadn't Sarah done the same thing? "How long have you been stealing other people's information, Lucy?"

Her chin rose higher. The flicker in her eyes turned flinty. "Ten years."

He had to repeat the mental calculations twice. "You were *fourteen*?"

"Yes." Blunt, with no apology.

Wade's breath caught in his throat like a fishhook. There was air in the room somewhere, but he couldn't seem to find it. He lurched to his feet, toppling the chair over in his haste to get away. He wiped a hand across his mouth. "I can't stay. I gotta go."

Chapter Eight

Lucy adjusted the sling. The contraption hindered her movement, but wasn't that the point? The clock said ten fifty. She was starving. Should she go in search of food or wait for someone to come get her?

Using her knee, she nudged the chair Wade left by her bedside the night before and walked it across the room to its proper place by the window. A tug at the lacy curtains let the early light flood the room. Squinting, she got her first look at a real ranch. Unsure what to expect—a barn, horses and cows, maybe a few chickens—the vista left her speechless.

The windows in this room faced white-topped mountains that made a jagged slash against the horizon. Evergreens edged the foothills and climbed up the slopes.

Pulling the terrycloth robe she found in the bathroom tight around her, Lucy plopped down in the chair to enjoy the view.

The ranch sat on a slight rise overlooking a valley that stretched from the base of the hills in the north to as far south as she could see. A river split the verdant basin, a silver slash in a sea of green. The scene resembled a watercolor framed by a sky of purest blue, stunning in its purity. With all the sophisticated technology available today, computers couldn't capture the true colors unveiled by nature.

"I brought some food and clothes for you."

Lucy turned and grinned at the familiar face. She walked to the door, hand outstretched. "You have to be Mallory. I knew you and Cassie were twins but ... wow. Are you identical?"

Imperfect Trust

"No." Mallory ignored Lucy's greeting, set a small tray on the dresser, and dropped a large plastic bag on the bed. "Mom said you might be hungry. Lunch is in an hour so I brought a muffin and some orange juice to tide you over. Mom also asked me to pick up some clothes since you don't seem to have any." Her tone wasn't hostile, but neither was it warm or welcoming.

Lucy's smile slipped. It looked more and more like she'd made a mistake coming to Idaho. "Thank you, but that wasn't necessary. I'll leave soon."

"Oh?" Mallory's eyes raked over her. "Wade said you'd moved into my sister's apartment."

That people often disliked her didn't bother Lucy, but it usually resulted from something rude she'd said or done. Not that she set out to insult or wound anyone. Tact just wasn't one of her strong points. But she'd only met Mallory, what, three minutes ago? This had to be Wade's influence.

"James said Cassie asked him to look after you. He stopped by last night, by the way, but you were passed out from all the drugs." Her lip curled a little. "He'll be over today for lunch, so maybe you ought to get cleaned up."

Lucy's cheeks warmed from Mallory's tone and dismissive looks. "James wants to see me?"

"Yes. We don't get many strangers in Hastings Bluff, so I'm sure he just wants to make sure you're not up to no good. Why are you here, Lucy?"

Okay, the snotty attitude was beginning to tick her off. She picked her battles, and this wasn't one she wanted. She chose her words with care. "I needed to get away. Your sister offered her apartment. It seemed like a good idea at the time."

Mallory sniffed and waved one hand toward the bag she'd brought. "Do you need help?"

"No. Thank you." Not from her.

Mallory left with a shrug that said 'I don't care' and

closed the door behind her a fraction too hard.

Phew. Lucy downed the juice in one, long drink. Cramming half the muffin in her mouth, she rummaged through the stuff Mallory brought. The package of white cotton granny panties that were two sizes too big prompted a chuckle, but her laughter faded at the discovery of the front-closure sports bra—one size too small. And then she unearthed the shapeless gray sweats big enough for two people. *Nice, Mallory.*

A few off-brand toiletries, a toothbrush, and a travel-size plastic hairbrush and comb completed the treasure trove. Lucy decided Mallory was either really, really cheap or she had a chip on her shoulder and intended to take it out on Lucy. But why?

The better part of an hour passed while Lucy struggled through a shower and dressed in the shapeless, but clean clothes. After a vain attempt to towel-dry her hair, she attempted to detangle the sodden mess with the sad excuse for a comb. She gave up after two teeth broke off and she had to dig through her hair to find them. What she wouldn't give for a large hairclip.

The puzzle of Mallory bothered Lucy. Cate liked her well enough and the sheriff seemed fine with her being here. Jonas acted like he didn't care one way or the other, despite their initial run-in. Wade's dislike she got. But not Mallory's.

Well, she'd be gone soon enough.

A knock drew Lucy's attention to door.

"Come in."

Cate pushed the door open a crack and peered in. "I came to see if you needed help, but it looks like you've managed all—oh, dear." Her eyes narrowed as she took in Lucy's appearance. She made a tsking sound. "Is that what my daughter brought for you?"

Lucy put on her brightest smile and twirled around.

Imperfect Trust

"Clean clothes are a gift from heaven. Thank you so much."

"Stay put, I'll be right back."

"No, it's fine …" *Great.* Lucy deflated. Now she'd landed Mallory in hot water with her mother.

Cate returned in minutes with a pair of well-worn jeans, a western-style girly shirt with pearl snaps instead of buttons, and a pair of scuffed moccasins. "I robbed Cassie's closet. She's a mite more robust than you, but her stuff will fit better than those shapeless sacks Mallory brought. I'll help you change. James is in the family room, and lunch is almost ready."

With an extra pair of hands, Lucy stripped off the sweats, redressed in Cassie's clothes, and had her sling back in place in no time. She sat in front of the bathroom vanity while Cate fetched her own personal comb and brush to fix Lucy's hair.

"There. Much better," Cate said, smoothing the heavy braid. Her hands rested on Lucy's shoulders. "Now you look like the beautiful young woman I knew was in there."

Their eyes met in the mirror.

No one had ever looked beyond the mask of indifference Lucy wore. Until now. She patted one of the older woman's hands, her throat tight with emotion. "Thank you."

"Go see what James wants. I have to see about lunch." Cate gave Lucy a gentle squeeze, pointed her toward the front of the house, and headed off to the kitchen.

Two steps into the foyer, she heard a man's annoyed voice. "It's none of your business."

James.

"She's staying in my home. That makes it my business."

Mallory.

"You know nothing about Lucy," he snapped.

"I know she's involved with drugs."

The overheard words stung but sent a clear message. Lucy turned away. She wouldn't stay here a minute longer.

Mallory barreled from the room, eyes shiny with unshed tears. She stopped short when she saw Lucy.

"I'm sorry, Mallory," Lucy said. "I shouldn't have come here."

Mallory stormed past her with a glare. A moment later, a door slammed upstairs.

"I'm sorry you heard that."

Lucy turned to find James in the door of the family room. Tall as Wade, though not as muscular, he filled out his police uniform quite well. The star on his chest and the gun at his hip added a hint of danger—a heady combination.

"Should I get Cate to check on her?"

"No. Let's give her some time. She'll be mortified once she calms down."

Watching James gaze up the stairs where Mallory had disappeared, all the pieces slid into place. Those two had it bad for each other and jealousy had Mallory in its grip. And James, poor guy, had no clue.

"She's unhappy that I'm here."

He looked dazed. "Mallory's not like this."

"Okay." Lucy had no idea what to say. Not that it mattered. She would give James his time and then ask him for a lift into town. There had to be bus to somewhere this afternoon, and she intended to be on it.

He looked away from the stairs, straightened his shoulders, and took on a whole new persona. The sheriff had returned. "I'll deal with Mallory later. Right now, I want to ask you some questions about yesterday. Let's go in the family room."

He thought he could deal with Mallory? Lucy held back a smile and followed James. Too bad she couldn't stick around. It would be fun to watch cupid shoot the studly sheriff full of arrows.

James sat on the sofa across from her. His intense hazel

Imperfect Trust

eyes demanded her attention. He didn't have the same blatant charisma Wade and Jonas oozed. His charm was more subtle, with a gentleman's manners and a killer smile he used with great effect.

Was she trying to talk herself into an attraction for the sheriff? Hey, as Bennie, one of the staffers she worked with back in Atlanta, used to say, if you don't look you might as well be dead. *Yeah, but Bennie's a troll with a comb over.*

Lucy looked at James again. A clinical observation, that's all. Tall, lean, muscular. He had a decent job, was respected, could hold up his half of a conversation, and had all his teeth. All definite pluses. He seemed clean and had manners. Good looking? Oh yeah, though sizzling might offer a better description.

And yet, James didn't do it for her. Zero chemistry. End of story.

Not a surprise. She'd learned long ago that men tended to shy away from women with sharp tongues and big IQs, the gorgeous guys in particular. So she shied away first. But Mallory's possessive instincts left Lucy with an envious feeling. What would it be like to feel that way about a man? And him feel the same way about you?

"Start at the beginning, when you first saw Wade and Jonas."

Lucy cocked her head to one side. She might not be as beautiful or sexy as Mallory, but she wasn't a dog either. Guys checked her out often enough, sent her that "yeah, Baby, I want to get close to you" vibe. Until she spoke and cut them off at the knees.

Not James, though. She liked him, but in a like-only way. He cleared his throat.

"Sorry. So, there I was, walking down the sidewalk, minding my own business …" She paused to gauge his reaction and grinned when the corners of his mouth lifted.

Good. Tension defused. She went on to describe her trip to the grocery store, right down to each item in the two bags, their brands, and sizes.

"You remember all that?"

She nodded. "Expiration dates, too. It's a quirk of mine."

To his credit, he accepted her claim without a quibble. "Go on."

She related the mad dash across the street, Wade's pursuit, and what transpired in the sheriff's office right up until she hit the floor. "The next thing I remember is hearing two men discuss my medical history. Not long after, Cate stormed in and took over."

James hesitated before he spoke. "Why did you feel threatened by two men you'd never seen before?"

"Well, they're kind of big. They blocked the sidewalk so I couldn't pass." The words sounded lame even to her. Argault had made her suspicious of everyone.

"I'm big. You didn't run from me. Half the men in town would fit your description."

"But you're the sheriff," she sputtered. "You're supposed to help people in trouble."

"Are you in trouble, Lucy?"

Could she trust him? "You said a stranger would stand out here. Those two wore suits. They didn't dress like the other men I saw. I didn't like the way they targeted me."

"Tell me why you're scared, Lucy. I want to help you."

She could trust him. She knew it instinctively. "It's compli—"

A voice interrupted from the doorway. "I can tell you."

Startled, she whirled around.

Wade leaned against the jamb, her backpack in one hand and a sheaf of papers in the other.

"She was involved in a drug deal in Atlanta." He took a step inside the room. "It's all over the major news stations."

"Shut up, Wade." James stood. "You don't know what you're talking about."

Wade ignored him and moved further into the room. "It's all here." He shoved the papers at James's chest. "I printed them out for you."

James grabbed the papers to keep them from scattering.

"Cassie told us how you got hurt when the authorities moved in," Wade taunted Lucy. "Go on. Read it. You're famous."

"You're out of line." James stepped in front of Lucy and blocked Wade.

"She's got five thousand dollars in small bills in here." Wade held out the backpack. "Who carries around that much cash? Did you steal it from Cypher, Lucy? Is that why he's after you?"

"I said back off," James snarled. Feet planted wide, chest thrust out, he looked ready to do battle.

Lucy rose to her feet, touched by James's need to defend her but furious over Wade's snooping. Last night, he'd promised no accusations or judgment, just truth. She'd wanted to believe him. Had planned to tell him some of her story ... but then, he'd condemned her out of hand. And now he'd drummed up enough information to justify his actions. Would she ever learn?

Lucy skirted James and confronted Wade with a fingernail jabbed in his chest. "I wanted to like you." She snatched the backpack from his hand and slung it over her shoulder. "Foolish me."

"I won't let you put my family in danger."

"You already have, you arrogant jerk." She had to get out of here before she lost it.

Wade lifted that single cocky eyebrow and caught her arm to stop her from leaving. "Tell me I'm wrong, Lucy."

"You're wrong, Wade. Worse, you're so caught up in your

own misery it makes you stupid." She wrenched free of his hold, but only because he let her go.

"You're way off base, Wade." James shoved his friend.

Wade returned the shove. "You got different information? Then spill it."

James glared at Wade, and then looked at Lucy with a heavy sigh. "I spoke to a guy at the Bureau of International Intelligence this morning. A special agent in Atlanta, name of Whitaker."

Lucy whipped around. James had spoken to Ed?

"I didn't tell him where you are, Lucy. I didn't have to. He already knew. Look, I'm sorry—"

"Don't." She held up a hand to halt him.

James took a step toward her. "Let me explain. It's not what you think."

"It never is." She laughed to cover the catch in her voice.

"Wade, what's going on, son?" Cate stood in the doorway.

An older man hovered at her side, one arm around her shoulders. He had to be Cody Cameron, Cate's husband. So this was how Wade would look in thirty years.

Jonas and Mallory joined them, cementing the family resemblance.

Lucy's throat constricted. She would not cry in front of these people, would not give them the satisfaction.

"Lucy?" Jonas took a hesitant step forward. "Are you okay?"

Wade's betrayal didn't deserve the dignity of a response. Digging deep, she found strength to lift her chin high. With a frosty glare for both James and Wade, she left without another word.

Back in her room—no, the guest room as Wade had pointed out—Lucy dropped the backpack on the bed next to the stack of clothes she'd worn from Atlanta. Cate must have washed and folded them.

Imperfect Trust

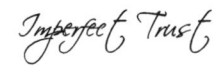

Someone knocked at the bedroom door. "May I come in?" Mallory eased the door open and peeked in.

"No." Lucy went into the bathroom to gather up her bargain basement toiletries.

Mallory came in anyway and perched on the side of the bed. "James told us—"

"I need a ride into town." Lucy found it difficult to stuff her things into the pack one-handed.

"Lucy, please don't go."

"Fine. I'll call a taxi."

"Look, I don't blame you for wanting to leave. I feel terrible—"

"Does terrible ease your conscience?"

"What? No."

"Here's a clue, Mallory. Not everything is about you."

Mallory looked like she'd been slapped.

Lucy threw the denim jacket around her shoulders and grabbed the backpack by the straps. "Look, I'll leave with or without your help. Will you drive me into town or not?

With shoulders slumped, Mallory gave in. "All right, I'll take you."

"Good. Let's go out the back. I've had enough drama for one day."

The two of them slipped out the kitchen door. A few moments later, they were in Mallory's truck, speeding down the long drive. When they reached the outskirts of Hastings Bluff, Lucy motioned to the side of the road. "You can let me out here."

Mallory shook her head and didn't stop until she pulled up in front of her sister's apartment. "I really am sorry."

Lucy laughed. James said Mallory would be mortified.

"I know you have no reason to believe me, but the way I acted, that's not me." Mallory's eyes glistened with unshed tears. "Look, I'll come by tomorrow when our emotions aren't so raw. We'll talk. Clear the air. Please give me a chance to make up for my bad behavior, Lucy. I think you need a friend. I know I do."

"Sure thing, Mallory. Thanks for the ride."

Lucy got out, closed the door behind her, and hurried toward the apartment without looking back. She couldn't wait to get out of this place.

After she heard Mallory drive off, Lucy waited another five minutes before setting out for the Greyhound station eight blocks ahead and left at the grocery store. At least this time, she could carry her one bag on her shoulder. Physical pain she could handle. It was the emotional sucker punches that left her eviscerated.

The denim jacket she'd slipped on offered little protection against a stiffening breeze. Florida was looking pretty good about now, or anywhere above seventy degrees.

Inside the terminal, she paid cash for a one-way ticket on the first bus out.

Imperfect Trust

Chapter Nine

Wade paced like a caged animal through the family room. Lucy had an unsavory past and a very questionable present. She was evasive, uncooperative, and waspish, and he wanted her out of his home and away from his family.

James had taken her side, though, a turn of events Wade didn't like.

Why did Cassie ask the sheriff to help Lucy? Why didn't she come to her own family? Lucy's words from last night were a splinter under his skin, impossible to ignore.

"What's wrong with you, man?" James threw the news articles onto the coffee table. "Since when do you believe everything the media writes?"

Was there more to her story? James seemed to think so. No, Wade had seen the news stories, searched the online channels. He'd learned enough to know Lucy Kiddron was bad news for his family. "They might stretch boundaries, but there's always a nugget of truth at the core."

"Never thought I'd say it, but you're a fool, Wade. A mule with blinders can see more than you." James pointed toward the long hallway where Lucy had disappeared moments before. "She came here for help. Not to get slapped down by a sanctimonious know-it-all."

"She—"

"Shut up and listen."

Wade took a deep breath, held his hands out, let them flop to his side, and took a seat on the sofa. "Preach it, brother."

James's eyes had gone stone cold. "Here are a few facts,

pal. Yes, Lucy was involved in the Atlanta drug bust. Yes, she got injured in the course of the op. And yes, she's on the run."

Wade tamped down his satisfaction. His friend had gone into sheriff mode, which meant he had more.

"Here's another fact. Lucy is an agent with the Atlanta office of the Bureau of International Intelligence."

Wade's head jerked up. "The same group you and Garrett worked for?"

"Yes. I got the scoop this morning from Special Agent Ed Whitaker. He's in charge of the Cypher case. Been after him for three years. Whitaker pulled in a few favors and got Lucy reassigned to his task force in a last ditch effort to take Cypher down. He needed her 'magic.' His words, not mine. Turns out she's a computer whiz like you."

The hits kept coming.

"She infiltrated Cypher's systems, got the account numbers and pass codes for seventeen Grand Cayman bank accounts, the names of all his distributors on the east coast, and details on six new pipelines in Costa Rica and Honduras. The bust was huge, Wade. This one op netted more than forty million dollars from those offshore accounts."

Regret punched Wade in the gut. He slumped against the sofa, head shaking. Intuition and a keen ability to read people had kept him and his teams alive through three overseas tours. How could he be so wrong?

A small, inner voice reminded him that same sixth sense hadn't worked so well with Sarah, either.

"Whitaker captured fourteen men that night, but Cypher got away." James dropped into the chair across from the sofa and settled in.

"Is he the one after her?"

"Yeah," James nodded. "You ready for the rest of it?"

From the fierce glint in James's eye, whatever he had to say would kick Wade's butt.

"Whitaker put Lucy in an armored van for the duration of the op to keep her safe, but something went wrong. Cypher's goons found the van. They also grabbed one of the advance scouts, a new recruit fresh off the assembly line in Virginia. They stood him up where Lucy could see him, put a gun to his hand, and pulled the trigger at point-blank range."

The visual brought a rush of bile. He'd witnessed too many atrocities over the years, seen the depths of evil inflicted by men. But he'd never gotten used to it. "Go on."

"When she didn't budge, they shot him again, in the leg. And then threatened him in the gut. The girl you accused of mixing with the scum of the earth left her safe haven to give the task force a few extra minutes to get there. She saved that agent's life and almost lost her own."

Shame burned in Wade's gut. "She didn't deny my accusations."

"Would you have believed her?"

No. He hadn't wanted to believe her. She'd gotten under his skin, and with her hacker confession, she handed him the perfect excuse to push her away. "Why is this Cypher after her?"

"She used his technology to take him down." James leaned forward, arms on his knees. "His men said he went nuts when he figured out what she'd done. Before her team arrived, he carved his initials into her chest. Swore he'd finish the job, and darn near did but for Cassie."

Wade swallowed hard. He deserved whatever she thought of him. But then, rage ignited in a wave of bloodlust, ugly beyond anything he'd experienced before. His brothers battled with their anger. Dad, too. But not him. Not until now.

Fists clenched, his mouth twisted in a snarl. He wanted to—

His mom's distressed cry broke the spell. She and Mallory stood in the doorway across the room, Mal with a hand clapped over her mouth.

His dad pulled them into his arms, but over their heads he locked eyes with Wade. Who better than Cody Cameron to understand the battle his son waged against a fury so powerful it relegated sanity to a dark closet?

His dad nodded, a subtle tilt of the chin, but it was enough to convey a father's understanding and confidence in his son.

Wade choked the anger off and returned the nod. "Is that everything?"

A wry smile twisted James's lips. "Other than the dead guard outside the hospital room, terrorizing Lucy, and his threat to Cassie if she got in the way? Cass had enough faith in all of us to think Lucy would be safe in Hastings Bluff. Lucy didn't have any other options, so she grabbed the chance and ran. She probably thinks your nosing around will draw Cypher here. I think she might be right."

Mallory sobbed and fled.

"Is Cassidy in danger?" his father demanded. "Do I need to go to Atlanta and get my daughter?"

James shook his head. "I don't think so, Cody. We—Wade, Jonas, and I—spoke to her yesterday. She's stubborn. Still has a few weeks left on her internship, and doesn't want to leave. The locals assigned her a bodyguard, but I sent Derek to watch over her. He won't let anything happen to her."

His father leveled a considering look at both James and Wade, one that promised more questions later, but he said no more at that moment.

Wade got to his feet to pace and slipped into the Zen-like mindset that let him work through complicated plots. With help from his family and James, Lucy would be safe here at the ranch. Even if he had tipped Cypher off. But he needed information.

"Okay, I was wrong. Show me what you've collected on this creep," he said to James. "I want to see everything." His head had to be screwed on straight if he wanted to help Lucy through this nightmare, and that meant going back to the basics—Intel, a plan, preparation, and execution.

"That's why I came out here today. I thought if Lucy volunteered the story, she'd be more willing to cooperate in any plan we devised. I doubt she'll trust any of us now."

"She won't have a choice."

"Yeah, right," James said with contempt. "*That* attitude will send her off for sure."

"Well, this explains why she won't consider surgery," his mother said. "Since lunch is ready, why don't you boys go clean up? Mallory and I will try to coax Lucy to join us. After you apologize …" She glared at Wade. "You can discuss your ideas with her."

A few minutes later, Wade, Jonas, their dad, and James all stood around the dining room table while they waited for the women to join them. As the seconds ticked by, Wade grew uneasy.

His mom hurried into the room, wringing her hands. "Cody, Lucy's gone. Her things are, too. And I can't find Mallory."

"Told you she'd run," James grumbled. "Ten bucks says if you check the barn, Mallory's truck won't be there."

A stone settled in the middle of Wade's chest. He'd run Lucy off. Whatever happened to her now was on his neck. "I think I know where she went."

Everyone stared at him.

"The only places she knows are the bus station, Cass's apartment, the grocery store, James's office, Doc's place, and the ranch. If she's running, she'll head for the bus station."

James started toward the front door. "My truck's out front. You can ride with me."

Wade followed after him until his mother caught his arm at the front door.

Imperfect Trust

"Bring her home, son. It's more than her shoulder hurting."

"I will, Mom. I promise." Wade folded her into a hug.

James broke the speed limit by a wide margin on the way into town.

"Slow down, man." Wade grabbed the handle above the passenger window and hung on. "You might be the sheriff, but you can still get a ticket."

"Nah, being boss comes with a few perks."

"I messed up." Said aloud, the words didn't lessen his remorse, but it needed saying.

"Yep." James looked away from the road for a moment and met Wade's eyes. "Look, I get it. Sarah messed you up, and now you don't trust anybody. But Lucy's not Sarah.

"I know."

"Not sure you do. There's some serious stuff at work between you and Lucy. It's got you freaked."

"James, she's only been here two days."

"Just saying. Be a shame to miss it."

"Like I'd take advice on women from you." Wade rapped his fist against the passenger window. "You can't face up to what's going on between you and Mallory."

"Don't change the subject. Mal and I are friends. That's all."

"Right."

"Look, Wade, It's not about love. Lust either for that matter, though I wouldn't cross it out. I know it's too soon, but you act like the boogeyman's jabbing you with a cattle prod."

Wade turned away to stare out the window.

Unfazed, James pushed on. "I'm serious. Lucy's a pretty little thing. I suspect there's a real sweet girl hiding behind all that sass and brass. You need to be careful she doesn't get snatched up under your nose."

"She's smarter than that."

"Do yourself a favor, Wade. Follow the breadcrumbs. See if this thing between you and Lucy goes anywhere. You'll regret it if you don't."

"Sometimes you regret if you do."

James didn't respond.

"There's the bus station," Wade pointed ahead. "Let me out here. Give me five before you come in."

Before Wade could open the door, James grabbed his arm. "You need to figure this out before Lucy gets hurt any worse."

"I meant what I said. Alone, she's vulnerable to every pickpocket, hophead, and sexual predator out there." Wade got out of the cruiser and leaned down to finish what he had to say. "I'll go with her if I can't convince her to stay."

"She's not your responsibility."

He knew he had trust issues, but James was right. This crazy attraction to Lucy was worth exploring. But he had to keep her close to do it. "I'm making her my responsibility."

He closed the door, ignoring the smirk on James's face and hurried inside the terminal.

Four people stood in line at the ticket window, none of them Lucy. He perused the room again, slower this time, and spotted her small figure huddled in the far corner, hidden in part by a plastic ficus tree. She sat sideways on the row of interconnected chairs, her knees drawn up, feet planted on the adjacent chair, and forehead resting on her knees.

From the corner of his eye, he saw James enter the terminal. Wade motioned for him to wait.

Moving with slow, deliberate steps, he took the chair across from Lucy. Should he call her name? Cough?

She turned her head and skewered him with those big brown eyes. "If you're here to make sure I get on the bus, it doesn't arrive for an hour and forty minutes."

Her words poured salt in his self-inflicted wounds.

"Lucy, I'm sorry."

"Right." She snorted and swung her feet to the floor. "You and Mallory. Shoot first, apologize later."

"I don't know what's up with Mallory, but there's no excuse for me. I jumped to the wrong conclusion, and you have every right to nail my hide to the wall. So, if you want to, go ahead. I deserve it. But don't punish the rest of my family or yourself for my actions."

She looked away.

"Please don't let me drive you away." If she wanted him to beg he would.

"Why?" At least she was looking at him again.

"Cassie thinks you need protection, and she knows we'll keep you safe."

She stiffened at his words. "I don't need your help. I have cash, which by the way is my own money. And I have the pills Dr. Burdette gave me. I can buy anything else I need." She waved a hand in dismissal. "Consider yourself released from any misplaced sense of duty."

"You can't run forever. The money won't last, and the pain medication knocks you out. You can't take the pills while on the move, not without someone to watch over you and your stuff."

Her thoughtful expression gave him hope, but then she shook her head.

"My family wants you to come back to the ranch. James does, too. *I* want you to stay. Please rethink your decision and let me take you home. I promise I won't hound you anymore."

She shook her head. "I can't. Staying depended on anonymity. I have no doubt your online searches have triggered all kinds of red flags. Argault will know I'm here. I can't risk your family."

He zoomed in on the dark circles under her eyes. What more could he say to convince her? "Look, James, a couple of his deputies, my brothers, and me—we're all combat veterans with extensive training. We have contacts and resources. There's also a whole town of cowboys we can call on. Taking Cypher out poses no problem for us."

"It's tempting," she said. But then her eyebrows flattened in a frown, and she started shaking her head again.

He ticked off what little he knew of Lucy. She was fierce and independent, smart but practical, and good with computers if the government had hired her. She also had a vulnerable side, try as she might to hide it. The girl wore her pride like a suit of armor.

James said she left Atlanta and everything she knew because she worried Cypher would hurt her friends and colleagues. Maybe a different tack would work.

"I've been thinking about what you said," Wade continued. "About what you do. I know I acted like a pompous, uh ... jerk ... last night, which I regret. But I have to admit I'm also curious. Maybe even a little hopeful. You see, I've got a hacker trying to break into my systems. That's why I freaked out. It's not a script kiddie doing it for kicks either. No lightweight software program off the Internet. These attacks are persistent and methodical. I wondered if this might fall in your area of expertise, and if you'd be willing to take a look."

Something flared in her eyes. Interest? Resentment? A challenge?

"You called me a hacker. And it wasn't a compliment. You don't know anything about me or my work."

"You're right. I don't. And despite my tendency to be judgmental, I find that I want to know you."

She studied him with a calculating look.

"Give me another chance, Lucy. I admit my fault. I'll even beg your forgiveness if you want. Just, let's start over."

Wade waited while the minutes marched by. The longer she remained silent, the more convinced he was she'd refuse. He understood how pride could stand in the way of need. The good Lord knew he'd been there often enough.

"Beg, huh?"

Was that a twinkle in her eye?

Relief left him limp, like he'd finished a twenty-mile run carrying a sixty-pound rucksack. He motioned James over. "If that's what it takes, then yes, ma'am. I'm begging you to stay. Now, where's your bus ticket? Our esteemed sheriff can get your money refunded."

She frowned trying hard not to smile but handed the paper ticket to James, who took it to the station agent.

"Let me carry that." Wade reached for her backpack.

She swatted his hand away.

The little tiger tried hard to be ferocious, and she was determined to be self-sufficient. He'd need a velvet touch with her. Not one of his strengths, but he'd try his best.

Chapter Ten

Seven days they'd coddled her. A whole week of pampered comfort with the Camerons catering to her every need. If one more person told her to take it easy or to lie down and rest …

Lucy moved around the king-sized bed in the Cameron's guest suite and straightened the bed linens with one hand. She could do this much at least.

Wade had kept his promise not to hound her. Easy to do since he hadn't shown his face one time since bringing her home from the bus station.

Home? Where did that come from? She didn't do the whole family, hearth, and home nonsense. Her rented apartment suited her fine. One bedroom to sleep in and one for her computer lab.

Restless strides took her back and forth across the bedroom. This whole situation with the Camerons had her on edge. She kept expecting a cool reception, a polite nod, and an eventual dismissal. Instead, they treated her like family.

She grunted. *Foolishness.*

But was it foolish? Despite their rocky start, she and Mallory had formed a cautious friendship. Jonas even set himself up as her champion. James had dropped by the ranch to see her a few times, but Lucy suspected his visits were more about Mallory than her.

The oldest son, Garrett, and his fiancée, TJ, were another matter. TJ was staying in the absent Cassie's bedroom, which allowed the two love birds to spend a lot of time together—

Imperfect Trust

under the ever watchful eye of Cate, of course. When they deigned to notice others, they treated Lucy like she belonged.

And, of course, there was dear, sweet Cate who seemed intent on making up for all of Lucy's motherless years.

Cody surprised her most, though. She looked forward to their time after dinner each evening when she and the patriarch of the family would sit and discuss everything from world events to local politics, the number of foals he expected this year to the merits of a home school program versus public education. He told her stories about his rodeo days, of legal battles he'd faced with the setup of the wild mustang preserve, and of his pride and love for his family.

Lucy, in turn, regaled him with tales of her social misadventures as a too-young kid in college with a bunch of hormone-crazed young 'adults.' She spoke of the thrill of her martial arts competitions, and the flak she'd taken from her male peers after acing the Bureau's marksmanship trials.

Somewhere along the way, the wily old coot slipped in a directive for her to attend Sunday worship services with the family.

The idea intrigued her. She'd never attended church. After a little hesitation, she agreed to go. *Like she had a choice.*

"Never been, huh? Then it'll be a unique experience for you," Cody had said with a wink.

Wade remained AWOL the whole week, and Lucy couldn't say what irked her more: that he kept his distance or that she kept looking for him. Everyone knew the truth about her role in the drug bust now. He'd apologized and asked for her help, but she still remembered his contempt. *You're a hacker?*

Well, he wouldn't win any prizes either. Overbearing didn't begin to convey the man's personality, not to mention his control issues. Add in enough arrogance to shame Donald

Trump and the failed engagement to the infamous Sarah a year ago and …

Lucy gave herself a mental shake. She didn't want to think about him anymore, not after he'd treated her like last week's garbage. *He said he was sorry.*

She flopped in the chair by the window and snapped her fingers. That's how much she cared for Wade Cameron's opinion. Her work stood on its own merits, and she had the accolades to prove it. She'd illegally hacked a system only one time. And it had to be the State of Georgia website. And of course, she'd gotten caught. A shudder wracked her at the memory of that awful night. Ed Whitaker arrested her and her life changed again.

Lesson learned. She'd changed. Everybody changed. It was a fact of life. Hadn't her mother moved on?

Dark memories stirred. The Juvenile Detention Center. The windowless room. Mama standing by the door, shoulders slumped, her eyes full of sorrow. And then the life changing moment when she'd walked out of Lucy's life forever.

"Mama." Lucy whispered in a broken voice. "Why did you leave me there?"

The memories rushed in unchecked, her carefully constructed defenses breached. The car accident. Daddy and Sammy killed. Mama's broken legs that left her with a terrible limp. Only Lucy had walked away unscathed. Until Mama couldn't cope anymore. "Why did you throw me away?"

She'd not seen her mother since. Didn't even know if she was still alive.

Lucy scrubbed at her eyes with angry swipes. Tears weakened you. Showed the world you were vulnerable.

With the floodgates opened, scenes from her time in foster care flowed with relentless detail. The six long months spent with the Millers taught her how to survive. One-hundred-eighty endless days she'd stolen, fought, and begged for food. Moved up a grade level twice, ridiculed by the older kids in her classes, she'd found refuge in the library. Until Ed Whitaker returned and offered her a way out.

She had no idea how Ed wangled it, but she'd snatched at a chance to interview with the Admissions Office at Georgia Tech. By the end of her junior year in high school, at fifteen years young, she'd accumulated enough credits to graduate, aced the college entrance exams, and entered the university on a scholarship that covered tuition, books, dorm, and meals. Her ticket out of purgatory.

Lucy wiped her face with a shirt sleeve. Ed had given her a shot and she'd capitalized on it. Taking a tissue from the box on the nightstand, she blew her nose. Enough with the trip down memory lane. She needed to focus on the current problem, namely Jensen Argault.

Two weeks since she got hurt in the field op. One week since she arrived in Hastings Bluff. Her shoulder didn't hurt much anymore unless she overstressed it. Her body and brain, on the other hand, craved activity. She'd never lazed around like this. Worse, she had a deadline looming. The initial draft for the second video game was due in June.

She had the beta players all lined up. All that remained were a few loose ends in the programming, one more QA check, and confirm the testing schedule. Once she analyzed the beta results and made any needed changes, the video game would head to production with a projected launch right before Christmas.

The way she saw it, she had two choices—continue to lie low, be safe, and go crazy from inactivity, or get on with her life. If Wade were around, she'd ask to borrow a laptop from his office. Since he couldn't be found, she'd have to hitch a ride into town and buy one. Everything she needed was on the flash drive in her backpack.

Lucy went in search of Cate. She found Wade instead.

"Good morning, Lucy."

"Oh." His unexpected appearance after being absent all week left her tongue-tied. Speechless didn't happen to her often. Like never. "Good morning. Where's your mom?"

"Dad took her into town to do some errands. I doubt they'll be back for a few hours yet. Something I can do?"

His parted lips revealed an imperfection she hadn't noticed before. One incisor turned out. Wade had a crooked tooth. Why did that make her happy?

Garrett, the older brother, fit the Tarzan role to a T, while Jonas, the younger brother, was more of a Lothario. Wade remained a puzzle. He was bigger than his brothers and father, but gentle. Blunt and abrasive, but also considerate and caring. And more intelligent than any man had a right to be. He seemed too much like her, a loner, with no need for anyone else. And yet he'd asked for her help in thwarting a hacker—right before he disappeared for an entire week.

"I, uh, wanted to ask her for a ride into town. I need to catch up on my work and thought I'd buy a laptop. Is there somewhere I could work here? I don't want to be a bother."

"You can use Mom's office." He started toward the front of the house, motioning for her to follow.

"I can't use your mother's office. What if she needs it?"

"Mom's taking a breather between books. She won't mind if you set up shop in here. I do it all the time. If you don't mind a loaner, I've got some spare laptops at the office."

"Is that where you've been all week? Working at your office? I haven't seen you around." Somehow she managed not to groan out loud. She needed to just shut up.

His mouth stretched into a full-blown grin. "Working, but not at the office. Been roughing it up in Wyoming. Remember that buffalo herd I mentioned? They proved every bit as ornery as I expected. Bison are a lot harder to manhandle than cows or horses."

Imperfect Trust

"Forcing technology onto brute muscle, huh? Quite a challenge."

"Takes four strong backs and a squeeze chute to immobilize a two-thousand pound bull long enough to zap him with a sub-dermal chip. We didn't get back until late last night. Did you miss me?"

Flirtatious bunch, these Camerons. She decided to ignore that side of him.

"Who monitors the transmissions when you travel?"

"It's all routed to my laptop. I carry a satellite phone and have a hot-spot so I can get a signal from most anywhere."

She nodded, impressed with the slick setup.

"Uh ..." He cleared his throat. His eyes stared at something over her head, looked left, and finally settled on his boots. "Look, if you're still willing to check out my, uh, problem, I'll pay for your time."

"I wouldn't charge you. I already owe you and your family too much."

"Great. When can we start?"

Okaaay, she might be wrong about the loner theory. "Now?"

"Let me grab a drink first. Can I get you something?"

"No thanks."

"Be right back." He took off for the kitchen.

Before the bus station face-off, Wade made it clear he didn't like her. Now, he wanted to play nice-nice. His mood swings made her dizzy. The good news though—he had a computer she could use. She'd be able to meet the second game deadline.

Lucy dashed to the bedroom for the notebook and pen she kept in her backpack.

When she returned to his mother's office, Wade rose from his seat on the front side of the desk, a glass of soda on a coaster in front of him.

She had to give Cate credit. The woman knew how to raise gentlemen.

Wade waved her to the empty chair behind the desk.

"I'll take notes while we talk." Lucy settled in the chair and opened her notebook. "So, when did you first realize someone was fiddling with your system?"

"Last year, March 14th, nine thirty-five in the evening. It was a Friday."

She looked up from writing. Clients seldom surprised her. "Uh, most cybercrime victims aren't able to answer with such accuracy."

"I can."

"Go on." Sensing his internal struggle, she waited for him to continue.

"I play cards with friends on Friday once a month. Not far from the office. On the night I mentioned, I'd left my wallet at work. No ante means no play, so I sat out the first round and ran back to get my wallet. Imagine my surprise when I discovered my fiancée seated at my computer."

Lucy remained silent as he stared at a spot over her left shoulder.

His eyes refocused and met hers. "Sarah was talking to a man on the phone. She had him on speaker. I heard enough to know she'd already loaded a file and was trying to create a new access to bypass normal authentication."

"A backdoor," Lucy clarified when he paused.

He nodded. "The man—Ullah Ahmad Azizi I found out later—was a rebel I helped put away during my last tour in Afghanistan. At least I thought he'd been taken out of action. Guess not. Besides instructing Sarah on how to infiltrate my computer system, he also explained in explicit detail what he wanted to do to her. From the way she responded, I'd say they'd already indulged in most of it."

Lucy's heart ached for Wade as he related the sordid

details. She understood betrayal and rejection. But then, his pained expression turned dark. She sensed the violence he held in check.

"Sarah ran the office, but didn't know about the new security programs I'd installed."

Lucy suspected Wade Cameron didn't trust many people outside his immediate family, even before his engagement. "What happened then?"

"I made my presence known. Azizi hung up. Sarah tried to explain." He related the sequence of events like checking off a to-do list. "I called James but had a change of heart before he arrived. I took her phone and purse. Kept everything but her driver's license and cash. Told her to leave and never show her face around here again. So far, she hasn't."

"Why did you let her go?"

He got up and strode to the door, turned, and retraced his steps. His hands clenched and unclenched at his side. After a few seconds, he pulled himself together and sat again. "I made a mistake," he said in a soft voice. "I think Sarah's behind these attacks."

Lucy dropped her eyes to the paper in front of her. Time to move the conversation away from all the personal pitfalls. "How many attempts? How often? Is there a pattern? Are you able to reverse ping to determine if they originate from the same IP address? Or do they come from different computers?"

"Six attempts in the last two months. I run updates and backups at irregular intervals because the systems are most vulnerable then. None of the attacks occurred during those times. They're random—midday, one o'clock in the morning, right after closing—no pattern. I never thought to check if they originated from the same computer or not. I'll run a report."

"Besides the new security programs you implemented, what else do you use to stop the attacks?"

"I've been checking line-by-line through the source code

since the first attempt, trying to find whatever it was she added." He shrugged and held his hands out palms up. "I'm also realistic enough to understand someone smart and persistent will find a way in sooner or later. No system is failsafe. That's why I'd like your help."

"If you haven't found the file she inserted by now …" She smiled at him. "I doubt you will. My guess is she used a polymorph shell." At his curious look, she explained. "A self-modify command sequence that prompts a location change, most often at random intervals. It's the latest buzz. If you don't know what to look for or where, the odds you'll find it are astronomical. From all the activity, I'd say she's been unable to locate it, too."

Wade's expression turned sheepish. "In other words, I've wasted my time."

She couldn't stop her smile from widening into a grin. "Pretty much."

He laughed and let his head fall back.

This intelligent, arrogant, and dangerous man could laugh at himself. Okay, maybe he had a few redeeming traits.

Wade slumped in the chair, beaten for the moment but not defeated. "So, Miz Hacker Extraordinaire—and I mean that in the most respectful way—what's my next step?"

"I need to take a look at your operation, maybe dig into your system."

His facial expression didn't change. He didn't move, twitch, or even blink, but the tension in the room swelled.

"Look, Wade, if you want my help, it's yours. I'll do everything I can to help, but you have to trust me a little. I can provide professional references, though I'd prefer you not contact them for obvious reasons."

When he didn't react, she went on. "I'm not Sarah. You can watch every move I make."

"It's not what I can see that worries me."

Imperfect Trust

He might as well have slapped her. She remained silent, afraid of what she might say.

"I'm sorry. You didn't deserve that." He extended a hand across the desk. "Seems like all I do is apologize to you."

She understood how it felt to have all decisions taken from you, but that didn't stop her from ignoring his overture. Trust was a two-way street. In time, she would prove his fears about her were unfounded. But he had to prove he could be trusted, too. "Tell me why you think Sarah is the hacker."

The devastation in his eyes revealed unfinished business between Wade and Sarah, and not of the technological kind.

He withdrew his hand.

"Okay, scratch that. Not important."

She'd never worked on a project so fraught with emotional landmines and had no clue how to navigate them. One thing for certain, from here on out their interactions would remain on a strictly professional level. "I think a visit to your office is next up on the agenda."

If the request surprised him, he didn't show it. "Okay. Mom made you a follow-up appointment with Doc Burdette at noon on Monday. We can stop by my office in the morning and then head over to his place."

The darkness surrounding him lifted, but her irritation flared. Did the Camerons think they could run her life?

She remembered another comment Wade made during the course of their conversation. "If Sarah ran the day-to-day business before all this happened and you spent most of your time offsite like this last week, who runs your office now?"

"Mallory."

"Oh." She didn't see that coming. "Monday it is."

"Great." He cocked his head to one side and studied her for a moment. "You haven't been out much since you arrived, have you?"

"I take my coffee out on the patio most mornings.

Sometimes I sit with your father on the verandah after dinner."

He stood, walked around the desk, and held out his hand. "C'mon, I have a surprise for you."

Imperfect Trust

Chapter Eleven

Wade took Lucy's hand and tugged her from his mother's office.

"I don't like surprises." She let him pull her through the house and out the kitchen door.

He smiled at her words. "You'll like this one."

Shocked by his own spontaneous action, he wondered what he was doing. He never acted on impulse.

"Where are we going?" Lucy asked.

"You'll see."

Outside, a cloudless sky and warm sunshine supported his decision. The first fine day this spring. All the talk of Sarah had stirred the shadows in his soul. He'd known the instant his darkness touched Lucy. She'd retreated, throwing up mile-high defenses. He wanted those barriers gone because somehow this little too-smart woman with the tart mouth filled his tormented world with light.

"How about a hint?" She sounded a little breathless.

Ha. Wasn't a woman out there who could let the word *surprise* slide by.

He slowed down when he saw Lucy had to double-step to match his stride. "See that long, red building?"

The rambling barn lay straight ahead. He and his family housed their horses there, along with a fleet of trucks, cars, mowers, a wagon, and one prissy pink golf cart with a fringed top that his mother used to gad about the property. Supplies and feed filled the far end of the room next to the chicken house and the small pen for Edwina, the sassy old goat Mallory brought home close to ten years ago.

"We're going to the barn?"

Wade looked down at her face. "Not just a barn, milady."

He adopted a well-practiced medieval accent and loosed a carefree smile. "Yon is a magical and *tragical* kingdom, replete with knights and dragons, fair damsels and mystical beasties, a dangerous realm for a ten-year-old boy warrior. Dare ye venture in? I swear my fealty and wouldst give my life for thy safety."

Her giggle was a musical enchantment. "You played Knights of the Roundtable with your brothers? With Mallory and Cassie, too?

"Ha, those two don't require a magical kingdom to imagine their royalty."

"But you still treat them like princesses."

His ears burned.

Her look went far away for a moment. "I wish ..."

"Uh-uh. No room for dark memories in the kingdom, milady. Only sunlight, moonlight, starlight, and firelight. And your own special radiance, of course." Wade tugged on her hand and broke into a jog. "Hurry up, slowpoke."

The sparkle returned to her eyes. She laughed with him, the fantasy restored.

The barn doors stood twelve-feet high and just as wide. He gave a single shove and sent the precision-balanced door sliding to one side. The doors on the opposite side of the barn were already open, revealing the corral where several horses frolicked.

Wade guided Lucy inside where shadows filled the left half of the structure.

"Where ...?"

"Shhh." He laid a finger across his lips. "We dare not disturb the beasties in the tack room."

He pushed a door open and waited until their vision

adjusted to the dim light before pulling Lucy inside.

A dozen shiny eyes stared up at them.

Lucy gripped his hand tighter. "What kind of beasties?" she whispered.

"Kittens. Born about four weeks ago."

A mewling chorus erupted. Six tiny bodies flopped over each other in their escape from the blankets.

"Ohhh, they're so cute." Lucy let go of his hand and dropped to her knees.

Wade's smile broadened into a grin when she started with the goo-goo baby talk. He knelt beside her, scooped up a black fur ball, and handed it to her. "Momma Cat is around here somewhere. She won't go far, not for a few more weeks yet."

"What are their names?" Lucy nuzzled the tiny kitten and rubbed her cheek along its head.

"They're barn cats, Lucy. They don't have names."

She turned astonished eyes on him. "But you name your horses."

"That's different. We feed and interact with our mounts."

A frown drew her delicate eyebrows into a straight line. "You don't feed the kittens?"

"Mama Cat takes care of that. She has her own feast every day taking care of the rats. I promise. None of them go hungry."

She dropped into a cross-legged position on the floor, settled two of the babies in the circle of her legs, and reached for a third one. "They're precious." She looked up at him. "Please, can we name them?"

A wood nymph sat on his dirty barn floor while tiny kittens climbed over her legs, up her sling, and serenaded her. A shaft of sunlight spilled through the openings, making her lustrous brown hair shimmer like a halo. How could he say no? "Whatever you want, tiger."

The smile she gifted him stole his breath. When she patted

the ground next to her, he collapsed like a puppet.

Lucy came with enough baggage to fill a boxcar, but she had a simple, undeniable purity about her. His family thought she told the moon when to rise and the stars where to hang. Cassie gave her clothes and sent her here after knowing Lucy less than a day. Mallory claimed they were best friends. Mom had all but adopted her while Dad ... Wade sighed. His dad worshipped her.

Even Jonas, self-professed Romeo who'd made it his goal in life to love and leave every unattached woman in the state of Idaho, thought she was special. A growl gurgled deep in his chest at the thought of Jonas playing his games with Lucy.

She handed him three kittens, one calico and two black and whites. "You name those, and I'll name these. What do you call the mother?"

"Momma Cat."

"Really Wade?" She gave him an eye roll. "How do you tell ... I mean ..."

"Whether they're male or female?"

She nodded, spots of color tinting her cheeks.

Lucy was way cuter than the kittens. He settled two of the babies between his legs, lifted one of the black and white kits to eyelevel, and yanked its tail high. "Male."

Her gasp made him laugh. Country living was hard. Not much shocked folks around these parts. Sheltered city girls would be mortified by some of the things done on a ranch. He repeated the examination for the other two kittens. "Male. Female. I think we'll call this little girl Flower. See the daisy design these brown spots make?"

"Flower. That's good." She swapped her three cats for his three and picked up one of the males. "This one I'll call Inky because he's all black. And this other one is Grit because his tongue feels like sandpaper."

Wade repeated the examinations. "Two females—Gingersnap and Valentine." He swapped the two calicos for the last black one. "Cornelius."

"Cornelius?" Her pert nose wrinkled. "What kind of name is that for a kitten?"

"I wanted to name my first horse Cornelius, but Dad said no self-respecting stallion would stand for it."

Her disdain gave way to another fit of giggles. "Okay. I could get to like it."

Momma Cat slinked through the doorway then. Her hiss put an end to their fun.

Wade got to his feet and settled his three kittens back on the blankets, and then reached for hers. "Time to go, tiger. We'll back out nice and slow."

"Mama Cat won't attack, will she?"

"Don't think so. She's not feral, but I wouldn't call her domesticated." He positioned himself in front of the still hissing mother and nudged Lucy from the room.

"Okay, this way. There's somebody else I want you to meet." He twined their fingers together.

Lucy walked with him through the rear doors and squinted when they stepped into bright sunlight.

He steered her to the outside of the fence before letting himself into the corral through the gate.

"They're beautiful." She leaned over the rail and nodded at the horses.

"You ride?"

"Horses? Not a chance."

Wade pursed his lips and let out a shrill, two-note whistle.

The big, dun stallion lifted his head, perked his ears, and then trotted over to the fence.

"Lucy, meet Lancelot." Wade stroked the horse's velvety nose.

"Can I touch him?" She reached out with hesitant fingers.

Imperfect Trust

"Sure. Run the flat of your hand down between his eyes."

The stallion snorted and tossed his head.

Lucy jerked her hand back.

Wade caught the bridle and whispered in the horse's ear before looking at Lucy. "Try again. Horses sense if you're skittish. Don't let him boss you."

She reached again, with more confidence this time, and let her fingers caress Lancelot. "Oh my, his fur is so soft."

"Hair. Not fur."

Lancelot sidled closer and nuzzled her neck.

"I think he's taken with you. Want to go for a ride?"

Her gaze left the horse and met Wade's. Hope flared in her expressive eyes but was all too soon replaced by regret. "Not sure that's a good idea." She made a face and indicated her bum arm.

He touched her cheek. Soft as doeskin under his rough fingertips. "Like I'd let you ride alone your first time. Wait here while I get him saddled."

When he returned from inside the barn laden with reins, blanket, and a saddle, Lucy had advanced beyond a stroke on Lancelot's face. Standing high on the fence rails, she leaned over and trailed her hand along the horse's withers as far as she could reach.

Wade hefted the saddle over the top rail and clucked to get Lancelot's attention.

The stallion remained calm while Wade attached the reins, smoothed the blanket over his back, added the saddle, and cinched it tight.

"Follow us along the rail." He led the horse a dozen yards away from the barn until they came even with an elevated wooden stand outside the fence. "Climb up on the block and wait."

Wade mounted and directed the horse closer to the fence until his flank touched the rails. "Turn your back to me, Lucy.

I'm going to pull you onto my lap."

She did as he said.

A sense of rightness settled in his gut. "Don't worry. Lancelot's a gentleman."

"Yeah? What about you?"

Delighted with her playfulness, he wheeled Lancelot toward the gate. "My mother would be insulted by that question. Hold onto the saddle horn while I let us out." Satisfied she wouldn't topple off, Wade leaned down and lifted the latch.

"Well, hey there," Rascal called, strolling from the barn. He closed the gate behind them. "I heard tell we had a guest up to the house, but they didn't let on how pretty you are. I'm Rascal." He doffed his big cowboy hat.

"Lucy, meet Rascal Sutcliff. He's been Dad's foreman and best friend for about a hundred years. Rascal, this is Lucy Kiddron, a friend of Cassie's. She's staying with us awhile."

The older man chuckled. "Nice to meet you, Miss Lucy. Lancelot here will give you an easy ride." His eyes wandered to Wade. "*You* behave yourself, or I'll tattle to your momma."

Wade grinned. "You'll tattle anyway, you old gossip." He tapped his heels against the horse's sides, and Lancelot moved forward in a slow walk down the worn track.

"Where are we going?"

"Not far. Down by the river. Maybe catch a glimpse of the horses."

She lifted her face to the sun, letting her eyes flutter shut. "I'd almost forgotten what fresh air smelled like. Tell me about the ranch. What it was like growing up here."

An hour into the ride, she started squirming.

"Want to stop and stretch?"

She nodded with a sheepish grin. "Yes, please. My fanny is numb."

"Hold onto the saddle horn while I get down." After

dismounting, he reached up, hands spanning her waist, and lifted Lucy out of the saddle. She weighed about as much as a butterfly.

"This is part of your fairytale kingdom, only it's my fairytale now. Doesn't this splendor make you wonder how such majesty could form out of nothing?"

He snorted. "You're kidding, right? Please don't tell me you're an evolutionist or one of those Big Bang theorists."

Her smile wavered. "I haven't given it much thought."

"Aw, c'mon, Lucy. That would be like you dumping a trillion lines of code in a paper sack, shaking it up, and pouring out a program that would change the world. I mean, take a gander at those mountains. Look at the sky and the plains. You think something went *boom* and all this fell into place? You know chaos doesn't produce order."

She turned in a long, slow circle. "It's not without flaws."

"No, it isn't. But it's about as close to perfection as we'll get on this earth." He swept his arms wide. "All of this is part of a grand design, which means there has to be a Creator."

Her expression turned thoughtful as they wandered along the river bank.

Good. Seed planted. Lucy could no more ignore a challenge than a weasel could stay away from a hen house. She might be stubborn, but she was too smart to not see what he meant.

"You're right. It is beautiful." She shaded her eyes from the sun.

"And deadly. A dozen or more people, most of them from the city, will die or suffer life-threatening injuries this summer while mountain climbing. It's a harsh land full of sinkholes, rockslides, predators—"

"Are you saying ranch life is dangerous?" She looked up at him, surprise in her eyes.

"It can be. Work doesn't start at nine and end at five like

in the city. Out here, it's twenty-four-seven, every day, rain or shine. No holidays, sick time, vacation, or weekends off. Something always needs doing. Everybody has a job."

"Like the cats?"

He loved the twinkle in her eyes, the way her mouth twitched when she tried to hold back a smile. "Mousers, every one. They earn their living."

"And the children?"

He nodded. "Yep. Me and my brothers started out with chores around the house—fed the stock, mucked stalls, forked fresh hay, cleaned the tack. When we got older and stronger, we went on roundups, ran the herds to fresher pastures. A boy's greatest adventure, at least until the shine wears off."

"You loved it. I can tell from the size of your grin."

He took her hand and started back toward the horses. "It's boring, backbreaking, dirty work. When we drive the herds, we sleep on cold, hard ground and eat endless meals of beans and hardtack. We sleep for a solid day once it's over and taste trail dust for a week. And yeah, I loved it. Still do. It's my heritage. I might not work on the ranch fulltime now, but I can't imagine a life anywhere else."

"I envy you." Her eyes lost focus, looked far beyond the river.

The sadness he'd seen earlier had returned. He tugged her hand. "It's best we start back to the ranch."

"What about your sisters? What did they do?"

"I'll get you a copy of Mom's books. They're all about ranch life, the hardships she and dad survived, and raising a family out here. As for the twins, they had their own chores from the time they could walk. We teased them about having it easy, but those two more than pulled their load. Mallory still does. They're tougher than most men. Did you know Cassie is a champion barrel racer and calf roper?"

Imperfect Trust

Lucy raised her eyebrows. "I don't know what that means, but I'm impressed."

A low chuckle got away from him. Lucy was like a breath of fresh air, a pure mountain stream, a ray of sunshine on a summer day—all those stale clichés the old folks spouted. He hadn't felt this carefree since ... before Sarah. Before Afghanistan.

"I'll tell you my favorite story about Mal and Cass as kids. They must've been about five, maybe six. One of their jobs was to feed the chickens and boy, did they hate it. We all did." He leaned down to whisper in a conspiratorial voice. "Not sure if you know or not, but you need a rooster if you want fertile eggs that will hatch."

She didn't pull the punch to his ribs. "I took biology."

He straightened up with a laugh and rubbed his side. "Okay, okay. Anyway, we had this big, good-looking rooster. He had copper and black feathers that gleamed, and curly tail feathers. Dad named him Beelzebub because he was meaner than a bear with a sore ... uh ... paw. And he strutted around like he owned the place. The girls couldn't get their tongues around the name so they called him Belzabug."

Wade stopped near the river, sat down, and pulled Lucy with him. "This one day they went out to the pen with a pan of feed. Most days Belzabug would strut around and ignore them, but not that day. The girls no sooner got inside the pen than that old rooster went after them."

A chuckle rumbled up from the depths of his memory and stopped his tale for a moment. "Cassie squealed when he pecked at her legs. She scrambled up on top of the fence, but not Mallory. Mal might be girly, but she won't run from anything. She stood her ground against Belzabug but spilled all the feed. She got mad then and went after that old bird with the empty pan."

Another spate of laughter doubled him over as he gasped for breath.

"Go on. Don't leave me hanging."

"Garrett and I had come back from the field. We saw the whole thing and about fell off the horses laughing." Wade paused to wipe away tears.

Lucy laughed with him ... or at him. He didn't care. Seeing her carefree like this made the sun shine brighter.

"Cassie was perched on top of the fence, bawling like a baby. Mom raced from the house, apron flapping. Mallory, though ..." He couldn't hold back another belly laugh, and fell over on his back in the grass.

Lucy laughed and lay down beside him.

"Belzabub ..." He choked out. "He ... he chased Mal around the pen, but then she stopped and brandished the pan at him. Belzabug backed off but Mal chased him, and then they switched roles."

Lucy rubbed her own tears away with the back of her hand. "How did it end?"

"Garrett got there first and scared the rooster off. Later, after Dad got home, Mom showed him the peck-marks on Mal's arms and Cass's legs. He took both girls and walked them out to the woodshed for the axe and then over to the chicken house. We had a new rooster the next day and fried chicken for Sunday dinner."

Wade glanced at the sky where the sun sank lower on the horizon. He didn't want this time with Lucy to end, but they needed to head back.

Lancelot had wandered away to graze on the rich grass. The horse lifted his head at Wade's whistle and ambled over.

"Much as I hate to say it, we need to get going. Mom's a real stickler about being on time for supper."

Lucy sighed.

"Hey, you don't feel bad for that old rooster, do you?"

"No. So, how do I get up on Lancelot without the little platform?"

"It's a mounting block, and we don't need it." He put his hands around her waist and lifted her up to sit sideways on the saddle. "Grab the horn, swing your right leg over so you sit astride, and scoot forward to make room for me. This position will be more comfortable for the return ride."

"Wade," she said when he pointed Lancelot toward home. "Thank you for this afternoon."

Her skin had a rosy, sun-kissed glow. He'd have to get her a wide-brimmed hat for next time. Sunscreen, too. "The pleasure is all mine, tiger."

Chapter Twelve

Dinner with the Camerons that night was a loud, crowded, and boisterous affair. When James joined them, they somehow managed to cram nine people around a table better suited for eight. Not easy since five of the diners topped six feet, with each man packing more than two hundred pounds of hard muscle.

Lucy sat on one side with Mallory on her right and Cate to her left at the end of the table. "Thanks for looking after me, Cate."

"You're welcome, dear. Don't want anyone to jostle your arm by accident. Here, let me serve you some of this." She spooned mashed potatoes onto Lucy's plate and leaned over to whisper, "Save room for dessert. Roseanna made Huckleberry Buckle. It's the boys' favorite."

James sat on Mallory's other side with Cody next to him at the head of the table. Garrett and his fiancée, TJ, Jonas, and Wade—directly across from Lucy—rounded out the seating. A myriad of topics flowed through the room as each person tried to talk over the others. City ordinances, wild horse regulation, the caterer's suggestions, a pregnant mare's predilection for wildflowers, Wade's up front and personal experiences with the bison herd, a rash of vandalism against some of the outlying ranches ...

Between the volume and ever-changing subject matter, Lucy found it impossible to follow any one thread of conversation. She didn't mind. Most of the topics held little interest for her anyway, but the animated chatter fascinated.

Imperfect Trust

Their antics exposed a pang for something long gone. Vague memories stirred and sharpened. The present blurred, and Lucy found herself in another dining room, one she hadn't thought of in a very long time. Sammy, Mama, and Daddy were there with a younger her. They ate breakfast together, excited about the camping trip. Sammy clapped his hands while she giggled. Daddy said they'd canoe and hike, maybe fish off the dock and swim in the lake. And roast marshmallows over the campfire.

"S'mores," she'd shouted in her little girl voice. They couldn't have plain marshmallows. Mama laughed and promised to stop by the market for Hershey bars and Graham crackers on the way. They never made it to the store.

The buzz of conversation drew Lucy back to the present. Pulled her from the last meal her family ate together.

She caught Wade's concerned look and averted her eyes. They'd known each other such a short time, and yet he seemed to read her so well. She dabbed at her mouth with the napkin and laughed at something Mallory said.

After dessert—she *adored* Huckleberry Buckle—Roseanna bullied the guys into clearing the table while the women headed for the kitchen and divvied out clean-up duties. Lucy helped as best she could until Cate shooed her off to join the men.

Cody sat in his recliner, hidden behind a newspaper. The others played a video game with Wade and Jonas pitted against Garrett and James. Not one of the popular bloodthirsty violent games though. This one required hand-eye coordination and a fundamental knowledge of tactics and strategy.

Lucy sucked her upper lip between her teeth to hold back her smirk. These four brawny guys were playing her game. She didn't understand the all-consuming appeal—it was just a game—and yet *LA Kidd Game of Trust* had hit the top ten in sales only three months after its release.

As far as she knew, no one had beaten it yet, and that puzzled her. She'd even provided a hint embedded in the name. *Trust*.

She lurked at the rear of the family room while studying the men's play.

"Watch it." Wade groaned, his warning given too late.

Jonas's character took a mortal hit. "Agghh." He pounded the sofa arm and caught sight of Lucy where she lurked by the door. "Hey, Luce. Want to play?"

"No, thanks."

He turned back to the game.

"You've played before," said a hushed voice behind her.

Lucy whirled around. She hadn't heard Mallory approach. "What makes you think so?"

Of course she'd played—through every step of development, beta testing, and a complete-game run-through in preparation for the commercial release—but only with virtual players and online contacts. What would it be like to see her opponents' expressions?

"You rolled your eyes right before Jonas blundered. And jerked your hands." Mallory mimicked a corrective movement.

Lucy guarded her anonymity. Only Wilson Kofer, Ed Whitaker's brother-in-law, knew she'd created *LA Kidd*. Not even Ed knew.

Wilson, a successful entrepreneur in his own right, provided the real brains behind LAK Enterprises. He'd taken a chance on her and provided the start-up funds. Now, he ran the day-to-day operations while she wrote beautiful code, an ideal partnership with a net value approaching their first million.

Lucy shrugged her good shoulder. "It's a fun game."

"Would you play it with me?"

"Don't listen to her." Garrett called over his shoulder. "Mal always loses. She's hoping you'll be easy."

James elbowed him. "Get your head in the game."

Imperfect Trust

"I think your brother just insulted me," Lucy whispered to Mallory.

Mallory sighed. "Yes, he did. I love my brothers, but they're in serious need of an ego reduction. James, too."

Lucy pursed her lips. "I can help with that."

"Oh?" Mallory's interest perked up.

James and Garrett sat on the sofa in front of the television, both holding joysticks. Their bodies swayed as they maneuvered their avatars through an intricate maze. The two men anticipated each other's moves to capitalize on every treasure trove and weapons stash in the level.

Wade and Jonas weren't slouches at the game either, but they didn't possess the practiced, machine-like precision demonstrated by the other two.

"Two weeks," Lucy called out to the room.

Wade looked around. "What?"

"Two weeks," she repeated, raising her voice.

"Two weeks for what?" Jonas asked with a puzzled look.

Garrett gave her a curious glance, while James ignored her, his focus on the screen.

No retreat now. Would she ever learn to think before speaking? "Give me two weeks to work with Mallory and the two of us will take on whoever wins the game you're playing now. A grudge match, *LA Kidd*-style, complete with conditions and a referee."

James hit the pause button and swung around, his expression incredulous. "You're kidding." The sound he made might have been laughter. Worse, his three cohorts joined in.

That sealed it. One lesson in ego reduction coming up.

"Lucy," Mallory groaned through clenched teeth. "What are you doing?"

"Trust me."

"So, you're a player?" Wade asked.

She nodded. "I play."

"What conditions?" James asked. "You want us to spot you like a gazillion points? Play with one hand behind our backs?"

Her mouth dropped. Oh, no, he did not say that. "If I can play one-handed, you can, too."

His neck, face, and ears turned dark red when he realized his blunder. "Uh, that came out wrong. What I meant ..."

Lucy gave him what Ed used to call her "look of death." But then she let him off the hook. "Don't worry, Sheriff. I won't hold you to it. You'll need both hands. I won't."

Garrett lifted one smug eyebrow. "Smack-talk, sweetheart?"

Of the four, Garrett posed the biggest threat. He saw everything, could analyze a situation with a look, and never hesitated once he determined a course of action. Ruthless and intimidating, he'd pull out all the stops to win. Taking him down would be sweet.

"The conditions." Her index finger went up. "First, tomorrow and every day until the tournament, Mallory and I get exclusive access to this room and the game station." Another finger went up. "Second, none of you will interrupt or spy on us. The room is off limits while we're training."

Staring at each man in turn, she ignored their smirks and rude noises. "Third, we'll designate a knowledgeable but impartial judge to mediate any disputes, someone with no skin in the game. I'm sure we can find someone in town who knows their way around this game."

Wade nodded. "Casey, the kid from my office, would be my choice."

Mallory nodded.

"Who?" Lucy asked.

From the recliner in the corner, Cody lowered the newspaper, one eyebrow raised in a questioning look.

"Too easy ..."

Imperfect Trust

"Like candy from a baby ..."

"It breaks my heart to see a grown woman cry ..."

"Yuk it up, boys." Lucy cut them off. "Number four, the winner is the team that reaches the highest level. If both teams beat the final level or if neither team does, highest points decides the winner."

The guys nodded with knowing smirks.

"The last condition," she continued.

"Ah, here it comes," James broke in. "Mal always demands do-overs, don't you, princess? How many extra lives you want this time?"

Mallory's cheeks turned a brilliant shade of pink.

"None for us, but thanks," Lucy said. "How many do you want to request?"

James seemed flustered by her comeback. His grin slipped. "Gotta have stakes, ladies. What do we get when we win?"

"While it's unlikely you'll win, *if* you do, Mallory and I will provide maid service for a day." She shushed Mallory's outraged grumble. "Within reason, of course. However, when *we* win," Lucy batted her eyes. "All four of you will accompany us to Fancy's Salon for a spa day. That means a full body wax—chest, back, and legs—*and* a mani/pedi. We pick the polish and you wear flip-flops for the week. Gotta show off those pretty toes. All of this is at your expense, of course."

Over in the corner, Cody's other eyebrow rose as he peered over the top of his reading glasses.

Stunned silence filled the room for all of five seconds before Garrett, James, Wade, and Jonas erupted in a harmony of guffaws. When Jonas fell off the sofa and rolled on the floor, Lucy wanted to kick him but waited for them to quiet instead.

Garrett, no surprise, regained control first. "Agreed, but with one point of clarification. You two will fetch and carry for all four of us, for a whole week. Now, any more conditions?"

The idea of servitude to four testosterone-driven peacocks produced a shudder. Mallory would kill her if she let that happen.

"I'm adding one more, so listen up." She ignored their taunts and spoke in a syrupy southern drawl. "Y'all don't get to call us little girl, darlin', sweetheart, honey, cutie, angel, babe, baby, baby doll, sugar, kitten, or princess."

She didn't list Wade's pet name for her. She liked when he called her tiger, not that she'd admit it out loud. Her voice turned stern to match her scowl. "In return, we won't call you stud, cowboy, beefcake, muffin, Cisco, Poncho, Wild Bill, or jerk. You call her Mallory. I'm Lucy. Got it?"

Beside her, Mallory stood a little taller.

The four men looked at each other like they were holding a silent conversation. As one, they returned a snappy salute and replied in unison, "Ma'am, yes, ma'am."

Cody erupted in a fit of coughing, snapped the paper up, and buried his face behind it.

Lucy zombied her way through the house the next morning, nose lifted high to sniff out whatever made that amazing smell. She found Mallory in the kitchen, tipping muffins out of a tin.

Mal looked up with a smile. "Good morning."

"What is that wonderful aroma?"

Mallory picked at two stubborn muffins that clung to the pan, stopping every few seconds to blow on her fingers. "Wouch. Hot. Roseanna had leftover huckleberries from last night, so I whipped up some muffins."

"It's Saturday. Where is everybody?"

"Mom and TJ have an appointment with the caterer and the florist this morning. Dad and Garrett rode out to check on the new mustangs, which means Wade and Jonas got stuck with the ranch chores. Looks like it's just you and me. Want one?" Mallory gestured toward the steaming muffins.

"Uh, yeah." Lucy's mouth watered. "Can I help?"

"Glasses in the cupboard." Mallory pointed at a cabinet. "I want milk, but there's juice in the fridge, too. Don't forget the butter." She slid a couple of fat muffins onto two small plates.

Lucy set glasses on the breakfast counter and went to the refrigerator. Holding the butter dish in her left hand—small movements and minor weight no longer hurt—she grabbed the carton of milk.

Mallory giggled.

"What?"

"You." She snickered again and pointed. "I had this momentary vision of you smacking Wade with the milk."

Lucy laughed with her. "It wasn't funny then." She pried her muffin open, slathered butter inside, and took a bite. "Mmm. Sooo good."

"You act like you've never had a muffin before." Mallory started on her second one.

"Muffins, yes. Homemade and fresh from the oven, with butter dribbling down your chin? Not even. In Atlanta, I usually grabbed a glazed donut or bagel for breakfast. Most of my meals came from drive-thrus."

"Your mom didn't teach you how to cook?" Mallory asked.

"No." Lucy averted her eyes. "My dad and little brother died in a car accident when I was a kid. Mama had to work two jobs to make ends meet after that. Didn't leave much time for cooking, much less lessons. I lost her four years later."

When the silence reached an uncomfortable point, Lucy glanced at her friend.

Mallory set the remnant of her muffin down. She wore a look Lucy associated with pity. "I'm so sorry."

"Eat, Mallory." Lucy bristled. "It happened a long time ago."

"Didn't your relatives take you in?"

More often than not, nosiness about her past triggered a snide remark that stopped snoopy people cold. She couldn't do that to Mallory. Their connection was too new. Friendship didn't come easy for Lucy, and she wanted to nurture this one.

"Nope, no family. I spent some time in foster care, but I wangled a scholarship and got into college early. Been on my own ever since."

"Well, you're not alone anymore. You have us, Lucy. We're your family now."

Mallory smiled, her eyes ablaze with … friendship. Not pity.

Uncomfortable with the novelty of someone caring about her, Lucy changed the subject. "Hey, let's get these dishes cleaned up. We've got a game to play."

Other than one short break for a late lunch, they spent the day in front of the gaming console. The others didn't return until dinnertime.

"I'm worried we'll embarrass ourselves against James and Garrett," Mallory confessed as they helped Cate prepare the evening meal.

"Mal, you mastered six levels in one day. Another week, and you can play with anybody."

"I *completed* six levels."

"I told you, the treasure stashes, extra lives, and weapons caches are distractions. The more time you spend collecting them, the higher the risk. We get in and out as fast as possible. The most points at the end won't matter when we beat the final level and they don't."

Mallory gave her that *yeah, right* look.

Lucy understood her friend's skepticism. No woman wanted to look foolish in front of a man they cared about.

Imperfect Trust

"I believe in you, Mal. I won't let you down."

The tight lines around her friend's eyes relaxed. "Okay."

Later, during the evening meal, Cody rapped his knife against his water glass. "Your mother would like us to attend church tomorrow as a family." Eyes of blue steel squelched his sons' groans. "It won't hurt you boys none to visit the Lord's house once in awhile. That includes you, James."

James straightened up. "Yes, sir."

"Since we won't all fit in one vehicle, Lucy and Mallory will ride with your mother and me. I'm sure Garrett will take care of TJ. You three can figure out your own transportation." He nodded at Wade, Jonas, and James. "Be in the pew before the music starts."

A chorus of grudging 'yes, sirs' followed.

Lucy pulled Mallory aside after they'd washed and put away the dishes. "What do you wear to church?" she whispered.

Mallory conked her head with a fist. "Where is my brain? You don't have any clothes. Come upstairs with me. Between Cassidy's closet and mine, I'm sure we'll find something."

The girls got up extra early the next morning. Mallory helped Lucy don a knee length red dress of hers and added a delicate white sweater from Cassie's closet, but Lucy balked at the tan cowgirl boots Mallory suggested.

"I promise. All the girls wear them." Mallory posed in her own black, fancy-stitched Ariats.

Left with a choice of sneakers or the heelless scuffs Cate had provided, Lucy gave in and stuffed her feet into the medium-height Tony Lamas.

She brooded on the short drive to the church. She knew zilch about religion. After the horseback ride with Wade on Friday, his words had stayed with her. He was right. She needed to figure this Christianity stuff out for herself.

Mallory hooked her arm through Lucy's and led the way past rows of dark wooden benches to a seat near the front.

Cate and Cody followed close behind.

Wedged into the pew between Mal and her mother, Lucy tried hard not to gawk, but still managed to get a few discreet peeks in. She smiled at the sight of a familiar face coming their way.

A subtle nudge followed by a nod got Mallory's attention. Her face broke into a smile when James slid in next to her.

He bumped Mallory with his hip to make room, causing a chain reaction.

Lucy giggled. And then clapped a hand over her mouth.

Garrett and TJ arrived next. A few minutes later Wade and Jonas took their seats at the end of the bench.

When the organ music started, Lucy took her cue from the others and stood to sing when they did, stayed quiet during the sermon, and bowed her head for prayers. Some of the Bible verses the pastor recited raised more questions. She made a mental note of where to find them so she could read them for herself.

They exchanged pleasantries with the pastor at the conclusion of the service, and then the family descended the front steps en masse—and ran into a bevy of friends and neighbors.

Surrounded by strangers, Lucy's instincts kicked in. She took a step back. A second step landed her against a solid wall of flesh.

"Going somewhere, tiger?" Wade steered her back into the vortex with a hand pressed against the small of her back.

Cody and Cate shook hands, shared embraces, and tried their best to introduce Lucy to the entire town.

James and Mallory laughed and joked with everyone while Garrett tucked TJ's hand in the crook of his elbow and held it in place. His scowl kept most people at bay, but TJ ignored him. She smiled and greeted several people, and waved to others.

Lucy wanted to laugh at Garrett's pained expression.

Jonas, an obvious favorite with the women, turned his charm on high. Before long, several young, attractive women preened before him.

Through it all, Wade remained aloof to the crowd, while maintaining some type of physical contact with her—a shoulder bump, a touch, his chin on her shoulder as he whispered an explanation of the family's relationship to the people she met.

While they observed the niceties, Lucy studied the people around her and concluded that Cameron men—James included—were like catnip to women. Even Cate kept a protective—and possessive—grip on Cody's arm.

Several young women circled Jonas. One, a tall redhead who couldn't seem to work her way close enough, turned her attention on Garrett. Ignoring TJ, who was clamped to Garrett's side, she said, "Hey, Garrett. I haven't heard from you in awhile."

Garrett's Adam's apple bobbed up and down several times. "Uh …"

TJ reached over, grabbed the redhead's hand, and shook it. "Hi, I'm Garrett's fiancée. I don't believe we've met?"

Lucy clapped a hand over her mouth at the relief on Garrett's face. Well done, TJ.

The redhead muttered a few words before she turned to Wade, jostling Lucy in the process. "Hey, Wade. I haven't seen you around lately."

"Be careful, Tiffany. You bumped Lucy's injured arm." Unlike Garrett, Wade didn't care about making a scene. He turned his back on Tiffany and put his arm around Lucy's shoulders. "You okay, tiger? Did she hurt you?"

"Excuse me." Tiffany sniffed and stalked back to join Jonas's fans.

"I'm fine, Wade."

He led Lucy away from the crowd, on guard against anymore incidental contact. "I'm sorry about all that." He waved a hand at the girls around Jonas.

She grinned. "Sorry? For all these women who fawn over you and your brothers? No, you're not."

He grinned.

"If you could stop lightning, you still couldn't stop this. Your mom and dad should know better than to unleash all of you at once on the female population."

His neck took on a ruddy hue. He looked at the ground, back at the crowd, over at his truck … Was that a blush burning Wade Cameron's cheeks?

Imperfect Trust

Chapter Thirteen

Monday dawned with a deep chill in the air, breaking the promise of summer. Frost should be a memory by now, not crusted on the grass in late May.

Lucy huddled in the patio chair on the back deck and sipped her coffee. She refused to retreat inside because of a little cold weather. A few goose bumps were a small sacrifice for a chance to breathe in the purest air in the world.

A foggy mist hugged the land in a greedy embrace, only giving way as the sun climbed its ladder. She marveled at the unveiled beauty. Wild, but in complete harmony with the people who lived here. No, it wasn't perfect, but like Wade said, it came darn close.

The cup between her palms infused a little warmth, though not enough to stave off shivers. Forget mind over matter. Southern blood didn't adapt well to northern temperatures.

An unexpected contentment filled her. She felt safe here. How could anyone feel otherwise when surrounded by an army of rough and ready cowpokes?

"Don't get too comfy," she muttered to herself. Jensen Argault might be certifiable, but the man had an IQ off the charts. Like a Venus flytrap that waits for lunch, he would be patient.

Setting the now cold coffee aside, Lucy's fingers found their way to the spot over her heart where Jensen had left his calling card—J.A. Ugly red scars. The cuts didn't hurt anymore, at least not on the outside.

The kitchen door squeaked behind her.

Imperfect Trust

Wade stood in the doorway. He wore khakis today and had turned up the sleeves of a white button-down shirt.

"Second thoughts about your game challenge, tiger?" he asked. The unseasonable chill didn't seem to affect him.

"Nope," she said, rising from the chair.

He dipped his head, not quite hiding a cheeky grin. "You ready to roll then?"

"Yep." Lucy took her mug into the kitchen, rinsed it, grabbed her backpack from the table, and followed Wade to the front of the house.

"Truck's all warmed up." He reached for her bag.

"I got it." She hefted the strap higher on her good shoulder.

He lifted that quirky right eyebrow but didn't push the issue. He did insist on opening the passenger door of his truck, though. He also helped her up so she slid in without undue stress to her injured shoulder.

A girl could get used to this kind of treatment.

Wade climbed in on the driver's side, started the engine, and switched on the radio to George Strait crooning about Amarillo. He turned the volume down. "Tell me the truth, Lucy. You weren't serious, were you? About playing against Garrett and James? Because I have to tell you, those two don't play."

"Yeah, I figured that much out." Should she let him in on her secret or play it close?

"They won't cut you any slack. It's not in their DNA. *LA Kidd* isn't just a game to them."

"You know, it's wrong the way you four shut Mallory out. She's smarter than you realize. And deserves better."

"You think throwing her to the wolves will make her feel more accepted?"

He had a point but only if she and Mallory lost. "I'll let you in on a secret, Wade. I don't bluff."

He meant well, but she'd survived in a male-dominated industry for too many years to feel threatened now. Besides, she had an edge. A *big* edge.

They remained silent for the remainder of the ride, which gave Lucy time to go over her mental to-do list—check out Wade's office setup and catalog any physical weaknesses, determine who had access to his systems, get suggestions for someone to arbitrate their video game match, and figure out why Mallory still worked for Wade a year after Sarah left. Mal had a masters' degree in journalism, for goodness' sake.

Wade parked in front of his office and waved at an older woman who wore a trim, navy suit and carried a chic black briefcase. Her hair, a gorgeous array of salt and pepper, was coiled in an intricate bun at the nape of her neck. She returned Wade's wave before entering the bank two doors down.

Lucy strove for the same smart, professional look when she met with new clients. Her motto, *set expectations early*, went a long way toward alleviating concerns about her gender, youthful appearance, and experience. She glanced down at the clothes borrowed from Cassie's closet—worn jeans, faded shirt, and sneakers that had seen better days—and her confidence took a hit. "You know, under normal circumstances, I'd dress up to visit a client in his office."

Who was she kidding? They hadn't signed a contract. Wade wasn't a real client, and the circumstances weren't normal. Her only obligation was a verbal agreement to help him with the cyberattacks, but she wouldn't take a penny of his money.

Wade switched off the engine and shifted on his seat to face her. Resting his forearm on the top of the steering wheel, he tipped up his black Stetson and let his eyes roam from her chin to her toes. "You'll do. When we finish at Doc's, we'll shop for some decent clothes for you."

You'll do?

Imperfect Trust

Being an introverted social kumquat, the smart thing would be to suppress her attraction to him. Better to keep their relationship professional. Sometimes, though, her impulsive nature refused to cooperate with her brain. "We'll see. Let's get started, shall we?" Lucy snapped.

The Camerons all had formidable frowns. Wade turned his on her now. "I don't know. Depends on what you have in mind. You haven't been very forthcoming with what you intend to do."

She stiffened. So much for him trusting her even a little. "You want a plan? Fine. Today, I inspect your office for physical security deficiencies. I'll provide my findings in a report, along with a systematic action plan. It's the same process I use with contract clients."

He stared at her.

"What?" she demanded.

He remained silent a second longer before saying, "I figured you'd want to jump right into the code."

"Like all the digging you've done has had any results?" Lucy sniped. "Don't worry, Wade. Your source code is safe from me."

"You don't think my office is secure?"

"I find it best not to make assumptions."

"I have a state of the art alarm system, multiple locks on the two doors, and more alarms on the windows. My programs are patented, and I have no intention of marketing them. Since no one knows about them, the chances of someone lucky enough to hack in are too small to calculate."

"Then why are you concerned? Why ask for my help?" She reached for the door handle, done with this conversation.

"Because I'm a perfectionist. Most programmers are. I can't leave a loose thread hanging. Are you confident you can find whatever it was Sarah inserted?"

"Yes, I am." She opened the door, but his hand on her knee stopped her exit.

"Wait. I'll get your door."

"That's not—"

"My mother thinks otherwise. You don't want to get me in trouble, do you?" He slipped out of the vehicle.

She closed her gaping mouth before he reached her door. His capricious mood swings were going to land her in an asylum.

Wade helped her from the truck, and then held the door to Cameron Security Services for her. Two steps in, she stopped.

"Well, good morning, you two," Mallory greeted them. Dressed in a navy pencil-skirt, nylons, low-heeled pumps, a white silk blouse, and frou-frou scarf, she put another dent in Lucy's self-esteem.

Maybe she should take him up on the shopping after all.

Wade closed the door and removed his hat. "Hey Mal, any messages?"

"A few." Mallory handed him a stack of papers. "One from Mathis Farms in East Texas. They run eight hundred head of beef. Andy Milligan's referral. Ralph Mathis is expecting your call at eleven."

Wade grinned. "Told you word of mouth works better than spending a fortune on fancy advertising. You can't sell cattlemen with four-color ads or radio spots."

Whistling, he turned and started down the hall.

"Invoices are on your desk," she called after him. "I need them back today. And Casey's free this week. Something about assessments he's already aced. I told him he could come in and work."

Wade waved a hand in the air without looking back.

"One more thing. Dr. Hadde called."

That stopped him in his tracks. He turned, wearing an expression Lucy didn't recognize.

Dr. Hottie? Lucy looked from brother to sister—right, left, right, left—like a spectator at a tennis match.

"Ramona's back?" he asked.

Mallory nodded. "Got in two days ago. Jonas called her out to look at the new mares. She asked if you'd be there this afternoon."

"I'll call her." His eyes flickered toward Lucy for all of two seconds before he disappeared inside his office and shut the door.

He was interested in this Ramona. The realization hit like a sucker punch to the gut.

Mallory turned to Lucy, all business now. "Casey works out of the lab in the back but there's an empty office next to Wade's you can use."

Shoving thoughts of Wade and the mysterious Dr. Hottie aside, Lucy focused on Mallory. Who was this bossy, prissy, I'm-in-charge person? "Who's Casey?"

"A high-school student and a whiz with computers." Mallory jabbed a thumb toward her brother's office. "Wade gave him an afterschool job to keep him out of trouble." She glanced at the clock on the wall. "He should be here soon."

What was Wade thinking bringing a tech savvy teenager into his office? When you discover evidence of a computer breach, the logical step is to eliminate the potential threats, not add new ones. How much access did the kid have? *And who the heck is Dr. Hottie?*

"How long has Casey worked here?"

"A week."

Oh. He wasn't around when the hack attempts started, not that it earned him a pass.

"Hey, about the challenge to the guys ..." Mallory crossed her arms in a classic confrontation pose. "You do realize I have a job, right? I can't play video games with you all day."

"Trust me. I have a plan."

"You keep saying that."

"I know. Mind if I work over here instead of in the office?" She pointed to the counter behind the reception desk. "Wade mentioned something about a laptop I could use."

Mallory shrugged. "No problem. Casey can set you up. Do you need printer access? Internet? We have wireless."

Sniffers loved wireless. One more complication. "Printer, yes. No internet. Mind if I look around until Casey gets here?"

"Knock yourself out," Mallory said, already engrossed in the stack of papers on her desk.

The office had a comfortable feel, tasteful and upscale, but unpretentious. Wade opened his door as Lucy wandered past.

She ignored him and continued down the hall.

A conference room and an empty office lay beyond Wade's. Another room at the end of the hall had a locked door. A spare office? A storeroom? More likely the server room. She found an open area across from the locked room where waist-high counters spanned one wall. Computer hardware in various stages of breakdown cluttered a workbench. Was this Casey's lab?

On the return circuit, she passed an exit door, complete with chain-lock, a deadbolt at the top and another at the bottom, and a security keypad mounted nearby on the wall just as Wade had described. There was also a bathroom, a small storage closet, and a tiny break room. Two thousand square feet of efficient office space. Not many concerns about the layout.

She stopped in the break room to grab a cup of coffee before settling in at her temporary desk.

For Lucy, quiet mode came natural. She disappeared into the background with little effort, a survival trait acquired while in the foster care system and honed during her early college years. Being the youngest or weakest in any group put you at a decided disadvantage. Survivors learned to avoid attention.

Imperfect Trust

She pulled her notebook from the backpack, opened it, and added a few questions—and kept an eye on Mallory.

Her friend was an enigma. She answered phones, scheduled appointments, argued with vendors, and did the bookkeeping with easy efficiency—a simple challenge for someone with Mallory's education and personality.

Shortly after ten, a gangly teenage boy arrived. His baggy clothes were clean and neat, but a year's worth of home-cooked meals wouldn't fill out his skinny frame.

"Hey," he said to Mallory but stopped cold when he saw Lucy. "Who're you?"

His wariness gave her a sense of kinship. "You must be Casey."

Red cheeks and a nod rewarded her question.

"I'm Lucy. Wade asked me to look at his computer security." She touched Casey's arm. "I hear you can set me up with a loaner laptop and access to your printer."

Casey looked ready to jump out of his skin. He tore his eyes from Lucy and looked over at Mallory. When she nodded, he muttered, "Uh, okay. Let me put my stuff down." He scurried off.

"Are you flirting with Casey? He's like fifteen, Lucy," Mallory hissed.

"It's easier to do my job if he doesn't fight me every step."

Mallory frowned, gave a short nod, and returned to the Word file open on her computer. She didn't minimize the document. Made no attempt to hide what she worked on. "Holler if you need me," she said over her shoulder.

"I'm good."

When Mallory resumed typing, Lucy took a long look at the file and trusted her strange ability to retain images.

The document had a ponderous title—*The Dynamics of Autistic Children Immersed in a Public Education System.*

Heavy stuff. The references cited people with titles and alphabet soup designations longer than their names. What did such a subject have to do with Wade's business?

Nothing.

Lucy committed Mallory's article to the part of her brain that allowed selective recall and hoped it would stick. A photographic memory like hers wasn't all Technicolor. More often than not, her mind served up jumbled images that made no sense. Thankfully, she'd learned to filter the important stuff for the most part.

"Here's a laptop. I gave you access to the printer," Casey said.

"Thanks. She smiled at him again, a glimmer of an idea forming. "Can I ask you a personal question?"

Casey gnawed at his lower lip and frowned, hesitating before he nodded.

"Do you play video games?"

"Yeah."

"Would you help Mallory and me with a project?"

What was she doing? All she'd done since the night of her run-in with Jensen Argault was make rash decisions. Why should this one be any different? Besides, both Wade and Mallory thought he'd be perfect.

"What kind of project?" Casey asked.

"A computer project," she told him. "There's no pay."

He looked curious but didn't say anything.

"You ever play *LA Kidd*?" she asked.

"Yeah."

"You any good?"

"Yeah."

Okay, this could work. "What's the highest level you reached?" Lucy grilled.

Casey's scowl returned. "Ninety-nine, but that's because the game's rigged. You can't beat it."

He'd given up too? "Mallory wants to learn. Her brothers won't help her, and I've got a bum arm."

Definitely a spark of interest.

"What happened?" he nodded at her sling.

"Shoulder dislocation. Hey, since you're out of school this week, maybe you could spend the mornings and work with us? We need to get her through as many levels as soon as possible so she can play against her brothers in two weeks."

"But I have to work here," Casey said. The spark in his eyes dimmed a little.

Lucy leaned forward and lowered her voice to a conspiratorial whisper. "I can show you how to beat the final level."

His eyebrows shot to his hairline. "No way. I follow the blogs. Nobody's beaten the last level."

"I did."

"Lucy," Mallory growled through clenched teeth.

"Mal, we have two weeks to get you ready," Lucy frowned at her friend. "We need all the help we can get. I'll explain later."

To Casey she said, "I've beaten it. Are you in?"

His grin lit up the room. "Shoot, yeah." He shot a glance at Mallory. "That is, if Wade's okay with it."

Lucy wanted to do a fist pump but restrained herself. "I'll make it okay."

He grinned. "Okay, then. When do we start?"

"You got a car?"

He shook his head.

"Then Mallory will pick you up tomorrow, here, at 8:00 a.m. sharp, and every day this week. She'll bring you out to the ranch and you can both return here at two o'clock to do your work. I'll figure out what to do about next week and let you know. Oh, and we want you to arbitrate the actual match. Okay?"

If anything, his grin grew bigger. "Like a referee? You sure this won't mess up things with Wade?"

Mallory shook her head. "I won't let it interfere with your job, Casey. I promise."

"Sweet." He swaggered off down the hall.

Mallory stood with arms akimbo and confronted Lucy. "I can't abandon Wade to play games. He depends on me."

"That's a crock and you know it. The work you did this morning took one hour and twenty-five minutes. There hasn't been a single call since I got here, and this isn't a walk-in business. Your brother doesn't need a babysitter. He can handle any calls that come in."

Mallory blinked.

"Let me put it another way—how much does he pay you?"

Her mouth opened and closed. "He ..."

Bull's eye.

"No pay, no benefits, and I bet no time off, either."

Unable to maintain eye contact, Mallory tried to argue. "I don't need the money. Dad gave us all shares in the ranch. And I have ... other income. Look, I can't just walk out on—"

"Mallory, I'm not asking you to leave him in the lurch. Come to work at two with Casey. You'll both have plenty of time to do what needs doing. Wade's a big boy. He can manage the phones and any visitors until you get here. Better yet, he can use an answering service or hire someone. And pay them. After the match, you can go back to your old routine if you want."

"You don't understand. When Sarah—"

"The blowup with Sarah happened more than a year ago. Wade needed you then. Now it's an artificial need. One you've cultivated. Tell me about the article you're working on."

Mallory's mouth flopped open. "What—"

"I saw the document on your computer. Early autism? Public schools? It's very good."

Imperfect Trust

Mallory looked at the darkened computer screen and back at Lucy. "You couldn't have read it."

Lucy's studied her toes. Few people believed her when she tried to explain her strange ability. Plopping into a chair, she rolled over to where Mallory stood. "Sit down. It's confession time."

Mallory sat.

"I have this weird ability. It's like near perfect recall. What I see sticks."

"You have an eidetic memory?" Mallory's voice hummed with excitement.

Eidetic? Lucy stared, stunned by her friend's enthusiasm. Most people didn't know the word, much less how to use it. "Uh, no. Eidetic is more about the senses—smells, sounds, touch, taste, and sight. An eidetic memory recalls everything in exact detail. A photographic memory is images. Flat, two-dimensional pictures. That's me."

"Wow."

"Definitely not wow-worthy. I can't always control it."

"Did you really beat the game?" Mallory scooted her chair closer.

Can't turn back now. "Yeah, well, about that. I have another confession, but you have to promise under threat that I'll torch your shoes if you tell a soul."

Eyes wide, Mallory looked like a kid who'd seen the Tooth Fairy. She crossed her heart. "I swear. Please tell me you're not going to cheat."

Lucy bit her lip and winced when she drew blood. She looked over her shoulder to make sure they were alone, took a deep breath, and said, "I don't have to. My name is Lucy Alice Kiddron ... as in *LA Kidd*."

Chapter Fourteen

Wade thumbed through a stack of magazines on the side table. He chose an issue of *Field and Stream* magazine, thumbed through it, and then set it down in favor of a *National Geographic*. Perched on one of the straight-back chairs in the waiting room, he propped an ankle on his knee and settled down to wait.

Color snagged his attention on one of the pages. He'd traveled to many places while in the service, seen a lot of strange and beautiful—and some not-so-beautiful—things. Maybe that's why the pictures drew him in. On one full-page glossy he saw a forlorn koala bear in a fire-ravaged outback. A second photo on the same page showed an equally tired-looking firefighter who tipped up a bottle of water for the thirsty animal to drink. A few pages further, a scuba diver petted a spotted moray eel, much like you would a puppy. Another story featured a 500-pound Siberian tiger cuddled up to a baby antelope. Why did the pictures seem like shades of him and Lucy?

He uncrossed and re-crossed his legs, trying to find a comfortable position in a chair not designed for someone his size. Impatient, he tossed the magazine aside. Why was he here? Waiting rooms were for loved ones. Not strangers. Maybe he should have let Mom or Mallory bring her.

He dropped both feet to the floor and leaned forward to brace his forearms on his thighs. Being here with Lucy—for Lucy—seemed too familiar, too intimate. He rolled his wrist and glanced at his watch.

Imperfect Trust

A half hour had passed since they arrived. Fifteen minutes since Doc's nurse took Lucy back. "How long can a simple checkup take?" he grumbled under his breath.

Sandy Reeves, a girl he'd gone to school with, looked up from her seat behind the reception desk and smiled. "Sorry about the wait, Wade. We had a drop-in. It shouldn't be much longer now."

Somewhat chastened, Wade nodded and reached for another magazine and turned a few pages. Several minutes passed before he realized it was an old issue of *People*. He tossed the rag aside in disgust.

The office phone rang again, but this time Sandy's agitated voice grabbed Wade's attention. "Oh my gosh. How bad? Hold on. I'll get Doc."

He got to his feet, watching as she hurried toward the back rooms.

That didn't sound good.

"Doc." Sandy pounded on one of the exam room doors before opening it a crack. "Coot Harbins fell off his cultivator. Melinda says he's cut his leg half off. She got a tourniquet on him but can't get him in the truck and the paramedics are over in Challis on another call."

Doc Burdette stuck his head out. "It's an hour's drive to their place. Call the sheriff's and get the emergency chopper. Tell them I'll be at the helipad in five minutes. Have Melinda call me on my cell phone."

He disappeared into another room and reappeared seconds later with a scuffed leather satchel and cell phone clutched in one hand and patting at his pockets with the other. "Reschedule the other patients. Leave Mrs. Akins' chart on my desk. I'll finish writing it up when I get back."

Wade followed the doctor through the front door and down the newly repaired step. "Doc, what about Lucy?" he asked, making a mental note to send Casey over to paint the steps and the entryway.

Doc's cell phone rang. He waved Wade off with a brusque, "Bring her back next week. Hello, Melinda?"

Wade slapped his black Stetson against his leg and went back inside. Coot's injury sounded serious, maybe life-threatening. Of course, it would take precedence over a routine checkup, but it was still frustrating. Lucy's shoulder didn't seem to be getting any better. She never complained, though, and he doubted the rest of his family gave it a second thought.

No. Mom would notice. She saw everything.

And he knew. He recognized the pinched look she sometimes got, the fine lines around her mouth and the glazed look in her eye.

Lucy returned to the waiting room.

"Well," he said and helped her with her jacket. "Looks like we're done for today. You up for some clothes shopping?"

"No."

The blunt answer reminded him of her earlier reserve. He'd said or done something wrong on the drive into town.

"I want to talk to you about something, though," she said.

Words to make a man tremble.

Lucy left the doctor's office without waiting for him.

Wade had to hurry to open the passenger door of the truck and help her inside.

He'd enjoyed the horseback ride with Lucy last week, and the time they spent together. They'd talked and laughed, and she'd let her guard down, opened up a little. Even better was the way she'd felt in his arms, all soft curves and sweet smell. He liked the weight of her leaning against his chest. How her eyes crinkled when she smiled. Didn't hurt that she was pretty, either.

Wade chuckled on the walk around the front of the truck. He'd spent most of Friday with her without stepping wrong, but he'd sure put his foot in something this morning.

Inside the truck, he turned to her. "You sure? About the shopping? There's a couple of stores close by."

"You didn't seem concerned about my appearance this morning. Why now?"

He stared at her for a long moment, stumped by her question. "I, uh ... I'm not concerned. I mean you look nice, it's just ... I thought women ..." He looked away, afraid to say anything more, afraid not to. "What I mean to say is ... Don't you want clothes that make you look good?"

"Oh," she said, sounding like he'd knocked the wind out of her.

"That didn't come out right." He backed out of the parking spot.

Time moved like a drunken raccoon while his mind searched for words to rescue him from the hole he'd dug. He sneaked another peek at her when he looked both ways and pulled onto the main road.

Her expression didn't waiver. Flat. Closed off.

Maybe he'd do better to keep his stupid mouth shut the rest of the day. "Look, I'm sorry. Again. Every time I open my mouth I seem to hit a tripwire, so I'll just shut up." He kept his eyes focused on the road ahead.

"You'll do." The flat tone of her voice was anything but reassuring.

"Huh?" He glanced at her. "What's that mean?"

"I asked you this morning if I was dressed appropriately for your office. That's what you said. 'You'll do.' If you don't care that I dress like one of the hands, why should I?"

So that was it. He'd hurt her feelings. "Tiger, you'd make burlap look amazing."

Her head snapped toward him.

Yep. That did the trick. Her eyes had gone all soft, the lines around them smoothed out. Had he finally said something right?

"Thank you, Wade."

"You're welcome, Lucy." He allowed himself a mental *hooyah*, but kept his face devoid of expression.

"I really do want to talk to you about something."

His short-lived relief disappeared like smoke up a chimney. "Okay."

"It's about Mallory. She's worked for you since Sarah left, right?"

"Yeah," he said. His instincts screamed for caution.

"How much do you pay her?"

Okay, that was a low blow. He clamped his jaws shut and kept his eyes pointed straight ahead.

"And what about benefits? Vacation?"

He rubbed a hand through his short hair. "Look, Mallory's great at her job. She likes to feel needed. I tried to pay her, but she refused to accept anything. I can't very well fire her. And it's not like she doesn't have money. I mean, we all get a payout from the ranch profits."

Lucy chuckled.

"What's so funny?" He took a deep breath and tried to tamp down the rising irritation.

"Nothing. Well, maybe it's a little funny."

Her easy smile helped loosen the steel band around his chest. "Explain."

"You think you're doing Mallory a favor by giving her a job that makes her feel needed. She thinks her emotionally damaged brother can't function without her. I get that you Camerons don't do the touchy-feely stuff, but come on. You two need to talk."

Wade couldn't deny what she said. He hadn't paid Mal a dime in all the time she'd worked for him. Having Lucy point it out sat about as well as learning Mallory thought he was—what had Lucy called it—emotionally damaged.

A muscle ticked in his jaw. He wanted to snort, but a flicker of doubt held him in check. Was he broken?

"You think Mal does this because she feels sorry for me?" He did snort then.

"Why else would she work for her brother and take no pay? Are you aware your sister is a successful writer? That she's a regular contributor to a Seattle newspaper? Does anyone in your family know about all the articles she's had published in several high profile magazines?"

Wade looked hard at Lucy but saw only truth staring back. "The road, Wade."

He yanked the steering wheel to re-center the truck in his lane. Apparently his failure at relationships included sisters. How could such an epic communications failure occur in a family as close knit as his? Lucy had been in Hastings Bluff such a short time. How could she know these things when he didn't?

Beside him, Lucy shifted sideways in her seat until she faced him. Her brown eyes sparkled with laughter, but her smile ...

Eyes on the road. Eyes on the road.

What she said made sense. He'd taken advantage of Mal's good will, thinking she needed him. Had she made sacrifices in her career for him? "What do you suggest?"

"Tell Mallory she can take mornings off this week to train with me on the video game. She and Casey can come into the office at two and have plenty of time to do their work. Once the match is over, take her out to dinner and discuss your professional relationship. Tell her where you see your business going. Ask about her goals. Figure out together where you both see things going. I think you'll be surprised by what you learn."

Lucy spotted the turnoff ahead on the right. She'd been out of it when Cate first brought her here, thanks to Doc's special pills, and hadn't seen much. Now, after Wade turned onto the private drive, she got her first good look at the family's brand—three horseshoes adorned the arched gate, stacked on top of one another and canted sideways to look like C's—the Triple C Ranch.

The gates stood open to the private drive.

"Must be company," Wade muttered. "We usually keep the gates closed."

As they made the final winding curve, the ranch house came into view. A shiny white truck with a magnetic sign on the door was parked in front—*Dr. Ramona Hadde, Veterinarian.*

Hadde. Not *hottie.*

Wade's expression changed. He became ... animated. The same way he'd acted this morning after Mallory told him of Dr. Hadde's call.

The front door opened and Jonas came out onto the porch followed by an auburn-haired woman.

So that was Ramona.

For the first time since she'd met him Wade forgot his manners. He opened his door and stepped from the truck but didn't come around to help Lucy down. Instead, the tall redhead in her form-fitted shirt and snug jeans drew him like an iron rivet to a magnet.

Lucy fumbled for her door handle, unable to look away while the scene unfolded. Ramona wasn't Hollywood beautiful. More like striking with her fiery hair that floated like a cloud around her shoulders. Worse, she stood a lot closer to six feet than Lucy did, with legs that seemed to go on forever. And she moved with the grace of a cat on the prowl.

The Amazon locked eyes with Lucy for all of two seconds before she devoted her full attention to Wade again.

Imperfect Trust

Lucy's breath hitched at the obvious dismissal. She'd been overlooked and disregarded all her life. Being underestimated gave her an edge. So, why was her nose out of joint now?

The truth crawled out from its hiding place. She liked Wade, was attracted to the man in a way she'd never experienced before. And jealousy's claws had sunk deep.

Garrett, TJ, and Cody joined the others on the porch, all of them laughing like the old friends they were.

Ramona dashed down the front steps and launched herself into Wade's arms.

He caught her up with ease and swung her around, his head thrown back in a laugh. "Look at you, Ro. All grown up."

Ramona kissed him.

A different kind of pain settled in the area of Lucy's heart, a hurt she had no business feeling.

Wade moved at the last minute so Ramona's lips landed on his cheek, but there was no doubt they'd been close at one point.

Unwilling to watch the happy reunion, Lucy slipped from the truck and did what she did best—faded into the background. Beyond a mutual interest in technology, she and Wade had nothing in common. How could a computer geek compete with a woman like Ramona?

Slow, deliberate steps took her around the corner of the house undetected. Out of sight, she headed for the patio. The start of a headache tapped at her skull. These new feelings disturbed her. She needed solitude and quiet to work through them.

"There you are." TJ popped through the kitchen door perhaps ten minutes later. "Cody wondered where you'd gone."

Lucy managed a smile for Garrett's fiancée. Cody wondered. Not Wade. Did he even notice her absence?

"We're heading over to the big barn," TJ said, joining Lucy on the patio. "Ramona—she's a vet, you know—is here to give the new horses a clean bill of health. You haven't seen the big barn yet. You should come with us."

For a side-by-side comparison of the ugly duckling and the swan? "No, thanks." She had her pride.

"Wade said you might be tired. Cate's at a neighbor's house but should return soon. Will you be okay by yourself while we're gone?"

"Of course. Don't worry about me."

Not to be put off, TJ dragged a chair to Lucy's side. "Look, the Camerons mean well, even if they do overwhelm at times."

"At times?" The unladylike snort got away.

TJ nodded. "Yeah, more like always. They have their faults, but they're good people, Lucy. There're just so many of them."

Lucy nodded, unsure how to respond.

"Garrett has this overbearing personality that scares women, children, and most of the male population," TJ said with a chuckle. "But he's really a big teddy bear. Now, Wade is the smartest person I know, but he can make you feel dumber than dirt when he cocks that arrogant eyebrow at you. They all do the eyebrow thing, you know. Except Cate. And boy, does she hate that she can't. I caught her practicing in front of the mirror in the foyer one day when she thought everyone was gone. Oh my, the facial contortions ..." TJ's laughter tinkled like wind chimes. "You should have seen her expression when she saw me behind her."

Lucy grinned. She didn't know TJ well, only what Wade had told her—that TJ had also come to Hastings Bluff to escape a ruthless enemy and wound up falling in love with Garrett. Now, she and Cate spent most days absorbed with wedding details. Why was she so chatty all of a sudden?

TJ wiped her eyes and leaned forward. "All three of the brothers are hot enough to melt an icecap, but Jonas is Don

Imperfect Trust

Juan reincarnated.

Lucy clapped a hand over her mouth, unable to hold back a belly laugh. She'd seen Jonas in action after the church service with all the sweet young things gathered round him. "What about Mallory and Cassidy? I thought twins had some special connection, an intuitive bond that made them aware of each other all the time. According to Mallory, they're not close at all."

TJ's smile faded a little. "I don't know. The guys don't see it, the distance. Cody either. Cate senses it but brushes it off, because it's always been that way I think. In the family albums, when the girls were little, they were hugging each other in every picture like they were inseparable. I couldn't tell them apart because they dressed alike. All that seemed to change with the school photos. Not many pictures of them together after that. It might be my imagination. I mean, Cassie hasn't been here much, but when she is, she and Mallory seem to avoid each other."

A deep sadness filled Lucy's heart. How could sisters—twins—not cherish each other? If she had her baby brother back, her father, even her mother, she'd make sure they never doubted her feelings for them.

She had to let the old hurt go, though. Wishing wouldn't change the past.

"Well, enough of that." TJ dusted her hands. "I know I've acted like a refugee from an insane asylum since you arrived … all these wedding plans. Ugh." The harried look returned.

"Why not elope?"

TJ's laugh had more than a hint of frantic in it. "I suggested an Elvis wedding in Vegas. No cake, no flowers, no worry that I left someone important off the invitation list."

"What did he say?"

"That would be a big, fat no." TJ's cheeks deflated on a big exhale. "I think he likes all the fuss and bother, not that he'd admit it. I know Cate does."

"He is her first to get married," Lucy said. And that man was so in love, it hurt to watch him around TJ. The emotions on the other woman's face prompted feelings Lucy had never entertained. Thoughts of her own white wedding, blue-eyed children, and a rosy future.

"Lucy?"

Her attention snapped back. TJ had asked a question. "Sorry. My mind wandered. I had a vision of you in a white gown and veil, walking down the aisle. You'll be a beautiful bride."

TJ blushed. Her quiet joy chased the chill from Lucy's heart once more.

"Thanks for the sweet compliment. Look," she jumped up. "I have to scoot before Garrett comes for me. First, though, I want to give you some advice. The Camerons are the best. There's no artifice with them. Let them in, Lucy. Let Wade in. Give him a chance. I promise. You won't regret it."

"Go on, now," Lucy waved TJ off with a shooing motion. "Don't worry about me. I enjoy peace and quiet."

"Okay, see you at dinner."

Would they invite Ramona? Of course they would.

A dull throb settled in at the base of her skull. She dug her fingers into tight neck muscles, but no amount of rubbing seemed to help. Perhaps she should skip dinner tonight and barricade herself in the bathroom for a long soak in the tub. With water as hot as she could stand. Maybe some bubbles. Afterward, a few stretches and then off to bed for a good night's sleep.

Lucy went inside to write Cate a note. She'd plead a headache. It was true. Her head did hurt. And the last thing she wanted was to listen to Wade and his brothers relive their glory days with Ramona.

Chapter Fifteen

The next morning, after a restless night, Lucy grabbed a cup of coffee and started toward the family room to wait for Mallory and Casey. She'd waited for Wade to leave at his normal time to go do whatever ranch chores claimed him every day, and then rushed to get settled with her loaner laptop in the family room before he returned.

No way could she spend hours with him in Cate's tiny office. He took up all the air, was too much of a distraction. Besides, she needed to help Mallory train on *LA Kidd*.

As she neared Cate's cozy little office, the clacking sound of fingers on a keyboard caught her ear. She peeked in. Wade had returned early.

He worked from the wrong side of the desk, his attention shifting between an Excel spreadsheet on his laptop screen and a pile of papers beside him. From the number of manila folders scattered about, it looked like he planned to work from here for the foreseeable future.

The business side of the desk remained clutter free. She flushed, denying a pinch of guilt. It wasn't like they'd agreed to share the office. They weren't tied at the hip or anything. He'd made that clear last night when he went off with Dr. Hadde and forgot Lucy even existed. And he didn't seem all that anxious about his mystery bug either.

The grandfather clock in the foyer chimed once. A quarter past eight. Mal and Casey should roll in any minute. When Wade turned away and reached for a file, Lucy tiptoed past the open door.

Imperfect Trust

In the family room, the curtains were opened wide to allow in the morning light. She stood by one of the windows and marveled again at the beauty of the land. This place tugged at her heartstrings, made her yearn for something she couldn't put into words.

Enough of that nonsense. She left the window and curled up in one of the overstuffed chairs.

Wade's blasé attitude about the potential threat to his systems puzzled her. He exhibited no sense of urgency about finding whatever it was Sarah had uploaded to his computer. In his shoes and given the recent hack attempts, Lucy knew she'd freak out. Not him, though. Of course, he'd already spent countless hours in search of the intruder file. Some of his confidence had to be because he'd written his own security programs and designed the firewalls, all in a programming language unknown to anyone else. Factor in the failed break-in attempts, and yeah, she could see why he might not be worried.

Still, the thought of a foreign file in his systems had kept her awake for most of the previous night. They'd missed a clue.

She took a last sip from the cup and set it on the end table. The commercial anti-viral programs had come up empty, as had the enhanced search program Wade wrote specifically for the problem. Whatever it was Sarah had introduced didn't act like a virus, worm, trojan, or any other kind of destructive program. Logic said it posed no malicious threat after all this time, but instinct told her it did.

Her overnight musings began to gel. What she'd learned so far suggested the file wasn't tethered to a specific command, which could explain why Wade hadn't found it. Sarah made it impossible for anyone to find, including herself. Why?

Sarah hadn't completed the insertion sequence because Wade interrupted.

That made sense, but it left them with a free radical bouncing around. Not a problem ... until it caused a malfunction somewhere in the system. Or until an unfriendly someone stumbled onto it. And the odds said they would. No security system remained impervious to attack forever.

Lucy chewed on her bottom lip, her finger tracing the pattern on the chair arm. Wade wrote all of his own programs. Every programmer had a unique 'voice.' Like fingerprints and snowflakes, no two were alike.

That's it.

Instead of a search for malware ... they needed to tailor their search to identify anomalies in his writing style. A simple comparative program. Pattern recognition. Only in this case they'd search for what didn't match.

Frenzied excitement gripped her. She could revise a simple search program. Use some of his code to establish a pattern baseline ...

Her enthusiasm dropped a notch. Wade had yet to share much about his programs.

Unable to sit any longer, Lucy got up and paced. Okay, *he* could write the new search app. No, he would *have* to write it—in the same proprietary language employed in all his programs. She needed to talk with Wade.

She stopped, did an about face, and picked up her laptop. First things first. They needed a clear project plan. She'd work on it once Mallory and Casey got started. And after she got more coffee.

In the kitchen, Lucy found Cody standing by the coffeemaker and marveled anew at the strong likeness between him and his three sons. His daughters too, though in a softer way.

"Want some?" Cody asked as he filled a cup for himself.

Lucy nodded and extended her mug.

He poured hers full, handed it to her, and opened the fridge to get the half-and-half. "Sit down a minute, Lucy."

She settled on one of the tall bar stools at the breakfast

counter, poured the creamer into her cup, and stirred. Conversations with Cody made her day. Their easy camaraderie touched on everything—horses, babies, forest fires, politics, extreme weather, baseball, and recently quite a bit about religion. Too bad he didn't have an interest in technology. She could use a sounding board right now.

"You're at it again, girl."

Ed often called her *girl*. At least he used to. He hadn't been available the last few times she'd tried calling him. He and Cody were alike in many ways. Both accepted her, warts and all. "At what?"

"You get this look on your face sometimes, like you're thinking too hard."

She smiled. Was it possible to think too hard? But then she noticed how serious he looked. How he scrubbed a hand over his short hair ... just like Wade. A sure sign that whatever he wanted to talk about didn't come easy for him.

"I think you know me well enough by now," Cody said. "I shoot straight. No sugarcoating, but I don't kick puppies. You understand what I'm saying?"

Lucy nodded, worried now.

"I had to pound some sense into Garrett awhile back. He insisted on being pigheaded like you and almost let TJ slip through his fingers."

Lucy took a sip to hide her surprise. Of all the topics he might have chosen ... She wasn't sure she wanted to hear this.

"It's a father's duty to steer his kids in the right direction. That's why I'm having this same talk with you. So don't interrupt 'til I get my piece said."

He saw himself as her father? "Okay."

"We all got baggage, but what you're carrying around is more than a freight train can bear. Hard luck's a part of life, but it don't make us who we are unless you let it. Now, the Lucy I know is a beautiful young woman, inside and out." He cleared his throat and began to pace around the kitchen.

Lucy waited for him to continue.

"What I'm trying to say is, we all have regrets, but they don't have to influence your future." Cody leaned on the counter so they were eye to eye. "Wade's got a ton of regrets, but since you came to town he's let go of the bitterness. Now, it's your turn."

Lucy's throat closed up on a rush of emotion. This rugged old cowboy had clarified in a few simple sentences what she hadn't gotten straight in her own mind for … how many years? Her memories of Mama, Daddy, and Sammy hurt, but they were also precious. She should take joy in them, not shut them away because they reminded her of all the losses in her life. *Because they make me feel too much.*

"I seen the way you get all dreamy-eyed looking at him when you think no one's around. All I ask is don't shut him out. I tried that when I first met Cate. Now, I thank the good Lord every day that she's more stubborn than that cantankerous old goat Mallory saddled us with."

Leave it to Cody to make her laugh while she fought tears. She took the paper napkin he offered and blew her nose.

She didn't know when it happened or how it came about, but she trusted the Camerons. Cody and TJ had it right, she needed to let Wade in. Maybe in time he'd come to trust her, too. And if he walked away today, tomorrow, next month, or twenty years from now, her heart might break, but she'd survive. And have the memories to treasure.

"If what I think is brewing don't pan out …" He shrugged. "Then you've lost nothing. If there is something, though, and you run from it, that's a regret you'll never let go of."

Lucy leaned over the counter and grabbed the front of Cody's shirt. "How'd you get so wise, you old Nosey Parker? You deserve a kiss for that."

Imperfect Trust

He winked at her and let her pull him toward her. His blue eyes twinkled like a ten-year-old boy bent on mischief. "Some things you learn the hard way."

Lucy planted a loud smack on his leathery cheek. "I'd rather take your advice."

The front door squeaked open. Footsteps and laughter announced Mallory's and Casey's arrival. Lucy looked up from her makeshift workspace in the corner of the family room when they entered.

Wade followed a few steps behind them, both his hands up in a defensive gesture. "Before you say anything, I know I'm not allowed in here. But since you haven't turned the video console on yet, in technical terms I'm not in violation. I wanted to say good morning before you got started."

His eyes moved from Mallory to Casey and settled on Lucy. "I see you decided not to work in the office."

With him. He didn't say the words aloud, but the implication was clear. Censure or disappointment? Or was she reading too much into his words? "Seemed practical since I have to work with Mallory. And from the way you're spread out in there, I think you'll need all the space."

"There's room enough for two. I know how to share." A ghost of a smile teased the corners of his mouth. "Besides, I thought Casey was working with Mal."

A glance at Mallory and Casey showed the two of them ping-ponging between Wade and her with identical stunned expressions.

Great.

Stunned described the way she felt too, because her brain wanted to forget that he'd abandoned her yesterday in favor of the redheaded Amazon.

Wade broke the awkward silence. "Guess I'll leave you alone. Good luck, Mal. For what it's worth, I hope you win."

After he left, the air returned. Lucy took a deep breath.

"Well, that was interesting." Curiosity filled Mallory's eyes.

Casey looked like he wanted to be somewhere else.

"Well, let's get started." Lucy ignored their questioning looks. "Casey, we covered levels one through six over the weekend. Let's start Mallory on level seven this morning. Let her get familiar with the controller, do the jumps, use the weapons, get through the mazes, and learn where the traps are. Show her how the replay works so she can repeat a level as often as she needs."

The two players settled on the sofa in front of the television and launched the game.

Lucy found it easy to work in the same room with them. Why weren't they a distraction? She ignored the nagging thought and worked on the project plan for her idea for pattern exclusion software.

When the clock in the hallway chimed twelve, she set her work aside and fetched the sandwiches from the fridge Cate had left for them. The food disappeared in record time, scarfed down in less than five minutes. Mal and Casey returned to their game still chewing.

Casey's expertise at playing *LA Kidd* wasn't brag. The boy had a natural instinct for the game and a knack for teaching. Mallory thrived under his tutelage.

Lucy came and went while they played, unnoticed for the most part. After they left to head into the office, she spent the rest of the afternoon on *LA Kidd II* to finalize the specs for its beta test. Could she meet the deadline?

Wade didn't attend the family dinner Tuesday night. His mom said he had other plans.

Lucy looked for him Wednesday after breakfast. She wanted to brainstorm about her idea for a pattern recognition search, but when he didn't show, she spent the day making a few minor alterations to *LA Kidd II*. A test run identified nine bugs, which meant the deadline was doable. A few more days and she'd have it ready for the beta testers.

Wade didn't put in an appearance all day and missed dinner again.

Frustrated, she called his cell phone around eight o'clock. He didn't pick up. "Wade, this is Lucy," she said in a voice message. "I plan to probe your computer system tomorrow. Didn't want you to think it was a legit attack. And I think I found a way to locate your rogue file. I wanted to talk to you about it, but since you haven't been around ..." She hung up, afraid she'd say more with her rambling than she wanted. Maybe he'd call her back. Or better yet, come home.

On Thursday, he was still missing in action. And her one attempt at an overt hack failed in spectacular fashion. She slammed the lid on her laptop. When he didn't come to dinner again, she determined he was through with her. So be it.

Wade stopped by the family room on Friday after Mallory and Casey left. "Guess your superior hacking skills ran into a brick wall."

Plenty of gloat but not a hint of where he'd been the past two days and nights.

She glared at him. Losing—at anything—irked her almost as much as his smirk. For once, though, she kept her smart mouth under control. If she explained her reason for failure was due to conventional methods to probe his firewall, he'd hear sour grapes. No need for him to know about Quicksilver. Or that she could get into any system, his included. Not yet, anyway. The real question was, once she got in, could Hermes manipulate Wade's operating system?

She could test it. He'd never know. Yeah, and if he found out she'd hacked his system, he'd never trust her.

"Look, I want to know if you really want to find the file Sarah uploaded. Or did you ask for my help as a way to keep me here to make your mother happy? Because I don't like wasting my time." So much for keeping her mouth shut.

The humor slid from Wade's face, supplanted by the stony countenance he'd worn after she clobbered him with a quart of milk. "I stopped in to let you know Mom made another appointment with Doc Burdette. You see him on Monday at two. I thought we'd stop by my office on the way. You can tell me all about your brilliant ideas then."

Brilliant ideas? How did he do it? Avoid the question and push her buttons at the same time. She sucked in a deep breath. "All right."

His cell phone rang.

"One o'clock." Wade lifted his cell phone to his ear and walked out the front door. "Hey, Ramona, you recovered from last night?" He chuckled. "Yeah, I had fun, too."

Lucy stomped back to the family room, her suspicions confirmed. He'd been with *her*.

CCC

"You know, Casey made an interesting point yesterday," Mallory said. "I think we should consider it."

When Casey finished with Mallory on Friday, she'd reached level forty-eight. Excellent progress. Better than expected. But all good things came to an end sooner or later. Casey had to go back to school on Monday.

"Hmm. What point?"

Lucy stuffed the last bite of chicken salad in her mouth and waited. Now, working with Lucy, Mallory had made it to level fifty-nine before they'd stopped for lunch. Not bad for a Saturday morning. At this rate, they'd have enough time to get through all the levels and get a practice game in from start to finish.

Mallory set her empty glass down.

"Well?" Lucy stacked their plates on a nearby table.

"He says two players aren't necessary. He hates getting

Imperfect Trust

matched up with an unknown partner so he creates a fictitious second name and plays both roles." She looked up at last.

Ahhh, Mallory had a bad case of chickenitis. "What else?"

"I thought, I mean, what if I can't master the higher levels? I thought, maybe you could finish?"

Lucy sighed. She should have expected this. The seconds ticked by while she chose her words with care. "Casey is somewhat right. One person can play both roles, but only up to the final level. That's not our goal."

Mallory huddled into the sofa.

"In theory, I could run the game. But that won't help you, Mal. This challenge isn't about winning, at least not all of it. The guys need to acknowledge you as a worthy opponent, and the only way that happens is if you show them you're capable."

"But—"

"No, let me finish. What Casey doesn't understand because he's never beaten the game is that *both* partners are needed for the final level. One player can't beat the game. One player assuming both roles can't either. Simultaneous decisions and action are required. The partners have to work in a coordinated effort. And trust each other."

"I don't follow what you mean about trust."

Lucy rubbed her forehead. How to explain? "Imagine you're in a race. You've entered the final stretch and lead the pack. You look back and see your teammate fall. Is he your partner or your opponent? Would you stop and help him if it meant giving up your chance to win? If it means he would win instead?"

She thought about it for a moment and shook her head. "No."

"Exactly. In a way, Casey has it right. It is a no-win situation—for anyone who chooses self over team. The higher you go in the game, the greater the need becomes for teamwork. The final level is the true test of what you learn along the way. That Casey could even reach it playing alone says a lot about his skill and perseverance. But he'll never complete the final level without a partner. The game's name is a hint."

"*LA Kidd*?"

"The rest of it," Lucy prompted.

"*Game of ... Trust.*" A glimmer of understanding flitted across Mallory's face. Her scowl slipped away. "What you're saying is you have my back and I have yours."

"No matter what."

"Well, in that case, let's get to it. I need your help. And you need mine."

Lucy grinned. "Don't tell Casey. I want him to see for himself. And you need to understand—only one thing can hold you back and that's you."

By the time they called it quits Sunday afternoon, Mallory had conquered level eighty-one. Well, conquered might be a stretch, but it was a huge jump nonetheless. She had excellent hand-eye coordination, a good familiarity of the mazes and traps now, knew her way around all the levels she'd played, and could identify the threats the game threw in at random. Better yet, she had an excellent grasp of the overall strategy required for the upper levels. All she needed was familiarity with the higher levels and a big boost of confidence, the kind that only came with experience.

Jonas stopped by, saw them putting the game console away, and invited them out to the barn. "Got another new mare. Thought you'd want to see her."

"I would love to," Lucy groaned. "I need the exercise, even if it's just a short walk. Maybe we can check on the kittens while we're there."

"Kittens?"

"What kittens?"

Apparently, Jo and Mal weren't in the know. "The litter of

Imperfect Trust

kittens in the tack room. They're adorable." An impish thought took root. "Wade and I gave them names. I wonder if Momma Cat is still over protective. She almost took our heads off when she found us playing with her babies."

Mallory and Jonas looked at her like she'd grown a cauliflower for a head.

"Wade was playing with kittens," Mallory deadpanned.

"Uh-uh. Not Wade. He wouldn't be caught dead ..." Jonas scratched his head.

Mallory started laughing. "You are so bad!"

"That's just wrong, Luce," Jonas added with a chuckle. "What did you say the kitties' names were?"

"I didn't, but they're Flower, Inky, Grit, Gingersnap, Valentine, and Cornelius."

Mallory hooted. "Wade always wanted to name one of the horses Cornelius, but Dad wouldn't let him."

Jonas doubled over, wheezing with laughter. "Ramona will be at dinner tonight. She's gonna bust his chops good."

Lucy's humor dimmed. The jab at Wade didn't seem so funny now. Not with Dr. *Hottie* on the prowl.

A heavy sigh didn't help.

Lucy had hidden in her bedroom since the glorious Dr. Hadde arrived more than an hour ago. Much longer, and someone would come drag her out. That, or sic Doc Burdette on her. She shuddered. He'd dose her with some nasty tonic.

Girding herself, she checked the mirror again. Nothing had changed since she donned the little red sundress and cowgirl boots. She'd done her best with what God gave her, but how do you compete with someone who looked like Ramona?

"Hey," Mallory said from the doorway. "Dinner's almost ready. Everyone's worried about you." She came into the room. "What's wrong?"

So much for hiding her worries. "I'm a little achy from all

the time we spent in front of the computer, that's all." She nudged her friend and smiled. "Let's go before your brothers eat all the food."

"Don't hide from me, Lucy. Partners trust each other, remember?"

Lucy melted under Mallory's meaningful look. "Yeah, well I've never had a partner—or a friend—before."

Mallory crossed her arms, not giving an inch. "You do now."

Another long breath and Lucy took the plunge. "It's just … I feel a little inadequate next to Ramona." Oh mercy, here came Mother Nature's tattletale heat firing her cheeks. She dropped her gaze and studied the intricate stitchery on the boots.

Her friend's soft chuckle didn't help.

"Lucy, Lucy, Lucy. You've got it all wrong."

She met Mallory's amused gaze. "In what way?"

"Ramona and Wade went to school together. They fished, hunted, and played cowboys and Indians. Those two have been pals for like, ever. She wanted to join the rodeo when they were teens."

"So did your sister."

Mallory shook her head and continued with the grin still in place. "Ramona wanted to ride bulls, Lucy. They called her Butch, for Pete's sake. And she's still bigger than most guys. I promise there's nothing between her and Wade, not what you're thinking anyway."

"She doesn't look like one of the boys," Lucy muttered. "You mean, Wade thinks of her like a sister?"

Mallory snorted. "More like a brother."

Imperfect Trust

Chapter Sixteen

Ramona and the Cameron siblings had learned the trick of growing up without growing old. All the pokes and prods, tickles and punches made it dangerous to be near them, so when Cate announced supper, Lucy was the first one out of the family room. She scooted ahead of Cody and took her seat on the far side of the dinner table, glad to be away from all their horsing around.

Sure enough, when Jonas reached to pull out his chair, Ramona leveled a well-placed elbow into his side.

Jo flinched away. "Geez, Ramona. What are we, still in grade school?" He glowered when she plopped down in the chair next to Wade where he usually sat. Grumbling his way around the table, he took the empty seat next to Mallory.

Ramona stuck her tongue out at him. "You know this was always my place." She tossed her head and the mass of auburn waves tumbled over one shoulder. The action, like everything else about the tall redhead, was big—her size, personality, her laugh.

Envious of the easy camaraderie Ramona shared with the brothers, Lucy looked away. Her experience roughhousing as a child meant a daily fight for food. Or mad scrambles to escape her vile foster father. Not this playful tease and tussle.

After Cody said the blessing, the childhood tales began. Each adventure grew wilder, the tales more raucous. Even Cate and Cody weighed in with their own reminiscences.

The conversation whipped around the table, but somehow never quite included Lucy. A reminder of her outsider status.

Imperfect Trust

She smiled and laughed with them anyway, intrigued by the glimpse into their past.

On the opposite side, TJ exchanged a disgusted look with Lucy. Being stuck between her oversized fiancée on one side and their overzealous visitor on the other looked hazardous. After one arm wave came close to clocking her in the face, TJ scooted her chair back.

Lucy smothered a laugh when she and TJ rolled their eyes at the same time. They'd formed an alliance of a sort. Maybe even a friendship.

During a lull in the banter, Jonas called down the table to his brother. The twinkle in his eyes promised mischief. "Wade, I heard a story about you, man. I want to know if it's true."

"You listen to gossip now, Jo?" Wade snorted as he raised his glass.

"Just want to get my facts straight. Is it true you named the new litter of kittens? Let's see, there's Inky ..."

Wade choked on his drink, which earned him a few hefty thwacks on the back from Ramona. After catching his breath, he glared at Lucy.

She wanted to crawl under the table.

"And Grit, Gingersnap, Flower and, uh ..." Jonas grinned and snapped his fingers a couple of times. "Oh yeah. Cornelius."

Silence filled the room for all of two seconds. And then the laughter erupted. Not the polite, ha-ha kind either. Deep, gut-wrenching guffaws that left everyone wiping tears away.

A red flush started up Wade's neck.

Lucy clapped a hand over her open mouth. Jonas had thrown her under the bus ... just like she'd done to Wade. Her chest tightened with dread. One commonality the Camerons all shared—they lived for payback.

"You never gave up on that, did you, son?" Cody's laughter left him wheezing. "Cornelius." He lost his breath and wound up doubled over, hands slapping his legs.

Garrett piped in. "Imagine the names from that bloodline—Corny, Cornball, Cornpone, Cornbread ..."

The look Wade shot Lucy promised retribution. Maybe slow torture.

Of course, the whole story about the visit to the barn spilled out after that. As Jonas predicted, Ramona razzed Wade about the kittens long after the others gave up. Unable to get a rise out of him, her voice grew louder and shrill.

Cate cleared her throat. "I think that's enough joking for one meal. You boys know better than to act the fool at my table."

"Yes, ma'am," the brothers answered, Jo and Garrett trying to quell their chuckles.

"And you, Ramona," Cate turned her unhappy stare on their guest. "You're still as loud as a rooster at daybreak. Tone it down, please."

Red blotched Ramona's cheeks. Hers was not a pretty blush. She tucked her head. "I'm sorry, Mrs. Cameron."

Mrs. Cameron? Not Cate?

Trying to smother one last snicker, Ramona turned her attention to Lucy. "So, what brings a city girl to the Triple C Ranch?"

The chatter around the table ceased.

Wade lost his grip on his corn-on-the-cob and almost knocked a glass over before corralling the slippery ear.

"Sorry." He set the corn on his plate and wiped his hands with a napkin.

Ramona leaned in, crowding him. "Butter fingers."

Lucy set her fork down and waited until Ramona stopped sniggering. "I knew Cassidy in Atlanta. After I hurt my shoulder she urged me to come to Hastings Bluff to recuperate."

"So, how bad is it?" Ramona nodded at Lucy's sling.

"Shoulder separation." Lucy lifted her injured arm a few inches. "Nothing serious."

Wade coughed, but didn't say anything.

"The Camerons were kind enough to take me in. What about you, Ramona? I'm guessing from all the stories tonight that you grew up around here."

"You could say that. My daddy worked for Mr. Cameron. We lived in one of the cabins over on the north side of the ranch. Wade, Garrett, Jo, and I—well, we were tight. The four of us went to school together. Hung out in the afternoons and during the summers."

"But you left." Lucy turned the focus back on Ramona.

"Been gone ten years After high school, my parents moved to Florida. They were sick of the cold. Being from the South, you wouldn't know about our winters."

Lucy didn't care for Ramona's smirk.

"Anyway," the vet went on, "I went to the University of Idaho in Boise—Goooo Vandals! Did my undergrad and post grad there and then stayed on for an internship. I'm back now, though." She smiled and let her eyes wander toward Wade. "I'm planning on the long haul."

"Good. We can use another vet," Cody joined the conversation. "Ask Tom Blackburn. He's been the only one in the area for more than twenty years. Has more work than he can handle."

"Tom's the one who called Ro. He asked her to fill in for him for three weeks so he can go off to Canada for a fishing trip," Jonas explained. "Hey, remember when we used to camp out in the upper pasture for a whole week in the summer? All we did was fish, hunt, and swim. Man, that was living."

"Yeah, and we'd have starved if Roseanna hadn't provided a sack of food." Garrett added. "You jokers thought we could live off the land."

"Yeah, we wrestled for Roseanna's fried chicken." Ramona tossed her head again, not bothering to hide her smirk.

The comment didn't seem to sit well with Jonas. He looked like he'd eaten something sour. "You only say that because you always won."

"Remember when you rolled into that mound of fire ants? You couldn't shuck your britches fast enough. Seeing your scrawny shanks gave me nightmares for months."

Lucy winced at Ramona's hearty laugh. Vivid pictures of four skinny kids rolling on the ground flitted through her mind, but she couldn't reconcile the images with those same adults at the table now.

The chuckles started up again. Ramona snaked her hand around Wade's arm. Her laugh deepened to a throaty purr. She was staking her claim and Wade appeared to have no clue.

"This must be so boring for you, Lucy. But then, you must be used to it by now, what with everyone else working?" Ramona stared across the table. Her perfect eyebrows lifted an infinitesimal amount.

"Oh, she stays plenty busy. Wade asked her to help him with a project. Those two have their heads together all the time." From Mallory's expression, she appeared to be rethinking the "boyish" friendship between Ramona and Wade.

Lucy sent her friend a silent *thank you* look.

Ramona's nose lifted a fraction. Her plump lips formed a pout. Was that a spark of fire in her green eyes? "Well, I know how smart Wade is, so your little project shouldn't take much time. When do you plan to leave?"

"No term limits on Lucy's visit," Cody answered. "And we hope she'll make it a good, long stay."

Cate's head bobbed up and down, agreeing with her husband. "Having Lucy here is like having another daughter."

Ramona's nose gained more altitude.

"Thanks," Lucy murmured. "You've been so generous

Imperfect Trust

and kind. I love it here." She risked a quick look at Wade. Did he enjoy the way Ramona fawned over him?

He met her stare, blue eyes dark with a heated intensity. A moment more and he scooted his chair over an inch. Away from Ramona.

She looked at her plate, fighting a tremulous smile.

Talk soon turned to horses and the Cameron's breeding program, another topic Ramona could converse about at length but with which Lucy was unfamiliar. Idaho was a foreign country to her with its mountains, rivers, trucks, ranches, and slow-as-a-slug pace. Lots of horses and cows, too. She needed a Starbucks.

"Isn't that right, Lucy?"

She jerked her head toward Jonas. "Sorry, I missed what you said."

"I told Ramona how you challenged Garrett and James to an *LA Kidd* grudge match. How you and Mal have practiced all week, like that's gonna help." Jonas grinned, his head nodding up and down like a bobble head doll.

Mallory jabbed her knuckles in his arm.

"Yeow," Jonas hissed. He leaned away from his sister and rubbed the injured spot. "What is it with everybody hitting me?"

"Behave, Mallory," Cate seldom had to scold her children, but tonight they seemed to test her boundaries.

"Who's James?" Ramona's question caught everyone's attention. "And what is this *LA Kidd*?"

A collective groan went up from Wade, Garrett, and Jonas.

"Where have you been hiding, Ro?" Jonas's tone conveyed both disbelief and derision. "*LA Kidd* is only the hottest video game on the market. I can't believe you don't know that." He shook his head.

"Vet school doesn't leave much time for playing kids games." Ramona lifted her nose on a sniff. She seemed to do that a lot.

"Garrett's partner is James Evers." Wade told her. "He's the sheriff now. You left before he landed here."

"He and Garrett were in the same unit overseas." This from Jonas.

"Hmm. Maybe I should stop by and introduce myself to the sheriff. He sounds interesting."

Mallory opened her mouth to say something, but shoveled a forkful of roast beef in instead. She wore her feelings like most people wore clothes and wouldn't be able to hold her tongue for long.

Sighing, Lucy offered herself up as a distraction. "James and Garrett are formidable opponents, but Mallory and I can handle them."

Sure enough, all eyes turned her way.

Another round of brags, boasts, and blusters followed.

"We'll see." Lucy's unworried shrug became a wince. Darn shoulder. The slightest unguarded movement provided a reminder of the seriousness of her injury.

Across the table, Wade's eyes narrowed. He didn't miss much. Pulling free of Ramona's clutches, he rested his elbows on the table and clasped his hands together.

Maybe he wasn't so enamored of his grown up childhood friend after all. At least not the way she wanted.

Not to be denied, Ramona leaned forward with him. "It appears you're in some discomfort, Lucy. You should call the doctor tomorrow and see if he can fit you into his schedule. I can drive you. That would give us a chance to get better acquainted and maybe do some shopping." Her eyes flickered over Lucy's borrowed clothes.

"She already has an appointment with Doc Burdette tomorrow," Wade said using that arrogant, no nonsense voice

Imperfect Trust

he often employed. "I'm taking her, and when she's ready I'll take her shopping, too."

Mallory, Cate, and TJ smirked.

Cody, Garrett, and Jonas each raised a quirky eyebrow.

Wade returned their stupefied looks with a cocked eyebrow of his own.

Beside him, Ramona sat openmouthed and, for the first time since she'd arrived, had nothing to say.

"Well," Cate said, jolting everyone from their surprise. "Let's move this party to the family room. Ramona, why don't you and Mallory help me with the dessert and coffee?"

CCC

For once, Lucy was grateful her bum arm kept her out of the kitchen. She excused herself from dessert and ducked into her bedroom. Sometimes—like now—she needed to get away. Be alone. Escape from the sensory overload that crowds and large groups brought. And tonight, the challenge of Ramona's unexpected animosity.

Too many emotions churned inside her. Too much unprocessed turmoil. Times like this were when her lack of a filter got her into trouble.

Lucy waited until Cate and Ramona finished in the kitchen before she slipped out the back door and sank down in her favorite chair on the patio. Several deep breaths of pollution-free air helped clear her head as she ran through a few breathing exercises. The tightness between her shoulders relaxed. Tension seeped away in slow dribs. Time passed. How much, she had no idea. It could have been five minutes or forty-five.

Quiet footsteps broke through her reverie. The soft thuds approached from the side of the house. Odd they wouldn't come from the kitchen behind her. She looked up and saw a man striding her way. His dark suit blended with the gloom making him appear insubstantial, almost ghostly.

A spurt of fear sent her heart rate soaring and left a metallic taste in her mouth.

Stupid. So stupid. She'd become complacent. Forgotten why she ran.

Lucy scrambled up from the chair, her legs like jelly. She stumbled, banged a hip on the wrought-iron table, and dashed for the kitchen door.

"Wait, don't go. I didn't mean to startle you. My name is Kevin Fowler. Ed Whitaker sent me."

Lucy slipped inside and peered through the screen door at the intruder, one hand ready to slam the heavier wooden door. Ed sent him?

"I knocked at the front door," he went on. "But no one answered. With all the vehicles parked in the drive and the lights on inside, I figured the family must be out here. I didn't expect to find you here, alone in the dark."

Her good hand clutched at her throat. It hurt to breathe. Ed gave up her location?

The man—Fowler—had stopped some yards away. He held his arms out in a beseeching gesture. "Please. Get any of the Camerons. They know me."

Torn between flight or staying to hear what the man had to say, Lucy said, "Ed doesn't know where I am."

Fowler uttered a cynical laugh. "Your accomplice in Atlanta, Miss Cassidy Cameron, is a lousy liar. Your colleague, Agent Whitaker, surmised from something she said—or maybe didn't say—that you were here, with her family. Whitaker's known your whereabouts almost from the moment you arrived."

Lucy's knees threatened to collapse. It explained so much—why Ed no longer asked her whereabouts. Why he didn't send out the threatened APB. Why this man was here. Poor Cassie. She wouldn't fool a seasoned agent like Ed. James's call would confirm Ed's suspicion.

Imperfect Trust

Another, more terrifying thought surfaced. If Ed knew her location, then Jensen Argault couldn't be far behind. *OhNoOhNoOhNo!*

She turned away, one panicky thought in mind. *He'll kill them. Kill Wade. I have to leave.*

"Wait," the stranger called out before she could go. "It's very important that I talk to you."

"Who are you? What do you want with me?"

His laugh was raspy, like desiccated autumn leaves. It made her shiver. "You're smart not to trust. As I said, my name is Kevin Fowler and, like you, I work for the Bureau of International Intelligence. Out of the headquarters office in Virginia."

When she didn't respond, he took a step forward. "As for why I want to see you, your success on a recent operation has become the talk of the Bureau. When I contacted the man in charge of the Atlanta sting, Special Agent Whitaker sang your praises." He laughed again. "I need your computer voodoo to neutralize an international terrorist-turned-hacker. The same one who's taken an interest in Wade Cameron's business affairs."

The harsh sound of a shotgun being pumped somewhere behind him made Fowler freeze mid-step. He lifted his arms out to each side, elbows bent and hands spread wide.

The next moment, the kitchen door creaked open behind Lucy and Garrett moved in front of her, gun in hand. After hitting the switch for the flood lights, he stepped outside, closed the screen door, and took the three steps to the patio in one bound, weapon pointed at the interloper.

Glued to the spot, her breath came in shallow pants.

Fowler raised his arms inch by slow inch until his hands were even with his ears.

Wade emerged from the shadows, shotgun at his hip, the barrel leveled at their unexpected guest's back.

"Fowler?" Garrett sputtered. "Is that you?"

"Yeah." Another raspy laugh. "How about you and your brother aim those peashooters somewhere else?" His tone was derisive, but he kept his hands in the air.

Garrett chuckled, clicked the safety on his gun, and shoved it in the waistband of his jeans. "Can't you knock on the front door like a normal person?"

"I did," Fowler answered. "No one answered. How is TJ?"

Garrett scowled. "Fine, no thanks to you."

Wade joined them holding the shotgun in the crook of his arm, the business end angled toward the ground. He took up a position next to his brother—blocking her view. The two of them made a formidable barrier.

Safe.

Lucy sagged against the doorframe, her whole body atremble. She sucked in a big breath. Any minute now her legs would collapse and leave her in a puddle on the floor. Anger flared. Argault did this. He ruled her life even from a distance. Painted every moment with fear. She couldn't live like this, but how …?

"You can drop your arms, Fowler. You should have called first. Why are you here?" Wade didn't mince words.

"I didn't call because your guest would have bolted." Fowler raised his voice. "Ms. Kiddron, I really do need to speak with you. In private. The government has need of your services, and I have a proposition I think you'll find of interest. Garrett here will vouch for me."

Garrett crossed his arms over his chest and grumbled, "Don't bet on it."

Not much of an endorsement.

"A personal reference isn't necessary, Mr. Fowler," she said. Her anger climbed higher. Argault controlled her every move and now this man thought he could come in and take charge? She threw her shoulders back and stood as tall as her

Imperfect Trust

five feet four inches allowed. It was time to take back control of her life. "Since you and Ed have compromised my location and put everyone here in jeopardy, you've left me no choice. I have to leave." Turning, she found the rest of the Camerons crowded into the kitchen, hemming her in. Everyone except the lecherous veterinarian. Where was Ramona?

"Lucy," Wade yelled as he came inside behind her. "You're not going anywhere."

She should have known Wade, with his control issues, would weigh in. Did everyone think her incompetent? Whipping around to confront him, she said, "Watch me."

Chapter Seventeen

A deep breath of the crisp night did little to slow Wade's heart. He'd gone looking for Lucy and heard her talking to someone out back. What had she been doing outside, alone?

The woman drove him crazy. And then the fear in her voice registered. He reached for one of the guns they kept in a gun case near the kitchen door. Who knows what he'd have done if Garrett hadn't followed him.

She zapped his ability to reason. His first inclination was to lock the bullheaded woman up somewhere, but that wouldn't work. Lucy was a wild creature, skittish, and untrusting. Spook her and she'd run. Back her into a corner and the claws came out. If she didn't tear the house down around her, she'd rip off his head. He chuckled.

A smart woman, even brilliant. But predictable. Argault could bide his time, learn her habits, and wait until she let her guard down.

He handed his brother the shotgun and followed her inside the house.

The rest of his well-meaning but nosy family clogged the kitchen, blocking the only other way out.

Lucy confronted them, hands clenched, back stiff as a telephone pole. Was he the only one who saw the edge of panic she tried to suppress?

Wade moved in close behind her. "Breathe for me, tiger." His hands settled on her shoulders. Tension coiled in her deltoids. His fingers kneaded the tight muscles, digging his thumbs in with gentle pressure. "You know you're safe here,

Imperfect Trust

right? We'll never let anyone harm you. Anyway, you can't leave. You have a job. You work for me."

"I hate to disillusion you." Fowler crowded in through the open door. "The truth is you both work for me now."

Turning from Lucy, Wade glowered at the agent.

"For goodness' sake, get inside before the bugs move in." Cate shoved them aside until she could close the door. "You can talk in the family room."

Lucy looked around, as if searching for escape.

Fowler greeted each member of the family by name before turning to Cate. He took her hand and kissed it. "Would you mind, dear lady, if I borrowed your little office instead? I need to have a private conversation with Lucy and Wade."

"I don't keep secrets from my family, Fowler. You can spit out whatever it is you have to say right here." Wade hadn't liked the man when he worked on TJ's case. Still didn't.

Fowler laughed. "Then I'd have to kill them. Top secret, Wade. Need to know. Have you forgotten the rules?"

Wade's jaw clamped down. He had no choice. With a brusque nod, he pressed a hand against Lucy's back and steered her toward his mother's office.

Fowler followed.

Lucy resisted. "I don't think I'm going to like what he says."

"Shhh, tiger. Let's hear him out."

Before she could argue more, Wade guided her toward one of the overstuffed armchairs.

She sat, crossed her legs, and tapped out a tattoo on the chair arm with her fingers.

Maybe that was the key to Lucy—don't let her think. He took the seat beside her and covered her hand with one of his, stilling her restless fingers. "All right, Fowler, spill."

Fowler settled on the loveseat across from them. "Ullah Ahmad Azizi is in the States."

"Tell me something I don't know." Wade growled.

"Intel suggests he's after a special computer application, one written in a language that has way too much in common with a top secret government program. An application that can track tagged objects and receive detailed positioning data from said object. Sound familiar?"

"My work was vetted by every security agency the government could throw at me." Wade bristled. "They all approved the language and I agreed to not market it or any programs I wrote with it. I haven't. I'm not responsible for Azizi's activities."

"If I suspected your involvement in any form or fashion, you'd be in a six-by-six solitary cell with a slop bucket for company. Azizi wants your blasted program for a new extremist group on the rise and wasn't above using your fiancé to get it. He plans to tag and target American military assets for easy elimination and sell the program to the highest bidders."

"Sarah is working with this Azizi?" Lucy asked.

Fowler broke his stare-off with Wade and looked at her, one hand rubbing the back of his neck. His eyes closed for a moment while he took a measured breath and met Lucy's stare again. "I am not at liberty to discuss Sarah Porter, but you can both rest assured, she is no longer a threat. Azizi is. And that is why I'm here for you, Ms. Kiddron."

A block of ice settled in Wade's chest. "Lucy's helping me."

"And now, I am, too." Fowler folded his arms across his chest. "Whether you like it or not, we're in this strange, symbiotic relationship together. You both need me, and I need both of you. Azizi represents a verifiable threat to the security of the United States and the safety of our troops on foreign soil. That means the country needs all three of us. This case falls under the jurisdiction of the Bureau of International

Imperfect Trust

Intelligence, which means your problem and my problem are now the same."

Kevin Fowler was known for being heavy-handed. He'd almost cost TJ her life last year when he used her as bait to catch the drug dealer, Castillo. While Wade had no doubt about the agent's loyalty and patriotism, it would be a hot summer day at the South Pole before he left Lucy's safety in Fowler's hands.

"We believe Sarah inserted a backdoor into your computer," Fowler said. "Azizi will use any means necessary to obtain your program. And yes, I am aware of the ongoing cyberattacks against your computer system."

He faced Lucy. "You wrote a computer program called Quicksilver, is that correct?"

She nodded.

"And this program can identify individual computer signals and provide exact geographic coordinates, all without the user's knowledge. Is that also correct?"

She nodded again.

"You also developed a software application that was used in the Atlanta sting and which subsequently allowed the Bureau to dismantle the network of the drug dealer, Cypher."

Lucy's face turned ashen. She cast a brief, sideways glance at Wade before nodding once more.

"Is what Agent Whitaker said true? Did this trojan lock onto Cypher's signal, infiltrate the slack space on his computer, and take control of the operating system?"

"Yes," she whispered "It's more subtle than the lead pipe method."

"The what?" Fowler frowned.

"A joke, you know—the lead pipe, in the library, Colonel Mustard?"

Wade squeezed her hand, willing her to look at him.

Wounded brown eyes stared at him for all of two seconds, and then her defenses snapped into place. Lucy's beautiful face could have been a porcelain mask for all the animation she showed. Turning away, she stiffened her spine, and squared off with Fowler again.

"Whitaker also said this Cypher discovered the trap." Fowler pushed on, seemingly unconcerned with the undercurrents raging between Wade and Lucy. "Can you fix it?"

"Yes." Her shoulders went back as she responded without hesitation.

"Good. I want your programs installed on Wade's computers so we can catch Azizi."

The very idea of a hacker with free rein in his systems made his gorge rise. But this was Lucy. He'd asked her to entrust her life to him. The least he could do was believe in her integrity.

"No," she said.

"Yes," Wade overruled her.

That got her attention. She turned those fawn eyes his way, wary, but curious now.

"If it means being rid of the cyberattacks and whatever backdoor Sarah scripted, so be it. But I have a condition, and it's not negotiable."

Fowler surged to his feet, nostrils flaring. "We will do this, Wade. Don't make me call in reinforcements."

Glad of his superior height, Wade rose, drawing out the movement. He had a good six inches on Fowler and fifty pounds, maybe more. "Call your reinforcements. You'll need them."

"C'mon, guys," Lucy said.

Wade continued his glare, but the agent didn't back down.

"At least listen to him, Agent Fowler. We listened to you. And it is his business." Lucy played the mediator role well.

Imperfect Trust

Fowler didn't budge and neither did Wade.

"Okay, that's it. I've had enough." Lucy stood and forced her way between the two men. "You guys can take the caveman act outside where you can beat the snot out of each other without damaging Cate's house. Let me know who wins so I can pay my lack of respect. And for the record, I refuse to help either of you." She flounced away, fire burning in her eyes.

"Tiger wait—"

"Lucy, please—"

She kept walking.

"Lucy?" Wade caught her arm in a firm, but gentle grip. "Please don't run from me anymore. We can work through this. I have to know you're safe."

"I'm afraid you don't have a choice in the matter, Lucy," Fowler said.

With a shake of his head, Wade closed his eyes and tried hard not to smile. And here come the claws.

Wielding anger like a whip, Lucy whirled toward Fowler and shook her finger at both of them. "I have no idea why you two have to spread testosterone all over the place, but one thing I do know. Neither of you get it. Ed figured out where I am. That's bad enough, but then he told you." She jabbed Fowler in the chest. "And we all know how well the government keeps secrets."

Wade winced. He knew what that finger felt like.

Fowler stepped back and rubbed his sternum.

Lucy followed him and got in another jab. "And I assure you, Mr. Fowler, I *do* have a choice."

"Look, I apologize for my heavy-handedness, Lucy. If you'll let me explain—"

"No. You talk too much and don't say anything. Try listening for a change. You've drawn a map, painted a bull's eye on it, and express-mailed it to Jensen Argault. I will not lure that spawn of Satan here. I will not let him hurt these people." She whirled and reached for the doorknob.

Locking her up sounded more and more like the right solution.

"But that's part of my proposition," Fowler hurried on. "I can provide you a protection detail. In exchange, you will use your prodigious skill and help us neutralize and capture Azizi. While you work on our behalf, at full pay I might add, the Bureau will launch a full scale effort to capture—or kill—Argault. That should resolve all our problems."

He turned to Wade. "All right, Cameron, let's hear it. What's your sticking point?"

Wade couldn't help it. He laughed until tears blurred his vision. When Lucy scowled, he wiped his eyes and pulled himself together. "My point is I want the same thing—a protection detail for Lucy and a task force to capture Argault. I'm tired of her running scared."

Lucy shuffled back a step. Her mouth fell open.

Fowler continued to glare. After a moment, he shook his head and chuckled. "So be it. What do you say, Lucy? You can help your country, Wade, and yourself with this effort."

No turbulence remained, but she got that stubborn look, the one that said you couldn't reason with her. She drew a deep breath, exhaled, and faced Fowler.

"I have my own conditions."

The agent threw his hands in the air. "Now what?"

"First, Wade must agree before we change his systems. If he says no, that's it."

She demanded his approval? Emotion swelled inside his chest, making it difficult for Wade to swallow.

"Second," she went on. "You will include me in every facet of the plan for taking down Jensen Argault. Every. Single. Detail. Do you agree?"

Fowler studied her without a hint of his thoughts. No

Imperfect Trust

smile, no frown, only a gleam in his eye. "After this is over, Miss Kiddron, I'd like to offer you a job."

Wade clenched his fists and took a step toward the man, but Lucy stopped him with a touch.

"Thank you, but no thanks. I don't like the government controlling my life. So, do we have an agreement, Agent Fowler?"

"You, Miss Kiddron ..." He tapped her forehead. "Are a handful. I agree to your conditions, as much as I can."

From the way her eyebrows drew together, Lucy didn't like his response. "What do you mean?"

"You can't go outside, not to the barn, the yard, or even the patio where I found you tonight, without escort by one of these rowdy Camerons. Remember, a marksman can hit his target at a thousand yards. Farther if he's good."

"She sees the doc tomorrow about her shoulder. We'd planned to do a little shopping afterward."

"Reschedule."

"No can do." Wade shook his head. "Appointment was already put off. She needs her shoulder fixed. The longer she waits, the worse it gets."

Fowler crossed his arms over his chest. "Then you or one of your brothers will accompany her. That means she doesn't breathe unless it tickles your ear. And forget the shopping expedition."

Lucy opened her mouth like she wanted to say something but then closed it again and nodded.

"A team will be here by 1800 tomorrow. I'll return at 2100. We'll meet then with you, your brothers, and your father. James, too, if he's available, plus any deputies he wants to include. And Lucy, of course." He gave her an abbreviated bow.

Wade wanted to rub his hands together. He winked at Lucy instead.

Chapter Eighteen

Wade cranked the engine and started down the long drive that led from the ranch to the main road. As he made the turn toward town, he caught a glimpse of his scowl in the rearview mirror. Well, bloody heck. No wonder Lucy didn't have much to say. He looked like a munitions dump about to blow.

Beside him, Lucy remained quiet. She'd been that way all morning.

He took a deep breath and let his jaw muscles relax. The truth was, she'd been subdued ever since Fowler's visit the night before. And that worried him. He got nervous when she went all introspective.

"You know, it's bound to get crazy around the ranch with Fowler's men underfoot. Might be hard to concentrate on a video game. Garrett and James would understand if you wanted to postpone the *LA Kidd* match."

"No," she said, leaving no room for argument. "I'm not a quitter, Wade. Neither is Mallory. I'm sure James and Garrett would understand, but no thanks. Don't you remember what James said? Her voice dropped in imitation of his friend's voice. "'Do we have to spot you a gazillion points? Play with one hand behind our back? Heh-heh.'" She pressed her lips together and made a rude noise.

"Just saying …"

"We stick to the original schedule. Unless …" Lucy's eyes lit up with what he could only describe as pure mischief. "They want to bail?"

Imperfect Trust

Ah, there it was. The mischievous side she did her best to hide. A short bark of laughter erupted from his throat. "Garrett back off a challenge? Yeah, that's about as likely as him renaming his horse Cornelius. And James would tear his head off, right before he threw himself off a cliff. No, tiger. They scent blood."

That smug, I-know-something-you-don't-know smile appeared. The same one she'd worn when she issued the challenge. "Then I say bring it on."

The Cheshire cat grin told him clearer than words that she had an edge and would employ it without mercy. Lucy might not have the combat skills or experience Garrett and James did, but Wade suspected she was every bit as ruthless and calculating. And a whole lot smarter.

He preferred this teasing, confident woman, even the irritated spitfire who'd reamed him when he disappeared and didn't call last week. Anything but the fearful, withdrawn little fawn she sometimes succumbed to.

Yet fear was a potent drug, one that might keep her alert. And alive.

Until Fowler's visit, Wade hadn't fully realized the danger that shadowed Lucy. The threat had seemed vague. Distant. Garrett had fallen into the same false sense of security last year, only to be blindsided by Castillo's attack on the ranch. The thought of how close the drug lord had come to snatching TJ still brought shudders.

Well, Wade wasn't complacent anymore. The promised protection detail would arrive soon. Until then, he would be more diligent. His dad had already alerted the hands to watch for strangers and signs of trespass. James had briefed his deputies as well.

He returned her grin. "So be it. Look, we got an hour before your appointment with Doc. I'd like to stop by the office and check on a few things. Maybe hear this plan you came up with to find the Sarah bug."

"You mean my brilliant ideas?"

He wanted to laugh but didn't dare. Snark and sass were bricks in the wall she'd built around herself. A defensive barrier. One he intended to infiltrate.

Now, if he could just get past his own reserve and stop thinking of her as a hacker.

"Sorry. I'm not good with ... with ..." Blood rushed to her cheeks.

"Relationships?"

Her look of revelation—and subsequent vulnerability—chased away any doubts that lingered. She cared but wasn't ready to admit it yet. He didn't blame her. Opening yourself up, leaving your soul exposed sucked.

She'd surprised and pleased him last night when she defended his ownership rights. Fowler hadn't offered him many options. Cooperate and give Lucy free rein or have the government take everything.

He'd trust Lucy over the government any day.

"Yeah. Relationships. Not something I've had a lot of experience with. And I know it's hard for you to trust someone like me."

Someone like her? The words left a knot in his gut. Is that how he made her feel? Like something you wipe off the bottom of your shoe? "Don't, Lucy. I'm the one at fault here, not you."

Lucy turned up the radio and hummed along with the Garth Brooks classic. "You know what?" She laughed. "This twangy music grows on you. Honkytonks, whiskey, boots, trucks, and love gone wrong—what more can a girl ask for?"

Baby steps. Rushing would only spook her. Not a problem. He had patience in spades.

CCC

Imperfect Trust

Wade did a quick scan around the area before he led Lucy down the steps from Doc's office. With her pressed against his side, they hurried to the truck where he lifted her inside and buckled the seatbelt for her.

The afternoon sun highlighted the sweat glistening on her forehead, but the tight lines around her eyes and the way her lips were pinched worried him most. She huddled in the passenger seat of his truck, pale and withdrawn, with her injured arm hugged close.

Wade backed out of the parking space, careful to avoid any quick motions that might jar her. He shifted a little in the driver's seat so he could keep an eye on her. "You okay?"

"Fine."

The short, clipped answer said otherwise. What had Doc done? "Mom texted me while you were in the exam room. Said she's been in the kitchen all morning. A bowl of her chicken stew, homemade bread, and one of Doc's pain pills, and you'll be good to go in no time."

"I'm sorry."

Her words puzzled him. "About the chicken stew? Or the bread? 'Cause if it's Mom's chocolate chip cookies you're craving, I'll bet we could get her to whip up a batch."

"No. Your mom's a wonderful cook." She averted her head to look out the window.

"Then what, tiger?"

Good. His nickname for her coaxed a smile. Tremulous and all too brief, but a smile nonetheless. And then she turned those big brown eyes on him. "I'm sorry I came here. Put your family in danger and brought the government down on you. I always mess things up."

"I'm not sorry in the least. Now, tell me what Doc said."

She seemed to deflate even more. "He says my shoulder won't get better without surgery. There's a fifty-fifty chance

I've already got some permanent damage. If I don't get it fixed—soon—the damage will get worse."

"Then we factor in a trip to Idaho Falls and see that shoulder specialist Doc likes so much."

She let out a long breath. "I despise how weak I've become, the helplessness. And I loathe imposing on you and your family. I'm such a loser." Her voice broke on the last word.

A chuckle popped out of his mouth before he could contain it, the sound like a rusty hinge that hadn't been used in a long time. "You? Helpless? I don't think so." He reached over and tapped the side of her head. "Up here, you're one of the strongest and smartest women I know. That makes you anything but helpless. Your shoulder is just a temporary inconvenience."

Lucy cocked her head to one side and stared at him like he'd grown antlers.

"I'm serious as a fat lady at a church supper. We'll set aside some time each day and do some muscle strengthening exercises."

That got a chuckle. And then her frown turned thoughtful. "I could do my Tai-Chi flows. Don't know why I didn't think of it before now."

"Sounds good. And forget that nonsense about an imposition. My family adores you. And if you hadn't come into my life, I'd still be buried nose deep in code."

That earned him another smile. "You'd have figured it out sooner or later."

"I talked with Mal the other night about what you said. You know, regarding our lack of communication. She agrees."

At last, Lucy laughed, easing some of the tension around her eyes. "It isn't funny, and yet it is. You and Mallory are like some weird Push-Me-Pull-You in an Idaho rendition of *My Fair Lady*. Mallory won't leave because she's afraid you've

Imperfect Trust

become dependent on her, and you won't tell her to go for fear of hurting her feelings."

"I don't think either of us is ready to walk away from the current setup, but we recognize the rut we're in. Once this business with Fowler is done and the wedding is over ..." He sneaked a quick peek at Lucy. "Well, Mal and I will come up with a plan for the future."

He wanted to touch her, reassure her, but the only part of her within reach was her injured arm. Or her leg, He settled for a wink instead. Her shoulder was hurt and her leg was off limits. All of her should be off limits.

She locked eyes with him. Her lips parted.

A horn blared.

Wade jerked the wheel and got the truck back into their lane.

Lucy's hiss made him grip the steering wheel, angry for the pain caused by his lapse of attention.

"I'm okay, Wade. Doc's poking around hurt like the dickens, but it's better now. I want to talk some more about Mallory. Casey, too."

"What about them?"

"Did you know Mallory wants to write a book?"

His head whipped sideways again. At this rate, he'd have whiplash before they reached the turnoff to the ranch.

She pointed at the windshield, mouth twitching.

He snapped his attention to the road again. "She never mentioned it. Mom didn't—"

"Cate doesn't know. Mal wants to succeed on her own merits, not by your mother's reputation."

His little sister an author? "What about Casey?"

Her eyes got that soft look, like when they'd played with the kittens in the barn. "He's so bright. I mean genius level. Hastings Bluff is a great place for a kid, all the fresh air and the great outdoors. But Casey needs more."

"More?"

She nodded. "He's smarter than all of his teachers. They can't do anymore for him. He's bored. The job you gave him helps, but he needs a school where the answers don't come easy."

"You just met the kid. What makes you an expert on what kind of education he needs?"

Her answer didn't come fast. "He's been at the ranch every day for the last week. I've had plenty of time to observe and talk with him. I understand his situation maybe too well."

"What's that mean?"

A deep breath preceded her answer. "I went to Georgia Tech in Atlanta when I was sixteen. I earned a double-major in Computer Science and Applied Mathematics, and then a graduate degree in Information Systems and one in Information Security." She took another breath and let it out. "I was nineteen when I left."

"Wait." Surely she didn't mean—Not all those degrees in—"You mean ..." Three years? She got—She was—His brain didn't want to process what she said.

"I understand what you're feeling." Her head dropped, long hair swinging forward to shield her face. "I get it. Really, I do. Yours is not an atypical reaction. It's a fact of life. Guys are uncomfortable around smart girls. I mean, the old 'me Tarzan, you Jane' jungle mentality gets turned upside down when Jane kicks his butt in the real world. Male ego, and all that. I guess. Anyway, I'm used to it. Doesn't bother me in the least. In fact, it's easier to work in a male-dominated field since it eliminates other expectations. Not a problem. I'm good. Happens all the time."

Huh? What was she rambling about? If anything, her intelligence was a huge turn on. Very few women spoke his language. Heck, not many guys could either. Wade tapped the brake and slowed until he could pull onto the shoulder without

Imperfect Trust

jostling her sore shoulder.

"Why did you stop?"

He shoved the gear shift into park and turned sideways in his seat.

She glanced at him for a brief second, all her vulnerability revealed. And went back to hiding behind her curtain of hair.

"Lucy, look at me."

A headshake.

He reached over, touched her chin with a finger, and nudged. "Please, tiger. Look at me."

She let him turn her face to his but kept her eyes planted on his chest.

He applied a little pressure. "Hey, up here."

Her eyes met his then, but her expression was filled with so much wariness it made his heart ache. "There's so much more to you than your incredible brain. More than any man deserves."

A tiny breath hitched in her throat.

Wade slid his hand behind her head and cupped the nape of her neck. His fingers itched to press the button on her seatbelt and haul her over the console onto his lap, but he didn't dare. Not with her in pain, and not on the side of the road. But he could do this.

With gentle pressure on her neck, his hand pressed her head forward as he leaned closer. His mouth hovered over hers, savored the warmth of their mingled breath. The vein in her neck beat a rapid pulse under his thumb. And then his lips found hers. Soft. Sweet. A taste of heaven.

A second more and she returned the kiss. Her mouth opened beneath his.

A sense of rightness filled him.

Long moments passed until the need for air broke the spell. He pulled away, breathing hard.

The windshield shattered.

Chapter Nineteen

Glass showered the inside of the truck, pelting Lucy's exposed skin. She yelped and threw her arm up to protect her face.

Beside her, Wade bellowed an ugly word. He reached across his body, clapped a hand to the back of her head, and shoved her face down into the seat. "Keep your head down," he yelled and fumbled for the gearshift.

The truck lurched, tossing her against the passenger door. The rear end slewed sideways. Gravel sprayed. The tires screamed. And then they found the pavement and surged forward.

The sudden acceleration pinned Lucy against her seat. What did he mean *keep down*?

Her ponytail whipped around like a wild thing. She caught it. Pulled it out of her eyes. And saw the destroyed windshield. Her heart stuttered and then tried to match the racing engine. "What happened?"

Wind whistled through a golf ball-sized hole in the center of the glass. Cracks radiated outward in a crazed spider web pattern, and yet somehow the damaged windshield held.

"Somebody shot at us." Wade's head shifted in one continuous movement between the road ahead and the rearview and outside mirrors. Their speed climbed.

She twisted in her seat to look over her shoulder. A dark vehicle followed at a distance.

"Keep down," he yelled. His breathing seemed as ragged as hers, but his harsh voice left no doubt who was in charge.

Imperfect Trust

The fierce warrior she'd first met had returned.

Fine. She had no problem with him taking over. Ducking down in the seat again, she latched onto the grab handle, her eyes fixed on the outside mirror on her side. "Cypher found me, didn't he?"

"Maybe."

Something pinged off the rear of the truck.

Wade slid as low as he could in his seat. "We got company."

A solid thud hit the truck this time. The vibration sent a chill up her spine.

In her mirror, the vehicle—a black SUV—closed the gap. The driver held his arm out the window, a gun in his hand.

Fear filled her veins in a rush and left her trembling. "Wade, he's shooting at us."

"No kidding." He yanked hard on the steering wheel. The truck swerved across the road and back again, tires squalling.

The sharp, jerky motions tossed Lucy from side to side. Thank goodness for the seatbelt.

"Get my cell phone, Lucy. It's on my belt." Wade's voice sounded strained.

She turned her head to look for the phone … and saw the dark, wet blotch on his blue shirt. Spreading. His right arm hung limp at his side. "Wade, you're shot!"

Was that strangled voice hers? Her already racing heart ratcheted higher.

His knuckles were white from the grip he had on the steering wheel.

"Password—seven-five-four-eight. Find favorites. Call Garrett." He spared another quick glance at his side mirror and jerked the wheel left and then right once more.

Lucy leaned across the console and reached for his cell phone. Blood smeared her fingers. Sticky. Hot.

"Hurry." He shook his head like a driver trying to stay awake, his face pale.

She wiped her hand on her jeans, pressed the phone's on button, tapped in the pass code, and pressed the number.

"Hey," Garrett's familiar voice answered. Wade's older brother was gruff, bossy, and arrogant beyond belief, but right now he sounded sweeter than an angelic choir.

"We need help," she blurted.

"Lucy? What's wrong? Where's Wade?"

"He's been shot." She clenched her teeth, willing away the tears that threatened to choke her. No time for histrionics.

"Put him on speaker," Wade directed.

Somehow she found the right button.

"Sniper took a shot at us," Wade yelled. "Black SUV on our tail. One man. Open the gate. We're coming in hot."

"ETA?"

"Two minutes."

The rear window shattered.

Lucy screamed.

"Talk to me, Wade," Garrett yelled.

"Get that gate open." Wade pressed harder on the accelerator and swerved again. His skin was ashen now.

"Using the remote. Gate is opening. Stay with me, little brother. We'll meet you there."

"Lucy." Wade's usual rich baritone sounded hollow. "Need you."

A freaky calm settled over her, not unlike the zone she sought when competing in martial arts matches. "Tell me what to do."

"Gun. In the console. Get it. Just in case." His breathing had grown harsh and rapid.

She dropped the phone in the cup holder and fumbled one-handed for the Sig Sauer P938, chambering a round. "Done."

He swerved hard left and back right again. "Turnoff up ahead. Can't slow down."

Another ping ricocheted off the tailgate.

"What do I do?"

"Unhook your seatbelt. When I tell you, slid over here and grab the wheel. Need help to hold it." His words sounded slurred.

She freed herself from the seatbelt. "Ready."

The passenger side mirror exploded.

Wade let loose a string of defiant curses. "Almost there. Five hundred yards. Four hundred. Three. Get ready."

She pushed with her feet, got one leg over the console, and pressed tight against his side. Ahead, the terrain sped by like they moved in fast forward.

Beside her, Wade tensed. "Now."

Lucy grabbed the wheel and helped him wrench it to the right. Too fast. Too fast.

The truck's front end made the turn, but the rear wheels screamed in protest. Still fishtailing, they slithered sideways.

The wheels on her side left the ground. The tilting motion slammed her against Wade's side. "Let go," he shouted.

She did and the wheel whipped the other way.

Somehow, the truck didn't flip. They jolted down on all four tires again, the impact snapping Lucy's teeth together. When the tires caught again, the vehicle surged forward.

The steering wheel jerked back and forth in Wade's one hand like a renegade fire hose in full stream. He groaned. "Help me. Can't hold it," he hissed, his hoarse voice.

She locked her fingers on the wheel again, every muscle in her body rebelling.

The rear end slid to the right this time while the front end raced in the opposite direction. Great clouds of dust filled the air around them.

Their speed dropped, but not enough. Worse, they were now on a collision course with one of the thick, wooden side posts that supported the arched entryway twenty yards ahead.

More gunshots peppered the truck. A tire blew out sending them careening to one side.

Wade let out a ragged groan. "Lucy—" His left hand dropped from the wheel. His body slumped against her.

"Wade," she screamed. "I can't do this." She leaned forward and grabbed the wheel with her left hand. Her shoulder screamed with the effort.

He flopped behind her.

"Oh, God, help me. Please," she pleaded. She lined the truck up with the opening and prayed.

The truck slammed against the pillar on the driver's side. A metallic screech followed, but they scraped through.

Using a little hip action to make more room, she wound up splayed across Wade's chest. She still held the steering wheel but couldn't reach the brake.

His foot remained on the accelerator, no longer pressing it but not allowing the vehicle to stop either.

A few wiggles and she managed to force her torso between his chest and the steering wheel—she'd have bruises tomorrow. If she survived. "Move your foot," she yelled with an elbow to his belly.

He groaned.

She kicked his leg. "Get off the pedal."

His foot moved, but not enough.

The drag of the blown tire played havoc with the steering. They were headed for the shallow culvert that ran the length of the drive. "Oh, dear sweet Jesus." *Pleasepleaseplease*. She hauled on the wheel again—more difficult now that she'd wedged herself in tight—with all her strength. Somehow they missed the ditch.

Too much. Now they were heading for the other side.

Imperfect Trust

Her injured shoulder shrieked at the abuse heaped on it. How long before the pain became too much? Another correction, softer this time.

The vehicle straightened out.

Ahead, four pickups raced toward them, barreling through the fields on either side of the dirt road. Men with handguns leaned out of the windows. More men stood in the back, braced against the cab, rifles at their shoulders. Pinpoints of fire erupted from the weapons.

Stretching her right leg, she reached for the brake with her foot. Nothing. He had the seat all the way back to accommodate his height.

She screamed in pain and frustration and tried again. Why did he have to have such long legs?

Wade made a sound, more a growl than a moan, but he shifted and gave her some wiggle room.

Her toes touched the pedal—but now she couldn't see out the windshield. And his foot remained in the way.

She bobbed up, peeked through the shattered glass, adjusted their course, and kicked him once more, hard this time. "Move your foot," she yelled.

His boot shifted out of the way.

Taking a deep breath, Lucy slid down and stamped on the brake with all her strength.

Their speed dropped. The truck slowed. Rolled to a stop.

Crammed in the awkward position with her hip lodged against the gear shift, she couldn't maneuver the lever into park. And dared not take her foot off the brake.

Wade stirred behind her, beneath her. She had no idea how they'd gotten so tangled up, but she couldn't move. Not yet. His chest rose and fell. He breathed. That was all that mattered.

Garrett's face appeared in the driver's window. "Lucy?"

She stared up at him ... and burst into tears. "I can't get it in park."

Garrett flung the door open and leaned in. His touch was gentle as he brushed the hair out of her face. Reaching across her, he yanked up the hand brake.

The passenger door jerked open on the other side. Jonas crawled in. "Hey girl, we got you now. You're covered in blood, Lucy. Where are you hurt?"

She looked down at her shirt, soaked with Wade's blood. "Not mine," she managed to choke out.

"Let's get you out so we can get to Wade." Jonas got a hand under her hip and shoved the gearshift into park. Looping a finger through her belt loop and a hand under her armpit, he tugged. "Work with me, sweetheart. Use your feet."

Jonas dragged her across the console. Her chest ached and her shoulder throbbed, but the pain was small compared to seeing Wade sprawled across the seat.

When her legs came free, Jonas scooped Lucy into his arms. He pulled her from the cab, carried her to the front of the truck, and set her on her feet. "Sit down before you fall, Lucy."

She sank to the ground.

Sirens sounded in the distance.

"James made good time," an unfamiliar voice said. "Ramona's here."

Someone—a woman—called out, "She okay?"

"A few scratches. Nothing serious," Jonas answered.

Ramona directed Garrett and two other men carrying Wade to lay him on a blanket. "Let's get his shirt off." She opened a large leather bag, snapped on a pair of latex gloves, and pulled out a stethoscope.

Lucy struggled to stand. Wanted to be closer to Wade. "Why is she here?"

Jonas put his hands on her shoulders to hold her down. "She's a doctor. He needs medical attention."

Imperfect Trust

"Will he be okay?" So much blood.

She'd never prayed before, only those frantic pleas in the truck. Did they count? If it would save this man's life, she'd offer a prayer every day. "Please, God," she whispered, unable to put her most desperate desire into words. "Please."

Cody and Garrett huddled on Wade's other side, blocking him from Lucy's sight.

Ramona started reciting, "Pupils are good. Lung sounds clear. Breathing is stable. Heart rate is elevated, but normal. No obvious bone fractures, which is pretty amazing. Let's look at the wound."

"Ow, that hurt, Ro."

Lucy took a choppy breath. "Wade?" Crawling on her hands and knees, she closed the few feet that separated them. She had to see for herself if he still breathed.

One of the ranch hands tried to block her way.

"Let her be, Rascal," Wade croaked.

Now she recognized him. Rascal. The Cameron's foreman. She'd met him when Wade took her riding.

Lucy crept to Wade's head and reached out a trembling hand to touch his cheek. His day-old beard rasped against her fingers.

His eyes met hers—and then his whole body jerked. "Sheesh, Rowena. I'm not dead yet."

"I need to see if the bullet's still in you," she crabbed back.

"No bullet. Exit wound." Wade ground out through clenched teeth

Garrett and James chuckled.

Red flooded the vet's face. "Sorry. I don't see many gunshot wounds in my patients. Roll him onto his left side and hold him there. Jonas. I need another pair of hands." Ramona pointed to her medical bag. "Put on some gloves and grab a package of gauze pads."

She leaned behind Wade and snipped the rest of his shirt away with a pair of scissors. "Ugh. This isn't an exit wound. It's a crater."

Jonas snapped on the gloves and opened a packet of gauze pads. "You want pressure on the entry wound?"

"Yes. Reach over and put pressure on this one, too. I want to check his vitals again."

Jonas pressed one hand to Wade's chest and the other to his back.

"Good work, Doc," Cody said, kneeling close by.

"I've treated colic, rain rot, Listeriosis, distemper, infections, and parasites, but never a gunshot wound. At least he didn't kick me," she grumbled.

"I'm not a horse, Dr. Hadde," Wade muttered. "And I'm not your patient."

"Horses are more civilized. They don't whine, either. Or go around blowing holes in each other. And you are my patient for the moment, big boy." Ramona patted Wade's hip, and proceeded to tape the thick bandage over both wounds.

Wade hissed at her rough handling.

"Cut him some slack, Ramona," James said. "Gunshots hurt like the devil's jabbing you with a pitch fork and a blow torch at the same time."

Lucy closed her eyes against a wave of nausea. She ducked her head and sucked in deep breaths.

"You okay, tiger?"

Wade's voice penetrated the fuzzy cloud around her brain. She leaned in close, the words she had to say for his ear only. "I thought you were dead. I was so afraid." She wiped his face where her tears spilled.

"Not a chance." He touched her cheek. "Not leaving you. You did good back there."

Ramona sat back on her heels and stared at them. "So, it's like that?"

Imperfect Trust

"Yeah, it is," Wade answered without hesitation.

The police siren cut off with a single, drawn-out whoop that trailed off like a dying cat. It broke the stare down between Ramona and Wade.

James stepped out of the cruiser, mic in hand. "Doc Burdette's twenty-five miles off in the other direction delivering a baby. I called for a Life Flight. ETA in ten. Anybody get a description of the shooter or his vehicle? A license plate number would be good."

"Life Flight?" Lucy scrambled to her feet. "But, Ramona said ..." Why was everything spinning?

"Dad," Wade yelled.

Strong arms caught her before she crumpled. "Hey, girl. Don't wimp out on us now. You rode that truck like Lane Frost going eight on Mr. T," Cody teased and lowered her to a sitting position. "The worst is over now. Wade's gonna be fine. Take a deep breath. That's it. Now let it out through your mouth, real slow."

She forced herself to do as Cody instructed. "Lane who?"

He chuckled. "Lane Frost. Best bull rider in the history of rodeo. And Mr. T was the meanest bull ever. Better now?"

She managed a nod. "I'd like to see a rodeo."

"She okay?" Worry shaded Wade's voice. "What about her shoulder?"

"A little dizzy is all." Cody crouched beside Lucy. "Listen up, girl. Accidents happen out here all the time. With the closest hospital in Idaho Falls, it makes more sense to send serious injuries on a thirty-minute helicopter ride rather than bounce them around in an ambulance for a couple of hours. Ramona, here, thinks he'll be fine, but he needs to be fixed up in a hospital. That's why we called for the airlift."

"Oh." She felt her cheeks heat up. "What about the man shooting at us?"

Garrett leaned over. "He had too much of a lead to give chase. Anyway, we were distracted by a crazy kamikaze truck barreling down the drive." He flashed a heart-stopping grin.

When he smiled, Garrett's entire demeanor changed. The hardened cowboy disappeared. The frown lines smoothed out. His eyes took on a twinkle that made him look so much like Wade it made her heart ache. She'd caught glimpses of this side of Garrett before but only when he was with TJ, the love of his life.

"James will put out an APB with the SUV's description. We'll find him." Garrett patted Wade's knee. "And don't worry about this guy. This isn't the first time he's tried to get out of the spring roundup."

Wade chuckled. And then groaned. "Dipstick."

The distinctive *whop-whop* sound drew their attention to the tree line where a sleek, blue and white helicopter popped over the horizon.

"Looks like my work here is done." Ramona gathered up her medical gear. "I'll send you a bill."

"Can I go with him?" Lucy didn't think she would survive if another person died—if he died—because of her.

"Afraid not," Garrett said. "Only one person goes. Has to be a family member who can make decisions on his behalf. We also want somebody who can protect him until we get more boots on the ground there. Dad's already claimed the job."

She nodded. It was Cody's right to safeguard his son.

Wade spoke then. "Garrett, take Lucy home. Keep her safe."

Garrett grinned. "Got it covered."

"Jo?"

"Right here," Jonas answered.

"Have Casey pull the plug on my computers. Mal knows the passwords."

Shut down his systems? "Wade," Lucy said. "You can't do that. Your clients won't be able to monitor their herds if you're down. You might as well close your doors on a permanent basis."

"Can't risk Azizi getting in while I'm out of commission. There's no one else I can trust to deal with him."

Chapter Twenty

There's no one else I can trust.

Wade's words hit Lucy like a physical blow.

"Lucy's right," Garrett said. "Shut down now and sure, they don't get the software, but you'll lose everything you've worked for. There has to be another way."

In the field off to the right, the helicopter's blades thrummed the air, stirring dust and debris as it set down. Two men hopped out. The shorter one grabbed a stretcher and tucked it under his arm. The second, taller one hefted a long metal box. They set off at a lope, heading for the group clustered around Wade and his bullet-riddled truck.

Lucy released Wade's hand and scooted back a few feet. Time to face reality. She didn't belong here and it was past time to get out of Dodge. Or in this case, Hastings Bluff.

"Lucy?" Wade called to her. "Don't."

She jolted at his words. Did he read minds now, too? "Don't you, Wade," she retorted. "I can manage your systems. And keep them safe. You know this. Why can't you trust me?"

"Not about trusting you," he gritted out. "I let this joker get too close. Let you down. I need to know you're safe." He held his hand out to her. "Please. Don't run."

Her hand fluttered to her chest, fingers fanning wide. She couldn't make her mouth form words to answer him, could hardly think when he looked at her like that. Blast his blue eyes. He thought he'd let her down? Silly man. He'd saved her life. She pushed the thought aside. Right now, he needed to agree to let her help. Kneeling, she took his hand again, unable

Imperfect Trust

and unwilling to squelch the naïve part of her that still hoped for more from him. Did she trust him? Yes. To a point. Did he trust her? Maybe. He was beginning to. Could they build a relationship based on such an imperfect trust?

Something the pastor had read came to mind. "Be strong and courageous. Do not be terrified; do not be discouraged, for the LORD your God will be with you wherever you go." She'd borrowed Cody's Bible that night after church, looked up the verse from Joshua, and memorized it. How many times today had she called on God?

And He'd answered.

She looked over at Jonas and Garrett with a silent plea for support.

"Lucy's right, Wade," Garrett said. "I'll send some of the hands into town."

"I posted one of my deputies at your office before I headed out here." James dropped to one knee beside Wade.

The EMTs arrived, interrupting the conversation. After Ramona gave them a summary of Wade's condition, they performed their own examination, started an I.V. line, and pronounced him stable and ready to transport.

"Wait," Lucy called. They hadn't settled anything. "Wade? Let me do this for you."

He rubbed his chest. "Man, this hurts."

Jonas grinned and batted Wade's hand away. "Leave the bandage alone. You need to stow your wounded pride and listen to Lucy. She's right and you know it."

Wade closed his eyes.

Lucy sighed and tried to pull her hand free, but he wouldn't release it.

"Garrett?" Wade said through gritted teeth.

"Yeah?"

"If she does this, you have to swear you'll keep her safe."

Hope rising, Lucy looked up at Garrett. Did this mean …?

"I swear it, little brother. Nobody gets to Lucy. She's family." He took Wade's hand from hers. "Brothers' pact."

"Count me in." Jonas leaned over and added his hand. "Brothers' pact."

"Okay, let's roll," the taller paramedic said packing up his gear.

James waved to some of the men. "Need a couple of guys to help carry Wade to the chopper."

Four brawny men thrust their weapons aside, hurried over, and elbowed the two medics out of the way.

James turned to Wade's father next. "Cody, are you armed?"

Cody patted his side. "You boys tell your momma not to worry none. I'll call her later on this evening once I know something."

"Roger that," Garrett answered.

Lucy squeezed in and leaned down to whisper in Wade's ear, "Thank you."

"For what, tiger?"

"For everything. You saved my life, wouldn't let me run, and now you're trusting me with your business."

He reached up to rub his thumb along her cheek. "I should thank you."

Jonas pulled her into his arms as the ranch hands headed for the helicopter. She smothered a half-laugh, half-sob at the sign of Wade's feet hanging off the end of the stretcher. Those long legs of his.

Cody and the EMTs followed.

"Well, Missy," James said. "I got a ton of questions for you."

"Let's get her home." Garrett put an arm around Lucy's shoulder. "From the way she keeps rubbing that shoulder, some of Doc's special pain pills might be in order."

CCC

Imperfect Trust

An hour later, after a hot shower, clean clothes, a bowl of Cate's chicken stew, and a handful of ibuprofen—she refused to take any more of the pain medication Doc had given her—Lucy recounted the day's events. Twice.

"What I don't understand is why Wade pulled off on the side of the road in the first place," James said. He'd dragged a chair from the dining room and positioned it in front of her.

Lucy pressed her fingers to her temples and rubbed. The ache in her shoulder had eased, but her head still felt like an overfilled balloon. "Do we really have to go over it again?"

Her mind buzzed with overload. She needed down time, somewhere quiet to process all that had happened today. The appointment with Doc. Their discussion about Mallory and Casey. The windshield shattering. She shuddered, recalling all the blood, the bullets pinging off the truck, and their mad escape.

And the kiss. Like she could forget that.

"Yes," James said. "Again. While it's still fresh."

"But I promised Wade—"

"Mallory and Casey have an eye on things at the office," James said. "She'll call if there's any funny business."

"You're worse than a dog with a bone," she muttered under her breath.

Garrett laughed. "You don't know the half of it."

Slipping her shoes off, Lucy folded her legs under her and relaxed against the sofa arm. It didn't look like they'd finish up here anytime soon. She took a deep breath and released it with a huff. "Wade wanted to talk. He pulled over. The windshield exploded. Wade got the truck going again. We took off. The shooter followed. I used Wade's phone to call Garrett. That was when I first realized he was bleeding. We turned onto the road to the ranch and, well, you saw the rest. I still don't know how we didn't flip."

James shook his head. "It doesn't add up."

"What doesn't add up?" Lucy asked.

Garrett sat on the sofa next to Lucy. "The bullet hit the windshield dead center, struck Wade in the fleshy part of his right shoulder, plowed through, and tore a hole in the back of your seat. I know my brother's a good-sized boy, but he's not that big."

Her face flamed.

"Garrett's right." James nodded. "What aren't you saying, Lucy?"

That Wade had leaned over to kiss her. None of their business.

She sat up. Her feet hit the floor with a thud. "I thought Jensen Argault had found me. You think Wade was the target?"

James scooted his chair closer. Their knees bumped. "What did you and Wade talk about?"

"Wade said something. I took it wrong. He wanted to discuss it without the distraction of driving, so he pulled off." The stares from the others fanned her embarrassment.

"Go on."

She looked down, her gaze fixed on the fancy tooled leather of James's boot. "He doesn't like it when I shut him out."

James put a finger under her chin and lifted. "You mean, like you're doing now?"

She nodded but still wouldn't meet his eyes. "He, uh, leaned over the console and, uh, put his hand behind my neck." If they kept this up, she'd soon be glowing like Rudolph's nose. "He kissed me."

"About time." Jonas's chuckle came from somewhere off to her left.

"Hush, Jonas," his mother admonished.

When had Cate come in?

"What happened next, Lucy?" James coaxed.

She glared at him. "If you mean did we rip each others'

Imperfect Trust

clothes off, the answer is no. We pulled away—"

"Came up for air, you mean?" Garrett quipped.

Anger flared. They joked at her expense, and she was tired of it. In one smooth motion, Lucy turned toward Garrett, drew her right elbow back and drove her open palm against his sternum. She pulled the punch at the last minute, not wanting to do any real damage—just shut him up.

"Ow." He recoiled, rubbing his chest. "I was kidding."

"Well done, Lucy. If you boys can't have a little respect, I'm calling a halt to this interrogation." Cate could be fierce in defense mode. "Get to your point, James."

In the corner, TJ clapped. "You'll learn to ignore them. All men revert to adolescence on a regular basis. They can't help it. It's built into their DNA."

James cleared his throat. "Go on, please."

Her death stare dared Jonas or Garrett to tease her again. "That's when the windshield exploded. I threw my arm up and ducked. I didn't see much. The next I knew we were on the move and Wade yelled at me to keep my head down. That's when he told me to call Garrett."

"How long was the kiss, Lucy?"

She stared at James, her mouth dropping. "What?"

There was no humor in his expression. No tease in his tone. "I know this is difficult, but bear with me. I want to understand the timing."

The timing? Of a kiss?

"I ... I'm not sure. A few seconds."

Someone whistled. Jonas again.

A muscle twitched along James's jaw. "Think. How long from when you separated and the windshield shattered?"

Where was he going with this? "A second. A fraction of a second." She shuddered. "I felt the air displacement. From the bullet."

James looked over at Garrett. "You thinking what I am?"

Garrett, no longer amused, nodded. He turned sideways on the sofa. "Turn toward me, Lucy. I want to reenact the scene. Pretend I'm Wade. Try to remember your exact movements after the kiss."

"What? No. You're kidding, right?"

He stared her down. Didn't even blink. "It could be important."

Was this more teasing? She didn't think so. Wade getting shot wasn't a laughing matter. "Okaaay."

Garrett put his right hand behind her neck and pulled her forward. "This hand? Like this?" He leaned toward her until their foreheads almost touched. "Did you lean in more?"

She pulled back a fraction. "More like this."

"Okay, you kissed. And then you separated. Show me."

Eyes closed, she recalled the way Wade's lips had felt on hers. Soft, but firm. Exciting. She gripped Wade's—no, Garrett's—left wrist and pulled him closer until their foreheads touched. "Close your eyes. Stay like this," she whispered.

Seconds passed, maybe minutes before she eased away. "Okay, now lean back a little, but don't let go." Her eyes drifted open, mere inches away from those too-blue eyes. Wade's eyes. Except they weren't. She blinked.

Jonas slapped his hands together. "And the windshield explodes."

She jerked free and turned her face to the other side.

Garrett let her go, but he didn't move from the position. "Got it?"

A grim-faced James said, "Yeah. When you separated, your head moved back, but your shoulder stayed put because your hand was still holding Lucy's neck. If our theory about high ground is correct, my bet is on Trotter's Ridge. It's the only elevation between here and town."

"Makes sense for how fast he got on their tail, too."

Imperfect Trust

Lucy stared from one man to the other, not following their logic. "What are you saying?"

Jonas answered. "Simple. The shooter—whether Azizi or Argault—had Wade's head in his sights."

The room expanded around Lucy and then caved in. She couldn't breathe.

Garrett pressed her face down between her knees. "Breathe, sweetheart. That's it."

The shooter had aimed for Wade.

When the dizzy spell passed, she straightened up. "Sorry. I'm okay now."

"So, what's your best guess?" James asked the room. "Lucy's stalker, toying with her by removing Wade? Or has Azizi run out of patience?"

"Seems too desperate, given what we know about Argault," Jonas offered. "But then again, Azizi might be panicky."

"We have to believe Azizi saw the Medevac chopper, which means he knows Wade's out of the picture for the moment," Garrett said. "He'll either make another hack attempt soon or try to steal the computers from the office."

"Are Mallory and Casey safe? Does she know what's going on?" Cate asked, one hand cupping her forehead. Worry etched sharp lines around her eyes. "They're all alone there."

"I sent a deputy over when the call first came through. Some of your ranch hands are there, too." James told Cate.

"I called Fowler and left a message," Garrett said.

James got up to pace. "The protection detail he promised will arrive by six. For now, we secure the office and the ranch. Once Casey powers all the machines down, we'll bring him and Mal here."

"No," Lucy shot back. "That's not what we agreed upon. I promised Wade I'd look after his business."

"You're safer here at the ranch. We're only guessing Wade was the target, which means you're not out of danger. And I don't have enough men to protect both the office and the ranch," James said through clenched teeth. "You'll have to do your work from here."

Lucy touched Garrett's arm. "Please. I have to be in the office."

"She's right," Jonas said. "Shutting his systems down is more than hitting the off button on a few computers. The servers have to be powered down in a specific sequence to avoid serious damage. Lucy's the only one who knows the proper order, not to mention the only one who can stop a hack attempt. Hey …" He turned to Lucy. "Any chance we could set up the servers here? I mean, Wade's worked out of Mom's office for the last week."

Lucy frowned, running the possibility through her mind. It could work. "Does the house have the electrical capacity?"

Garrett scrubbed a hand across his short hair. "I have no idea, but Cal Echols will know. He rewired the house and barns three years ago when Wade insisted on upgrading the security system. I suspect we might need to add a couple of dedicated circuits. The next question is where do we put the darn things?"

All heads turned to her.

Lucy closed her eyes and conjured up a picture of the server room. "Six servers, each about yea big." She squared her hands to indicate the size. "Six desktop computers. We'll need the two printers. I think they'll fit in the sitting room in my room ... I mean, the guest room."

"Your room. And it makes sense." Cate turned to Jonas. "Have some of the men haul four of the long folding tables from the barn. They'll do for counter space."

To her oldest son, she said, "We need to move the loveseat and chairs, maybe put them in the attic."

"I'm ready. Let's go." Lucy headed for the front door.

Imperfect Trust

Jonas nodded, texting as he followed her to the door.

"Wait," Cate called out. She pressed a bottle of ibuprofen into Lucy's hand. "You're still kneading that shoulder."

Lucy hugged Cate. "Thanks." These Camerons would be her undoing yet.

CCC

Ten hours later, Lucy sat back on her heels and waited. One by one, the computers blinked on. Soft whirrs filled the room. "Mal, turn the printer on. Casey, queue up a report on the Bar-M account and print it."

Casey crammed the last bite of a candy bar in his mouth, one of at least a dozen he'd already consumed since they started. He crumpled the wrapper and tossed it at the wastebasket in the corner. Swoosh—nothing but air. Wiping his hands on his jeans, he ran nimble fingers across the keyboard. In seconds, the printer started spitting out sheets of paper. "Yes." He gave a fist pump.

Lucy let out a slow breath, and let the tension slide away. They'd needed two additional dedicated circuits but they'd done it. Cameron Security Services was up and running in its new home at the Triple C Ranch.

Cate came in with a covered tray. "You three need to eat some real food. Casey's mother will never forgive me if I don't put more than chocolate in his belly."

"Where are Garrett, Fowler, and the others?" Lucy asked. She'd been so focused on Wade's systems she'd forgotten about them.

Casey got to the food first. One bite and half a turkey sandwich disappeared.

Mallory didn't lag far behind. "In the family room. They've been strategizing ever since Kevin Fowler arrived." She looked at her wristwatch. "Four hours ago."

Rats. She'd forgotten Agent Fowler too. And he hadn't bothered to call her down. Not that she would've joined them.

Wade's computers took first priority. Now that they were running again—

"Soft drink or water?" TJ lugged in a small cooler.

Lucy took a bottle of water but wondered if coffee might not be a better choice. They still had a lot of work left before she could call it a night. And she had no idea what Fowler and the other men were up to.

With food distracting Casey and Mallory for the moment, Lucy slipped to Cate's side. "Any word from Cody?"

"He called right before I came up," Cate told her with a smile. "Said the surgeon was happy with the results of the surgery—no broken bones, nothing was nicked, severed, or otherwise damaged beyond repair. Cody says they'll keep him drugged through the night and most of tomorrow."

"How's Cody holding up?"

"Kyle, one of James's deputies, arrived at the hospital while Wade was in surgery. He's in a private room now. They'll take turns through the night keeping watch. Rascal will take a change of clothes and shaving gear for them in the morning."

Lucy sighed. "I wish I could go with Rascal."

Cate patted her shoulder. "Wade needs you here. Anyway, I doubt the men downstairs would let you go. Don't worry, sweetie. My boys take after their father, which means Wade will fuss and nag until they kick him out. I give him a day before he bullies his way out of there."

Anxiety over Wade's health eased, but Lucy had another concern. How would he feel about her hatchet job on his systems? She'd done what she thought best given the circumstances.

Imperfect Trust

Chapter Twenty-One

"Son, if this is how I acted whenever I got hurt, I owe your mother a ton of apologies. I've never heard a grown man grumble and whine as much as you do."

Wade glared at his father. Was it too much to ask for his own clothes back instead of wearing a split tailed gown that showed his backside every time he got up?

He wanted a shower, the I.V. in his arm gone, his own clothes, and a steak as rare as he could get it without the cow still mooing. Not necessarily in that order, either. More than anything else, though, he wanted out of this prison.

A nurse came in, but not the sweet-faced cutie who'd insisted on wrapping her arm around his waist when she got him up on his feet to go to the bathroom. "Doctor's orders," she'd said ... and pouted when he refused her help. There were some things a man needed to do for himself.

The door opened and another angel of mercy entered, this one a forty-plus Jane Wayne who looked like a Marine. "You come to punch some more holes in me?"

"Careful what you say. You don't want to stir up more than you can handle, boy." Her nametag read C. Steel. Appropriate. Big around as she was tall and none of it fat, she had a no nonsense posture and matching frown.

Heavy footsteps carried her to his bedside. "Now, I'm going to check your vital signs while you lie here all nice. Going forward, you will mind your manners with my nurses. If you can't find it in you to smile and say, 'Yes, ma'am' and 'thank you, ma'am,' then I've got the doctor's written orders that say I can drug your sorry carcass. I can also have Nero give you a very thorough sponge bath. Capice, Roger Ranger?"

A choking sound erupted from the corner. "I'd do what she says, son. I've met Nero."

His dad had described the brute with the effeminate laugh and funny walk with extreme detail. No way that guy was getting anywhere near— "Yes, ma'am."

In the doorway, Rascal cackled. "Woo-wee, boy. This Nero fellow gave me directions to your room just now. I wouldn't want him doing any personal favors for me. That spunky little blond out there, that's another story."

Wade held his arm out so Nurse Steel could wrap the blood pressure cuff around his bicep. "When's the doc coming?" He tried to ask in a polite voice. "I want to ask him about getting out."

The nurse stuck the stethoscope in her ears and ignored him.

He choked back his irritation.

"Dr. Schmidt does rounds between seven and ten. An injury like yours should keep you here three or four more days."

"But—"

She quelled his argument with a look. "As I was saying ... it's barely been a day since your surgery, but you're strong and healthy. If your attitude improves, I might be persuaded to give you a good report. Maybe even get you out of here sooner."

He managed to choke out a "Thank you, ma'am."

With a stiff nod, she departed.

His father clapped a hand over his mouth and turned to stare out the window, shoulders shaking.

"I brought you both a change of clothes." Rascal dropped a gym bag on the foot of the bed.

"Good." Wade tossed aside the covers, swung his legs over the side—and almost did a nosedive.

"Whoa, hold on there." His dad hauled him back onto the bed. "Don't get ahead of yourself, son."

"I took a bullet before. I know the routine. Right now, I want a shower. By myself."

"Your mother always said you and your brothers didn't have a lick of patience. Right now, I'm of a mind to agree. Try to be smart. Take it slow and get your bearings before I call that old war horse back in here to add a little sleepy time juice to the tube in your arm."

Wade glared at his father. He'd do it, too. For spite. "I'm worried about Lucy and what's happening at the ranch."

Cody nodded. "Rightfully so. Can't say I remember anybody ever getting shot in Hastings Bluff before, at least not on purpose. There was that time Myra Devoe dropped the shotgun and peppered her husband's butt with buckshot. Ray Ruder wore the badge back then and wrote it up as an accident, but it always seemed a little suspicious to me. Cliff Devoe hasn't set foot inside Sidewinders or had a sip of whiskey since."

"I remember." Rascal added. "Cliff couldn't sit a horse for a month. Been all 'yes, Myra' ever since. Waste of a good man, if you ask me."

Wade tried hard not to laugh. He ended up groaning instead, a not so gentle reminder of why he'd landed in the hospital.

Two quick raps drew Wade's gaze to the door. Dr. Schmidt entered, his long white lab coat unbuttoned. "The nurses tell me they're ready for you to leave, but from the looks of that wince you just made, I'd say you're still hurting. I think you should stay another day."

"I'm good, Doc." Wade sat up straight and pointed toward Rascal and his father. "It's their fault. Tell them to stop making me laugh."

Imperfect Trust

"You're as sour as lemonade without sugar." His father harrumphed. "Worse than that old goat Mallory brought home. Ungrateful, too."

"I am not ungrateful." Affronted, Wade looked at the doc's raised eyebrows, spotted the knowing smile on his father's face and an outright grin on Rascal's, and had to chuckle. "Just a little out of sorts is all. I want to go home."

The doctor sighed. "The nurses want that, too. Give me a couple of hours. The discharge papers will take time, but we should be able to get you out of here this afternoon."

Wade grinned.

"You know you were lucky, don't you? The wound was clean as gunshots go, but I had to put in a lot of sutures. You'll have to be very careful for awhile. Follow the discharge instructions to the letter and absolutely do not use that arm for at least two weeks. Follow up with Dr. Burdette when you get back to Hastings Bluff. Any questions?"

"I've taken a bullet before, Doc." Wade held his left hand out for an awkward handshake. "Thanks."

Dr. Schmidt squeezed his hand. "My pleasure. No wrestling grizzly bears either."

Wade's father came forward, hand extended. "Thanks for fixing my boy."

The doctor nodded and headed for the door.

"How soon can I get this needle out?" Wade asked. "I want a shower ... without anyone's help."

The doctor laughed. "I'll send one of the nurses in."

Two hours later, his dad folded up his six-foot-two-inch body like a taco and squeezed into the back seat of Rascal's truck. "Couldn't be bothered to take one of the bigger trucks or Cate's car?"

"Quit whining. You got plenty of room."

"Yeah, well, then you crawl on back here, and I'll drive."

"When the moon turns purple and rises at noon on Groundhog Day." Rascal cackled. "You're just mad 'cause your old bones are giving you fits. Try a visit to Doc's like Cate's been nagging you to do."

Wade hissed as he settled into the front passenger side. "Can we grab some burgers from a drive-thru? I'm starved. And then I want a rundown on what's happened since I got carted off in the chopper."

With a sack of double cheeseburgers and two large orders of French fries, Wade set the biggest soda they had in the cup holder and fumbled for his cell phone.

Dead. He borrowed Rascal's phone and dialed Garrett.

His brother answered on the first ring "Hey, Rascal. How's my ornery brother? I hear he's been acting like a bear with a sore—"

"This from a guy so whipped he helps his fiancé pick out window treatments? Ask me yourself, wuss." He put the call on speaker.

Garrett's laughter filled the truck. "Good to hear you're still alive. We make a fine pair, don't we? Parade a pair of sexy legs, a curvy figure, and gorgeous eyes in front of us, and we're done."

"Yeah, yeah," Wade grumbled. Was he that far gone over one slight, brown-eyed girl? "We're on our way home. What's happened since they hauled me off?"

Garrett regaled him with how Lucy honchoed the relocation of Cameron Security Services to the ranch and got it up and running overnight while everyone else slept.

Outrage battled with relief and admiration. She coordinated the move, oversaw the shutdown, consulted with the electrician, and worked with Casey and Mallory to bring everything up again. Lucy had promised to protect his systems, and she'd done it. Not how he would have tackled the job, but it made sense given the circumstances.

Imperfect Trust

"Fowler's men arrived as promised. Him, too," Garrett said. "We brought everyone up to speed last night. This morning we hashed out possible scenarios and next steps and came up with a plan. Lucy's being difficult about it, though. Maybe you can talk some sense into her."

When pigs took up knitting. "No promises. She's, uh—"

"Yeah, we know. I thought TJ was stubborn, but Lucy makes Edwina the goat look meek." A chorus of male voices added their agreement over the speaker.

They rode in silence for a long while after the call ended. Sometime later, his father tapped him on the shoulder. "You know, Wade, a betrayal like Sarah's, it's like the sun goes down and never rises again. No color left in your life. That's where you've been for the past year. Existing. Even your work, what used to be your passion, is no more than busyness now."

"Dad—"

"Hear me out. It's funny, 'cause I see Lucy doing the same thing. Did you know she lost her father and little brother when she was only eight?"

Wade nodded.

"Did you also know her mother had to work two jobs after that? Left a lot of unsupervised time for a young girl smart as her. She took a dare she shouldn't have and got caught hacking a government website by this friend of hers, Ed Whitaker. She wound up in juvenile where her mom left her."

She'd opened up to his dad?

"Lucy ended up in the foster care system. I can't imagine the hard knocks she faced there. Anyway, my point is she's experienced betrayal, too. By someone she loved and trusted, someone who was supposed to love her back."

Wade swallowed hard. He knew some of Lucy's story but not all the details. Not the devastation she must have felt being abandoned by her mother. "Make your point, Dad."

"When you live, it's with people. When you exist, you go it alone. I hate to see you or her wither away because you're both too doggone stubborn to give an inch. Or is it that you're too afraid to let someone get close again? You're all grown up now. It's not for me to tell you to do this or to do that. I'm already proud of who you are. I'd just want to see you happy, maybe settled down with the right woman. A passel of grandkids wouldn't hurt either. They'd sure make your mother happy. Me, too."

"You think Lucy is the right one?" Wade asked.

"Don't know. That's your job to find out."

"She is pretty amazing."

"You know, a smart man wouldn't hesitate when something amazing crosses his path. He'd be on the hunt in a heartbeat."

"Grandkids, huh?" Wade shook his head. Why had it taken him so long to realize how smart his dad was? "Don't you and Mom have enough to keep you busy with Garrett's and TJ's wedding? You should be planting these little seeds with them. They're further along in the process."

"Your mom calls herself 'the constant gardener.' She expects all her seedlings to take root."

Wade laughed at his words. It hurt, but it felt good, too.

"Bottom line, it don't matter none what me or your mother think. You mind what your gut tells you."

◦◦◦

"He won't fall for it," Lucy exclaimed for what had to be the tenth time. "I keep telling you, Jensen Argault is not stupid. He'll see through the ruse."

"It will work," Fowler insisted. "My men found a little cabin in the woods not far from here. We'll flaunt the lookalike agent around town, let it be known that Lucy has moved out, and have the double drive to the cabin with one bodyguard. From there she'll use Lucy's computer to send a few e-mails. If

Argault's in the area, he'll trail her. If he's somewhere else, he'll track her computer signal to the cabin where we'll have a cordon of men hiding in the woods. As soon as he puts a foot anywhere near the property, we'll pounce. It's like cheese in a mousetrap. Irresistible, simple, and foolproof."

Lucy laughed. "A ten-year-old kid wouldn't fall for it."

Fowler's face turned purple, like he might go supernova any second. He threw his hands in the air and turned to Garrett and James. "When does Wade get home? Maybe he can reason with her."

"You have another plan, Lucy?" James asked.

Yes, she did, but there were still a few details to iron out. "I'm working on something."

"Yeah, well I'm getting married in three weeks," Garrett announced. "I want this finished before then. And you ..." Garrett pointed at Lucy. "Forget leaving. That's not an option."

Fowler took a seat next to Lucy at the breakfast table and patted her arm. "You keep working on your little plan. I'm moving ahead with what the rest of us agreed on."

Condescending Neanderthal. She hated Fowler's supercilious attitude. And what did he mean about Wade reasoning with her?

"Sorry, Lucy," James said. "Fowler's right. You're safer out of sight. We'll use the decoy."

Even James had joined forces against her. Why was her life more important than her lookalike's?

All the worry over embroiling the Camerons into her mess, and now she was tangled so deep in Wade's problems they couldn't separate the two. Everyone was at risk. Even Casey.

If Wade wanted to reason with her, he could try. None of them knew Argault like she did. Their prevent defense wouldn't work.

Cate sat at the end of the table, worry lines etched in her pale face.

James was on the phone again, giving directions to his deputies.

Garrett and Jonas snapped out orders to three hands who'd just come in, men she didn't know. They had watches to set up. Shift rotations to schedule. Guns. Ammunition. Supplies. Tactics when they needed strategy.

"Excuse me," she murmured and left the room.

No one noticed her leave caught up as they were in the urgency of the moment.

Grabbing her laptop from the guest bedroom—her room—Lucy slipped into Cate's office and closed the door. The din faded to a distant buzz.

Think.

Their opponent had made a daring strike. If Azizi, what was his motive? To eliminate a key player? Create a diversion? Maybe run a flanking maneuver while the Camerons were preoccupied?

Whatever the reason, the move had worked. The family was distracted and on the defensive. First imperatives often changed when loved ones were involved.

But all remained quiet on the cyber front.

The shooter could be Argault. He wouldn't blink at killing Wade to get to her. But the same defensive philosophy applied to him as well. You can't defeat the enemy by circling your wagons. With time on his side, Jensen could pick off the men one by one.

The warriors beating their chests would eventually figure it out, but time could cost lives. How did she make them understand they had to go on the offensive?

A simple analysis would work. Something they could see with their eyes and roll around in their heads. A strategic plan with teeth.

Her area of expertise.

When the laptop finished loading, Lucy pulled up the worksheet she'd started, a template created for the design phase of a video game—the Strategy Formulation Methodology. Whether video game, corporate objective, computer hacking, or a military operation, the philosophy remained the same. Define the problem, clarify it, splice it into manageable/achievable tasks, create viable solutions, create alternative solutions, choose the action most likely to work … and put it into action.

She shivered.

The only difference? In a video game you got do-overs. In real life, when people died they stayed dead.

Chapter Twenty-Two

Sweet relief flooded Wade as they turned onto the gravel drive that led home. The Triple C brand over the arched entrance had never looked so good. "Rascal, are you trying to hit every pothole?" he griped. "Or just the big ones?"

"Thought you was anxious to get back." The old foreman smirked when the truck hit another dip in the road.

The right side of his body hurt from his neck down to his hip. The hole in his shoulder burned like someone had poured liquid fire in it. The last dose of pain reliever, taken back at the hospital before they left, had long ago worn off.

"Well, I for one can't wait to be peeled outta this truck." His father squirmed in the cramped back seat, his knees finding some give in the middle of Wade's spine. "I feel like a fifty-pound sack of potatoes stuffed in a five-pound bag. Might as well mash me up and add some butter 'cause I don't know if I'll ever stand straight again."

A welcoming committee waited outside for them. Garrett and TJ, Jonas, Mallory and James, even Kevin Fowler waved when they drew up to the porch. A second later his mom elbowed her way through and scurried down the steps to the truck.

But no Lucy.

The depth of his disappointment surprised Wade.

"Hey, man, show us your war wound." Garrett called.

Wade wiggled his arm … and then wished he hadn't. Why'd it have to be the right arm? He was a crack shot with both hands, could hit a target every time, but simple stuff, like

Imperfect Trust

shaving and brushing his teeth posed a challenge. He hated—hated—the sling forced on him by Nurse Steel before she would release him. "Wear the sling or stay another day, your choice." Sadistic old harpy. He didn't know how Lucy tolerated hers.

He managed a smile for his mother and opened his left arm.

She approached him with caution but then got all teary-eyed and wrapped him in a hug.

Blazes, but that hurt. Wade groaned and somehow managed to loosen her grip. "I'm fine, Mom, but I won't be if you keep squeezing me like you're wringing out a wet towel."

She let him go, walked straight into his father's arms, and burst into a crying jag. Didn't that make him feel ungrateful?

"He really is fine, Catey-Cat. Got a few stitches is all." His dad pulled her into a tight embrace and ran his hands up and down her back.

Catey-Cat. His dad's pet name for the love of his life. Like Garrett's Angel. And his tiger? He tucked the thought away for later consideration.

"What was it like having all those gorgeous nurses strip you naked?" This from Jonas, of course.

Mallory jabbed Jo with an elbow, hard from the way he yelped and moved away from her.

"You boys leave your brother alone. He doesn't need your teasing," Mom scolded. She could be counted on to take the side of the underdog, in this case, him. "Let's get you inside, son. I put fresh sheets on your bed."

Wade spotted Casey waving from the doorway with a grin big enough to catch bugs.

And then he saw her, half hidden by the lanky teenager. Wade had never known anyone who skirted attention the way Lucy did. How did an attractive woman like her hide in plain sight? She blended into the surroundings like a chameleon.

Their eyes met. Locked. Held.

The others parted as he approached the front steps.

"Lucy," he breathed her name. "I hear you worked a miracle. Took down all my computers and moved them to the ranch." He touched her cheek. "Thank you for that."

Her eyes widened with surprise. Right before her chin dropped.

He knew what she'd say. In her short time at the ranch, Lucy helped where she could but never took credit for anything.

"Everyone pitched in."

"Don't listen to her," Jonas said. "Lucy pretty much singlehandedly—pun intended—ran the show. She was everywhere. Told us what to do, when to do it, and where to stick it." He snickered, planted a loud kiss on her cheek, and draped an arm around her.

Wade stared at his brother's hand on Lucy's waist and then turned his glare on Jonas.

The arm fell away. "Uh, yeah. Lucy's great." When Wade's frown didn't lift, he moved a few steps away. "Like having another sister."

Wade didn't bother with a response. He stepped between Jo and Lucy, and crowded into her space. Time to stake his claim.

Lucy's face flooded with color. "You're not upset? About what I did to your servers?"

"Do they work?"

Her head bobbed up and down.

Wade drank in the sight of her. He loved the way she blushed. "Then I have no reason to be upset. Show me." He'd missed her soft voice and snippy comebacks.

The gaping mouths of his family assured Wade he had surprised them as much as he'd surprised himself. He didn't care. Garrett's behavior made sense now. His father's, too.

Imperfect Trust

Wade hadn't realized how much Lucy had gotten under his skin until this moment.

She shivered beneath his stare, shadows in her eyes. A wariness he'd put there. Now it was up to him to fix things between them. Somehow, he had to prove he wouldn't leave her alone in this mess.

For the first time in a long while, fire burned in his soul. He felt alive. Lucy was his. She just didn't know it yet.

"C'mon, tiger. Show me your magic." He glanced at their audience before following her inside. Like a chorus of crickets, they stood wide-eyed and open-mouthed.

Wade couldn't believe what she'd accomplished. Lucy had not only dismantled and reassembled his entire setup of six servers, six computers, one printer, and a printer/scanner/fax machine, she'd rebooted the entire system, got it running again, and written an alert program that would issue an audible alarm when an unauthorized access was attempted. Why hadn't he thought of doing that?

"Is it okay?" Her voice quivered a little. Did she expect him to chastise her?

He opened the administrator page, pulled up his biggest account to study the data trends, and glanced at the security checkpoints and history. "Did you run a test report?"

She nodded.

"Is this what you did for the Bureau? Evaluate programs and make them better?"

She nodded again. "For the most part. But I didn't change any of your fundamentals. I checked with Jonas and Mallory first before adding any enhancements. They thought you'd be okay with what I suggested. I put them in a separate file so they're easy to uninstall. I'll show you."

He tucked a strand of chestnut brown hair behind her ear. "Shhh. Don't fret, Lucy. I don't need Jonas and Mallory to affirm your decisions. You're smarter than all of us. I trust your decisions. Thank you for covering my six."

She cocked her head to one side. "For ... your what?"

He laughed, soft and easy because it hurt too much to do more, but a lighthearted release nonetheless. "My six. Like six o'clock. Military lingo. Means you got my back."

She smiled then, a blast of sunshine that blinded him to all else. Her shoulders drew back, all her apprehension melted away on a sigh. "Really?"

"Yeah, really." He tucked another rogue curl behind her other ear.

"There's so much more I want to tell you, share with you." She pulled him over to another computer. "What you've built is fantastic. I mean, the concept is so far beyond today's constructs—it's the future of computing. But, it could be so much more, Wade."

The excitement in her voice raised goose bumps on his arms. When had he ever been this excited?

"I have programs that can complement yours," she forged ahead. "Let me show—"

"Slow down, tiger. Much as I'd love to see it—and I will—right now, there are more pressing issues. Like who shot at us. I need to talk with Garrett, James, and Fowler. Hear their plan."

The light in her eyes didn't dim so much as change. Her excitement faded, but anger blazed in its place. "Fowler has a crackbrained scheme to draw Argault here, while Garrett wants to hole up and wait it out. I've tried to explain why neither option is viable, but they—"

"You have another plan?"

She nodded and reached for a sheaf of papers on one of the tables.

He caught her hand, stalling her. "Hold up. I want to hear what the guys have to say first. After that, I want you to explain

Imperfect Trust

your plan to all of us. First, though, I'm in desperate need of some ibuprofen."

"Wade, I'm so sorry. I didn't even ask how ..." Her voice lost power as the words trailed off.

"Not to worry. I blame Rascal's driving. I swear he found every pothole in the road on the way home."

His mother announced dinner.

Wade checked his watch and wondered where the last hour had gone. He hated to relinquish his time with Lucy. After the spectacle he made of himself on the front porch, his family would be ruthless in their teasing. How would she handle it? "C'mon, tiger. I'm starved."

Wade claimed the seat at the end of the table that Lucy always took for herself. He pulled out the middle chair for Lucy. When everyone stopped and stared, he pointed between his sling and Lucy's. "This way we don't get bumped."

Lucy let him scoot her chair forward, which turned out to be tricky with only one hand.

Fowler was absent, preferring to share his meals with his men, but his family and James had crowded around the table.

His mother settled a pork chop on his plate and then proceeded to cut it into bite-size pieces. "Would you like me to slice up your green beans, too, dear?"

"No, thanks, Mom." He tried not to glower.

Beside him, Lucy smothered a laugh as she leaned in and whispered, "Get used to it. She'll do mine next."

The sound of her chuckle erased his scowl. His injury had an end date. Hers depended on a surgery that might or might be successful and couldn't be scheduled until they neutralized Argault. It didn't seem right that she had to wait.

His mother set two apple pies on the table for dessert. She dished out large slices while Mallory added a scoop of vanilla ice cream to each plate and passed them around.

Wade inhaled his and eyed the remaining slice in the pie dish in front of him. When Jonas reached for it, Wade got there first. He grabbed the pie plate and, with a deft, one-handed twist, let the wedge plop onto his saucer.

"Hey, I wanted that." Jonas complained.

Giving his baby brother a grin, Wade stuffed a huge, flaky forkful of fruit and pastry into his mouth until his cheeks bulged like a well-fed squirrel.

Jonas crossed his arms over his chest and sulked like a scolded toddler while the rest of the family laughed at the familiar antics.

Lucy giggled and clapped a hand over her mouth.

He liked seeing her happy. She held her own with one-on-one discussions but seldom joined in with the group. He wanted to change that, but he'd made so many mistakes with her.

Dinner finished, Wade rose from the table and pulled Lucy's chair out for her. His shoulder still ached, but the ibuprofen had taken the edge off. Tired as he was right now, anything stronger would knock him out. And he still needed to hear Garrett's and Fowler's plan. Lucy's, too.

Fowler arrived a short time later and joined them in the family room.

Wade sat next to Lucy on the love seat ... and yawned. Listening to Garrett's recital of all they'd done to shore up the defenses around the house almost did the job of a pain pill. Safe and thorough, that was Garrett. Wade found no flaws with his plan.

His confidence fled when Fowler took the floor. The agent's plan bothered him from the start, but he held his thoughts. Maybe after a night's rest, using Lucy's decoy as bait wouldn't seem like throwing chum in the water to attract a shark.

And then the spotlight turned to Lucy.

Imperfect Trust

She held a crumpled stack of papers, a sure sign of nervous energy. No one hated attention more than Lucy. But then she took a deep breath and her entire demeanor changed. Gone was the shy, reluctant girl. An energized businesswoman stood in her place. She asked Mallory to pass around the handouts. When the paper rustling subsided, Lucy stood and met each person's stare with bold confidence.

"We have identified two possible suspects for the shooter," she began. "Azizi or Argault. We have reason to believe Ullah Ahmad Azizi is behind the cyberattacks on Wade's computer system. Jensen Argault, a.k.a., Cypher, has issued multiple death threats against me and anyone who impedes him in his endeavor. There is a third possibility—that neither is behind the shooting—which leaves us with a random unknown."

Wade nodded with the others.

"The plan I'm about to present focuses on the first two known possibilities."

"We know this already," Fowler butted in. "What's your point?"

"Let her have her say," Cody reprimanded him.

"We also don't know the shooter's target," she went on. "Azizi could have been shooting at Wade to remove him from the picture or at me to create a distraction while he launches another attack. On the other hand, Argault could have taken a shot at Wade to send a message, or he may have intended the bullet for me. Regardless of who the shooter was, the threat is real."

She made eye contact with each person in the room.

"Since we don't know the shooter or his target, we have to consider all scenarios. We have to plan for all eventualities. This will stretch our limited resources and could impact the Cameron ranch operations and Wade's business."

Much as he wanted to support Lucy, Wade had to admit that Fowler was right. Other than stating facts in a clear, succinct summation, she hadn't presented any miraculous solutions. "What do you propose we do?"

She seemed surprised by his interruption but didn't let it disrupt her thoughts. "Garrett's plan is a tactical action that will work for the immediate future, but it's a stop-gap measure only, and not sustainable. Circling the wagons didn't work for the pioneers. It won't work for us. We're sitting ducks on someone else's timetable."

Now that made sense. Wade smiled encouragement.

Garrett's chest swelled. He opened his mouth but Lucy short-circuited his rebuttal with a hand gesture.

"I'm not saying you're wrong, Garrett, but you have to ask yourself—would you follow this course of action if the people involved weren't members of your family?"

Wade could almost hear gears churn in Garrett's head.

"To use a sports analogy," she went on. "You can't *win* by keeping your opponent from scoring. You can only win if *you* score. In this case, the advantage goes to the aggressor and that's not us. Whether the overt threat is Azizi or Argault, both have displayed extreme patience."

She let her words sink in for a long count of ten. "Now, Agent Fowler's plan on the other hand is a two-prong action: capture Azizi with technology that can pinpoint his location, and lure Argault into a trap. The first idea might work. The second won't."

Fowler started to rise.

"You had an opportunity to present your plan without interruption, Agent Fowler," she told him. "Please extend me the same courtesy."

Wade wanted to laugh when Fowler froze halfway up from his chair. From what both TJ and Garrett had said of Fowler, the retired Bureau director turned contract agent wasn't

Imperfect Trust

used to having his decisions discounted.

"Please look at the paper Mallory passed around as I explain why Agent Fowler's plan won't work. Page one is the analysis I just spoke of. I used the military's Strategy Formulation Methodology."

Across the room, James and Garrett nodded.

"For those not familiar with SFM, I laid out the six steps." She ticked them off using her fingers. "Establish the objective, clarify it, determine achievable tasks, define every possible solution, agree on a course of action, and then act on it."

Lucy gave them a few more moments to look over the document.

"You can study the paper in depth later. For now, it's late and I know Wade needs to rest. Let me summarize. Agent Fowler believes simple is best. I agree. His plan to capture Azizi should work because Wade's systems are more secure than any I've seen. And I've hacked the best. All legal, of course." A smile tugged at her lips.

"Explain." Fowler said.

"With a couple of program enhancements, we can locate any cyber intruder's geographical coordinates. Using said coordinates, you and your men can take them down. Do their stuff." Her smile broke free this time.

Fowler nodded and relaxed in his seat.

"As for why the plan to lure Cypher won't work, let's consider the adversary."

A telephone rang somewhere in the house.

"Sorry." His mother jumped up. "We've had that landline for forty years. I'll get it." She hurried from the room.

Lucy's intensity had chased away Wade's weariness. She believed in what she'd laid out and showed her passion with every word and movement. She made him believe, too.

"Cypher is a drug dealer, but he's not your typical street heavy or Mafioso wannabe. This man brokered multi-million dollar trades and avoided capture for years. He's still eluding the authorities. A few weeks ago, the Bureau's Atlanta Office set up a sting, one so secret only three people knew of it right up until the time it went down. The op was a success except Cypher got away again."

Every eye remained riveted on Lucy as she spoke.

"Cypher is the alias of Jensen Argault. I went to college with Jensen. He was the school's resident computer genius with a documented IQ of 175. If you don't understand what that means, most American adults have an IQ between ninety and 110. If you take an IQ average of all the 4.0 college students in the U.S. today, you'll come up with a median of 135."

Wade sat up straight at that, along with everyone else in the room.

She took a deep breath. "Jensen is smart, but also strange. I mean, the man had an advanced degree in psychology and was finishing up another in Computer Engineering when I knew him. But he also had these survivalist ideas. Claimed anarchy was coming and he was getting ready. He spent his summers working as a wilderness guide in the north Georgia mountains."

"So," Fowler interrupted. "We have a street-smart felon who can use a compass, has unlimited financial resources, and a scary IQ. I get that you were involved in taking down his drug network, but why is he still after you, Lucy? I mean, you said he was smart."

"People with big IQs have big egos. I used his own technology against him. Frankly, that would stick in my craw, too."

Mouths dropped open on that tidbit of information.

"By now he's learned all there is to know about me, every nuance, right down to the way I walk, my body language, and how I phrase things. He will map out every detail of this ranch, the nearby towns, and surrounding area. He'll know all about the cabin you found. He'll make your lookalike agent before she takes five steps. The government has underestimated Jensen Argault for years. I beg you to heed me. He won't play your game. You will have to play his. And I'm the only shot you've got."

Wade couldn't sit still any longer. "We're not using you as bait." He rose to pace the room. "I won't dangle you in front of him like a worm on a hook. We'll find another way."

"Not a good idea, Lucy," Jonas added.

"It's too dangerous." Mallory looked like she might pass out.

His mom came back in the room wringing her hands. "Ed Whitaker from Atlanta is on the phone. He wants to speak with Lucy. He says it's urgent."

Chapter Twenty-Three

"Ed?" Lucy's hand shook as she held the telephone receiver to her ear.

"Lucy, I've missed you. How's your shoulder?" Ed's voice sounded both relieved and anxious, neither of which reassured her.

She knew her old friend too well. No amount of urging would extract the real reason for the call until he was ready. "I've seen a local doctor. He confirmed Doctor Beaumont's recommendation. I declined the surgery for the moment, so I'm still in the sling.

"That's good."

Good? Whatever he had to say must be terrible if he wasn't listening. "Should I ask about Phyllis now? The team? Or how you knew where to find me?" She couldn't stave off her irritation any longer. "Or why you gave me up to the Bureau? That agent you talked to tracked me down."

Nothing.

"Why did you call? Cate said it was urgent."

"Cypher's gone off grid. No sign of him since he killed the guard outside your hospital room."

Not nearly enough for this disciplined man to break protocol, even off duty. "I know that."

"Todd Delacroix is recovering. He had reconstructive surgery and now faces a long road of physical therapy. The doctors think he might regain partial use of his hand."

Imperfect Trust

Great news about Del, the agent Argault shot at point blank range. Not that it relieved her worry. Ed never skirted issues like this. She remained silent.

"A busted hand didn't affect his brain, though. When it comes to technology, I'd rank him right up there with you." Ed would be rubbing his head about now. Thumb on his temple and two fingers on his forehead—his one tell when the stress got to him.

Lucy snorted. "Apples and oranges, Ed. Del is like, Mr. Ace-is-the-Place Hardware. I'm the Radio Shack princess."

"You know, Lucy, I thought I had Cypher so many times. It drove me nuts how he always got away. It was as if he knew where we'd be and when."

She didn't like the direction of the conversation. "Are you saying …?"

"I've suspected an internal leak for awhile now. Todd confirmed it yesterday. I arrested Diane Lunden last night."

"Diane?" Lucy didn't know what to say. She liked the secretary, considered her a friend. Not the confiding secrets kind or someone who'd be your wingman when you partied, but she'd gone to lunch with her a few times. She was the girl next door. Dressed like a librarian. Diane wouldn't catch Jensen Argault's eye. Or fall for his charisma. "How? Why?"

"Blew me away, too."

"What aren't you telling me, Ed?"

"I have your laptop and your file in a safe in my office. Only one other person besides me knows the combination. She gave you up, Lucy. Cypher knows where you are. Diane has fed him information for the past two years. Todd was suspicious of her all along. I thought he wanted to prove his value, so I let him set up a covert camera. The video showed her digging through the files in my safe and snapping pictures with her phone."

Lucy fought back panic. Argault knew about Hastings Bluff. And the Camerons. She'd never doubted he would find her, but not like this. He would come. Maybe he was already here.

A hand pressed down on her shoulder.

She turned and let Wade pull her against his chest. His heart beat in a steady rhythm under her cheek. Strong. Calming. Cassie's words from the hospital room in Atlanta echoed in her mind. "In Idaho, we don't tolerate jerks that hurt women or children. You'd be safe there."

Gentle as his touch was, even injured, she could feel the coiled power in him waiting to be unleashed. How did he make her feel so many different things? Some uncomfortable, others wonderful, all of them confusing. But always safe.

Lucy ignored the voice in her head that screamed run and listened to her heart instead. The answer came without hesitation. Wade Cameron could keep her from harm. He wanted to protect her. The only thing required was her trust.

"Lucy? Are you there?" Ed's voice broke the spell. "We need to get you into protective custody ASAP."

"Still here, Ed. Look, we both knew Jensen would find me sooner or later. I think I'll take my chances with the Camerons. I'm safer here than any place you can stash me."

Wade loosened his one-armed embrace and pushed her away a fraction to look deep into her eyes. Something fierce and feral stared back at her. Argault might be deadly, but he wouldn't stand a chance against this man. She'd bet her life on it. Hers and many more.

※ ※ ※

Lucy's expression struck a primitive chord inside Wade. Trust and confidence shone in her eyes. He vowed in that moment to do whatever he had to, anything to keep her safe.

After she hung up with the Atlanta agent, Wade pulled her close again. His hand ran up and down her spine in a slow circuit like it had a mind of its own. "You're safe here, tiger," he whispered.

She snaked her good arm around his waist and squeezed. "I know I am."

They were a fine pair, her with her busted left shoulder and him with his almost useless right arm. Together they were invincible, and that made him happier than he'd been in a very long time.

"So your Bureau friend thinks Cypher found you."

She nodded. "Someone inside has been feeding Argault information all this time. It's why he always got away whenever we got close." She turned her face up. "He knows I'm here."

Wade kissed her forehead and then her nose. "Doesn't change a thing except now there's no need to lure him in."

She rubbed her cheek against his chest like a cat, the movement one of the most erotic things he'd ever experienced. So innocent and yet—

He stopped that line of thought before it went any further. He needed to put some physical distance between them before he did something stupid. "He'll have to go through me and the rest of the men to get to you, and that won't happen. So, how about you show me this fancy program of yours, the one you think will boost my security and maybe catch us a thief."

"Okay." She nodded, still rubbing her face over his chest but not moving away.

Tongues of fire licked at his brain. His body hummed with desire. Lucy fit like a missing puzzle piece, but he stepped back and took her hand instead. Their connection was too new, too fragile. He refused to mess it up for a moment's gratification. He wanted the long haul. Wanted her to want it, too. "You realize this knocks Fowler's plan out of the water, right?"

She grinned. "Yeah. I can't wait to see his face when we tell him."

The imp was back, and he couldn't be happier.

Half an hour later, Wade sat next to Lucy at his mother's desk, staggered by what she'd shown him. She might think Argault was a genius, but Wade knew she was. "This is incredible. And you say you threw it together on the fly to catch Argault? Developed it in less than a week?"

He got her typical response—a one-shoulder shrug and rosy cheeks. "I can't claim all the credit. The basis is derived from Argault's work. I just happen to have very good recall and applied some of his code to the problem. That's what I do you know—build on others' work. For the most part."

Lucy looked away, but her eyes darted back to assess his reaction before concentrating on her nails.

For the most part. He almost snorted. His tiger was so honest she didn't realize how her own words betrayed her. She was smart, naïve, sweet, humble, and sassy. A contradiction if ever he saw one. And she couldn't lie worth a darn. Good thing she didn't play poker.

"Let me describe how I think my Quicksilver program will work with your Switchback." Funny how she always diverted to a new subject whenever someone sang her praises. "If I recall, anyone who gets past your firewall winds up in a loop—"

"Not a loop, a maze," he corrected.

"Even better. Circular loops are easy to recognize. A maze will hang them up longer, which will give Quicksilver time to lock in the intruder's signal. Kind of like lassoing a steer, huh?" Mischief danced in her eyes, giving him a glimpse of one pert dimple.

"Yeah, but without the bruises." He loved this side of her.

"That's when we launch Hermes."

"What is Hermes?"

"I like to call it a stealth program, but it's really just a fancied up trojan designed to slip in and steal documents, data files, executables, whatever. I named it after the Greek god of thieves. Ed freaked when I explained how it worked. He's a black-and-white kind of guy. No gray. Which is why I double encrypted the original. He'll feel obligated to explain it to his higher ups."

Wade had to admit it freaked him a little, too. In the wrong hands, her genius might very well destabilize the world economy. "Where is this little gem? Who, besides you, has access?"

"The original is on my computer back in Atlanta, in Ed's safe. Don't worry. Access requires an optical scan. If the intruder somehow manages to circumvent the optical requirement, all the files on the hard drive get eaten by a fast acting worm."

"You have backups?"

"Of course. I keep them in a vault at an offsite location. And I have a copy on this." She pulled the small memory stick from her pocket. "I ran the program that broke Cypher's network from it. Oh, and now there's a copy on your computer."

Well, if that wasn't a show of trust, he didn't know what was. "Explain to me how it works."

For the next hour she walked him through the logic that had brought Hermes to life and then through every conceivable scenario where she thought her applications might help him snare Azizi.

Thoughts sped through his mind faster than he could process. "Would it work with Argault again?"

Lucy shook her head. "He won't make the same mistake twice."

∞

The rooster's crows brought Lucy wide awake with a groan. All the crawling around on the floor and under tables over the last two days shouldn't have made her sore, but she'd grown sedentary since Atlanta. Or lazy. Wade was right. She needed to start exercising.

First, she had to check on Wade's computers in the adjacent room. Satisfied all was as it should be, she headed for the bathroom to brush her teeth, pull her hair into a sloppy ponytail, and don her baggy sweats.

In the family room, Lucy used her knee to push the coffee table aside. She moved into position, planted her feet shoulder-width apart, and stretched her right arm to the sky. The pull along her ribcage felt wonderful. Breathe in. Fill the lungs. Inhale the good air. Hold it. Stand tall. Now, exhale the used oxygen. Slow. Feel the lungs contract. Repeat.

The yoga disciplines she'd employed for years in her martial arts workouts soon prompted a burn. She'd missed this. After days of inactivity, lethargy fled. Muscle memory kicked in. Cautious of her shoulder and limited flexibility, she performed the movements with precision.

Before long, perspiration dotted her forehead. She paused long enough to slip off the sling, determined to work the now flaccid muscles of her left arm. Only a little, though. She knew the difference between the ache of working muscles and real pain.

Seated on the floor, she spread her legs wide and bent from the waist to reach for one foot and then the other. She leaned to each side in a slow, graceful stretch. On her feet, she widened her stance and placed her palm on the floor. Her balance was off using only one hand, but she pushed up onto her toes and flexed the calf muscles.

Sweat trickled from her temples and beaded on her upper lip. Wisps of hair stuck to her neck. She increased her efforts and felt a burn in the unused muscles of her legs and back. The good kind of pain. Endorphins had kicked in.

Imperfect Trust

Physical exertion worked like a computer reboot for her. It cleared the sensory overload that gummed up her brain. Chaos subsided.

Movement in her peripheral vision caught her attention. Wade leaned against the doorframe, a cup of coffee in his hand.

She smiled at him from an inverted position and continued her exercises. When she finished, he handed her a towel. "Coffee?" He had morning voice, two octaves lower than normal.

A tingle ignited in her chest and spread. A delicious, forbidden feeling that made her nerves jangle.

In the kitchen, she perched on one of the tall stools at the counter where she and Mallory often took their breakfast.

Wade set a steaming mug in front of her. "Creamer?"

"Please." She reached for the sugar bowl.

He set the carton of half-n-half in front of her and watched while she fixed the coffee to her liking—light and sweet.

They sipped in silence.

When her cup was half empty, he extended the coffeepot for a refill.

She covered her mug with a hand. "No thanks."

He refilled his cup.

Other than the terse, one-word questions, he didn't speak until he finished the second cup. "I didn't sleep much last night, too keyed up about your programs. I'd like to give it a shot, but first you'll need a crash course on Switchback since it uses a different machine language. And I need to better understand Quicksilver."

His incredible blue eyes turned her brain to mush. A brisk head shake helped her reclaim the clarity she'd spent the last hour capturing. "My schedule happens to be free this morning, if that works for you."

Crinkle lines formed around his eyes when he smiled.

"Funny, mine is, too. Why don't you grab a shower and meet me in Mom's office in say, thirty minutes?"

"Okay."

Imperfect Trust

Chapter Twenty-Four

Wade's shoulders slumped in defeat. He handed over the currycomb. "Thanks, Rascal."

"No problem."

Long strides carried him out of the barn and into bright morning sunshine. Overhead, birds chirped and flitted through the trees. Year-old foals newly separated from their dams frisked and frolicked in a nearby pasture. The smell of fresh mown hay filled the air.

Wade spat on the ground. Yesterday, he'd sat on his butt in front of a computer for hours on end while Lucy worked her magic on his systems. Last night, Mom had asked if he needed help shaving—her not so subtle hint that maybe his razor technique was lacking. Today, he couldn't even groom his own horse. He hated being indebted, but lately he seemed to owe everybody.

An unlucky clod of dirt found the toe of his boot as he started toward the house. It disintegrated with a kick. No doubt Mom waited in the kitchen. To help him. He glanced down at his shirt and bit back a disgusted huff. He couldn't even tuck his shirt in properly. The tail flapped in the breeze and the buttons were done up wrong.

The hard truth was he needed help. From all quarters. Lucy monitored his computer security. Mal and Casey kept his business running. Dad, Garrett, and Jonas had divvied up his ranch chores. Rascal was taking care of his horse. And Mom. He shook his head, unable to stave off a smile. She'd do

Imperfect Trust

anything he needed, even if he didn't want it. All so he could recuperate.

How did Lucy stand all the hovering? She never complained, not about the pain, the forced inactivity, her dependence on strangers, all the mothering, not even leaving her whole life behind.

The kitchen was empty when he entered. Relieved, he got the coffee from the pantry and managed to fumble off the lid. Eight scoops. Pour in the water. All he seemed good for these days was to make the morning coffee and keep Lucy company. What a pair they made. Two invalids with mirror image slings.

The thought stopped him cold. Lucy was no invalid. And she would bust his chops if she could hear his thoughts.

His sour mood faded. What a pansy he'd become, a grown man grousing over a little downtime while she was stuck in limbo.

He took his cup into his mom's office and settled down to wait. The fresh brewed coffee aroma began to fill the house. Shouldn't be long now. Lucy would appear any minute, her nose in the air like a bloodhound. That girl sure loved her caffeine.

He blew steam from his cup and waited for his laptop to power up. A week had passed since Ed Whitaker's call. Seven days without a sign of Argault. Azizi either, for that matter. Nothing from Fowler or his resources. They still had no idea of the shooter's identity or his intended target.

The alarm program Lucy had written and installed on his computers also remained quiet. All this waiting around ... A series of pings sounded from his laptop. Several new e-mails dropped into the inbox. He read the first one with pleasure. A new customer. Great. That made three in the last week alone. As he read on some of his satisfaction dissipated. Another buffalo herd. In Yellowstone, no less. He groaned. Massive, ornery brutes. Bison were dumb and required twice the effort to tag as cattle or horses. He'd have to bring on additional wranglers because who knew when he'd get back to full strength.

"Thanks." Lucy lifted her mug in salute as she traipsed back to her room. She was a hot mess with her tangled hair, loose pajama pants and … wait. Was that his tee shirt?

He tension began melting away. "Morning, tiger."

"Mmm," she grunted and kept going. Thirty minutes and she'd be back.

A grin stretched his mouth wide. Moments alone with Lucy were becoming fewer and more precious as Garrett's and TJ's wedding approached. A subtle frenzy had settled over the house of late. The ceremony at the church didn't pose much of a concern, but the nighttime reception planned for the backyard of the Triple C promised to be a nightmare. With more than two hundred guests expected, Fowler had already pulled out most of his hair over the security. They could use more bodies to man the entire perimeter.

Meanwhile, they still had Mom and TJ to deal with. Every night Garrett, Jonas, and Dad drew straws to see who played escort for them the next day. And every morning the two women—with said escort—left the house around nine armed with a list of errands. Flowers, menus, napkins, clothes, and music. Nothing else existed for them. Which left him the appointed babysitter/champion for Lucy and Mallory.

The two girls spent every day until noon in front of the video console. He'd tried on numerous occasions to talk them out of going through with the *LA Kidd* match only to have them laugh in his face. Mule-headed women. He didn't get it. They had one good player and one untested novice. Why would they set themselves up for failure?

He made a mental correction—the girls had one *maybe* good player. He hadn't actually seen Lucy play yet.

Imperfect Trust

Hard as Mallory trained, he didn't see how she and Lucy could beat Garrett and James. *LA Kidd* was like a holy grail to the two veterans. Besides their skill at the game, they had years of military experience working as a team. It was uncanny sometimes how they seemed to know the other's thoughts.

The match would happen tomorrow night. They'd find out then whether Lucy and Mal could hold their own.

The grandfather clock in the foyer struck seven. This was what his life had been reduced to. Waiting. Constrained by the promise to stay away while Lucy taught Mallory the fine points of *LA Kidd*, he would idle the morning hours away, alert for the sound of Lucy's laugh. And those two laughed a lot.

After lunch, his sister would retreat to her bedroom, claiming a need for privacy and quiet to produce the tracking reports he needed. Which meant Wade had Lucy to himself for the rest of the afternoon. He glanced at the clock in the bottom right corner of his monitor. A few more hours yet.

Settled behind his mother's desk, Wade took a sip of his coffee and let his thoughts run free. A sense of contentment had crept into his life. Did it bother him? Yeah. Not really. His body shook on a silent chuckle. What worried him most was Lucy's safety. They needed to find Argault pronto. Azizi, too. So many cyber attacks in such a short span of time. And then nothing. Didn't make sense.

No matter. Thanks to Lucy, the next hack attempt would provide a nasty surprise. Stubborn and one-handed, they'd gotten in each other's way a lot, but they'd stayed at it until she got the Quicksilver program synched with Switchback. Now, they waited.

ece

After supper that evening, Wade followed Lucy to the family room. It bewildered him how she and Dad could spend half an hour on the pros and cons of Google to look up phone numbers instead of thumbing through the paper tome the telephone company still delivered. Or text messages versus the hardwired telephone his dad still favored. They never argued, though. Even when they disagreed, they laughed it off.

Sure enough, she curled up on the hassock next to his father's recliner.

Wade took a seat across the room, watched his father monopolize her time, and tried to figure how to wheedle his way into their conversation.

Sweet Pete, he had it bad. Now he was jealous of his own dad.

Short bursts of sound droned in the background. Soft and persistent, it wormed its way to the front of his mind. Wade cocked his head to one side and listened. Too rhythmic to be the refrigerator. Too low for the air conditioner. Not his phone either, but some kind of alarm.

He bolted up from the chair. "Lucy," he yelled and raced for her bedroom. "It's happening."

The sound grew louder when he opened Lucy's door. The alarm. This was it. Azizi—or whomever. Wade didn't know what excited him more, that the waiting had ended at last or seeing the super-spy program in action.

Lucy followed on his heels and sat at the makeshift desk in front of the systems laptop. Her fingers flew over the keyboard. "Call Fowler. Tell him to open the computer portal and alert his team."

The Quicksilver icon appeared. Block letters filled the screen, soon replaced by a blinking cursor.

Wade dialed the agent. "Fowler, Wade Cameron here. It's happening. Open the portal and get your team ready."

Fowler asked a few questions and hung up.

Wade turned to Lucy. "He's ready. Launch Quicksilver."

"Not yet. Let Switchback pull him in first."

Wade stared at her. He was supposed to be calm one.

Imperfect Trust

"Quicksilver," she spoke at last. "Identify all signals attempting access."

A spinning circle materialized on the screen. Seconds later a list of four IP addresses appeared. The first one housed his firewall and security programs. The second ran a constant monitor on all tagged herds and stored the data. The third address belonged to the computer they sat in front of.

The last he didn't recognize. *190.227.1.24.*

"Quicksilver," Lucy instructed. "Acquire signal one-nine-oh, point two-two-seven, point one, point two-four."

Another spinning wheel and then—*Signal acquired.*

"Yessss." Lucy pumped her fist. "Quicksilver, send acquired signal coordinates to Fowler portal."

A tiny popup opened with a visual of the connection.

"Sweet." Wade stared at the screen and then at Lucy.

She looked up. Her brown eyes sparkled. "Ready for more?"

"Oh, yeah."

"Quicksilver, open Hermes."

A knot of excitement formed in his gut. Could it be this simple?

The spinning circle returned.

"How long?"

"Patience, grasshopper." She leaned back in her chair to wait. "Invasion without detection is delicate work."

New words formed. *Hermes ready. Launch?*

"This is it," she exclaimed. "Quicksilver, launch Hermes."

The wait took longer this time, but then Wade's mouth fell open as file paths filled the screen, scrolled up and off, only to be replaced by hundreds more. Maybe thousands. "What are all these files?"

"Everything on his computer. Hermes confiscates program files, data files, executables—you name it. I didn't design in selectivity."

"These aren't copies, are they? Hermes strips the target computer and … removes everything?"

She nodded. "Quicksilver. Transmit file cache acquired by Hermes to Fowler portal."

The popup connection to Fowler's portal changed. *Transmitting* appeared along with a bar at the bottom that began to turn green.

Ten minutes passed before she looked over at him. A frown drew her eyebrows together. "I think we hit the mother lode. This is way more than what we got from Argault."

Fascinated, Wade kept an eye on the bar that measured the transfer progress. Heavens above, they'd done it, but at what cost? Lucy's program was way more powerful than he'd imagined. Dangerous. And Fowler would recognize the potential military applications. They'd have to remove Quicksilver and Hermes from his computer. He didn't trust Fowler not to make a grab for them.

His cell phone rang. The devil himself. Wade put the call on speaker. "Any luck?"

Fowler's raspy voice seemed lower over the phone. "GPS shows the hacker in the Challis area. We have him bracketed. The teams are closing in. What's all this stuff you're sending?"

"Thought you might want to see what's on his hard drive," Lucy answered.

Fowler was silent for a long moment. "You got his files?"

Wade could almost hear the agent's mind working. "Yeah, we got lucky." He looked a Lucy and motioned her to silence with a finger over his lips.

"Huh. I'll let you know when we have him in custody."

"Roger that." Wade disconnected the call and pulled Lucy in for a hug.

She held him off. "What did you mean, *lucky*?"

He hated dashing their moment of victory, but they needed to discuss the implications of their actions. "Tonight was a

Imperfect Trust

huge success, but we have to consider what might come next."

The light in her eyes dimmed. "What do you mean?"

"Fowler. That man leans so far right, he's almost as wrong as the bad guys."

"You think he'll try to take our programs." She shook her head side to side, ponytail flapping. "That can't happen."

"Depends on what's in those files we sent him. We have to uninstall both Quicksilver and Hermes from my computer soon as this op is over."

She nodded. Her frown deepened. "He'll know we're thwarting him. I'm not a very good liar."

"No worries, tiger. I can handle Fowler."

ⓒⓒⓒ

The last file path rolled off the screen a few minutes before ten o'clock. Three minutes later, *Transmission complete* appeared on screen.

Wade's cell phone rang a few minutes later. "Was it Azizi?" Wade said, pressing the speaker button.

"Yes." The agent's response sounded giddy. "Put me on speaker. Lucy should hear this, too."

"I'm here," she answered.

"Azizi made it to an abandoned air strip a mile west of Challis. Had a Lear jet waiting."

"And?" Wade asked.

Fowler's laugh was dark and devoid of mirth. "Aircraft can't fly with their tail blown off."

"So, he's in custody? What about Sarah? You said she wasn't a concern but never explained why." Wade persisted.

"We nabbed Azizi, three of his henchmen, and the pilot tonight. Sarah has been a guest of the government under the guise of cooperating with the Bureau of International Intelligence. We picked her up a month after you let her walk out."

Sarah had been in jail all this time? "If it was Azizi all along, why did he stop?"

"Don't know. Directions from someone higher up maybe. Do either of you have any idea what those files contained?"

Dread settled somewhere in the region of Wade's stomach. He looked at Lucy. "Nope. It was a fluke we even got them."

Fowler cleared his throat. He took a long time to answer. "A fluke. Right. Okay, you don't know any of this, understand?"

"Yes," Lucy and Wade responded in unison.

"Azizi's bank records were in the lot, account numbers, passwords, and wire transfers for multiple accounts. We know how much, who paid, and who received. Better yet, we can access the accounts and take the money. And that's only a few of the files. This is mega. You two are heroes."

Lucy's worried eyes locked with Wade's.

"Uh, Fowler?" Wade said. "Lucy and I would rather you take the credit. Plead confidential resources or whatever it is reporters claim, but keep us out of it."

When the silence grew uncomfortable, Lucy added a plea. "This could impact our lives in a very negative way."

Fowler's sigh whistled over the line. "You two are killing me. Okay, I'll keep your names out of the reports … on one condition."

Wade held his breath.

"I'm sure you realize your programs have immense value," the agent went on. "I understand your reservations and will protect your interests, but you have to agree to cooperate with me if and when I need you."

"That's not—"

"You can't—"

"No, it's not fair. And yes, I can. You both know if I snap my fingers, you and your work will disappear."

Imperfect Trust

"We want refusal rights." Wade's heart drummed way too fast. Fowler held all the power. How far could he push? "You can't involve either of us in anything we consider illegal, unethical, or immoral."

Fowler didn't hesitate. "Granted."

"Or if it disrupts our lives or the lives of those around us," Lucy added.

"Granted." Not even a quibble.

Wade waited. There was always a *but*.

"If that's all, I have my own conditions. When—if—I need your special expertise or require the use of your programs, I expect your immediate response. You may decline and, if it's a reasonable refusal, I will accept your decision. However, if I deem it to be in the interest of national security, I will override your refusal. Mine is the final decision. Are we in agreement?"

Wade saw fear and uncertainty on Lucy's face. He took her hand and squeezed. They'd have the specter of Fowler behind them forever, but it wasn't like they had much of a choice.

He nodded. "Agreed."

She gifted him with a smile and said, "Agreed."

"Then we have a deal. For what it's worth, you have my word that I won't abuse your trust." Fowler cleared his throat. "Regarding the outcome of this mission, I will tell you what I can, but everything that went down tonight is top secret. You speak of it to no one. Not even family."

Once again Lucy and Wade concurred.

"Then our business is finished. For now. You can tell the others we have Azizi in custody. The search for Jensen Argault continues. Agent Duncan, who runs Lucy's protection detail, will keep you apprised of developments. For now, on behalf of our country, please accept my sincere thanks for a job well done."

The line went dead.

"Quicksilver," Lucy said. "Close Hermes. Close Fowler portal. Close acquired signal. Shutdown."

Wade watched until the screen went black. They'd resolved one threat, but the other remained. And now they had Fowler to contend with.

"You're thinking about Argault." A statement, not a question. How well she'd come to know him.

"He's still out there."

Lucy's brown eyes seemed luminous in the dimmed light. A man could drown in those eyes.

"Don't." She reached for his hand. "We'll dismantle the programs and worry about Argault tomorrow."

"You're going ahead with the *LA Kidd* challenge, aren't you? With Cypher still lurking in the shadows."

"Fowler's team is here. Your men are watching. I think we need the distraction." She snaked her arm around his waist.

A protest lingered on his lips, but with Lucy pressed up against him he couldn't form the words. She chased away his darkness. And while his brain didn't function at the moment, all his circuits sizzled when she lifted her face and met his kiss.

Imperfect Trust

Chapter Twenty-Five

The grandfather clock came to life at the top of the hour. Lucy counted twelve strokes. The witching hour. No wonder her body ached. They'd been playing *LA Kidd* for hours.

Her lungs released a slow breath. She and Mal had done it. They'd gotten through all the levels with only the last one left—the one everybody said couldn't be beaten.

The guys took the controllers for their turn at ninety-nine. Bet Garrett Cameron never played catchup in his life. Their taunts had ended somewhere around level thirty-five, about the time Mallory stepped up her game.

Lucy allowed herself the tiniest of smiles.

In a perfect world, the guys would have started the match first. Then, when they reached the final level and failed to complete it as was usual for them, she and Mal would have swept through the final level and taken the victory.

The world wasn't perfect, though. Garrett won the coin toss and, like the gentleman Cate had raised him to be, insisted on ladies first. Which meant the guys watched—and learned—as Lucy unveiled too many secrets.

Chewing on her bottom lip, she wracked her brain for a way to guarantee victory for her team. They had a big edge in time, but Garrett and James had garnered a ton of points. If the impossible happened and both teams made it through, would their time bonus beat the guys' points?

Unable to sit any longer, Lucy stood, stretched, and tried to ease the tightness between her shoulder blades.

Imperfect Trust

Mallory rose with her. "We got this, Lucy. I can smell a win."

"I don't know, Mal. They have seven extra lives. If they figure out level one hundred ..." She shrugged. "It's too close."

In a chair adjacent to the sofa where she and Mal sat, Garrett's body jerked in sync with his online avatar, Mars, the Roman god of war. His character, a muscle-bound giant dressed in battle gear and carrying a full complement of weaponry, suited him. Mars forged ahead, sweeping every obstacle out of his way.

In contrast, James remained still in the chair next to his partner, only his hands moving. His avatar, Pallas, another Greek god whose passion was war, also appeared as an overly large warrior dressed in camo and loaded with armament. They sped through mazes and climbed impossible precipices, all to gain an extra life or a sack of coins, while they took out enemy combatants. Without a single wrong move, they snagged all the level had to offer, defeated the surprise elements, obstacles, and enemies, and then dashed through the exit with their loot and precious little time on the clock.

Where was the apparition when you needed it?

During the design phase, she'd added random enhancements to spice up the game. Some were helpful, others hindered a player's actions, and a few were lethal. Like the apparition, a ghostly creature that appeared and disappeared without warning.

A kernel of guilt pricked at Lucy's conscience. Garrett and James had watched her root out unseen power sources and take shortcuts through hidden chambers while ignoring the allure of treasure chests, extra lives, and fantastic weapons. They never questioned her expertise, but neither did they waver from their own strategy.

"Here you go, girls." Garrett handed over the two controllers with a flourish and a smile.

Casey, who'd acted as their bipartisan judge, stood in front of the television and tapped his wristwatch. "Five minute break before the home stretch."

"I have drinks if anybody wants one." Cate gestured to a table against the wall where she'd set up a tray of soft drinks and water.

After a few sips, Lucy recapped the water bottle and set it down. Two weeks of intensive training. Mallory had become quite a skilled gamesman. No matter the outcome of tonight's match, she'd accomplished her goal, and Lucy couldn't be prouder. Mal could hold her own against her big bad brother and the sheriff.

Garrett and James bumped fists. "Let's finish this."

Wade stood off to one side, one finger stroking his chin.

When everyone was seated again, Casey handed the controllers to Lucy and Mallory. "Level one hundred. The final level. Are you ready, ladies?"

Mallory looked like a scared rabbit.

Lucy nudged her shoulder. "We got this."

Mallory's pale face flushed with color. She took the proffered controller, sucked in a deep breath, and let it out. "Yeah, let's do it."

Lucy's avatar, Brienne, took the lead like they'd practiced. She sprinted up steps that led to the top of the mountain while Mallory's Asha stayed back to protect her flank. Right on schedule, colorful bullet-shaped forms descended from the sky, falling in lazy spirals only to zip to one side when you least expected it. Relatively harmless, their only threat was to slow you down ... except for the metallic ones. The silver bullets could disable. The gold ones killed.

Brienne vaporized all the bullets that came near her, regardless of their threat level, freeing her partner to guard her back from below.

"Spike. Six o'clock," Mallory's Asha called.

Imperfect Trust

Lucy's character turned and blasted the nail-like projectile speeding her way. The spike disintegrated.

She continued on, her goal the pale yellow radiance at the very top. The guys couldn't know the exit door there hid a deadly surprise. By going first, she would reveal the roiling shadows that consumed a player's life force. Not the scenario she'd hoped for.

Fighting on, Lucy planned each step with careful deliberation.

"Hurry," her beleaguered partner pleaded. The hailstorm of bullets and spikes had focused on Mallory.

One more step and Lucy lunged. To enter meant death. She thrust her hands into the golden aura instead, letting it bathe her arms until she too glowed with absorbed power.

"Whoa," Jonas said. "Never saw that before."

"Me either," James answered.

Beside Brienne, the writhing shadows calmed. The blackness within faded, leaving behind a transparent veil and a kingdom beyond. So tempting. And misleading.

"Shhh," Casey rebuked them.

"Aaaaah." Mallory's Asha had fallen.

Lucy's Brienne climbed higher, to a plateau where she could spread her arms wide. The golden glow infused her whole body and wrapped her in a shield.

The alien spikes fell in a barrage, drawn to the power she held.

She knew the lush paradise was a false promise and yet it tempted her. With a last look, Lucy turned away. Her downed partner needed her. With calm deliberation, she stepped off into air and let her newfound power slow the descent. To win this game of trust required two.

"What are you doing?" James threw his hands in the air. "You had a chance to win."

She ignored him and took up a defensive position as the vapor settled over her partner. A moment passed, and Mallory's Asha opened her eyes.

"You did it," Mal whispered.

"No, we did it. Now it's your turn." Lucy/Brienne tugged her partner upright.

Mallory/Asha took the lead. One behind the other, they raced along the bottom of the canyon toward an impenetrable rocky expanse … and a tiny crevice that hid a door. They claimed no booty in their race to the finish, took none of the extra lives displayed in abundance. Empty-handed but for the weapons they wielded, they fought off more bullets, spikes, and drones, and dodged two apparitions. They reached the nondescript opening and stepped through, leaving the alien realm behind.

Silence fell over the room as the screen went black.

A loud crescendo left Mallory covering her ears. A riot of colorful explosions erupted on the screen.

Garrett, James, Jonas, and Casey stared openmouthed at the text box superimposed over the tumult.

CONGRATULATIONS WARRIORS ASHA AND BRIENNE! YOU COMPLETED ALL LEVELS. ENTER YOUR INITIALS HERE TO POST YOUR SCORE.

Lucy peeked around the room, her heart thudding hard enough to make her forget about the pain in her shoulder.

Beside her, Mallory squealed and pulled her into a ruthless hug.

Cate and Cody looked bewildered and maybe a little pleased the marathon game had ended.

Only Wade and TJ seemed unfazed.

Casey let out a whoop. "You did it, you did it. I watched and still can't believe it. Woohoo!" He high-fived everybody in the room.

Imperfect Trust

"We did it," Mallory squealed. "Just like you said we would."

Garrett and James stared expressionless at the screen.

"Type in your initials, Mal." Casey pointed at the screen.

"MMC," Mallory said as she tapped in the letters. "Mallory Michaela Cameron. Your turn, Lucy."

Without thinking, she typed in LAK and hit enter.

"What's the A stand for?" Jonas asked.

"Yeah, what's the A stand for, Ms. Kiddron?" Mallory repeated, her voice smug.

"Alice."

Jonas, Wade, and TJ huddled at the rear of the room, heads together and whispering.

"We still have a turn, don't we?" James demanded.

Lucy swallowed. The little grain of guilt plaguing her all night long threatened to choke her now. Garrett and James were fine players. They deserved the truth. Well, some of the truth. But if she told them ... she would blow it for Mallory.

"Yeah, you still have a turn."

Garrett sat up straight.

A gleam returned to James's eyes.

"Hold on," Wade called. "We have a question first." He and Jonas took a stance in front of the television.

Uh-oh.

"Maybe it's a coincidence, but we noticed your initials. LAK." Jonas pointed at the typed initials on the screen.

"Lucy Alice Kiddron." Wade's lips twitched. "Is there a connection to *LA Kidd*?"

Another delighted squeal erupted from Mallory. She clapped her hands together, unable to suppress her grin. "They figured it out. I told you they would."

TJ sidled up to Garrett, a huge grin on her face.

Casey groaned and slapped a hand to his forehead. "I should have known."

Jonas grinned. "I knew something was off. TJ did, too, but Wade's the one who put it all together."

Garrett and James wore identical thunderstruck expressions.

In the back of the room, Cate and Cody joined the laughter but seemed to have no idea what was so funny.

"I love it," TJ said from where she stood near Garrett. "You *played* them, girls. Beat them at their own game."

Lucy didn't know what to say.

"This is your game? A bit like cheating, don't you think?" James asked, but his grin took the sting from the words.

"Lucy and Mallory don't cheat." Casey bristled in their defense. His chin lifted, eyes filling with heat. "They worked hard, saw an advantage, and used it. It's no more than what you did to Mallory."

Garrett and James frowned at the boy.

Casey quailed a little but stood his ground. Good for him, but he'd need more than bravado to go toe-to-toe with two former Army Rangers.

In the time it took to exhale, the tension in the room broke. Garrett punched James in the shoulder and grinned. "He's right."

"Couldn't have said it better, Casey," Wade stated between chuckles.

"Well," Mallory said. "Are you two going to roll over and play dead or take your shot?"

"Yeah. Let's lock and load," James said.

"Too bad we got ten times the number of points you have." Garrett smirked, all his audacity resurfacing. "All we have to do is—"

"Uh, guys?" Mallory interrupted. "I hate to break it to you, but did you notice how fast we moved through the levels? Those points you're so proud of? Yeah, they don't mean

Imperfect Trust

anything. You have to actually beat the final level to have a chance. And let me think—you've never done that, have you?"

Lucy laughed. Little Sis wanted to milk this moment for all it was worth. Good for her.

The two brawny warriors eyed each other. Some kind of silent communication sizzled between them. "If we beat this level, what's the deciding factor?" Garrett asked.

"Points and time differential. It's too close to call at the moment."

James nudged his partner. "We got seven lives. We can do this."

Lucy shivered. He was right. They could still win.

Garrett and James started the final level. Half way up the mountain, Garrett missed a shot and took a hit, using up one of their lives. When it happened a second time, he and James traded places.

James clawed his way higher until the soft yellow glow above was revealed. He lunged for it.

"No," Lucy yelled, but too late.

James hit the pause button, but his character had already bitten the dust. They'd used up another life. He turned to Lucy. "What?"

"You have to watch out for the chthonic creatures," Lucy explained. "See those tiny red threads oozing out of the mountain? Yeah, they're attracted to quick movements, so you have to go slow. Oh, and they can't be killed."

James made it all the way up the mountain the next time, but the golden glow didn't appear. "How do I trigger the aura?"

On the far left of the screen, a green ball appeared, fading in and then out again. The size of a thumbtack and webbed, Lucy was sure no one else saw it. "Pause the game."

James froze the screen. Both he and Garrett looked at her.

She couldn't believe she was going to do this, tell them how to beat the level. With every life lost, their precious points dwindled. She and Mallory now had almost as many points as they did. There was no mathematical way Garrett and James could win now, even if they beat the level.

Except there was. If the right element showed up. And it had.

In all the times she'd played this game, she'd never encountered the Neural Net. Taking a deep breath, she pointed out the green sphere. "That is a Neural Net. Capture it and everything changes. See the little timer?" She pointed at the alarm clock icon in the bottom left corner of the playing field.

"Hey, that wasn't there before," Garrett griped.

"No, it wasn't. The Neural Net controls time—in other words, you can run your clock count backward. That will give you time to capture this treasure …" She pointed at the screen again. "Here and here. They aren't just a cache, they're mother lodes. That will get your points back. If you can capture the Net."

"We could match your time?" This from Garrett.

Lucy nodded.

"How do you capture this net thing?" James asked.

She sighed. "I'm not sure."

"But you wrote the program." Garrett's voice had turned hard, his eyes cold and flat.

"The Neural Net, the Chthonic threads, all the other random oddities that show up are added enhancements, elements designed to throw a monkey wrench into the game. They're programmed using a complex algorithm with a kicker—a random integer that drops in and locks. It allows any of four enhancements in a given level. The Neural Net comes with an additional set of random kickers and is a cerebral design. That means it learns. You have to outsmart it."

Garrett looked at James and shook his head. "Shouldn't be too difficult. I mean it's a machine with no more than four possibilities. Humans have endless possibilities."

Imperfect Trust

"Say we capture the Net. Do we lose it if we die?"

"No. They remain constant in the current game. You start up again where you left off." She looked at her opponents. "The Net poses four possibilities. You have five lives left. Capture it by a process of elimination. I suggest you take a moment and map out a strategy."

She'd done everything except win the game for them. Time to shut up.

Mallory leaned over and threaded her fingers through Lucy's. "I'm not mad. I've already won."

Not many people got her, but Mallory did. Lucy had found herself a real friend.

Half an hour later, amid whoops and backslaps, hoots and whistles, the pandemonium died down. For the first time, *LA Kidd Game of Trust* had been beaten, not once, but twice.

Mallory asked the question Lucy dreaded. "Okay, guys. You won. We owe. So, when are you calling in the debt?"

Three pairs of blue eyes and one hazel set focused on Lucy.

"Wade, since it was your idea, why don't you tell them what we decided," Garrett said, pushing Wade to the front.

"Uh, we don't want maid service. Mal might be a neat freak at work, but her bedroom is a warzone." Wade laughed with the others joining in. "With Lucy one-handed, I don't see her doing much. And since neither one of you can cook worth a darn, we changed the bet."

Lucy squeezed Mallory's hand.

"Hey, you can't do that," an outraged Casey yelled.

"It's a school night. Shouldn't you be tucked up in bed, Junior?" James scolded.

Cate wrapped her arm around Casey's waist. "I called his mom. Told her we'd make sure he got to school on time."

Wade never took his eyes off Lucy. The intensity of his stare unnerved her.

"Okay, I'll bite. What's the new price?" She let out a resigned sigh.

"Doc Burdette called in a favor. His nephew, Charlie Wilkes, is one of the best shoulder specialists in the northwest. He's coming for a visit next week and wants to see you while he's here. If he recommends surgery, you get your shoulder fixed right after the wedding."

"Wade, you know I can't do that." The thought of lying helpless in a hospital bed while Jensen Argault roamed the world made her nauseous.

"I'm not finished."

The man was impossible. She motioned him to get on with it.

"Mal and Mom will take care of you when you come home. Doc promised to come out to the ranch to check on you."

Lucy turned an accusing stare on her partner.

Mallory beamed, not an ounce of remorse in sight.

"Cassie will be home in two weeks. She's agreed to oversee your rehab."

Hope flickered just out of reach. Could it be this easy? "You've been busy putting all these little pieces of the puzzle together, but it still doesn't address the fact that my name in a hospital database will draw Jensen like a moth to a bug zapper."

"And if he shows his face there, he'll get zapped." Garrett crossed his arms over his chest.

"Doc's nephew knows the situation, and Fowler strong-armed a few people. The hospital will accommodate however many guards we want to take. Two of us will be by your side every minute." Wade looked around at his brothers. "Fowler's men will patrol the floors and the grounds."

"But—"

"No buts, tiger. You need the surgery. Given different circumstances, it would already be done. Will you trust us to do this? To keep you safe? I'd really like to hold you in my arms without fear of hurting you."

Defeated, not by logic but by the allure of those big, strong arms of his wrapped around her. "Okay."

Chapter Twenty-Six

Almost two weeks had passed since the night of the *LA Kidd* challenge. A month since he'd been shot, and nothing since. The men grew more restless as days passed with no sign of the attacker. And that worried Wade. Over time, constant vigilance wore down even the best trained soldier.

Other than Lucy's insistence that her stalker wouldn't give up and Whitaker's revelation of the leak in the Atlanta office that gave away her location, all they had was Azizi's insistence that he wasn't the shooter. Which left Argault. Who should be in jail by now given all the resources Fowler had thrown at finding him. Wade's hand curled into a fist.

"So, we concur," Fowler announced to the group gathered in the family room. "Operation Mousetrap is a go."

Each person there nodded in agreement—Garrett, Jonas, Dad, James, and Agent Duncan, the head of Lucy's protection detail. Lucy, too.

Outvoted. Great.

Wade's loud exhale conveyed the depth of his disgust and drew every eye. Tough. He'd made it plain on more than one occasion how he felt about the fool plan. Operation Mousetrap—stupid name for an op—would parade Lucy in public because Fowler actually thought Argault would try to kidnap her rather than kill her outright. He couldn't believe she'd agreed to Fowler's nonsensical plan.

Score another point for Argault. He'd struck the first blow by shooting Wade and made Fowler and the rest of them blink

Imperfect Trust

first. Now they had his brother's wedding only a few days away. A security nightmare and the reason for this powwow.

The ceremony wasn't the issue. With everyone contained inside the small church, they could easily guard the approach and the building. The reception afterward posed a much greater concern. Two hundred people milling around the backyard of the ranch, out in the open, at night, framed by floodlights, and with three miles of open tree line. They could draft every man in the county and still not cover the entire perimeter.

"All right." Fowler stood and began to pace the room. "Phase one begins now. We put Lucy in the public eye as much as possible over the next three days. See if we can make something happen. I want an armed escort with her at all times." He turned to Wade. "I suppose that's you."

"Yes." Like he'd let anyone else.

"Be sure you update Duncan on any changes to her schedule. As the leader of her protection detail, he'll ensure we have extra eyes on her at all times, as well as backup. Make sure your cell phones remain charged and keep your guns loaded. And Wade, she doesn't breathe without tickling your ear. Got it?"

Wade nodded. He'd be so close she'd mistake him for a fur coat.

What's your first excursion, Lucy?"

"Oh, you're talking to me? I wasn't sure you realized I was standing right in front of you."

Some of the men coughed or cleared their throats at the snippy retort while others chuckled.

Wade kept a straight face. "She's right. You need to include her in your plans. Not talk around her."

Fowler's face turned red. He looked like he was trying to swallow his tongue. At last he said, "My apologies."

She gave him a gracious nod. "Shopping."

Several groans dispelled some of the tension.

"I need a dress for the wedding. I refuse to borrow any more clothes. Mallory said she would take me."

The hair on the back of Wade's neck bristled with the thought of Lucy and his sister running around town. "No. I'll take you. We can head out right after lunch."

"And you know what about women's clothes?" The sweet tone didn't go with the poison darts Lucy's look sent his way.

Fowler saved him. "Wade's right, Lucy. I'm sure you can find something without Mallory's assistance."

Throwing her a sop, Wade added, "We'll check with Mal to see which stores she recommends."

From the face she made, Lucy didn't think much of their idea.

Jonas, who sat beside her on the sofa, leaned in with an overloud whisper, "We don't want to provide another target."

Her chin dipped, all the fight gone.

He had to hand it to her. Lucy had been alone and self-reliant for the majority of her life and while she made it plain she didn't like handing over control, she did it with grace and dignity ... and just enough spunk to make sure they understood it was temporary.

"Lucy has an appointment with the shoulder specialist tomorrow at Doc Burdette's office in town. We'll head into my office at nine, to the diner around eleven thirty for lunch, and then to Doc's at one. If the exam with the orthopedic doc goes anything like her last visit, she'll want to come home afterward."

Agent Duncan gave an absentminded nod and typed notes with one finger into his iPhone.

"Okay, that takes care of today and tomorrow," Fowler said. "What about Friday?"

Lucy sent a wishful glance at Wade. "I wouldn't mind another horseback ride."

Imperfect Trust

Wade lost the power of speech. Of all the things she could ask for, why'd it have to be that? He'd love to hold her on the saddle in front of him again and ride for hours. Maybe show her the property where he planned to build his own home someday. But not now, not with a death threat over her head.

He made a silent vow to himself. Once Argault was apprehended, after Lucy got her shoulder fixed, they'd ride horses as often as she wanted.

Garrett saved him this time. "Not a good idea, Lucy. A ride poses the same problem as the wedding reception—too much ground to cover. You'd need a posse to go with you, and I doubt that's what you had in mind."

"I agree with Garrett," Fowler said. "Let's stick to public places where we can position backup and control the setting."

Control the setting? Wade exchanged glances with his brothers and James. Was he kidding? The best they could do was plan for every conceivable scenario and even a few inconceivable ones, and then hope you reacted in a way that wouldn't get you or your buddies killed when the enemy didn't follow the rules. His time in war-torn Afghanistan had beaten that into his head. "And if Argault doesn't bite, what then?"

"Ready to go shopping?" Wade asked Lucy. He slipped his jacket on, covering the gun in his inside-the-waistband holster. He wanted this excursion over and Lucy tucked away safe again.

"More than ready." Excitement put a spark in her eyes. She looked like a kid at the circus.

Hard to fault her for wanting out of the house. She'd been cooped up inside for weeks. He opened the front door and stepped onto the porch first, shielding her with his larger frame, and took a long hard look around. His newly repaired truck stood fifteen steps away.

"Stay close, okay?" He pulled her into his side and hurried her down the front steps. When they reached the truck, he bundled her inside and closed the door. No more than ten seconds.

Trailing his hand along the new paint job, he quick-stepped around the front and climbed in on the driver's side.

A green truck had already started down the long, private drive. One of the agents assigned to her protection detail. Wade followed at a distance, aware that a second agent would fall in behind them. With several others already stationed in town, they had all aspects covered. Or so Fowler believed.

"Thank you for taking me shopping."

"My pleasure, tiger. Delilah's Dress Shop, here we come."

She laughed.

Three stores and two hours later, she'd purchased jeans, shirts, a pair of boots, some killer heels, and not one, but two dresses for the wedding. He scratched his head over that. Maybe she couldn't decide which one she liked. He shrugged it off and made a mental note to come back another day. With summer coming on, she'd need a wide brimmed hat for riding.

He loaded her bags into the backseat of the truck.

"Do we have time for one more stop?" She touched his arm.

"Sure. Where to?"

Her cheeks turned a lovely shade of pink. "Lavender and Lace."

Lingerie. She wanted him to go with her while she shopped for fancy underwear. Or what passed for underwear. He hadn't seen that coming. For the first time, Wade questioned the wisdom of leaving Mallory out of today's excursion.

After a tenth glance at his watch, Wade retreated to the front door of the boutique. He could keep Lucy in sight from

Imperfect Trust

there. But then she held up a frilly, white, barely there ... something.

He did an about face, tugged at the open neck of his shirt, and focused on the light fixtures. The front window. Anywhere but at Lucy with the merchandise pressed against her ...

When was the last time he field stripped and cleaned his gun?

Clear the chamber. Remove the mag. Pull the slide back. Release the pin. Lift off the frame. Remove the recoil spring and guide rod.

Uh-oh. She held up two pairs of what might be panties—one red satin and the other white lace.

Take out the barrel. Clean the carbon buildup on the extractor. Use the soft cloth. Solvent. Hoppes 9 Oil. Brush. Cleaning patches.

"I'm sorry, Wade," she said to him a few minutes later. "I know you don't want to be here."

The Sig's image slipped away, replaced by full lips that smiled up at him and a pair of seldom seen, peek-a-boo dimples. Her chin dropped.

She'd bewitched him. It was the only answer. "Baby, look at me."

Warm brown eyes lifted to hold his gaze.

"I'm in a women's underwear shop. All these lacy ..." He waved his hands about. "Scraps—are distracting. I can't help but—" He coughed.

Her eyes widened.

"Forget that. This isn't about me. Yes, I feel like a bull in a beauty parlor, and yes, it's uncomfortable. But I said I'd take you shopping, so you take as long as you need. I'm good."

She graced him with a smile, making all the awkwardness worthwhile. Five minutes later he added two pretty lavender bags with ribbon handles to the stash in the truck, and let out a long, relieved breath.

His phone rang on the return drive to the ranch. The display read—*Cassie*. "Hey, Brat. Are you home?"

"Yes. Praise the Lord. We pulled in about fifteen minutes ago. If I had to spend one more hour cooped up in a car with Derek Naughton, you'd have to spring me from a jail cell. He yelled the whole time I drove. 'Slow down, speed up, watch out for this, turn your blinker on.' I swear that man was born without a funny bone."

Wade laughed. He'd missed his chatterbox little sister.

"When will you be home? I'm dying to see Lucy again."

"Passing the city limit sign as we speak."

"Great. See you soon."

He disconnected the call and said, "Cassie's home."

CCC

Wade started for the barn after dinner and left his father to man the fort. Garrett and Jo had escaped earlier, claiming work at the big barn. He should have gone with them.

With Cassie's return, female hormones saturated the house. A man couldn't turn around in there without girl squeals and chatter assaulting his ears. From the precise color of their bouquets to which shoes looked best with whose dress, what hairstyle flattered, favorite perfume fragrances, the merits of garters versus some crazy hosiery they called thigh-highs, and stuff he dared not think about for fear the summoned images might sear his brain.

Yeah, the next couple of days would be tough. Tomorrow, Mom and TJ would take Cassie to get her dress fitted—darned if he understood why she didn't buy one that fit in the first place. Mallory planned to work at his office in town. She claimed it was quieter there. Which left Lucy and her doctor's appointment.

So far, her calendar for Friday was empty, not that he expected it to remain that way.

Imperfect Trust

Mom had claimed Saturday morning for what his dad called a remodel—hairdo's, make-up, fingernails, and toenails and then later the wedding and reception. Maybe things would calm down come Sunday.

He blew a raspberry. Not if Garrett and TJ stopped by for brunch before they left for their honeymoon in the Bahamas. Everybody and their brother would likely drop by the house. Again. At least they'd be inside.

He turned his attention to Lancelot, leaning over the horse's stall to stroke the silky muzzle. "What do you think about all this, huh, Lance?"

Lancelot whickered and gave him a gentle head butt.

Wade laughed. "Always nosing around for a treat, aren't you, boy?" He dug in his jacket pocket for the baggie of apple slices he'd prepared ... and felt the bulge of the small box. One more way to safeguard Lucy if he could get her to accept the gift. And wear it. First problem was how to get her alone. He sure didn't want to do this with his family hovering.

Movement caught his attention. Backlit by the sun, a figure walked through the barn's wide door. A silhouette he'd know anywhere.

Lucy paused two steps in and looked around. "Wade?"

He moved away from Lancelot's stall and walked toward her. "What are you doing out here, Lucy? You know you're not supposed to leave the house without one of us with you.

"Rascal walked me over. He said you were here. I just needed to get away from all the wedding craziness for a minute."

A chuckle escaped before he could stop it. "I'm with you on that." He waved at the horse stalls. "You know Lancelot. This one next to him is Ranger, my dad's horse." Wade reached over the rail and extended a slice of apple to the big roan before moving on to the next stall where a big, black stallion snorted and bobbed his head.

"This bad boy belongs to Jo. His name is Malachi." He extended another apple slice.

"He looks a little ... spirited." Lucy remained several steps back.

"He is that." Wade moved on to the next stall. "This little lady might be more your style. Lucy, meet Buffy." The buff-colored horse stuck her head over the rail.

Lucy came closer this time. "She's beautiful."

"Cassie won the calf roping championship with Buffy the year she graduated from high school." He held his hand out, palm up, and the mare took the apple. "She's got some years on her now. Getting fat, too, since Cassie hasn't been here to exercise her. If you want, when your arm is better, I can give you some riding lessons on Buffy. She's as docile as they come. Here." He handed an apple slice to Lucy.

She held the fruit on her palm for Buffy. "Her lips are so soft."

Wade's gut tightened remembering the softness of Lucy's lips. "Come sit with me over here, tiger. I have a favor to ask." He led her to a bale of hale against the wall. "Sit here."

"Okay." She looked up at him, her eyes wide and filled with trust.

He fumbled in his pocket for the small box. "I'd like you to wear these."

She hesitated a moment before she accepted the blue velvet box. She opened it and gasped. "Oh, Wade. They're beautiful." She looked up at him, her eyes lit up with pleasure.

He tore his gaze away from those mesmerizing brown eyes and stared at the earrings—filigree discs rimmed with gold—on the white satin bed. "Practical, too."

"Practical? In what way?"

Now came the tricky part. "Uh, see the little bead in the center of the design?"

She ran her index finger over one of the discs, nodded, and looked up to meet his eyes.

"That's a ...um ... it's a GPS chip."

Lucy's expression underwent a subtle change, one most people wouldn't notice. She excelled at masking her emotions. But he saw the crinkled lines around her eyes smooth out, the curve of her mouth lessen. And the light in her eyes fade from pleasure to understanding.

"So now I'm one of your cows." Her laugh sounded forced.

"No, Lucy. You're much more precious than a horse or a cow. Or even a buffalo," he quipped.

She didn't crack a smile. Setting the box down beside her on the hay bale, she removed the simple gold loops she wore, and threaded the posts of the new earrings through her ear lobes. "They really are gorgeous. Thank you, Wade."

"I got the idea when you ran off to the bus station. I knew if you left, I'd never find you again. This way ..." He shrugged.

Chapter Twenty-Seven

"We're leaving the office for the diner," Wade said into his phone. Just because he thought Fowler's plan to expose Lucy was a ridiculous risk and a complete waste of time didn't mean he would drop his guard. "Alert the others. We'll take the truck. I'll let you know when we head over to Doc Burdette's office."

"Roger. I'll pass the word," Agent Duncan replied.

Wade turned to Mallory. After they restored the servers to their proper place in the office, she'd gone back to working early hours. Said it was quieter in the office. She could get both his work and her writing done faster. "You and Casey have done a great job, Mal. Remind me next week to rethink his pay rate. Boy deserves a raise." They still needed to talk about Mal's plans, but she and Casey had the office well in hand for now.

Mallory gave him an impish grin. "You got that right."

He turned to Lucy. "You ready for some lunch? I'm starving."

Once again, he led the way, pausing on the doorstep to scan the area. When he motioned her forward, Lucy slipped through the door and under his outstretched arm. Together they hurried to his truck. He would normally walk the few blocks to the diner. Not today, though.

"Look," she said once he'd buckled her in. "Isn't that Jonas's truck?"

Imperfect Trust

Sure enough, his little brother's black GMC rolled by and parked in front of the Calico Diner. "He's not part of today's security detail. Wonder what he's doing here?"

Jonas got out, walked around the front of his truck, and opened the door on the passenger side.

A woman leaned into his arms as he helped her hop down from the high seat. Wavy blonde hair spilled down her back.

Wade stared.

"You're at it again," Lucy said.

He glanced over at her. "What?"

"That arch thing you do with one eyebrow. It's arrogant, you know. Your whole family does it. Except Cate."

He frowned, drawing both his eyebrows together. "It's not intentional. I'm just surprised to see Jo out with someone is all."

"Why? You said he's the Romeo of the bunch. And Garrett always talks about the women Jonas dates."

"Jo is a Romeo, but he doesn't date. Not in the daytime, anyway."

Lucy looked thoughtful. "She looks familiar. Do you know her?"

"Name is Shan or Cheryl." He shrugged. "She's the caterer Mom got for the reception. She's a cook at the diner when she's not whipping up frou-frou food for fancy parties."

Wade tried not to appear obvious as he glanced around. No sign of the back-up detail. Good. He wasn't supposed to see them, but he still felt naked, like a newly shorn sheep. He pulled into the slanted parking space next to Jonas's truck and cut the engine. Before he could get out, though, a dusty blue Ford Bronco pulled in on Lucy's side. One of the guys on Lucy's protection detail got out, tipped his hat, and otherwise ignored them.

Good to know another gun was handy.

Inside the diner, Lucy gestured toward the booth where his brother and the blonde sat. "Should we say hi to Jonas and his friend?"

His little brother had a hound dog reputation, so for him to be with a beautiful woman wasn't a surprise. Out in public in the daytime was. And holding her hand in the diner? Every woman over forty in town would have his wedding planned by sundown.

Jo looked up and nodded their way.

Wade dipped his head in return. Folks would think it strange if they ignored each other.

The little blonde corkscrewed around to look over her shoulder, but his brother said something and recaptured her attention.

"No. I don't think he wants our company." Wade guided Lucy to a booth on the opposite side of the diner, one where he could put his back to the wall—like Jo had done—and keep an eye on the front windows and entrance. They passed the agent who'd come in right before them. He sat at the end of the counter, angled to the side so he could survey the entire dining room. Wade ignored him and kept walking.

DeeDee greeted them when they took their seats. She handed out menus and eyed Lucy with suspicion.

"Wade Cameron, you haven't been here in forever. Is this who I think it is?"

Of course, she would remember Lucy from their altercation on the sidewalk outside the diner's front door. DeeDee had come to Jo's rescue after Lucy maced him. Come to think of it, the little cutie sitting with Jo was there, too. Shea. Shea Townsend. Yeah, that was her name. She'd held Jo's head while DeeDee tried to drown him by dousing his eyes and face with water. Another vague memory surfaced. Shea had catered Mom's party last year when Castillo sent his band of guerillas after TJ.

Imperfect Trust

"Lucy, meet the one and only, DeeDee Guthrie, owner and proprietor of this fine establishment. DeeDee, this is Lucy Kiddron, Cassie's friend from Atlanta. She's staying at the ranch."

DeeDee nodded, her smile tight. "Nice to meet you, Lucy. How long you planning to stay?"

Lucy seemed to pick up on DeeDee's reticence, but she offered a genuine smile in return. "Thanks, it's nice to meet you, too. Cassie suggested I come for a visit while I recuperate." She gave a half-shrug with her left shoulder.

DeeDee nodded, eyeing Lucy's sling before she looked at Wade again. "Cassie's home?"

"Yeah. She got in yesterday. So, what do you recommend?" Wade opened the menu, anxious to get back to safer ground.

"Anything from the grill. Whatever you do, stay away from the chili. Shea's not in the kitchen today, which means Willard's cranky. I caught him shaking that can of crushed red pepper like a tomahawk. We do have one of Shea's pies for dessert, though. Coconut cream."

"I saw her come in with my brother."

"Shocked me, too. Not Jonas's usual type, but he knows I've got my eye on him. Shea's a sweet girl. Don't go out much. Now, what can I get for you two?"

Wade looked to Lucy.

"I would love a big, fat cheeseburger with French fries. Water is fine for me."

"I'll have the same but make mine lemonade. I'll see if I can talk her into a slice of that pie." Wade handed the menus over.

Movement through the window drew Wade's eyes to the front. He spotted one of Fowler's men across the street, back propped against the wall of the sheriff's office. Had he not seen the man before, Wade would've pegged him as a local in his western shirt, faded jeans, boots, and dusty Resistol hat. The agent removed a dangling cigarette from his lips, flicked it to the ground, and ground it out under his heel.

Wade chuckled. James would have the man's hide if he found cigarette butts on his sidewalk.

Lucy wanted to talk about the wedding while they waited for their food, about the guests in particular. Was she nervous?

After their burgers arrived, they chatted about his run-in with the bison herd a few weeks before and some of the places he'd seen during his time in the service. She told him about her one and only trip to DEFCON, the annual hackers' conference held in Las Vegas, and her stint at Georgia Tech as a teen.

When she gave up on her fries and pushed the plate away, Wade asked, "Will you share a piece of that coconut pie with me? DeeDee's slices are more like slabs, so one is too much."

She grinned. "I make it a rule to never turn down pie of any kind. Cake either, for that matter."

That's twice now he'd seen those dimples. He loved her lighthearted side. It was like her voice borrowed some of the sunshine streaming in through the windows and made the world inside the diner brighter.

After they finished off the pie, Lucy pulled some bills from her jeans pocket.

"Not happening, tiger. You're not paying."

She looked like she might argue but then smiled and put her money away. "Thank you."

"My pleasure. You ready to see the new sawbones?"

"Yes." One word and the fun side disappeared.

He couldn't blame her. Sick, injured, or vulnerable gave him hives. She wanted to trust him. That had to count for something.

CCC

"Well, Lucy. I agree with your orthopedist back in Atlanta," Dr. Wilkes said. "You need surgery if you ever hope to regain full use of your left arm. If you do nothing ..." He opened his hands and shrugged.

Lucy slumped in the comfortable armchair in Doc Burdette's office. Her lungs deflated like a balloon with a slow leak. She'd known the prognosis wasn't good and hadn't expected to hear different, and yet the news crushed her.

Dr. Charlie Wilkes, Doc Burdette's nephew, was a good-looking man. Tall, slender build, mid-thirties. He reached for a brochure on his desk and then moved his chair around to sit beside her. "Let me show you."

On her other side, Wade scooted his chair closer and draped his arm along the back of her chair, their knees touching.

"Dr. Beaumont sent the x-rays and scan he took in Atlanta along with his case notes. You have what we call traumatic anterior instability. Look at this illustration." He flipped to an anatomical schematic of an upper torso.

"The shoulder is a ball and socket joint and has more flexibility and movement than any other joint in the body. This means it also experiences more stress." He tapped the drawing with a pencil. "The socket, or glenoid, is concave like a golf tee."

The pencil moved. "The ball at the upper end of the arm bone, the humerus, is called the humeral head. It fits precisely in the center of the tee." Finished with the brochure, he tossed it back on the desk, balled one hand up, and cupped it with his other hand. "The concavity, the rotator cuff, the fibrous glenoid labrum, and several ligaments all help keep the shoulder stable. You following me?"

Lucy nodded.

"Injuries like yours occur when the ligaments and the labrum at the lower front part of the shoulder are stretched or torn by hyper-extending the arm outward—such as you described with your first injury. Unfortunately, they don't heal well on their own, which leaves the shoulder susceptible to additional dislocations."

She nodded, recalling the takedown that had ended her competitions. "So, surgery, huh?"

"Yes. Soon as possible. The longer you wait, the more scar tissue will build, and that can hamper rehabilitation." He pulled out his iPhone and opened his calendar. "I think I can get an OR room at Regional for a week from Monday. Let me confirm, and I'll get back to you."

Ten days. Oh wow.

"How long will she be in the hospital, Dr. Wilkes?" Wade leaned forward in his chair, almost shielding her with his body.

"If we do surgery on Tuesday, she should be out by Friday, barring complications. Uncle Wilton can follow her progress to ensure the wound heals properly, but I'll want to see her in Idaho Falls two weeks post op, and again at six weeks."

"Are you aware of the special circumstances surrounding Lucy's situation? Someone will have to stay with her twenty-four-seven. Someone who can protect her."

"I understand. My uncle and Sheriff Evers filled me in. Might I assume that person will be you?"

Wade nodded.

"All right. I'll make whatever arrangements are necessary to ensure her name stays out of the computers, and I'll clear the way for you to remain with her."

She wanted to laugh and cry—a sure sign hysteria was creeping in. "I don't think anonymity is an issue any longer." She exchanged a look with Wade. "Operation Mousetrap, Phase Two."

His fingers curled around the back of her neck in a gentle squeeze. For such a big man, he had a soft touch. "I'm with you on this, tiger. Argault will have to go through me and several more to get to you."

Imperfect Trust

She took a deep breath and turned back to the doctor. "I have insurance. Your office person will need to contact them for whatever kinds of approvals are needed."

Dr. Wilkes took her hand and held it. He had a kind smile. "I'll have Renee, my insurance manager, call you with the details. She can answer all your questions and expedite the approval process."

Beside her, Wade fidgeted. She leaned into him and stifled a smile, sensing his possessive nature rising. He might object to the doctor's bedside manner—or in this case, chair side—but she trusted Dr. Wilkes. Good thing, since she would soon be at his mercy. "Okay. Let the fun begin."

She thanked the doctor, shook his hand, and followed Wade to the front door.

"Let me take a look around before we go out."

He was so protective. All of them were. Would she ever get used to it?

"Okay, let's go. Remember, stay on my right side."

His wounds had healed, and he no longer needed the sling, but his injured shoulder still lacked strength and flexibility. Cassie had agreed to work with him on his physical therapy exercises, but in the meanwhile, he wore the discreet gun holster on his left side.

Garrett claimed Wade was equally proficient with a gun in either hand.

She tucked her fingers in the crook of his right arm and tried to match his stride. They'd parked in the middle of Doc's patient parking lot, in the only available space at the time. Now, his truck was the only vehicle left.

"Should have brought the truck to the door for you," he grumbled.

"Look, there's Jonas." She pointed down the street. "They had a long lunch."

Wade looked to where Jonas helped the same blonde from the diner into his truck.

"You still look surprised," she added, hoping he'd say more.

"I am." He didn't elaborate but urged Lucy forward again.

A dirty, older model pickup turned onto the street in front of Doc's office. The noise growling from the engine sounded like a death rattle.

Wade noticed it, too, and picked up their pace.

She grabbed her arm and held it close when he forced her into a jog. "Wade, slow down."

He increased their pace again instead. "Sorry. Just a few more steps. We have no cover out here."

She clenched her teeth. Dr. Wilkes had poked and prodded until she ached. The running made it worse. "Wade, I can't—"

Booom. The front end of the ratty old jalopy exploded in a fireball.

Imperfect Trust

Chapter Twenty-Eight

Wade knew it was too late, even as instinct took over. Years of training and multiple tours in 'do or die' Afghanistan had heightened his reflexes to the point he doubted he'd ever lose them. He kicked Lucy's legs out from under her, took her to the ground, and covered her body with his before she could react. "Are you hit?"

From the way she pummeled and pushed at his chest, he didn't think so, but he wouldn't move off her. Not yet. She could handle his weight a little longer. Until the area was secure. He ignored the pain in his shoulder from the impact of hitting the ground. His gunshot wound might be a shiny pink scar now, but he was still far from a hundred percent.

Heart pounding faster than a woodpecker on a sugar rush, he lifted his head and looked around.

Half a block down the street, the worn out old clunker that made his radar twitch came to rest against the curb. The flames he'd seen had died down, but smoke billowed from underneath the carriage. Steam escaped in hisses and spurts from under the hood. The driver—eighty if he was a day—was cussing up a storm, and then the old coot hauled off and kicked one of the tires, hands flapping all the while.

Beyond the truck, four men raced down the street in a diamond formation. They converged on the vehicle with guns drawn. Fowler's men. Two of them stopped at the truck, while the other two continued on to where he and Lucy lay sprawled on the ground.

Imperfect Trust

Stupid, stupid plan. It didn't matter the others thought it could work. He'd known it wouldn't. Lucy was his responsibility. He knew better. Had they been in a real war zone, military or urban, he and Lucy would both be dead.

Wade didn't wait for the agents. He scooped Lucy up in his arms and ran with her to his truck. Once he had her inside, safe and buckled in, his knees threatened to give way. The adrenalin drop left him weak and trembling. His shoulder throbbed. And his belly threatened to evict the cheeseburger he'd eaten for lunch.

He gripped the steering wheel and tried to get control of his anger. "We're done with Fowler's idiocy."

Lucy didn't say a word.

Calmer now, he turned and looked at her, taking in the big brown eyes wide with pain and fear. He took her head between his hands and searched every inch of her face.

A police cruiser pulled up behind the disabled truck. James got out, spoke with the old man for a few seconds, and then headed Wade's way. "Judd was trying to nurse his old rattletrap to the auto repair shop before it flamed out. Looks like he didn't make it."

Wade released Lucy and nodded without speaking. He'd already figured out what happened.

One of Fowler's men joined them. "I think our cover is blown."

James leaned down on Wade's open window. "You okay, Lucy?"

She nodded, still quiet.

Wade caressed her cheek one more time. "She's fine. Agent Duncan, tell whoever's lead to roll now. We're going home." He cranked the engine and pulled the gearshift into drive but kept his foot on the brake. "And you can let Fowler know we're done with his plan."

Friday was quiet. Other than a drive into town so Lucy could buy a wedding present—she insisted—Wade kept her inside.

He smiled, recalling her snippy remarks about his 'overbearing, over-protective, macho, arrogant, cowboy attitude.' But she'd gone along with his demands.

Saturday, the day of the wedding, dawned clear, sunny, and perfect. Wade stood guard outside Fancy's Salon while the women got their hair and nails done. When they left for the church later that afternoon, he and Jonas sandwiched Lucy between them. It was the first time he could recall carrying a gun into church.

The ceremony went as planned, thanks in part to TJ's insistence on minimal fuss. James stood as the only attendant for both bride and groom, and all he did was hand over the rings. A single moment of shock came when his dad walked TJ down the aisle. Tears trickled down his leathery cheeks and had everyone reaching for tissues.

Wade had never seen his father cry. Cody Cameron had reputation as a man who'd grown up hard and fast and had little tolerance for fools. Learning his old man had a soft spot was unsettling.

Even the reception went off without a hitch, much to everyone's surprise. Wade was sure Argault would make his move then. They all expected it, which was why thirty-six armed men not on the invitation list mixed with the more than two hundred people who swarmed the house and the grounds. It didn't hurt that most of their guests, men and women alike, had been alerted to the situation and carried their own concealed weapons.

All to no purpose.

Lucy described it best—anticlimactic. They'd been so sure, so tense and ready, like a string of cherry bombs waiting for a match.

Wade laughed.

She was so smart. Scared half out of her wits yet braver than most of the soldiers he'd known. The lavender dress she'd worn to the wedding hugged her figure. It revealed nothing, but promised everything. Then she'd changed after they got home, traded the sexy lavender for a cool mint green dress that swirled around her knees. Put her hair up in a fancy knot and left the sling off. "To confuse Argault, if he's watching," she'd confided. "And because it's time I had a little fun." She'd flashed those sassy dimples at him.

He got the first dance with her but couldn't get close after that. A line of hopeful cowboys dogged her and waited for their chance to spin Lucy around the floor. He'd kept watch over her from across the room, not allowing her to get too far away, and never out of his sight.

When the last dance was announced, she'd refused three different guys and made her way to his side. "Dance with me?" She held her arm out.

"Oh, yeah." At last, the sparkplugs in his brain fired. He set his drink on a nearby table, pulled Lucy into his arms, and thanked the band for choosing a slow, dreamy song.

Sunday came and went. Garrett and TJ left for their honeymoon mid-afternoon while friends and neighbors lingered. It had to be well past ten that night before the last well-wishers departed.

Wade carried the tray Lucy had filled with dirty glasses into the kitchen, and set them on the counter.

"Cleanup is over for now," his mom said and shooed him away. "Roseanna's two nieces will be here tomorrow to help with this mess."

"Yes, ma'am." He saluted and went to tell Lucy.

He found her stuffing napkins and other trash into a bag. "Hey, Mom says work's over for today. You look tired, tiger. Why don't you head for bed?"

"Are you?"

Spunky. And always concerned about others. "Soon as I take a final spin around the house and make sure we're locked up tight."

She set the garbage bag aside and smiled. "I am tired. Good night, Wade."

He kissed her forehead and sent her on her way, before starting his security check. Midnight had come and gone by the time he made it to his bed.

The sounds of Rascal Flatts jarred Wade awake sometime later. *Life is a Highway*, the ringtone he'd assigned to their foreman, blared in the quiet. He fumbled for his cell phone and noted the time on his bedside clock—4:45 a.m.

Dread made his gut clench. Good seldom came from calls in the middle of the night. "Yeah, Rascal?"

"Wade, we need you up to the big barn, quick." The foreman's rusty voice sounded troubled. "We got a fire."

He reached for the lamp, already on his feet. "On my way."

"I called the sheriff's office. They're notifying the fire department. I just spoke with Cody. Still need to get Jonas."

"I'll tell Jonas. We're on our way."

A million thoughts sped through Wade's mind as he banged on his brother's bedroom door. Five minutes to reach the barn. Fifteen minutes minimum before the volunteer firefighters could muster. Six pregnant mares in the stable, two of them days from foaling. Did Rascal get them out? What started the fire?

A premonition made the hairs on his arms stand on end. Maybe the better question was who started it.

Imperfect Trust

He made quick work of dressing and was pulling on his boots when heavy footsteps clomped past his door and down the stairs. Dad. No doubt, Mom was awake, too. And Lucy. She'd hear the ruckus and be worried.

His hands stilled. He couldn't leave her here alone, and he sure couldn't take her with him. He pulled his cell phone out and dialed the head of Lucy's detail.

"Duncan," the agent answered on the first ring. "Heard about the fire. On my way."

"Thanks." Relieved, Wade hung up and dug through his closet for the big bore Smith & Wesson .460. If Argault made an appearance, Wade wanted something that would leave a big hole.

Lucy waited at the bottom of the stairs, wrapped in a thick, terrycloth robe. "What's going on?"

Her right hand was stuffed in the pocket of the robe. From the bulge, he guessed she carried the small handgun he'd given her. "Fire at the big barn. Agent Duncan will stay with you while we sort it out." He smoothed the hair away from her face. "Don't worry."

Jonas clattered down the stairs, still buttoning his shirt.

"You boys coming?" His dad appeared in the kitchen door, a shotgun cradled in one arm.

Boots pounded on the front steps, right before a fist hammered on the door.

Jonas looked through the sidelights, saw it was Duncan, and opened the door for him.

Wade caught the agent's arm when he entered. "Lucy stays put. No one but family or one of your men comes in. Understand?"

"I know my job, Cameron. Now, go do yours." Duncan set a rifle down in the corner by the door, took his jacket off, and hung it on the coat rack. He wore a dual shoulder holster with a handgun under each armpit.

"Let's go," Dad yelled.

Wade went to Lucy again and brushed her cheek with his one finger. So soft. He loved touching her skin. "Do what Duncan says."

She nodded. "Be careful."

※

By Tuesday morning, Wade wanted to tear someone's head off. The barn fire, as it turned out, did little damage. It was catching the horses that took so long. Someone had used wire cutters to open up a twenty-yard swath of fence, and then ran a 4x4 around the lower pasture to stampede the horses through the break.

Rascal and five of the hands mended the fence while Wade, his dad, brothers, and a dozen other hands went after the runaways. But it was the dead horse, one of his dad's wild mustangs, found this morning out in Dice Canyon that couldn't be forgiven. The mare had a .22 caliber gunshot in its chest and had taken a long time to die.

Wade turned Lancelot loose in the corral. The animal's graceful movements helped soothe some of the fury that raged inside him.

His father was heartsick. The numbers of wild horses were dwindling, which was why he'd established the refuge. So the mustangs could roam free and safe.

What kind of deranged mind would shoot a horse and leave it to suffer?

A psychopath, that's what kind. Argault was a coldblooded killer. He wouldn't blink at slaughtering a horse.

And yet, something didn't fit.

※

When Fowler entered, Wade crossed his arms over his chest, in no mood for another of the agent's wild ideas.

"I have a plan," Fowler announced.

Imperfect Trust

Wade clenched his teeth at Fowler's words. Around the room, the others rolled their eyes.

"We use the cabin in the hills. It's about five miles north of here. I think we can lure Argault there."

Back to that? Kevin Fowler had to be the most arrogant man in the world. When he set a goal, he stuck to it, regardless of the consequences and no matter the collateral damage.

"We're stretched too thin," James said. "How do you propose we maintain security around Wade's office, the ranch, the barn, keep an eye on Lucy and the rest of the family, plus the animals and property, and add a new location miles from here?"

"We make a show of moving Lucy there. Let it be known she's distanced herself from the Camerons. I'll yank two men off her protection detail like we're cutting back on manpower, but they'll go covert. Take up sniper positions, along with six more men I'm bringing in. The other two agents will stay with her at the cabin."

Wade stared. How had this man risen to a leadership position within the government?

"That's lame, Fowler, even for you." Jonas made a sound of disgust.

A thundercloud settled over his dad's face. "We're not sending Lucy away."

James closed his eyes and rubbed his temple, while Duncan and another of the guards hung their heads.

Satisfied they were on his side this time, Wade let his shoulders relax. "Not happening."

"Wait," Lucy said from her seat on the sofa. "Where is this cabin?"

His stomach turned a flip. "No, no, no, no, no." He started her way. "I told you—"

Lucy raised her hand in the age-old stop gesture. "No, I told you Jensen Argault wouldn't play your game. Now, we do this my way. I need a piece of paper and a pen." She got up and headed for the dining room.

Wade followed with the others trailing behind him.

"This do?" Jonas handed Lucy a handful of what looked like paper from the printer in Mom's office.

James offered a pen from his pocket.

"Thanks." Lucy settled into a chair at the table. Putting pen to paper, she drew a star in the middle and added a small circle around it. A heavy line led away from the star. Using the pen tip as a pointer, she said, "This is the ranch house, and this is the drive. Where is the barn located? The one that burned?"

Wade reached over her shoulder and pointed at a spot off to one side.

She marked it. "And the fence he cut? The dead horse?"

He pointed at two locations and she drew more marks.

"Now, where is Agent Fowler's cabin in the woods?"

Taking the pen from her, Wade drew a couple of long squiggly lines and a bunch of inverted Vs on the far side of the barn. "Here's the river and these are the foothills. It's heavily wooded through here. The line shack is about here." He drew a square in the midst of the drawn trees. "We use it when bad weather catches us. Spring thunderstorms can be unpredictable."

The group gathered closer, some sitting while others leaned over the table, each one focused on Lucy's drawing.

She held up an index finger. "Everyone in town is aware of the situation with Argault, but no one has seen him. Therefore, we can assume he is not staying in town."

A second finger went up. "James alerted the law enforcement personnel in nearby towns, but they haven't seen him either. For the purposes of this exercise, I believe we can cross off any commercial lodging within a hundred mile radius. That doesn't rule out barns or abandoned buildings, but my money says he's set up camp in the woods somewhere around here. Out of the way so no one stumbles upon him."

"Doesn't fit the profiler's sketch," Fowler argued. "He's city born, well educated, and a technology genius. Not the outdoors type."

"Your profilers are wrong. Your people didn't do their homework. Remember I told you Jensen was a wilderness guide all through college. He led rock climbing expeditions in the North Georgia Mountains. It's how he earned extra money. Scholarships don't cover all living expenses."

Seconds ticked by in silence until Wade spoke up. "What are you suggesting, Lucy?"

"Fire here, discovered around 4:30 this morning. Fence cut here, found around 6:00 a.m." She used the pen as a pointer again. "And here's where your men found the horse this morning. Ramona placed the time of death around 10:00 a.m. yesterday. She estimates it took an hour, maybe two before it bled out, which means we have to figure the horse was shot between 8:00 and 9:00 a.m."

She was creating a storyboard, a timeline. Smart girl. James nodded.

Lucy frowned and tapped the pen over the last spot. "What's the distance from the barn to the canyon? Is it accessible by SUV?"

His dad shook his head. "Twenty-six miles as the crow flies, longer since there are arroyos to dodge. Vehicles muck up the ranges and scare the horses. I never intended roads. You can drive to the rim of the canyon, but it's too far for a rifle. A man would have to trek another four or five miles by horseback or on foot to reach a shooting distance."

One by one, the light bulb came on for the men gathered around the table. Twenty-six miles cross-country from the breeding barn to the canyon lip where the dead horse was found, and another twenty-six miles back. Two hours minimum for an all-terrain vehicle. More like three if you factor in travel at night with no road to follow. Add another two to three hours to walk or ride into the canyon.

"The timing is wrong," Jonas said. "He couldn't set the fire, cut the fence, stampede the horses here, and get to the canyon to shoot the mustang all on his timeline. What bothers me more, though, is how did he get close enough to set the fire? How did he know when to do it?" Jonas turned to look at Wade. "Why didn't the alarms go off? And why isn't there anything on the security cameras?"

Silence settled over the group.

"The house is compromised," Lucy whispered. Her pupils were huge.

"Gentlemen, I suggest we adjourn to another location," Fowler said.

"I know a place. Get your trucks and follow me." Wade took Lucy's arm. "You'll ride with me."

Jonas clamped a hand on Wade's shoulder. "Think I'll hang out here with Mom, Mal, and Cass. You can brief me later."

Wade nodded.

"Thanks, Jo. Keep your gun and cell phone handy. We won't go far." Just enough so Argault, who'd tampered with the security system, could no longer eavesdrop on their plans.

The picnic area he had in mind was less than ten minutes away by truck. Wade and his brothers used to sneak off to fish and swim in the river there before the state parks system claimed it.

They took three trucks. Fifteen minutes later, Lucy sat at a picnic table with the men crowded around her. The pseudo map she'd drawn now sported a large tic-tac-toe box. Using her pen, she tapped each square and explained how a grid-by-grid search would either locate Argault or flush him toward a route

Imperfect Trust

of their choosing—in this case, Fowler's little cabin in the woods.

"We need men who know the land around here, trackers who can spot signs of recent human activity," she said.

"Two of my men are excellent trackers," Fowler said. "They don't know the area, but can pair up with one of the locals." Fowler seemed to have bought into her idea.

"All the ranch hands grew up around here. They all know how to track." His dad looked over at Wade. "Might help to have a couple of Joseph Acaraho's grandsons."

"Who?" James asked.

"I forget you didn't grow up around here," Wade said. "Joseph's the old Shoshone who lives in the mountains near Morning Glory Pass. He must be ninety by now. With his help, we can clear the grids in no time."

"Give me your phone, son."

Chapter Twenty-Nine

"No, Lucy. It's a bad idea." Wade scrubbed a hand through his short hair. Why'd she have to become fearless now?

After they met in the park yesterday, they'd agreed to scour the area based on Lucy's grid. Starting out at daybreak that morning and with help from six of Joseph Acaraho's grandsons, they launched a twenty-four man operation that cleared six of the nine sectors by two in the afternoon. In the seventh sector, they hit pay dirt—a candy wrapper, the remains of a fire pit, and a faint trail of disturbed foliage, the kind made by two-legged animals. They'd surprised their quarry. Gotten too close too fast and left him no time to hide his presence. And if Argault was as good as Wade had come to believe, they might not catch him before he pulled another disappearing act.

Which is why Lucy came up with her screwball plan to dangle herself in front of him. A last ditch effort to draw out the monster.

Who was he fooling? Lucy wasn't fearless, but she did have more courage than anyone he knew. And more than was prudent. Argault would be more dangerous than ever. Cornered prey became desperate and took more risks.

Wade couldn't believe he was considering her idea.

"You said yourself there are fifty different ways off the mountain," Lucy added. "Let's give him a reason to hang around. If he sees me, it might be enough to flip his crazy switch. But if he gets away now …"

She didn't have to turn her pleading eyes his way to make

Imperfect Trust

him understand. Argault was like a cat with more than his fair share of lives. Add in the patience of a Tibetan monk and years might pass before he showed his face again. And he would. Revenge was important to psychopaths.

"Please, Wade. I don't want to look over my shoulder for the rest of my life. Let's end this."

Argault was meticulous, cold, and calculating. He would leave no room for chance. But he'd also been thwarted in every attempt to get to Lucy. Would seeing her here on the mountain be enough? "It's too dangerous."

She took his hand. "You've kept me safe this far. And it's only a possibility. He might choose caution."

They'd taken the trucks as far as they could, all the way to the foothills. From there, travel was by horse or on foot.

Over the ridge, on the western side, logging trails riddled the mountain. They'd found no sign of the shooter's black SUV in any of the cleared sectors. No tire tracks either. In all likelihood, Argault had stashed it on the far side and was making a run for it. He was too smart to be herded into a trap.

The warrior in Wade told him Argault would cut his losses and run. It's what he would do. Live to fight another day. But his gut said otherwise. He suspected Lucy's did, too. "You think he'll come after you. Why?"

"Logic is black and white. One plus one equals two. Two plus two equals four. But emotion doesn't follow logic's rules and right now Jensen Argault isn't thinking with his brain."

"So it's personal. Because you bested him back in Atlanta?"

She shook her head. "No. It goes back farther than the drug bust. We were in college together. I was a skinny, too young freshman, and he was the resident genius in a graduate program. I've always been too smart-mouthed for my own good." Regret dimmed her brown eyes.

"What happened?"

She did her one-armed shrug. "He made a presentation to the school and his advisory team. The next big breakthrough in computer technology, except I pointed out the flaws in his logic. A sixteen-year-old made him look like a fool in front of everyone. My life was a nightmare until he left several months later. Without his degree."

Ego. The male curse. Bruise it and common sense bailed. How well he knew.

The bad feeling that had nagged at him all day was still there. With only a few hours of daylight left, they'd have to move fast. "If we do this, you follow my orders. What I say, when I say. No questions. No arguments."

"Okay."

CCC

"Get inside." Wade pushed Lucy ahead of him into the cabin and closed the door against the rain. How had everything turned upside down so fast?

"Didn't anyone check the weather report?" she asked, wiping raindrops from her face.

She'd remained mostly dry, unlike him and the rest of the men. He'd thrown his poncho over her when they left the horses behind an hour ago.

"I told you, we use this shack when bad weather pops up. Squalls in the mountains aren't unusual in any season, but they seem to happen more often during this time of year. Can't blame the meteorologist."

But he could blame himself for not factoring in the possibility. They'd almost reached the cabin when the thunder started and the sky opened up. Slippery pine needles, mud, and fading daylight made descent an impossible task, especially given Lucy's one-armed limitations. So, here they sat, like fish in a barrel.

"Dad remembers this place from when he was little. He and Rascal rebuilt it about forty years ago, all but the fireplace.

Imperfect Trust

That's the only original part left. They think it dates back to before the turn of the century." Wade slapped a hand against the stone surround. "I've never seen a chimney this sturdy."

Ash filled the grate and soot blackened the cook pit—the last occupant hadn't bothered to clean it for the next visitor—but the thick granite slabs and smooth mortar fill looked strong enough to stand another century.

Lucy wandered around the one-room cabin. She examined the stone fireplace with the gridiron cook bar before moving on to the narrow cot in the corner and what passed for a kitchen. She trailed her fingers over the shallow enamel basin that served as a sink and opened the single cabinet where dusty canned goods were stacked. Picking one up, she brushed the label. "Peaches. I don't suppose you were a Boy Scout?"

"What?"

"You know, be prepared. Don't all boy scouts carry one of those gadget knives with a hidden can opener?"

He grinned and reached for the leather scabbard strapped to his leg. "You mean something like this?" The seven-inch KA-BAR knife, serrated on one side, razor-sharp on the other, slid free with a soft scrape. "I've opened many a can of beans with this."

Her eyes grew impossibly wide. She set the can of peaches back on the shelf and dusted her hands.

Wade found a hammer and a jar of rusty nails, and spent the next hour boarding up the two front windows from the inside. He also fashioned two block latches and nailed them to the doorframe. A deterrent. An early warning system, too.

The dense forest and atmospheric disturbance played havoc with cell reception. Communication with the others was spotty. Even so, his cell phone rang.

"Hey, James. We made it to the cabin and got it locked up."

Lucy inched closer to listen.

"... trouble." James's voice crackled over the line. "Argault ... two of our ..."

Sporadic static garbled the transmission, making it difficult to interpret what James was saying, but enough came through. Wade clenched his fingers around the thin phone. He met Lucy's eyes and saw her concern. "How bad?" he asked.

"One of Fowler's men ... knife ... thigh. The other ... head wound .... Both are okay. I sent Joseph's boys down with them."

"How did he get close enough to use a knife? Did you pick up his trail?"

"... minimal visibility. Maybe five yards. I think he ... PEC-Fours ..."

Night vision. Not good. Argault could see them, but they wouldn't see him.

Lucy mouthed a question. *What*?

"Hold on. Lucy's hearing this." He turned to her. "PEC-Fours. Night vision scopes. They let you see in the dark."

Her expression didn't change. Tough girl. She might be afraid, but she wouldn't freak.

"What's your twenty?" Given the change in circumstances, Wade was grateful James had taken charge of their mission. The man had more hot zone experience than anyone except maybe Garrett. That ought to count for something.

The rain slowed to a heavy drizzle. James's voice came through the line clearer now. "I split the men into three groups—five hundred yards south, southeast, and southwest of your position. You and Lucy sit tight and stay alert while we sweep the area."

"Roger."

Wade wished the rain would start up again. Night vision let you see in the dark, but didn't work so well in a downpour. The bad feeling he'd tried to ignore all day cranked up a notch.

Imperfect Trust

Half an hour later, the rain had stopped altogether, but a dense fog rolled in. Visibility dropped to mere inches. A plus for them. Scopes didn't work in fog either.

Wade studied the pitiful assets he'd amassed. Two dozen cans of beans and peaches that could be used as projectiles, a cast iron pot heavy enough to crack a man's head, and a walking stick carved from a thick knob of oak. Other than the wooden bed frame and rickety table and chairs, he had nothing to barricade the door. Heck, the whole cabin looked like one good hit with a shoulder would topple it over.

"Here." Lucy pulled a small canister from her jacket pocket and added it to the pile.

He chuckled but wouldn't discount the little can of Mace. She'd felled Jonas with it. Would've dropped him too, but for the sunglasses that protected his eyes. "You hang onto that, tiger."

Lucy slipped the can into her pocket again. She also had her gun and a spare magazine.

He patted his knife and the Smith & Wesson and felt for the extra ammo in his utility vest. The status quo had shifted. The hunter became the hunted. But not for long.

Wade closed the shabby curtains over the two windows, and glanced at his wristwatch. What little light remained would soon disappear. If Argault came for Lucy, it wouldn't be to kidnap her this time. If he came, it would be soon. Attack while the fog obscured his trail. Get in and get out while the fog obscured everything.

Kneeling by the fireplace, he pulled a penlight from one of the many pockets of his cargo pants. With a hand braced against the stone, he leaned in, and pointed the light up the flue. Dirty, but clear enough for their needs.

"What's the bar for?" Lucy pointed at the iron crosspiece that spanned the width of the fireplace.

"See this hook? Old timers used to hang cast iron pots over the fire." He reached in and yanked on the bar. Anchored deep, it didn't budge.

He motioned Lucy closer. "Come here."

"Uh-uh. You're all sooty."

"Listen, tiger. Argault knows you're in here. He's coming, and we can't leave. I want you to hide. In here." He pointed up the chimney.

She shook her head. "I'm not hiding while you play decoy. And I'm not climbing up there." Her button nose wrinkled with a look of disgust.

"Knowing you're safe gives me an edge. I can confront him on my terms. I can't do that if my attention is divided."

"No. I won't do it."

"Lucy, you said you trusted me. You agreed to do as I say. Please. We don't have a lot of time." He held his hand out and waited. He understood how her mind worked now. She'd evaluate what he said, size up the risk, and draw the same conclusion he had.

She slumped to her knees. "Ugh. What do I do?"

"Wiggle in here." He pointed at the fire pit. "Then push up to your feet and climb up on the crossbar. There's a shelf right above the fire pit where you can stand. It's high enough your feet won't show."

"What if he looks up the chimney?"

"Use your gun and blow his head off."

She wasn't shocked. "I can do that."

He took her hand and drew her closer. "Take a look. You'll fit."

"He'll see the ashes are disturbed." She sat on her bottom and scooted into the fire place.

"I'll fix them once you're settled."

A string of seconds passed before she started working her way into an upright position. "It stinks."

Imperfect Trust

Wade coaxed her on. "You're doing great. Step up on the bar. That's it. Now, brace your hands against the chimney wall for balance."

"Ugh, I hate this. It feels ... awful." Her feet shifted on the narrow bar, and then steadied.

"You'll get used to it. It won't be for long. Move your feet until you find the niche. It's about six inches higher than the bar."

One foot lifted. "Found it."

"Okay, the other foot. Lean against the wall. Use it for support. Remember, once you're in place, you can't move or speak."

"Ohhhh, this is awful. I can't breathe in here."

"Good. You won't make any noise then."

"Ha-ha. Very funny." She shifted her feet. Moved them again. "Okay. I guess this is as good as it gets."

"Can you get to your gun?"

"Yeah. No problem."

"Okay. I'm going to stir up the ashes and slip outside. Don't make a peep until James or I come for you."

Wade texted James to tell him his plan, silenced his phone, and pocketed it. Next, he scooped a handful of the fine gray residue from the fire pit and rubbed the ashes over his face, arms, and clothes, repeating the process until he looked like a ghost. Ash wouldn't wash away from a little rain. You had to scrub it off. He used the straw broom by the fireplace to sweep the hearth, and then made his way to the door. "I'm going out now, Lucy," Wade called. "Be quiet and don't move around."

With that, he raised the wooden latches and slipped out to become one with the mist.

A dense thicket stood near the side of the cabin. He made his way there, the wet ground aiding his need for silence. Fifteen steps along and all he could see of the structure was a dim outline. Hidden among the trees and saplings, he settled down to wait.

Rain dripped from the leaves overhead and trickled down his neck. By his best estimate, thirty minutes passed before movement off to his right drew his eye. A ripple only. And then another. The vague shape of a man stepped from the shadows. His dark clothing, invisible in the shadows, stood out in stark contrast against the gray fog when he left the shelter of the trees.

Wade's men all wore camo or khaki.

Step by slow step, the figure emerged from the woods, his head in constant motion, a handgun led the way.

Inch by inch, Wade eased out of the thicket and worked his way around behind the man. Fowler wanted Argault alive, but Wade had no qualms about putting down a rabid dog, if necessary.

The man moved faster now, on a direct line for the cabin door.

Wade picked up a small pebble and threw it wide left. Lucy was well hidden, but he didn't want the murdering scum anywhere near her.

Argault whirled, his gun tracking the sound. Spooked, he retreated back the way he'd come—right into Wade's path.

Wait for it.

Five feet separated them, and Argault still hadn't seen him.

Wade tucked the .409 in his hip holster. Three feet. Every muscle tensed. Closer. A quick lunge. He wrapped his arm around the killer's neck and grabbed for the gun.

They fell to ground, rolled in the mud and leaves, and grappled for control of the weapon. Argault moved like he'd learned to fight in a gym. Wade had grown up on a ranch where only the strong survived. And tempered in the mountains and deserts of Afghanistan where survival didn't have rules. He fought to win. It didn't hurt to have a height and weight advantage, either. During one of the wild rolls in the slop, he slammed Argault's hand against a rock and the gun flew away, lost in the fog.

Frantic, Argault clawed at the arm squeezing his windpipe.

Wade let go.

The unexpected movement threw Argault off balance.

Wade whipped around and rammed his knee into the smaller man's gut.

Argault collapsed, retched once, and rolled face down. A second later, he sprang at Wade, a rock in his hand.

Searing pain struck Wade's temple. He stumbled back but didn't go down. Snatching his pistol from the holster, he thumbed off the safety ... but Argault had disappeared. No, *wait*! There.

He took aim and fired.

Argault yelped and grabbed his left arm but didn't stop.

Wade ran after him. So close.

Boots pounded the ground. Voices called out, muffled by the fog and heavy air. Wade couldn't gauge their location. He took aim at the fleeing figure, and then thought better of it. He dared not take the shot, not and risk hitting one of his men. He lowered his weapon as his quarry disappeared and reappeared through the forest.

Argault looked right and then veered left around a bog, and doubled back toward the cabin.

"No." The denial left a sick feeling in Wade's gut. He brought his gun up again. Tracked Argault's movements. Fired. And missed.

More shouts erupted from the woods.

Wade lowered his gun and took off running. His men were too close.

Argault reached the front of the cabin, slowing enough to jab an elbow between the slats. Glass tinkled.

"No." Wade upped his speed, heart pounding.

Argault pulled something from a pocket, poked it through the broken window and then took off again.

"No." Wade screamed this time. He'd never reach her in time.

KABOOM.

The concussion lifted Wade and threw him several feet. His back hit the ground. Air whooshed from his lungs. A shower of splinters and dirt fell over the world, along with an eerie silence.

Please no, please no, please no. The silent screams drowned out the ringing in his head.

James knelt at his side. His lips moved, but no sound emerged.

Wade stared at the skeletal remains of the cabin. His dad had often claimed a strong wind would knock the place down. He was right. The framework remained. Mostly. There were gaping holes where the door and windows used to be, and the rear wall had collapsed, but the chimney remained.

It might stand for another century.

He watched in horror as the chimney swayed and then toppled over.

"Lucy," Wade screamed and somehow got to his feet.

"Hold on." James grabbed his arm. "It's not safe."

"Lucy ... the chimney." He staggered forward, ears still ringing, but he could hear James calling his name from a mile away. "A stun grenade. Not a frag. I have to get her."

Wade stumbled to the fallen chimney, still intact despite its age and the blast. A pair of small brown boots kicked and writhed in the opening.

"Derek," James yelled.

A dozen men entered the clearing, guns at the ready.

"Take your team and go after Argault." He pointed toward the path Lucy's nemesis had taken.

"Roger." Derek and six men set off at a run.

"Larry, Bob, over here," James waved to some of his men. "Wade, sit down before you fall down. And stay out of the way."

"We've got to get her out," Wade yelled. His heart raced so hard he thought it might explode.

James and the two men cleared away the rubble around what remained of the chimney's fire pit. "Lucy, honey," he called out. "It's James. We're going to pull you out."

Wade couldn't hear. "Is she okay?"

James ignored him and grabbed a flailing ankle. One of the other men grabbed her other foot.

"Ow. Take it easy."

The sound of her objection was sweeter than a host of angels.

A few more grumbles and she emerged.

Wade crawled to her side and let his hands roam up and down her arms, legs, and face. He choked off a sob. She was alive.

"You're hurt." She touched his head where the rock caught him and then swiped her thumb across his cheek to wipe away his tears.

Covered in soot and black as a stick of licorice, Lucy crawled onto his lap.

Wade wrapped his arms around and sat there on the wet ground for the longest time, staring at her. "Lucy Kiddron, you are the most beautiful sight I've ever seen."

Chapter Thirty

Wade looked up from his seat by Lucy's bed when Ed Whitaker stood and yawned.

"I'm going to stretch my legs and then grab a cup of coffee from the nurses' station. You want some?" Lucy's friend and long-time mentor hadn't been able to stay away after learning Argault had escaped again.

"No thanks, Ed. I'm good."

"When I get back you need to think about heading to the motel to get some rest. You haven't left her side in more than thirty-six hours. I can call in one of Fowler's guys to hang out here with me."

Wade's jaws opened involuntarily with a prolonged inhalation, followed by a loud exhale. Yawns really were contagious. No matter. He'd gone for longer periods without sleep and stayed awake through some hairy times. But he couldn't remember anxiety like this. Lucy upped the ante on everything.

He also didn't want her to wake up with a stranger in her room. She'd agreed to the plan—two men with her at all times. Fowler had provided four teams of two men each to patrol inside and out. Twelve hour shifts. Two teams on, two teams off. For a discreet op, they'd thrown a lot of firepower at keeping Lucy safe.

"I'm good." Wade waved Ed off. "I'll grab some zzz's here once you get back."

Ed, James, and his dad had taken turns partnering with Wade while he watched over Lucy, though only James understood why he refused to leave her side. He'd witnessed Wade's melt down on the mountain.

The memory of that night, almost two weeks gone now, still had the power to gut him. No. He wouldn't leave her while she was so vulnerable.

Ed nodded and slipped out, leaving the door ajar so a spill of light from the hallway filtered in.

A soft whir started up near the head of Lucy's bed. The automated blood pressure cuff attached to her arm inflated. Wade followed the numbers on the screen as they ticked down, and let out a sigh when they stopped. 110/68. Normal.

He stared down at the too fragile creature lying on the bed. Long brown hair fanned out over the pillows, providing a sharp contrast to the white sheets and mummy-like bandage on her newly repaired shoulder. An IV line in her right arm led to a bag on a pole and a cocktail of medications.

The better part of a week had passed since Argault slipped away in the fog. As feared, he'd stashed his vehicle near a logging trail on the western slope. Only minutes ahead of his pursuers, it proved to be enough for Lucy's enemy. The black SUV had disappeared in the night.

Wade pressed a feather-light kiss to Lucy's forehead and smoothed her bedcovers. She looked so young and free of worries. He thanked the Lord again for the miracle of Lucy's escape from the ruins of the cabin.

They'd discussed postponing her surgery, but in the end, she'd opted to go ahead with it. "I'll always be aware that he's out there, waiting, but I won't let him control my life anymore."

And so, they stuck to the original plan. They left the ranch at 0400 hours Monday morning. Had it been only yesterday? After two-plus hours on the road to Idaho Falls, more paperwork than any one person should have to deal with, and the 0800 pre-op, they took her back to the operating room.

Three long hours and another two in the recovery room—and he hadn't left her side since.

Drugs kept her comfortable and mostly unconscious since the operation. Her only lucid moment so far came when they got her up to go to the bathroom or woke her to eat the square of green Jello and a tiny cup of clear broth. Dr. Wilkes, the orthopedic surgeon she'd met with back in Hastings Bluff, assured him they'd cut back on the narcotics in the morning.

His wristwatch read 0015. The witching hour. That notorious time when evil is thought to be at its most powerful. A soft snort followed that thought. Not on his watch.

The night nurse wouldn't check her vitals again until 0400. Whitaker would check in with the outside team and then meet up with the inside team to compare notes before chatting up the nurses. Another ten minutes before he returned. Maybe fifteen.

Wade let out a long, drawn out sigh that seemed to go on forever, but then it morphed into a second yawn that threatened to dislocate his jaw. Shaking his head, he tried to throw off the cobwebs in his head. A splash of cold water would help. And then a couple of hours on the tiny bench they called a sofa.

Wade tugged off his boots and flexed his toes. Two more days. The doc said she could go home on Friday.

Another yawn. Man, he really was tired. Slipping into the bathroom, he left the door open a crack. Just enough light filled the room to find his way to the sink and turn on the tap. With his hands cupped, Wade splashed cold water on his face. Better.

Patting his face dry with paper towels, he leaned over the sink and stared at his shadowed reflection. He didn't need light to see the truth. His heart knew. He'd fallen in love with Lucy and would do everything in his power to convince her to stay in Idaho.

And if she wouldn't?

Imperfect Trust

A soft rustle drew his attention. Had Ed returned already? Was Lucy stirring? If she wanted to leave, he'd go with her—if she'd wanted him. They'd have that discussion soon. He'd tell her how he felt.

Wade used a finger to ease the door open, grateful the maintenance crew kept the hinges well oiled. The quiet of the night was peaceful.

A shadow moved by Lucy's bed. Someone stood there, studying her IV bag. A man. In scrubs and a surgical mask.

He frowned. Who …?

With the man's back to him, Wade couldn't see what he was doing … until he withdrew a syringe from his pocket.

The nurse administered pain medication less than an hour ago. Carried it on a little tray and flicked the low lights on to use the in-room computer.

The man removed the cap of the syringe and fitted it to Lucy's IV line.

"Hey," Wade called. "What's that you're giving her?"

Startled, the man jerked around and just as quickly turned back to IV bag. He fumbled with the syringe, fitted it to the port, and depressed the plunger.

All the weariness fled as Wade's inner voice screamed in warning. He didn't stop to analyze the man's actions. He reacted on instinct and launched himself at the man, shoving him away from the bed.

Argault.

Even in the dim lighting, he recognized the man whose pictures he'd studied and committed to memory. The man who'd sworn to kill Lucy.

The syringe …

He glanced back, and saw the hypodermic still imbedded in the access port of Lucy's central line. Fear clamped around his heart. Wade grabbed the tubing and yanked, knowing he had but seconds to keep whatever was in the syringe from reaching her veins.

She groaned. Her eyes fluttered, but didn't open. A dark stain spread over the sheets.

Wade turned back to the attacker.

Argault pulled a gun from his waistband.

Instinct kicked in. Wade dove for the weapon. He caught Argault's wrist, squeezed hard, and slammed his hand and the gun against the rolling table.

The impact tipped the table over with a crash. It skidded across the floor and slammed into the wall.

Argault howled.

Wade slammed the man's hand and gun against the bed's foot rail and the weapon sailed away to land on Lucy's belly.

A soft oomph escaped her lips. "Wade?" She sounded groggy and confused.

Argault landed a fist to Wade's ribs, grunted like a feral animal, and then punched him in the side of the head.

Wade staggered.

The two men spun around the room, locked in a deadly embrace. They ricocheted off the walls and furniture, knocked over a chair, bumped into Lucy's bed hard enough to move it several feet, and sent a vase of flowers crashing to the floor.

"Wade?" She called out, more coherent now, pain and worry in her voice.

Rage exploded in a fury unlike anything Wade had ever experienced. He muscled Argault away from Lucy's bed, caught his arm in a hammerlock, and wrenched it up behind his back. A sharp twist upward left Argault screeching.

Using his weight advantage, Wade ran his foe into the wall face first.

Argault screamed again. Blood smeared on the wall.

Wade followed him forward, ready to bash his head again, but lost his footing. His socks, wet from the spilled flowers, slid on the tile floor. He fell on his butt, hitting the floor at the same time Argault did.

Stunned, Argault struggled to his knees, tottered to his feet, and tried to stand, but he slipped in the water from the vase.

Wade crouched and confronted his foe.

Argault slowly pushed himself upright and groaned. He whirled, a knife in one hand. The switchblade snicked open to reveal a wicked six-inch blade.

Wade danced away from the slashing motions.

"Stop," Lucy cried out in a weak voice.

Both men cast a quick glance her way … and stopped.

She held the gun, the barrel pointed at Argault. The sound of the safety clicking off echoed in the silence.

Argault froze.

Wade took advantage of the distraction and made a grab for the knife, but Argault slashed out again, making him dodge back.

"Stop," Lucy shouted again, her voice stronger. "Don't make me shoot you, Jensen."

Argault ignored her and pressed his advantage.

Wade waited, drawing him in. He had Argault's measure. Could take him down. His muscles coiled tight as he prepared to—

The window exploded less than a foot from Argault's head. The drug dealer jerked around and stared at Lucy, his eyes wide, mouth open.

Wade barreled forward and drove his left shoulder into Argault's gut. He grabbed a flailing wrist. The momentum hammered Argault against the wall. His head clipped the corner of the wall-mounted television.

The door flew open. Light flooded the room.

Argault's eyes rolled back in his head. He slid down the wall, head lolling to one side, slumped in the corner. He didn't move.

"What in the ...?" Ed Whitaker skirted Wade and shoved Argault face down onto the floor. In one quick motion, he yanked the stunned man's hands behind his back and cuffed him.

Wade stumbled to Lucy's side. "Let go, tiger." He took the gun from her hand.

A nurse had entered behind Whitaker. She looked from Argault sprawled on the floor, face dripping blood, to Wade who huffed like he'd just run a marathon. Then she turned her attention to Lucy. "Merciful heaven, what happened?"

She didn't wait for an explanation. Donning a pair of latex gloves from the box on the wall, she used the sheet to staunch the blood that trickled from Lucy's arm.

A second nurse came in, and then two more. Orderlies arrived. The two inside agents appeared, along with three of the hospital's security personnel.

Chaos.

The first nurse on the scene turned a thin-lipped scowl on Wade. "I asked what happened here."

"I yanked her IV out." Wade pointed at Argault. "He tried to inject something in her line."

The nurse reached for the syringe hanging from the IV access port.

Ed caught her arm. "Leave it. We need fingerprints."

Lucy looked at Ed and then at Wade. "Argault? Is he ...?" Her voice was hoarse.

The nurse went back to tending Lucy's injury.

Wade leaned down to whisper in her ear. "Dead? Nah. But he won't bother you ever again."

"I didn't kill him?"

Imperfect Trust

"No, but you sure scared him." Wade chuckled and ran a fingertip down her cheek. "If it's any consolation, you killed the window."

When she smiled, the puckered frown lines relaxed. The nurse had a new IV line going and the narcotics were calling her back to dreamland. "I saw two." She yawned. "Aimed for ... one on the right ... his head. Guess I missed."

Wade swallowed hard. "Sleep now, tiger. I won't leave you."

Her eyelids closed.

"You're in the way here, Mr. Cameron." One of the nurse's aides crowded in.

Wade moved closer to the head of the bed to give them room, but refused to leave. Six different conversations filled the room, all vying to be heard. Medical staff hovered over Lucy. Fowler's two outside guards had joined the parade. And now a uniformed policeman had joined them.

Chairs scraped across the floor, furniture was righted, and at last Argault was hauled upright and hustled from the room. One of Fowler's men spoke to Wade. "Your father and Sheriff Evers are on their way."

Wade nodded.

Somehow he remained on his feet until the last aide left. As soon as the woman slipped out of the room, he dragged a chair to Lucy's bedside and collapsed. His hands shook. His legs quivered like the jelly his mom put up each summer. All signs of an adrenalin crash, something he'd experienced countless times, though never with tears. Those stymied him.

ccc

"I'm trying." Lucy wiped sweat from her forehead. Who knew physical therapy could hurt so much? Or that Cassie would turn out to be a sadist?

"Raise your arm, just one more inch. You can do it." Cassie tapped Lucy's arm.

For God has not given us a spirit of fearfulness, but one of power, love, and sound judgment. Today's Scripture came from Timothy. Cate had given Lucy the women's devotional when she came home from the hospital. *Home.* A smile touched her lips. Whenever the going got too hard, she repeated the words from this verse.

Gritting her teeth, she fought through the burn and finally reached a height that satisfied Cassie.

"Only two weeks post-op and you're ahead of schedule. Dr. Wilkes will be pleased with your progress. Good job."

"I'm not a puppy. Are we finished now?"

Cassie laughed and gathered up the stretchy tube-things they used for an isometric workout.

Lucy wiped her face and neck with a hand towel. "I'm taking a shower."

"Don't be long. TJ and Garrett will be here soon."

Lucy had just zipped her jeans and stuffed her feet into a pair of scuffs when shouting erupted from the front of the house. She hurried out, still buttoning her blouse. She didn't want to miss the newlyweds' arrival.

Hours later, after a sumptuous lunch and hilarious tales from the honeymooners' adventures, Lucy's stomach ached from laughing. TJ and Garrett left for their home amid congratulations, well wishes, and with a promise to return for a family dinner tomorrow. Tonight, they wanted to be alone.

Lucy waved from the front porch with a twinge of envy. To love someone the way TJ and Garrett loved each other, and be loved in return ...

Sensing a presence behind her, she smiled. Wade. Somehow she knew when he entered a room, not because she heard or saw him, not even from the enticing smell of his woodsy cologne or the unique scent that belonged to him alone. It was a connection that transcended earthly senses. She couldn't explain it.

Imperfect Trust

Did he feel the same way?

His big hands settled on her shoulders. Warm breath stirred the hair by her ear.

"Come with me out to the barn. I want to show you something."

She turned to face him. "More kittens?" She tried to keep her smile from widening but couldn't.

"Nah. Something better." He took her hand and led her out through the kitchen.

Lucy hurried along at his side, taking two steps to each of his, until she tugged on his hand. "Slow down. Not everyone has legs as long as yours."

He grinned down at her.

"Agent Fowler called this morning," she told him as their pace slowed. "He got the toxicology report back."

"The drug Argault tried to inject into your IV?"

She nodded. "Succinylcholine. It's a muscle paralytic used in surgery. It stops the heart and lungs."

Wade's grip tightened.

"Ease up there, He-man. He didn't succeed, thanks to you. Fowler says Argault may never see the light of day again."

"Good."

Inside the barn, Wade led her toward the horse stalls, not stopping until they reached the last one. A shaft of light slanted through the barn's rear doors, bathing the dainty mare inside in a golden glow. The horse whickered and thrust her head over the gate. Her warm honey gold coat and mane of white-blond hair glistened in the sun's rays.

Lucy stared, awed by the animal's beauty.

"Do you like her?" Wade asked.

"She's gorgeous. Like champagne and honey. What kind of horse is she? Does she have a name?"

He laughed. "Her registered name is Arabella Lady Pegasus. Jo wanted to call her Moon Pie, but I nixed that. I call her Honey instead, because of her coloring and sweet temper." He put some apple chunks in Lucy's hand.

Leaning over the stall door, hand outstretched, she crooned to the Palomino mare. "Here, Honey."

The horse stepped forward and nuzzled her hand, taking the bits of apple in dainty nibbles.

When the treats were gone, Lucy wiped her hand on her jeans and looked at Wade. "She's stunning."

He folded his arms and leaned on the top rail. "I got her for you."

"For me?" Her mind stuttered and came to a complete stop.

"Yeah. She's smallish, just over fourteen hands, and docile. She'll make a perfect horse for you."

He'd bought her a horse. She couldn't get her mind to move beyond that thought.

Wade straightened up and reached for a length of rope hanging on a hook. He let it unwind and then coiled it in loops, repeating the movements over and over. "I, uh, also cleaned out that empty office where I kept a lot of junk. Thought you could work there. If you want."

What?

"And I cleared my calendar next month. Thought we could drive down to Atlanta. Pack up the stuff in your apartment. Get you moved up here."

He wouldn't look at her, just rambled on about proper packaging for computers, who they would get to ship her stuff, accounts she needed to close, and storage.

He stopped talking and cleared his throat. After a long moment of silence, he finally looked at her.

"What do you mean?"

He shifted from one foot to the other. "I thought ... I mean, if you want ... It's okay if you don't ..."

She touched his arm. "What are you saying?"

Imperfect Trust

Framing her face with his hands, Wade stared deep into her eyes for a long time. "I want to teach you to ride. See you smile every day. Watch you get lost in writing code. Hear you grumble when I say something stupid."

Her breath joined her brain in the land of the lost.

"I want to take you on a date. And dance with you. Explore whatever this is between us." He rubbed his thumbs along her cheekbones. "Most of all, tiger, I want you to want it, too."

Her heart pounded. Her throat closed up. She wanted to laugh and cry at the same time but couldn't get a single word out. She wanted everything he did. All she had to do was reach out and take it. Did she dare?

For God has not given us a spirit of fearfulness, but one of power, love, and sound judgment. Lucy stretched up on her tiptoes and pressed her mouth to his. They would never have a future together unless she took a risk now. "I want it, Wade."

About the Author

Elizabeth Noyes—professional writer, aspiring author, dedicated dreamer—lives in the suburbs of Atlanta with her husband and best friend, Paul, who listens tirelessly while she regales him with all the tales in her head of damaged, but very human characters clamoring to be heard.

A native of the Deep South, she claims to still "speak the language," even after traveling around the world for most of her adult life. Recently retired from a career as a professional business writer and editor, she now fills her days editing, critiquing, reading, playing with the grandkids, learning more about Social Media than she ever wanted, and putting her stories into words to share with others. She also serves as Features Editor for the digital magazine *Imaginate*.

Imperfect Trust is the second book in the romantic suspense Imperfect Series. Book 1, the award winning *Imperfect Wings*, was released August 2014. She also co-authored two multi-author novellas, *A Dozen Apologies* and *The Love Boat Bachelor*.

Contact Information:
Elizabeth@ElizabethNoyesWrites.com
www.ElizabethNoyesWrites.com
www.facebook.com/Elizabeth.Noyes.54
www.linkedin.com/in/ENoyes1625
www.twitter.com/ENoyes5246

Amazon Author Page:
http://amzn.to/1HdjwOF

Imperfect Trust

Other Books by the Author

ELIZABETH NOYES

Imperfect Wings
Book One in the Imperfect Series

Evil stalks TJ McKendrick.

Three years after burying her father, TJ visits Honduras where he died. While there, she witnesses a murder and is forced to flee.

Don Castillo dreams of power. Funnel the drugs into the States and it's his. First though, he must kill the woman who dared spy on him.

The last thing Garrett Cameron needs is another woman interrupting his life, but when the feisty vixen that put a monkey wrench in his mission two years ago shows up at his ranch running for her life -- what's a man to do?

The attraction between TJ and Garrett bursts into flame in the midst of danger, a fierce desire that neither is prepared for. Her past is filled with betrayal. He's lived a life of violence, and love isn't for someone like him. Do they dare let go of past hurts and embrace a future together?

Only faith in God and trust in each other can overcome the deadly odds they face.

Available on Amazon in print and Kindle.

The Love Boat Bachelor

Romance is a joke.

After the love of Brent Teague's life came back into his world only to marry someone else, Brent is through with women. He might be through with being a pastor, too.

Brent was so sure that God brought Mara Adkins home to him so they could marry and live happily ever after. Six months after her wedding to another man, that theory is obviously a dud. If Brent could be so wrong about that, who's to say he's not mistaken about God calling him to pastoral ministry?

Tired of watching Brent flounder for direction, Brent's feisty older sister boots him out of Spartanburg and onto a cruise ship. Brent's old college buddy manages the ship's staff, and he's thrilled to finagle Brent into the role of chaplain for the two-week cruise.

As the ship sets sail, Brent starts to relax. Maybe a cruise wasn't such a bad idea after all. But there's just one little thing no one told him. He's not on any ordinary cruise. He's on The Love Boat.

What's a sworn bachelor to do on a Caribbean cruise full of romance and love? He'll either have to jump ship or embrace the unforgettable romantic comedy headed his way.

Available on Kindle.

Imperfect Trust

A Dozen Apologies

Mara Adkins, a promising fashion designer, has fallen off the ladder of success, and she can't seem to get up. In college, Mara and her sorority sisters played an ugly game, and Mara was usually the winner. She'd date men she considered geeks, win their confidence, and then she'd dump them publicly.

When Mara begins work for a prestigious clothing designer in New York, she gets her comeuppance. Her boyfriend steals her designs and wins a coveted position. He fires her, and she returns in shame to her home in Spartanburg, South Carolina, where life for others has changed for the better.

Mara's parents, always seemingly one step from a divorce, have rediscovered their love for each other, but more importantly they have placed Christ in the center of that love. The changes Mara sees in their lives cause her to seek Christ. Mara's heart is pierced by her actions toward the twelve men she'd wronged in college, and she sets out to apologize to each of them. A girl with that many amends to make, though, needs money for travel, and Mara finds more ways to lose a job that she ever thought possible.

Mara stumbles, bumbles, and humbles her way toward employment and toward possible reconciliation with the twelve men she humiliated to find that God truly does look upon the heart, and that He has chosen the heart of one of the men for her to have and to hold.

Available on Kindle.

IMAGINATE

Volume 1 | Issue 1   JUNE 2015

SERENDIPITY
An Interview with Mike Wendland,
Emmy-winning Journalist and RV Adventurer

Wrong Way Bob
by The Merry Sage

Nonfiction
~ Life-Changing View
~ Family Travel

Writing Craft
~ Fiction
~ Nonfiction

Book & Movie Reviews

Short Stories
~ Running on Fumes
~ Ride the Night
~ and MORE

Poetry
~ The Asphalt Road
~ Hundreds of Nowheres
~ Remembering
~ and MORE

Flash Fiction

Longing for Place

www.ImaginateZone.com

Look for other books

published by

Write Integrity Press

www.WriteIntegrity.com

and

Pix-N-Pens

Pix-N-Pens Publishing

www.PixNPens.com

Made in the USA
Charleston, SC
14 July 2015